PE

Lady

Mary E. Braddon (1835–1915) was born in Soho Square, London. When Mary was four years old, her Irish mother left her husband, a feckless Cornish solicitor, and took her three children to live in St Leonard's-on-Sea, Sussex, returning to London in 1843. Mary Braddon began writing at the age of eight, but in 1857, when her mother's money finally ran out, she took the name of Mary Seyton and became an actress – beginning with a part as 'Fairy Pineapple' in a pantomime. Three years later, however, support from an admirer allowed her to leave the stage and write. She began writing serial fiction for *The Welcome Guest*, *Robin Goodfellow*, the *London Journal*, the *Halfpenny Journal* and *Temple Bar*. Several of these were owned by the Irish publisher John Maxwell, with whom she lived until his death in 1895. As his wife was alive (in an asylum for the insane in Dublin), he was unable to remarry until after her death in 1874. He and Mary had six children, and also cared for Maxwell's five children from his first marriage. Two of her sons, W. B. and Gerald Maxwell, also became well-known novelists. Mary Braddon became a bestselling 'sensation' author with *Lady Audley's Secret* (1862) and *Aurora Floyd* (1863), which made her rich for life. Her reputation as 'Queen of the Circulating Libraries' was confirmed with *John Marchmont's Legacy* (1863), *The Doctor's Wife* (1864), *Birds of Prey* (1867) and *Charlotte's Inheritance* (1868). She wrote over eighty novels, gradually modifying her sensational style to produce acute satirical analyses of contemporary life. Though her work created a huge moral storm, it was read avidly by Tennyson, Dickens, Thackeray, Gladstone and Henry James. As well as her novels, she wrote plays and poems, and edited magazines such as *Temple Bar* and *Belgravia*. Mary Braddon lived to see her work transformed into a new and popular art when she attended the silent-film version of *Aurora Floyd* in 1913, two years before her death in Richmond at the age of eighty.

MARY ELIZABETH BRADDON

Lady Audley's Secret

PENGUIN BOOKS

PENGUIN BOOKS

Published by the Penguin Group
Penguin Books Ltd, 80 Strand, London WC2R ORL, England
Penguin Group (USA) Inc., 375 Hudson Street, New York, New York 10014, USA
Penguin Group (Canada), 90 Eglinton Avenue East, Suite 700, Toronto, Ontario, Canada M4P 2Y3
(a division of Pearson Penguin Canada Inc.)
Penguin Ireland, 25 St Stephen's Green, Dublin 2, Ireland (a division of Penguin Books Ltd)
Penguin Group (Australia), 250 Camberwell Road, Camberwell, Victoria 3124, Australia
(a division of Pearson Australia Group Pty Ltd)
Penguin Books India Pvt Ltd, 11 Community Centre,
Panchsheel Park, New Delhi – 110 017, India
Penguin Group (NZ), 67 Apollo Drive, Rosedale, North Shore 0632, New Zealand
(a division of Pearson New Zealand Ltd)
Penguin Books (South Africa) (Pty) Ltd, 24 Sturdee Avenue,
Rosebank, Johannesburg 2196, South Africa

Penguin Books Ltd, Registered Offices: 80 Strand, London WC2R ORL, England

www.penguin.com

First published in serial form 1861–2
Published as a Pocket Penguin Classic 2010

I

Set in 10.5/12.5 pt PostScript Monotype Dante
Typeset by Rowland Phototypesetting Ltd, Bury St Edmunds, Suffolk
Printed in England by Clays Ltd, St Ives plc

978-0-141-19233-8

www.greenpenguin.co.uk

Penguin Books is committed to a sustainable future
for our business, our readers and our planet.
The book in your hands is made from paper
certified by the Forest Stewardship Council.

Contents

VOLUME I

VOLUME II

VOLUME III

VOLUME I

CHAPTER I
Lucy

It lay low down in a hollow, rich with fine old timber and luxuriant pastures; and you came upon it through an avenue of limes, bordered on either side by meadows, over the high hedges of which the cattle looked inquisitively at you as you passed, wondering, perhaps, what you wanted; for there was no thoroughfare, and unless you were going to the Court you had no business there at all.

At the end of this avenue there was an old arch and a clock-tower, with a stupid, bewildering clock, which had only one hand; and which jumped straight from one hour to the next, and was therefore always in extremes. Through this arch you walked straight into the gardens of Audley Court.

A smooth lawn lay before you, dotted with groups of rhododendrons, which grew in more perfection here than anywhere else in the county. To the right there were the kitchen gardens, the fish-pond, and an orchard bordered by a dry moat, and a broken ruin of a wall, in some places thicker than it was high, and everywhere overgrown with trailing ivy, yellow stonecrop, and dark moss. To the left there was a broad gravelled walk, down which, years ago, when the place had been a convent, the quiet nuns had walked hand in hand; a wall bordered with espaliers, and shadowed on one side by goodly oaks, which shut out the flat landscape, and circled in the house and gardens with a darkening shelter.

The house faced the arch, and occupied three sides of a quadrangle. It was very old, and very irregular and rambling.

The windows were uneven; some small, some large, some with heavy stone mullions and rich stained glass; others with frail lattices that rattled in every breeze; others so modern that they might have been added only yesterday. Great piles of chimneys rose up here and there behind the pointed gables, and seemed as if they were so broken down by age and long service, that they must have fallen but for the straggling ivy which, crawling up the walls and trailing even over the roof, wound itself about them and supported them. The principal door was squeezed into a corner of a turret at one angle of the building, as if it was in hiding from dangerous visitors, and wished to keep itself a secret – a noble door for all that – old oak, and studded with great square-headed iron nails, and so thick that the sharp iron knocker struck upon it with a muffled sound; and the visitor rang a clanging bell that dangled in a corner amongst the ivy, lest the noise of the knocking should never penetrate the stronghold.

A glorious old place – a place that visitors fell into raptures with; feeling a yearning wish to have done with life, and to stay there for ever, staring into the cool fish-ponds, and counting the bubbles as the roach and carp rose to the surface of the water – a spot in which Peace seemed to have taken up her abode, setting her soothing hand on every tree and flower; on the still ponds and quiet alleys; the shady corners of the old-fashioned rooms; the deep window-seats behind the painted glass; the low meadows and the stately avenues – ay, even upon the stagnant well, which, cool and sheltered as all else in the old place, hid itself away in a shrubbery behind the gardens, with an idle handle that was never turned, and a lazy rope so rotten that the pail had broken away from it, and had fallen into the water.

A noble place; inside as well as out, a noble place – a house in which you incontinently lost yourself if ever you were so rash as to go about it alone; a house in which no one room had any sympathy with another, every chamber running off at a tangent into an inner chamber, and through that down some narrow staircase leading to a door which, in its turn, led back into that very part of the house from which you thought yourself the farthest; a house that could never have been planned by any mortal architect, but must have been the handiwork of that good old builder – Time, who, adding a room one year, and knocking down a room another year, toppling over now a chimney coeval with the Plantagenets, and setting up one in the style of the Tudors; shaking down a bit of Saxon wall there, and allowing a Norman arch to stand here; throwing in a row of high narrow windows in the reign of Queen Anne, and joining on a dining-room after the fashion of the time of Hanoverian George I to a refectory that had been standing since the Conquest, had contrived, in some eleven centuries, to run up such a mansion as was not elsewhere to be met with throughout the county of Essex. Of course, in such a house, there were secret chambers: the little daughter of the present owner, Sir Michael Audley, had fallen by accident upon the discovery of one. A board had rattled under her feet in the great nursery where she played, and on attention being drawn to it, it was found to be loose, and so removed, revealing a ladder leading to a hiding-place between the floor of the nursery and the ceiling of the room below – a hiding-place so small that he who hid there must have crouched on his hands and knees or lain at full length, and yet large enough to contain a quaint old carved oak chest half filled with priests' vestments which had been hidden away, no doubt, in those cruel days when the life of a man was in danger if he was discovered to have harboured a Roman Catholic priest, or to have had mass said in his house.

The broad outer moat was dry and grass-grown, and the laden trees of the orchard hung over it with snarled straggling branches that drew fantastical patterns upon the green slope.

Within this moat there was, as I have said, the fish-pond – a sheet of water that extended the whole length of the garden, and bordering which there was an avenue called the lime-tree walk; an avenue so shaded from the sun and sky, so screened from observation by the thick shelter of the over-arching trees, that it seemed a chosen place for secret meetings or for stolen interviews; a place in which a conspiracy might have been planned or a lover's vow registered with equal safety; and yet it was scarcely twenty paces from the house.

At the end of this dark arcade there was the shrubbery, where, half buried amongst the tangled branches and the neglected weeds, stood the rusty wheel of that old well of which I have spoken. It had been of good service in its time, no doubt; and busy nuns have perhaps drawn the cool water with their own fair hands; but it had fallen with disuse now, and scarcely any one at Audley Court knew whether the spring had dried up or not. But sheltered as was the solitude of this lime-tree walk, I doubt very much if it was ever put to any romantic uses. Often in the cool of the evening Sir Michael Audley would stroll up and down smoking his cigar, with his dog at his heels, and his pretty young wife dawdling by his side; but in about ten minutes the baronet and his companion would grow tired of the rustling limes and the still water, hidden under the spreading leaves of the water-lilies, and the long green vista with the broken well at the end, and would stroll back to the white drawing-room, where my lady played dreamy melodies by Beethoven and Mendelssohn till her husband fell asleep in his easy chair.

Sir Michael Audley was fifty-six years of age, and he had married a second wife three months after his fifty-fifth birthday. He was a big man, tall and stout, with a deep sonorous voice, handsome black eyes, and a white beard – a white beard which made him look venerable against his will, for he was as active as a boy, and one of the hardest riders in the county.

For seventeen years he had been a widower with an only child, a daughter, Alicia Audley, now eighteen, and by no means too well pleased at having a step-mother brought home to the Court; for Miss Alicia had reigned supreme in her father's house since her earliest childhood, and had carried the keys, and jingled them in the pockets of her silk aprons, and lost them in the shrubbery, and dropped them into the pond, and given all manner of trouble about them from the hour in which she entered her teens, and had on that account deluded herself into the sincere belief that for the whole of that period she had been keeping house.

But Miss Alicia's day was over; and now, when she asked anything of the housekeeper, the housekeeper would tell her that she would speak to my lady, or she would consult my lady, and if my lady pleased it should be done. So the baronet's daughter, who was an excellent horsewoman and a very clever artist, spent most of her time out of doors, riding about the green lanes, and sketching the cottage children, and the ploughboys, and the cattle, and all manner of animal life that came in her way. She set her face with a sulky determination against any intimacy between herself and the baronet's young wife; and amiable as that lady was, she found it quite impossible to overcome Miss Alicia's prejudices and dislike; or to convince the spoiled girl that she had not done her a cruel injury in marrying Sir Michael Audley.

The truth was that Lady Audley had, in becoming the wife of Sir Michael, made one of those apparently advantageous matches which are apt to draw upon a woman the envy and hatred of her sex. She had come into the neighbourhood as a governess in the family of a surgeon in the village near Audley Court. No one knew anything of her except that she came in answer to an advertisement which Mr. Dawson, the surgeon, had inserted in the *Times*. She came from London; and the only reference she gave was to a lady at a school at Brompton, where she had once been a teacher. But this reference was so satisfactory that none other was needed, and Miss Lucy Graham was received by the surgeon as the instructress of his daughters. Her accomplishments were so brilliant and numerous, that it seemed strange that she should have answered an advertisement offering such very moderate terms of remuneration as those named by Mr. Dawson: but Miss Graham seemed perfectly well satisfied with her situation, and she taught the girls to play sonatas by Beethoven, and to paint from Nature after Creswick, and walked through the dull, out-of-the-way village to the humble little church three times on Sunday, as contentedly as if she had no higher aspiration in the world than to do so all the rest of her life.

People who observed this accounted for it by saying that it was part of her amiable and gentle nature always to be light-hearted, happy, and contented under any circumstances.

Wherever she went she seemed to take joy and brightness with her. In the cottages of the poor her fair face shone like a sunbeam. She would sit for a quarter of an hour talking to some old woman, and apparently as pleased with the admiration of a toothless crone as if she had been listening to the compliments of a marquis; and when she tripped away, leaving nothing behind her (for her poor salary gave no scope to her benevolence), the old woman would burst out into senile raptures with her grace, her beauty, and her kindliness, such as she never bestowed upon the vicar's wife, who half fed and clothed her. For you see Miss Lucy Graham was blessed with that magic power of fascination by which a woman can charm with a word or intoxicate with a smile. Every one loved, admired, and praised her. The boy who opened the five-barred gate that stood in her pathway ran home to his mother to tell of her pretty looks, and the sweet voice in which she thanked him for the little service. The verger at the church who ushered her into the surgeon's pew; the vicar who saw the soft blue eyes uplifted to his face as he preached his simple sermon; the porter from the railway-station who brought her sometimes a letter or a parcel, and who never looked for reward from her; her employer; his visitors; her pupils; the servants; everybody, high and low, united in declaring that Lucy Graham was the sweetest girl that ever lived.

Perhaps it was this cry which penetrated into the quiet chambers of Audley Court; or perhaps it was the sight of her pretty face, looking over the surgeon's high pew every Sunday morning. However it was, it was certain that Sir Michael Audley suddenly experienced a strong desire to be better acquainted with Mr. Dawson's governess.

He had only to hint this to the worthy doctor for a little party to be got up, to which the vicar and his wife, and the baronet and his daughter, were invited.

That one quiet evening sealed Sir Michael's fate. He could no more resist the tender fascination of those soft and melting blue eyes; the graceful beauty of that slender throat and drooping head, with its wealth of showering flaxen curls; the low music of that gentle voice; the perfect harmony which pervaded every charm, and made all doubly charming in this woman; than he could resist his destiny. Destiny! Why, she was his destiny! He had never loved before. What had been his marriage with Alicia's mother but a dull, jog-trot bargain, made to keep some estate in the family that would have been just as well out of it? What had been his love for his first wife but a poor, pitiful, smouldering spark, too dull to be extinguished, too feeble to burn? But *this* was love – this fever, this longing, this restless, uncertain, miserable hesitation; these cruel fears that his age was an insurmountable barrier to his happiness; this sick hatred of his white beard; this frenzied wish to be young again, with glistening raven hair, and a slim waist, such as he had had twenty years before; these wakeful nights and melancholy days, so gloriously brightened if he chanced to catch a glimpse of her sweet face behind the window curtains as he drove past the surgeon's house; all these signs gave token of the truth; and told only too plainly that, at the sober age of fifty-five, Sir Michael Audley had fallen ill of the terrible fever called love.

I do not think that throughout his courtship the baronet once calculated upon his wealth or his position as a strong reason for his success. If he ever remembered these things, he dismissed the thought of them with a shudder. It pained him too much to believe for a moment that any one so lovely and innocent could value herself against a splendid house or a good old title. No; his hope was that as her life had been most likely one of toil and dependence, and as she was very young (nobody exactly knew her age, but she looked little more than twenty), she might never have formed any attachment, and that he, being the first to woo her, might by tender attentions, by generous watchfulness, by a love which should recall to her the father she had lost, and by a protecting care that should make him necessary to her, win her young heart, and obtain from her fresh and earliest love alone the promise of her hand. It was a very romantic day dream, no doubt; but, for all that, it seemed in a very fair way to be realised. Lucy Graham appeared by no means to dislike the baronet's attentions. There was nothing whatever in her manner of the shallow artifice employed by a woman who wishes to captivate a rich man. She was so used to admiration from every one, high and low, that Sir Michael's conduct made very little impression upon her. Again, he had been so many years a widower that people had given up the idea of his ever marrying again. At last, however, Mrs. Dawson spoke to the governess on the subject. The surgeon's wife was sitting in the school-room busy at work, while Lucy was putting the finishing touches to some water-coloured sketches done by her pupils.

'Do you know, my dear Miss Graham,' said Mrs. Dawson,

'I think you ought to consider yourself a remarkably lucky girl.'

The governess lifted her head from its stooping attitude, and stared wonderingly at her employer, shaking back a shower of curls. They were the most wonderful curls in the world – soft and feathery, always floating away from her face, and making a pale halo round her head when the sunlight shone through them.

'What do you mean, my dear Mrs. Dawson?' she asked, dipping her camel's-hair brush into the wet aquamarine upon the palette, and poising it carefully before putting in the delicate streak of purple which was to brighten the horizon in her pupil's sketch.

'Why, I mean, my dear, that it only rests with yourself to become Lady Audley, and the mistress of Audley Court.'

Lucy Graham dropped the brush upon the picture, and flushed scarlet to the roots of her fair hair; and then grew pale again, far paler than Mrs. Dawson had ever seen her before.

'My dear, don't agitate yourself,' said the surgeon's wife, soothingly; 'you know that nobody asks you to marry Sir Michael unless you wish. Of course it would be a magnificent match; he has a splendid income, and is one of the most generous of men. Your position would be very high, and you would be enabled to do a great deal of good; but, as I said before, you must be entirely guided by your own feelings. Only one thing I must say, and that is, that if Sir Michael's attentions are not agreeable to you, it is really scarcely honourable to encourage him.'

'His attentions – encourage him!' muttered Lucy, as if the words bewildered her. 'Pray, pray don't talk to me, Mrs. Dawson. I had no idea of this. It is the last thing that would have occurred to me.' She leaned her elbows on the drawing-board before her, and clasping her hands over her face, seemed for some minutes to be thinking deeply. She wore a narrow black ribbon round her neck, with a locket or a cross, or a miniature, perhaps, attached to it; but whatever the trinket was, she always kept it hidden under her dress. Once or twice, while she sat silently thinking, she removed one of her hands from before her face, and fidgeted nervously with the ribbon, clutching at it with a half-angry gesture, and twisting it backwards and forwards between her fingers.

'I think some people are born to be unlucky, Mrs. Dawson,' she said, by-and-by; 'it would be a great deal too much good fortune for me to become Lady Audley.'

She said this with so much bitterness in her tone, that the surgeon's wife looked up at her with surprise.

'You unlucky, my dear!' she exclaimed. 'I think you're the last person who ought to talk like that – you, such a bright, happy creature, that it does every one good to see you. I'm sure I don't know what we shall do if Sir Michael robs us of you.'

After this conversation they often spoke upon the subject, and Lucy never again showed any emotion whatever when the baronet's admiration for her was canvassed. It was a tacitly understood thing in the surgeon's family that whenever Sir Michael proposed, the governess would quietly accept him; and, indeed, the simple Dawsons would have thought it something more than madness in a penniless girl to reject such an offer.

So one misty June evening Sir Michael, sitting opposite to Lucy Graham at a window in the surgeon's little drawing-room, took an opportunity, while the family happened by some accident to be absent from the room, of speaking upon the subject nearest to his heart. He made the governess in few but solemn words an offer of his hand. There was something almost touching in the manner and tone in which he spoke to her – half in deprecation, knowing that he could hardly expect to be the choice of a beautiful young girl, and praying rather that she would reject him, even though she broke his heart by doing so, than that she should accept his offer if she did not love him.

'I scarcely think there is a greater sin, Lucy,' he said solemnly, 'than that of the woman who marries a man she does not love. You are so precious to me, my beloved, that deeply as my heart is set on this, and bitter as the mere thought of disappointment is to me, I would not have you commit such a sin for any happiness of mine. If my happiness could be achieved by such an act, which it could not – which it never could,' he repeated earnestly, 'nothing but misery can result from a marriage dictated by any motive but truth and love.'

Lucy Graham was not looking at Sir Michael, but straight out into the misty twilight and the dim landscape far away beyond the little garden. The baronet tried to see her face, but her profile was turned to him, and he could not discover the expression of her eyes. If he could have done so, he would have seen a yearning gaze which seemed as if it would have pierced the far obscurity and looked away – away into another world.

'Lucy, you heard me?'

'Yes,' she said gravely; not coldly, or in any way as if she were offended at his words.

'And your answer?'

She did not remove her gaze from the darkening country side, but for some moments was quite silent; then turning to him with a sudden passion in her manner, that lighted up her face with a new and wonderful beauty which the baronet perceived even in the growing twilight, she fell on her knees at his feet.

'No, Lucy; no, no!' he cried vehemently, 'not here, not here!'

'Yes, here, here,' she said, the strange passion which agitated her making her voice sound shrill and piercing – not loud, but preternaturally distinct; 'here, and nowhere else. How good you are – how noble and how generous! Love you! Why there are women a hundred times my superiors in beauty and in goodness who might love you dearly; but you ask too much of me. You ask too much of *me*! Remember what my life has been; only remember that. From my very babyhood I have never seen anything but poverty. My father was a gentleman; clever, accomplished, generous, handsome – but poor. My mother—But do not let me speak of her. Poverty, poverty, trials, vexations, humiliations, deprivations! *You* cannot tell; you, who are amongst those for whom life is so smooth and easy; you can never guess what is endured by such as we. Do not ask too much of me, then. I *cannot* be disinterested; I cannot be blind to the advantages of such an alliance. I cannot, I cannot!'

Beyond her agitation and her passionate vehemence, there was an undefined something in her manner which filled the baronet with a vague alarm. She was still on the ground at his feet, crouching rather than kneeling, her thin white dress clinging about her, her pale hair streaming over her shoulders, her great blue eyes glittering in the dusk, and her hands clutching at the black ribbon about her throat, as if it had been strangling her.

'Don't ask too much of me,' she kept repeating; 'I have been selfish from my babyhood.'

'Lucy, Lucy, speak plainly. Do you dislike me?'

'Dislike you! No, no!'

'But is there any one else whom you love?'

She laughed aloud at his question. 'I do not love any one in the world,' she answered.

He was glad of her reply; and yet that and the strange laugh jarred upon his feelings. He was silent for some moments, and then said with a kind of effort –

'Well, Lucy, I will not ask too much of you. I dare say I am a romantic old fool; but if you do not dislike me, and if you do not love any one else, I see no reason why we should not make a very happy couple. Is it a bargain, Lucy?'

'Yes.'

The baronet lifted her in his arms, and kissed her once upon the forehead; then, after quietly bidding her good night, he walked straight out of the house.

He walked straight out of the house, this foolish old man, because there was some strong emotion at work in his heart – neither joy, nor triumph, but something almost akin to disappointment; some stifled and unsatisfied longing which lay heavy and dull at his heart, as if he had carried a corpse in his bosom. He carried the corpse of that hope which had died at the sound of Lucy's words. All the doubts and fears and timid aspirations were ended now. He must be contented, like other men of his age, to be married for his fortune and his position.

Lucy Graham went slowly up the stairs to her little room at the top of the house. She placed her dim candle on the chest of drawers, and seated herself on the edge of the white bed; still and white as the draperies hanging round her.

'No more dependence, no more drudgery, no more humiliations,' she said; 'every trace of the old life melted away – every clue to identity buried and forgotten – except these, except these.'

She had never taken her left hand from the black ribbon at her throat. She drew it from her bosom as she spoke, and looked at the object attached to it.

It was neither a locket, a miniature, nor a cross: it was a ring wrapped in an oblong piece of paper – the paper partly printed, partly written, yellow with age, and crumpled with much folding.

CHAPTER II

On board the Argus

He threw the end of his cigar into the water, and leaning his elbows upon the bulwarks, stared meditatively at the waves.

'How wearisome they are,' he said; 'blue, and green, and opal; opal, and blue, and green; all very well in their way, of course, but three months of them are rather too much, especially—'

He did not attempt to finish his sentence; his thoughts seemed to wander in the very midst of it, and carry him a thousand miles or so away.

'Poor little girl, how pleased she'll be!' he muttered, opening his cigar case, and lazily surveying its contents; 'how pleased and how surprised! Poor little girl! After three years and a half, too; she *will* be surprised.'

He was a young man of about five-and-twenty, with a dark face, bronzed by exposure to the sun; he had handsome brown eyes, with a feminine smile in them, that sparkled through his black lashes, and a bushy beard and moustache that covered the whole of the lower part of his face. He was tall, and powerfully built; he wore a loose grey suit, and a felt hat, thrown carelessly upon his black hair. His name was George Talboys, and he was aft-cabin passenger on board the good ship *Argus*, laden with Australian wool, and sailing from Sydney to Liverpool.

There were very few passengers in the aft-cabin of the *Argus*. An elderly wool-stapler, returning to his native country with his wife and daughters, after having made a fortune in the colonies; a governess of five-and-thirty years of age going home to marry a man to whom she had been engaged fifteen years; the sentimental daughter of a wealthy Australian wine merchant, invoiced to England to finish her education, and George Talboys, were the only first-class passengers on board.

This George Talboys was the life and soul of the vessel; nobody knew who or what he was, or where he came from, but everybody liked him. He sat at the bottom of the dinner table, and assisted the captain in doing the honours of the friendly meal. He opened the champagne bottles, and took wine with every one present; he told funny stories, and led the laugh himself with such a joyous peal, that the man must have been a churl who could not have laughed for pure sympathy. He was a capital hand at speculation and vingt-et-un, and all the merry round games, which kept the little circle round the cabin lamp so deep in innocent amusement, that a hurricane might have howled overhead without their hearing it; but he freely owned that he had no talent for whist, and that he didn't know a knight from a castle upon the chess-board.

Indeed, Mr. Talboys was by no means too learned a gentle-man. The pale governess had tried to talk to him about fashionable literature, but George had only pulled his beard, and stared very hard at her, saying occasionally, 'Ah, yes!' and, 'To be sure, ha!'

The sentimental young lady, going home to finish her education, had tried him with Shelley and Byron, and he had fairly laughed in her face, as if poetry were a joke. The wool-stapler sounded him upon politics, but he did not seem very deeply versed in them; so they let him go his own way, smoke his cigars and talk to the sailors, lounge over the bulwarks and stare at the water, and make himself agreeable to everybody in his own fashion. But when the *Argus* came to be within about a fortnight's sail of England everybody noticed a change in George Talboys. He grew restless and fidgety; sometimes so merry that the cabin rang with his laughter; sometimes moody and thoughtful. Favourite as he was amongst the sailors, they grew tired at last of answering his perpetual questions about the probable time of touching land. Would it be in ten days, in eleven, in twelve, in thirteen? Was the wind favourable? How many knots an hour was the vessel doing? Then a sudden passion would seize him, and he would stamp upon the deck, crying out that she was a rickety old craft, and that her owners were swindlers to advertise her as the fast-sailing *Argus*. She was not fit for passenger traffic; she was not fit to carry impatient living creatures, with hearts and souls; she was fit for nothing but to be laden with bales of stupid wool, that might rot on the sea and be none the worse for it.

The sun was dropping down behind the waves as George Talboys lighted his cigar upon this August evening. Only ten days more, the sailors had told him that afternoon, and they would see the English coast. 'I will go ashore in the first boat that hails us,' he cried; 'I will go ashore in a cockle-shell. By Jove, if it comes to that, I will swim to land.'

His friends in the aft-cabin, with the exception of the pale governess, laughed at his impatience: she sighed as she watched the young man, chafing at the slow hours, pushing away his untasted wine, flinging himself restlessly about upon the cabin sofa, rushing up and down the companion ladder, and staring at the waves.

As the red rim of the sun dropped into the water, the governess ascended the cabin-stairs for a stroll on deck, while the passengers sat over their wine below. She stopped when she came up to George, and standing by his side, watched the fading crimson in the western sky.

The lady was very quiet and reserved, seldom sharing in the after-cabin amusements, never laughing, and speaking very little; but she and George Talboys had been excellent friends throughout the passage.

'Does my cigar annoy you, Miss Morley?' he said, taking it out of his mouth.

'Not at all; pray do not leave off smoking. I only came up to look at the sunset. What a lovely evening!'

'Yes, yes, I dare say,' he answered, impatiently; 'yet so long, so long! Ten more interminable days and ten more weary nights before we land.'

'Yes,' said Miss Morley, sighing. 'Do you wish the time shorter?'

'Do I?' cried George; 'indeed I do. Don't you?'

'Scarcely.'

'But is there no one you love in England? Is there no one you love looking out for your arrival?'

'I hope so,' she said, gravely. They were silent for some time, he smoking his cigar with a furious impatience, as if he could hasten the course of the vessel by his own restlessness; she looking out at the waning light with melancholy blue eyes: eyes that seemed to have faded with poring over closely-printed books and difficult needlework; eyes that had faded a little, perhaps, by reason of tears secretly shed in the dead hours of the lonely night.

'See!' said George, suddenly pointing in another direction from that towards which Miss Morley was looking, 'there's the new moon.'

She looked up at the pale crescent, her own face almost as pale and wan.

'This is the first time we have seen it. We must wish!' said George, 'I know what I wish.'

'What?'

'That we may get home quickly.'

'My wish is that we may find no disappointment when we get there,' said the governess, sadly.

'Disappointment!'

He started as if he had been struck, and asked what she meant by talking of disappointment.

'I mean this,' she said, speaking rapidly, and with a restless motion of her thin hands; 'I mean that as the end of this long voyage draws near, hope sinks in my heart: and a sick fear comes over me that at the last all may not be well. The person I go to meet may be changed in his feelings towards me; or he may retain all the old feeling until the moment of seeing me, and then lose it in a breath at sight of my poor wan face, for I was called a pretty girl, Mr. Talboys, when I sailed for Sydney, fifteen years ago; or he may be so changed by the world as to have grown selfish and mercenary, and he may welcome me for the sake of my fifteen years' savings. Again, he may be dead. He may have been well, perhaps, up to within a week of our landing, and in that last week may have taken a fever, and died an hour before our vessel anchors in the Mersey. I think of all these things, Mr. Talboys, and act the scenes over in my mind, and feel the anguish of them twenty times a day. Twenty times a day!' she repeated; 'why, I do it a thousand times a day.'

George Talboys had stood motionless, with his cigar in his hand, listening to her so intently that as she said the last words, his hold relaxed, and the cigar dropped into the water.

'I wonder,' she continued, more to herself than to him – 'I wonder, looking back, to think how hopeful I was when the vessel sailed; I never thought then of disappointment, but I pictured the joy of meeting, imagining the very words that would be said, the very tones, the very looks; but for this last month of the voyage, day by day, and hour by hour, my heart sinks, and my hopeful fancies fade away, and I dread the end as much as if I *knew* that I was going to England to attend a funeral.'

The young man suddenly changed his attitude, and turned

his face full upon his companion, with a look of alarm. She saw in the pale light that the colour had faded from his cheek.

'What a fool!' he cried, striking his clenched fist upon the side of the vessel, 'what a fool I am to be frightened at this! Why do you come and say these things to me? Why do you come and terrify me out of my senses, when I am going straight home to the woman I love; to a girl whose heart is as true as the light of heaven; and in whom I no more expect to find any change than I do to see another sun rise in to-morrow's sky? Why do you come and try to put such fancies into my head, when I am going home to my darling wife?'

'Your wife,' she said; 'that is different. There is no reason that my terrors should terrify you. I am going to England to rejoin a man to whom I was engaged to be married fifteen years ago. He was too poor to marry then, and when I was offered a situation as governess in a rich Australian family, I persuaded him to let me accept it, so that I might leave him free and unfettered to win his way in the world, while I saved a little money to help us when we began life together. I never meant to stay away so long, but things have gone badly with him in England. That is my story, and you can understand my fears. They need not influence you. Mine is an exceptional case.'

'So is mine,' said George, impatiently. 'I tell you that mine is an exceptional case, although I swear to you that, until this moment, I have never known a fear as to the result of my voyage home. But you are right; your terrors have nothing to do with me. You have been away fifteen years; all kinds of things may happen in fifteen years. Now, it is only three years and a half this very month since I left England. What can have happened in such a short time as that?'

Miss Morley looked at him with a mournful smile, but did not speak. His feverish ardour, the freshness and impatience of his nature were so strange and new to her, that she looked at him half in admiration, half in pity.

'My pretty little wife! My gentle, innocent, loving, little wife! Do you know, Miss Morley,' he said, with all his old hopefulness of manner, 'that I left my little girl asleep, with her baby in her arms, and with nothing but a few blotted lines to tell her why her faithful husband had deserted her?'

'Deserted her!' exclaimed the governess.

'Yes. I was a cornet in a cavalry regiment when I first met my little darling. We were quartered at a stupid sea-port town, where my pet lived with her shabby old father, a half-pay naval officer; a regular old humbug, as poor as Job, and with an eye for nothing but the main chance. I saw through all his shallow tricks to catch one of us for his pretty daughter. I saw all the pitiful, contemptible, palpable traps he set for big dragoons to walk into. I saw through his shabby-genteel dinners and public-house port; his fine talk of the grandeur of his family; his sham pride and independence, and the sham tears in his bleared old eyes when he talked of his only child. He was a drunken old hypocrite, and he was ready to sell my poor little girl to the highest bidder. Luckily for me, I happened just then to be the highest bidder; for my father is a rich man, Miss Morley, and as it was love at first sight on both sides, my darling and I made a match of it. No sooner, however, did my father hear that I had married a penniless little girl, the daughter of a tipsy old half-pay lieutenant, than he wrote me a furious letter, telling me he would never again hold any communication with me, and that my yearly allowance would stop from my wedding-day. As there was no remaining in such a regiment as mine, with nothing but my pay to live on, and a pretty little wife to keep, I sold out, thinking that before the money that I got for my commission was exhausted, I should be sure to drop into something. I took my darling to Italy, and we lived there in splendid style as long as my two thousand pounds lasted; but when that began to dwindle down to a couple of hundred or so, we came back to England,

and as my darling had a fancy for being near that tiresome old father of hers, we settled at the watering-place where he lived. Well, as soon as the old man heard that I had a couple of hundred pounds left, he expressed a wonderful degree of affection for us, and insisted on our boarding in his house. We consented, still to please my darling, who had just then a peculiar right to have every whim and fancy of her innocent heart indulged. We did board with him, and finely he fleeced us; but when I spoke of it to my little wife, she only shrugged her shoulders, and said she did not like to be unkind to "poor papa." So poor papa made away with our little stock of money in no time; and as I felt that it was now becoming necessary to look about for something, I ran up to London, and tried to get a situation as a clerk in a merchant's office, or as account-ant, or book-keeper, or something of that kind. But I suppose there was the stamp of a heavy dragoon upon me, for do what I would I couldn't get anybody to believe in my capacity; and tired out, and down-hearted, I returned to my darling, to find her nursing a son and heir to his father's poverty. Poor little girl, she was very low-spirited; and when I told her that my London expedition had failed, she fairly broke down, and burst into a storm of sobs and lamentations, telling me that I ought not to have married her if I could give her nothing but poverty and misery; and that I had done her a cruel wrong in making her my wife. By Heaven! Miss Morley, her tears and reproaches drove me almost mad; and I flew into a rage with her, myself, her father, the world, and everybody in it, and then ran out of the house, declaring that I would never enter it again. I walked about the streets all that day half out of my mind, and with a strong inclination to throw myself into the sea, so as to leave my poor girl free to make a better match. "If I drown myself, her father must support her," I thought; "the old hypocrite could never refuse her a shelter, but while I live she has no claim on him." I went down to a rickety old wooden pier, meaning to wait there till it was dark, and then drop quietly over the end of it into the water; but while I sat there smoking my pipe, and staring vacantly at the sea-gulls, two men came down, and one of them began to talk of the Australian gold-diggings, and the great things that were to be done there. It appeared that he was going to sail in a day or two, and he was trying to persuade his companion to join him in the expedition.

'I listened to these men for upwards of an hour, following them up and down the pier with my pipe in my mouth, and hearing all their talk. After this I fell into conversation with them myself, and ascertained that there was a vessel going to leave Liverpool in three days, by which vessel one of the men was going out. This man gave me all the information I required, and told me, moreover, that a stalwart young fellow such as I could hardly fail to do well in the diggings. The thought flashed upon me so suddenly, that I grew hot and red in the face, and trembled in every limb with excitement. This was better than the water at any rate. Suppose I stole away from my darling, leaving her safe under her father's roof, and went and made a fortune in the new world, and came back in a twelvemonth to throw it into her lap; for I was so sanguine in those days that I counted on making my fortune in a year or so. I thanked the man for his information, and late at night strolled homewards. It was bitter winter weather, but I had been too full of passion to feel cold, and I walked through the quiet streets, with the snow drifting in my face, and a desperate hopefulness in my heart. The old man was sitting drinking brandy-and-water in his little dining-room; and my wife was upstairs, sleeping peacefully with the baby on her breast. I sat down and wrote a few brief lines, which told her that I never had loved her better than now when I seemed to desert her; that I was going to try my fortune in a new world; and that if I succeeded I should come back to bring her plenty and happiness, but that if I failed I should never look upon her face again. I divided the remainder of our money – something over forty pounds – into two equal portions, leaving one for her, and putting the other in my pocket. I knelt down and prayed for my wife and child, with my head upon the white counter-pane that covered them. I wasn't much of a praying man at ordinary times, but God knows *that* was a heartfelt prayer. I kissed her once and the baby once, and then crept out of the room. The dining-room door was open, and the old man was nodding over his paper. He looked up as he heard my step in the passage, and asked me where I was going. "To have a smoke in the street," I answered; and as this was a common habit of mine, he believed me. Three nights after this I was out at sea, bound for Melbourne – a steerage passenger, with a digger's tools for my baggage, and about seven shillings in my pocket.'

'And you succeeded?' asked Miss Morley.

'Not till I had long despaired of success; not until poverty and I had become such old companions and bedfellows, that, looking back at my past life, I wondered whether that dashing, reckless, extravagant, luxurious, champagne-drinking dragoon could have really been the same man who sat on the damp ground gnawing a mouldy crust in the wilds of the new world. I clung to the memory of my darling, and the trust that I had in her love and truth, as the one keystone that kept the fabric of my past life together – the one star that lit the thick black darkness of the future. I was hail fellow well met with bad men; I was in the centre of riot, drunkenness, and debauchery; but the purifying influence of my love kept me safe from all. Thin and gaunt, the half-starved shadow of what I once had been, I saw myself one day in a broken bit of looking-glass, and was frightened of my own face. But I toiled on through all; through disappointment and despair, rheumatism, fever, starvation, at the very gates of death, I toiled on steadily to the end; and in the end I conquered.'

He was so brave in his energy and determination, in his proud triumph of success, and in the knowledge of the difficulties he had vanquished, that the pale governess could only look at him in wondering admiration.

'How brave you were!' she said.

'Brave!' he cried, with a joyous peal of laughter; 'wasn't I working for my darling? Through all the dreary time of that probation, wasn't her pretty white hand beckoning me onwards to a happy future? Why, I have seen her under my wretched canvas tent, sitting by my side, with her boy in her arms, as plainly as I had ever seen her in the one happy year of our wedded life. At last, one dreary, foggy morning, just three months ago; with a drizzling rain wetting me to the skin; up to my neck in clay and mire; half-starved; enfeebled by fever; stiff with rheumatism; a monster nugget turned up under my spade, and I came upon a gold deposit of some magnitude. A fortnight afterwards I was the richest man in all the little colony about me. I travelled post-haste to Sydney, realised my gold findings which were worth upwards of £20,000, and a fortnight afterwards took my passage for England in this vessel; and in ten days – in ten days I shall see my darling.'

'But in all that time did you never write to your wife?'

'Never till a week before this vessel set sail. I could not write when everything looked so black. I could not write and tell her that I was fighting hard with despair and death. I waited for better fortune; and when that came, I wrote, telling her that I should be in England almost as soon as my letter, and giving her an address at a coffee-house in London, where she could write to me, telling me where to find her; though she is hardly likely to have left her father's house.'

He fell into a reverie after this, and puffed meditatively at his cigar. His companion did not disturb him. The last ray of the summer daylight had died out, and the pale light of the crescent moon only remained.

Presently George Talboys flung away his cigar, and, turning to the governess, cried abruptly, 'Miss Morley, if, when I get to England, I hear that anything has happened to my wife, I shall fall down dead.'

'My dear Mr. Talboys, why do you think of these things? God is very good to us; He will not afflict us beyond our power of endurance. I see all things, perhaps, in a melancholy light; for the long monotony of my life has given me too much time to think over my troubles.'

'And my life has been all action, privation, toil, alternate hope and despair; I have had no time to think upon the chances of anything happening to my darling. What a blind, reckless fool I have been! Three years and a half, and not one line, one word from her, or from any mortal creature who knows her. Heaven above! what may not have happened?'

In the agitation of his mind he began to walk rapidly up and down the lonely deck, the governess following, and trying to soothe him.

'I swear to you, Miss Morley,' he said, 'that, till you spoke to me to-night, I never felt one shadow of fear; and now I have that sick, sinking dread at my heart, which you talked of an hour ago. Let me alone, please, to get over it my own way.'

She drew silently away from him, and seated herself by the side of the vessel, looking over into the water.

CHAPTER III
Hidden relics

The same August sun which had gone down behind the waste of waters glimmered redly upon the broad face of the old clock over that ivy-covered archway which leads into the gardens of Audley Court.

A fierce and crimson sunset. The mullioned windows and the twinkling lattices are all ablaze with the red glory; the fading light flickers upon the leaves of the limes in the long avenue, and changes the still fish-pond into a sheet of burnished copper; even into those dim recesses of briar and brushwood, amidst which the old well is hidden, the crimson brightness penetrates in fitful flashes, till the dank weeds and the rusty iron wheel and broken woodwork seem as if they were flecked with blood.

The lowing of a cow in the quiet meadows, the splash of a trout in the fish-pond, the last notes of a tired bird, the creaking of waggon-wheels upon the distant road, every now and then breaking the evening silence, only made the stillness of the place seem more intense. It was almost oppressive, this twilight stillness. The very repose of the place grew painful from its intensity, and you felt as if a corpse must be lying somewhere within that grey and ivy-covered pile of building – so deathlike was the tranquillity of all around.

As the clock over the archway struck eight, a door at the back of the house was softly opened, and a girl came out into the gardens.

But even the presence of a human being scarcely broke the

silence; for the girl crept slowly over the thick grass, and gliding into the avenue by the side of the fish-pond, disappeared under the rich shelter of the limes.

She was not, perhaps, positively a pretty girl; but her appearance was of that order which is commonly called interesting. Interesting, it may be, because in the pale face and the light grey eyes, the small features and compressed lips, there was something which hinted at a power of repression and self-control not common in a woman of nineteen or twenty. She might have been pretty, I think, but for the one fault in her small oval face. This fault was an absence of colour. Not one tinge of crimson flushed the waxen whiteness of her cheeks; not one shadow of brown redeemed the pale insipidity of her eyebrows and eyelashes; not one glimmer of gold or auburn relieved the dull flaxen of her hair. Even her dress was spoiled by this same deficiency; the pale lavender muslin faded into a sickly grey, and the ribbon knotted round her throat melted into the same neutral hue.

Her figure was slim and fragile, and in spite of her humble dress, she had something of the grace and carriage of a gentlewoman; but she was only a simple country girl, called Phœbe Marks, who had been nursemaid in Mr. Dawson's family, and whom Lady Audley had chosen for her maid after her marriage with Sir Michael.

Of course this was a wonderful piece of good fortune for Phœbe, who found her wages trebled and her work light in the well-ordered household at the Court; and who was therefore quite as much the object of envy amongst her particular friends as my lady herself in higher circles.

A man who was sitting on the broken woodwork of the well started as the lady's-maid came out of the dim shade of the limes and stood before him amongst the weeds and brushwood.

I have said before that this was a neglected spot: it lay in the midst of a low shrubbery, hidden away from the rest of the gardens, and only visible from the garret windows at the back of the west wing. 'Why, Phœbe,' said the man, shutting a clasp-knife with which he had been stripping the bark from a black-thorn stake, 'you came upon me so still and sudden, that I thought you was an evil spirit. I've come across through the fields, and come in here at the gate agen the moat, and I was taking a rest before I came up to the house to ask if you was come back.'

'I can see the well from my bed-room window, Luke,' Phœbe answered, pointing to an open lattice in one of the gables. 'I saw you sitting here, and came down to have a chat; it's better talking out here than in the house where there's always somebody listening.'

The man was a big, broad-shouldered, stupid-looking clod-hopper of about twenty-three years of age. His dark-red hair grew low upon his forehead, and his bushy brows met over a pair of greenish grey eyes; his nose was large and well shaped, but the mouth was coarse in form and animal in expression. Rosy-cheeked, red-haired, and bull-necked, he was not unlike one of the stout oxen grazing in the meadows round about the Court.

The girl seated herself lightly upon the woodwork at his side, and put one of her hands, which had grown white in her new and easy service, about his thick neck.

'Are you glad to see me, Luke?' she asked.

'Of course I'm glad, lass,' he answered, boorishly, opening his knife again, and scraping away at the hedge-stake.

They were first cousins, and had been play-fellows in child-hood, and sweethearts in early youth.

'You don't *seem* much as if you were glad,' said the girl; 'you might look at me, Luke, and tell me if you think my journey has improved me.'

'It ain't put any colour into your cheeks, my girl,' he said, glancing up at her from under his lowering eyebrows; 'you're every bit as white as you was when you went away.'

'But they say travelling makes people genteel, Luke. I've been on the Continent with my lady, through all manner of curious places; and you know when I was a child, Squire Horton's daughters taught me to speak a little French, and I found it so nice to be able to talk to the people abroad.'

'Genteel!' cried Luke Marks, with a horse laugh; 'who wants you to be genteel, I wonder? Not me for one; when you're my wife you won't have over-much time for gentility, my girl. French, too! Dang me, Phœbe, I suppose when we've saved money enough between us to buy a bit of a farm, you'll be *parlyvooing* to the cows?'

She bit her lip as her lover spoke, and looked away. He went on cutting and chopping at a rude handle he was fashioning to the stake, whistling softly to himself all the while, and not once looking at his cousin.

For some time they were silent, but by-and-by she said, with her face still turned away from her companion –

'What a fine thing it is for Miss Graham, that was, to travel with her maid and her courier, and her chariot and four, and a husband that thinks there isn't one spot upon all the earth that's good enough for her to set her foot upon!'

'Ay, it is a fine thing, Phœbe, to have lots of money,' answered Luke, 'and I hope you'll be warned by that, my lass, to save up your wages agen we get married.'

'Why, what was she in Mr. Dawson's house only three months ago?' continued the girl, as if she had not heard her cousin's speech. 'What was she but a servant like me? Taking wages and working for them as hard, or harder than I did. You should have seen her shabby clothes, Luke – worn and patched, and darned, and turned and twisted, yet always looking nice upon her, somehow. She gives me more as lady's maid here than ever she got from Mr. Dawson then. Why,

I've seen her come out of the parlour with a few sovereigns and a little silver in her hand, that master had just given her for her quarter's salary; and now look at her!'

'Never you mind her,' said Luke; 'take care of yourself, Phœbe; that's all you've got to do. What should you say to a public-house for you and me, by-and-by, my girl? There's a deal of money to be made out of a public-house.'

The girl still sat with her face averted from her lover, her hands hanging listlessly in her lap, and her pale grey eyes fixed upon the last low streak of crimson dying out behind the trunks of the trees.

'You should see the inside of the house, Luke,' she said; 'it's a tumble-down looking place enough outside; but you should see my lady's rooms – all pictures and gilding, and great looking-glasses that stretch from the ceiling to the floor. Painted ceilings, too, that cost hundreds of pounds, the house-keeper told me, and all done for her.'

'She's a lucky one,' muttered Luke, with lazy indifference.

'You should have seen her while we were abroad, with a crowd of gentlemen always hanging about her; Sir Michael not jealous of them, only proud to see her so much admired. You should have heard her laugh and talk with them; throwing all their compliments and fine speeches back at them, as it were, as if they had been pelting her with roses. She set every body mad about her wherever she went. Her singing, her playing, her painting, her dancing, her beautiful smile, and sunshiny ringlets! She was always the talk of a place, as long as we stayed in it.'

'Is she at home to-night?'

'No, she has gone out with Sir Michael to a dinner party, at the Beeches. They've seven or eight miles to drive, and they won't be back till after eleven.'

'Then I'll tell you what, Phœbe, if the inside of the house is so mighty fine, I should like to have a look at it.'

'You shall, then. Mrs. Barton, the housekeeper, knows you by sight, and she can't object to my showing you some of the best rooms.'

It was almost dark when the cousins left the shrubbery and walked slowly to the house. The door by which they entered led into the servants' hall, on one side of which was the housekeeper's room. Phœbe Marks stopped for a moment to ask the housekeeper if she might take her cousin through some of the rooms, and having received permission to do so, lighted a candle at the lamp in the hall, and beckoned to Luke to follow her into the other part of the house.

The long, black oak corridors were dim in the ghostly twilight – the light carried by Phœbe looking only a poor speck of flame in the broad passages through which the girl led her cousin. Luke looked suspiciously over his shoulder now and then, half frightened of the creaking of his own hob-nailed boots.

'It's a mortal dull place, Phœbe,' he said, as they emerged from a passage into the principal hall, which was not yet lighted; 'I've heard tell of a murder that was done here in old times.'

'There are murders enough in these times, as to that, Luke,' answered the girl, ascending the staircase, followed by the young man.

She led the way through a great drawing-room, rich in satin and ormolu, buhl and inlaid cabinets, bronzes, cameos, statuettes, and trinkets, that glistened in the dusky light; then through a morning-room hung with proof engravings of valuable pictures; through this into an ante-chamber, where she stopped, holding the light above her head.

The young man stared about him, open-mouthed and open-eyed.

'It's a rare fine place,' he said, 'and must have cost a power of money.'

'Look at the pictures on the walls,' said Phœbe, glancing at the panels of the octagonal chamber, which were hung with Claudes and Poussins, Wouvermans and Cuyps. 'I've heard that those alone are worth a fortune. This is the entrance to my lady's apartments, Miss Graham that was.' She lifted a heavy green cloth curtain which hung across a doorway, and led the astonished countryman into a fairy-like boudoir, and thence to a dressing-room, in which the open doors of a wardrobe and a heap of dresses flung about a sofa showed that it still remained exactly as its occupant had left it.

'I've all these things to put away before my lady comes home, Luke; you might sit down here while I do it, I shan't be long.'

Her cousin looked round in gawky embarrassment, bewildered by the splendour of the room; and after some deliberation selected the most substantial of the chairs, on the extreme edge of which he carefully seated himself.

'I wish I could show you the jewels, Luke,' said the girl; 'but I can't, for she always keeps the keys herself; that's the case on the dressing-table there.'

'What, *that*?' cried Luke, staring at the massive walnut-wood and brass inlaid casket. 'Why, that's big enough to hold every bit of clothes I've got!'

'And it's as full as it can be of diamonds, rubies, pearls, and emeralds,' answered Phœbe, busy as she spoke in folding the rustling silk dresses, and laying them one by one upon the shelves of the wardrobe. As she was shaking out the flounces of the last, a jingling sound caught her ear, and she put her hand into the pocket.

'I declare!' she exclaimed, 'my lady has left her keys in her pocket for once in a way. I can show you the jewellery if you like, Luke.'

'Well, I may as well have a look at it, my girl,' he said, rising from his chair, and holding the light while his cousin unlocked

34

the casket. He uttered a cry of wonder when he saw the ornaments glittering on white satin cushions. He wanted to handle the delicate jewels; to pull them about, and find out their mercantile value. Perhaps a pang of longing and envy shot through his heart as he thought how he would have liked to have taken one of them.

'Why, one of those diamond things would set us up in life, Phœbe,' he said, turning a bracelet over and over in his big red hands.

'Put it down, Luke! Put it down directly!' cried the girl, with a look of terror; 'how can you speak about such things?'

He laid the bracelet in its place with a reluctant sigh, and then continued his examination of the casket.

'What's this?' he asked presently, pointing to a brass knob in the framework of the box.

He pushed it as he spoke, and a secret drawer, lined with purple velvet, flew out of the casket.

'Look ye, here!' cried Luke, pleased at his discovery.

Phœbe Marks threw down the dress she had been folding, and went over to the toilette table.

'Why, I never saw this before,' she said; 'I wonder what there is in it?'

There was not much in it; neither gold nor gems; only a baby's little worsted shoe rolled up in a piece of paper, and a tiny lock of pale and silky yellow hair, evidently taken from a baby's head. Phœbe's grey eyes dilated as she examined the little packet.

'So this is what my lady hides in the secret drawer,' she muttered.

'It's queer rubbish to keep in such a place,' said Luke, carelessly.

The girl's thin lips curved into a curious smile.

'You will bear me witness where I found this,' she said, putting the little parcel into her pocket.

'Why, Phœbe, you're never going to be such a fool as to take that,' cried the young man.

'I'd rather have this than the diamond bracelet you would have liked to take,' she answered; 'you shall have the public-house, Luke.'

CHAPTER IV

In the first page of the Times

Robert Audley was supposed to be a barrister. As a barrister was his name inscribed in the Law List; as a barrister, he had chambers in Fig-tree Court, Temple; as a barrister he had eaten the allotted number of dinners, which form the sublime ordeal through which the forensic aspirant wades on to fame and fortune. If these things can make a man a barrister, Robert Audley decidedly was one. But he had never either had a brief, or tried to get a brief, or even wished to have a brief in all those five years, during which his name had been painted upon one of the doors in Fig-tree Court. He was a handsome, lazy, care-for-nothing fellow, of about seven-and-twenty; the only son of a younger brother of Sir Michael Audley. His father had left him £400 a year, which his friends had advised him to increase by being called to the bar; and as he found it, after due consideration, more trouble to oppose the wishes of these friends, than to eat so many dinners, and to take a set of chambers in the Temple; he adopted the latter course, and unblushingly called himself a barrister.

Sometimes, when the weather was very hot, and he had exhausted himself with the exertion of smoking his German pipe, and reading French novels, he would stroll into the Temple Gardens, and lying in some shady spot, pale and cool, with his shirt collar turned down and a blue silk handkerchief tied loosely about his neck, would tell grave benchers that he had knocked himself up with overwork.

The sly old benchers laughed at the pleasing fiction; but

they all agreed that Robert Audley was a good fellow; a generous-hearted fellow; rather a curious fellow too, with a fund of sly wit and quiet humour, under his listless, dawdling, indifferent, irresolute manner. A man who would never get on in the world; but who would not hurt a worm. Indeed, his chambers were converted into a perfect dog-kennel by his habit of bringing home stray and benighted curs, who were attracted by his looks in the street, and followed him with abject fondness.

Robert always spent the hunting season at Audley Court; not that he was distinguished as a Nimrod, for he would quietly trot to covert upon a mild-tempered, stout-limbed, bay hack, and keep at a very respectful distance from the hard riders; his horse knowing quite as well as he did, that nothing was further from his thoughts than any desire to be in at the death.

The young man was a great favourite with his uncle, and by no means despised by his pretty, gipsy-faced, light-hearted, hoydenish cousin, Miss Alicia Audley. It might have seemed to other men that the partiality of a young lady, who was sole heiress to a very fine estate, was rather well worth cultivating, but it did not so occur to Robert Audley. Alicia was a very nice girl, he said, a jolly girl, with no nonsense about her – a girl of a thousand; but this was the highest point to which enthusiasm could carry him. The idea of turning his cousin's girlish liking for him to some good account never entered his idle brain. I doubt if he even had any correct notion of the amount of his uncle's fortune, and I am certain that he never for one moment calculated upon the chances of any part of that fortune ultimately coming to himself. So that when one fine spring morning, about three months before the time of which I am writing, the postman brought him the wedding cards of Sir Michael and Lady Audley, together with a very indignant letter from his cousin, setting forth how her father had just married a wax-dollish young person, no older than Alicia herself, with flaxen ringlets and a perpetual giggle; for, I am sorry to say, that Miss Audley's animus caused her so to describe that pretty musical laugh which had been so much admired in the late Miss Lucy Graham – when, I say, these documents reached Robert Audley – they elicited neither vexation nor astonishment in the lymphatic nature of that gentleman. He read Alicia's angry, crossed and re-crossed letter without so much as removing the amber mouthpiece of his German pipe from his moustachioed lips. When he had finished the perusal of the epistle, which he read with his dark eyebrows elevated to the centre of his forehead (his only manner of expressing surprise, by the way), he deliberately threw that and the wedding cards into the waste-paper basket, and putting down his pipe, prepared himself for the exertion of thinking out the subject.

'I always said the old buffer would marry,' he muttered, after about half an hour's reverie. 'Alicia and my lady, the step-mother, will go at it hammer and tongs. I hope they won't quarrel in the hunting season, or say unpleasant things to each other at the dinner-table: rows always upset a man's digestion.'

At about twelve o'clock on the morning following that night upon which the events recorded in my last chapter had taken place, the Baronet's nephew strolled out of the Temple, Blackfriars-ward, on his way to the City. He had in an evil hour obliged some necessitous friend by putting the ancient name of Audley across a bill of accommodation, which bill not having been met by the drawer, Robert was called upon to pay. For this purpose he sauntered up Ludgate Hill, with his blue necktie fluttering in the hot August air, and thence to a refreshingly cool banking-house in a shady court out of St. Paul's Churchyard, where he made arrangements for selling out a couple of hundred pounds' worth of consols.

He had transacted this business, and was loitering at the corner of the court, waiting for a chance Hansom, to convey him back to the Temple, when he was almost knocked down by a man of about his own age, who dashed headlong into the narrow opening.

'Be so good as to look where you're going, my friend!' Robert remonstrated, mildly, to the impetuous passenger; 'you might give a man warning before you throw him down and trample upon him.'

The stranger stopped suddenly, looked very hard at the speaker, and then gasped for breath.

'Bob!' he cried, in a tone expressive of the most intense astonishment; 'I only touched British ground after dark last night, and to think that I should meet you this morning!'

'I've seen you somewhere before, my bearded friend,' said Mr. Audley, calmly scrutinising the animated face of the other, 'but I'll be hanged if I can remember when or where.'

'What!' exclaimed the stranger, reproachfully, 'you don't mean to say that you've forgotten George Talboys?'

'No, I have not!' said Robert, with an emphasis by no means usual to him; and then hooking his arm into that of his friend, he led him into the shady court, saying with his old indifference, 'and now, George, tell us all about it.'

George Talboys did tell him all about it. He told that very story which he had related ten days before to the pale governess on board the *Argus*; and then, hot and breathless, he said that he had a bundle of Australian notes in his pocket, and that he wanted to bank them at Messrs. —, who had been his bankers many years before.

'If you'll believe me, I've only just left their counting-house,' said Robert. 'I'll go back with you, and we'll settle that matter in five minutes.'

They did contrive to settle it in about a quarter of an hour; and then Robert Audley was for starting off immediately for the Crown and Sceptre, or the Castle, Richmond, where they could have a bit of dinner, and talk over those good old times when they were together at Eton. But George told his friend that before he went anywhere, before he shaved, or broke his fast, or in any way refreshed himself after a night journey from Liverpool by express train, he must call at a certain coffee-house in Bridge Street, Westminster, where he expected to find a letter from his wife.

'Then I'll go there with you,' said Robert. 'The idea of your having a wife, George; what a preposterous joke.'

As they dashed through Ludgate Hill, Fleet Street and the Strand in a fast Hansom, George Talboys poured into his friend's ear all those wild hopes and dreams which had usurped such a dominion over his sanguine nature.

'I shall take a villa on the banks of the Thames, Bob,' he said, 'for the little wife and myself; and we'll have a yacht, Bob, old boy, and you shall lie on the deck and smoke while my pretty one plays her guitar and sings songs to us. She's for all the world like one of those what's-its-names, who got poor old Ulysses into trouble,' added the young man, whose classic lore was not very great.

The waiters at the Westminster coffee-house stared at the hollow-eyed, unshaven stranger, with his clothes of colonial cut, and his boisterous, excited manner; but he had been an old frequenter of the place in his military days, and when they heard who he was they flew to do his bidding.

He did not want much – only a bottle of soda water, and to know if there was a letter at the bar directed to George Talboys.

The waiter brought the soda water before the young men had seated themselves in a shady box near the disused fire-place. No; there was no letter for that name.

The waiter said it with consummate indifference, while he mechanically dusted the little mahogany table.

George's face blanched to a deadly whiteness.

'Talboys,' he said; 'perhaps you didn't hear the name distinctly – T, A, L, B, O, Y, S. Go and look again; there *must* be a letter.'

The waiter shrugged his shoulders as he left the room, and returned in three minutes to say that there was no name at all resembling Talboys in the letter rack. There was Brown, and Saunderson, and Pinchbeck; only three letters altogether.

The young man drank his soda water in silence, and then leaning his elbows upon the table, covered his face with his hands. There was something in his manner which told Robert Audley that this disappointment, trifling as it might appear, was in reality a very bitter one. He seated himself opposite to his friend, but did not attempt to address him.

By-and-by George looked up, and mechanically taking a greasy *Times* newspaper of the day before from a heap of journals on the table, stared vacantly at the first page.

I cannot tell how long he sat blankly staring at one paragraph amongst the list of deaths, before his dazed brain took in its full meaning; but after a considerable pause he pushed the newspaper over to Robert Audley, and with a face that had changed from its dark bronze to a sickly, chalky, greyish white, and with an awful calmness in his manner, he pointed with his finger to a line which ran thus:–

'On the 24th inst., at Ventnor, Isle of Wight, Helen Talboys, aged twenty-two.'

CHAPTER V

The headstone at Ventnor

Yes: there it was, in black and white – 'Helen Talboys, aged twenty-two.'

When George told the governess on board the *Argus* that if he heard any evil tidings of his wife he should drop down dead, he spoke in perfect good faith; and yet here were the worst tidings that could come to him, and he sat rigid, white, and helpless, staring stupidly at the shocked face of his friend.

The suddenness of the blow had stunned him. In his strange and bewildered state of mind he began to wonder what had happened, and why it was that one line in the *Times* newspaper could have so horrible an effect upon him.

Then by degrees even this vague consciousness of his misfortune faded slowly out of his mind, succeeded by a painful consciousness of external things.

The hot August sunshine; the dusty window-panes and shabby painted blinds; a file of fly-blown play-bills fastened to the wall; the blank and empty fire-place; a bald-headed old man nodding over the *Morning Advertiser*; the slipshod waiter folding a tumbled tablecloth, and Robert Audley's handsome face looking at him full of compassionate alarm. He knew that all these things took gigantic proportions, and then, one by one, melted into dark blots that swam before his eyes. He knew that there was a great noise as of half-a-dozen furious steam-engines tearing and grinding in his ears, and he knew nothing more, except that somebody or something fell heavily to the ground.

He opened his eyes upon the dusky evening in a cool and shaded room, the silence only broken by the rumbling of wheels at a distance.

He looked about him wonderingly, but half indifferently. His old friend, Robert Audley, was seated by his side smoking. George was lying on a low iron bedstead opposite to an open window, in which there was a stand of flowers and two or three birds in cages.

'You don't mind the pipe, do you, George?' his friend asked quietly.

'No.'

He lay for some time looking at the flowers and the birds: one canary was singing a shrill hymn to the setting sun.

'Do the birds annoy you, George? Shall I take them out of the room?'

'No: I like to hear them sing.'

Robert Audley knocked the ashes out of his pipe, laid the precious meerschaum tenderly upon the mantel-piece, and going into the next room, returned presently with a cup of strong tea.

'Take this, George,' he said, as he placed the cup on a little table close to George's pillow; 'it will do your head good.'

The young man did not answer, but looked slowly round the room, and then at his friend's grave face.

'Bob,' he said, 'where are we?'

'In my chambers, my dear boy, in the Temple. You have no lodgings of your own, so you may as well stay with me while you're in town.'

George passed his hand once or twice across his forehead, and then, in a hesitating manner, said quietly –

'That newspaper this morning, Bob; what was it?'

'Never mind just now, old boy; drink some tea.'

'Yes, yes,' cried George, impatiently, raising himself upon the bed, and staring about him with hollow eyes, 'I remember all about it. Helen, my Helen! my wife, my darling, my only love! Dead! dead!'

'George,' said Robert Audley, laying his hand gently upon the young man's arm, 'you must remember that the person whose name you saw in the paper may not be your wife. There may have been some other Helen Talboys.'

'No, no,' he cried, 'the age corresponds with hers, and Talboys is such an uncommon name.'

'It may be a misprint for Talbot.'

'No, no, no; my wife is dead!'

He shook off Robert's restraining hand, and rising from the bed, walked straight to the door.

'Where are you going?' exclaimed his friend.

'To Ventnor, to see her grave.'

'Not to-night, George, not to-night. I will go with you myself by the first train to-morrow.'

Robert led him back to the bed, and gently forced him to lie down again. He then gave him an opiate which had been left for him by the medical man whom they had called in at the coffee-house in Bridge Street, when George fainted.

So George Talboys fell into a heavy slumber, and dreamed that he went to Ventnor, to find his wife alive and happy, but wrinkled, old, and grey, and to find his son grown into a young man.

Early the next morning he was seated opposite to Robert Audley in the first-class carriage of an express, whirling through the pretty open country towards Portsmouth.

They rode from Ryde to Ventnor under the burning heat of the mid-day sun. As the two young men alighted from the coach, the people standing about stared at George's white face and untrimmed beard.

'What are we to do, George?' Robert Audley asked. 'We have no clue to finding the people you want to see.'

The young man looked at him with a pitiful, bewildered

expression. The big dragoon was as helpless as a baby; and Robert Audley, the most vacillating and unenergetic of men, found himself called upon to act for another. He rose superior to himself and equal to the occasion.

'Had we better ask at one of the hotels about a Mrs. Talboys, George?' he said.

'Her father's name was Maldon,' George muttered; 'he could never have sent her here to die alone.'

They said nothing more, but Robert walked straight to an hotel, where he inquired for a Mr. Maldon.

'Yes,' they told him, 'there was a gentleman of that name stopping at Ventnor, a Captain Maldon; his daughter was lately dead. The waiter would go and inquire for the address.'

The hotel was a busy place at this season; people hurrying in and out, and a great bustle of grooms and waiters about the hall.

George Talboys leaned against the door-post with much the same look in his face as that which had frightened his friend in the Westminster coffee-house.

The worst was confirmed *now*. His wife, Captain Maldon's daughter, was dead.

The waiter returned in about five minutes to say that Captain Maldon was lodging at Landsdowne Cottages, No. 4.

They easily found the house, a shabby bow-windowed cottage, looking towards the water.

Was Captain Maldon at home? No, the landlady said; he had gone out to the beach with his little grandson. Would the gentlemen walk in and sit down a bit?

George mechanically followed his friend into the little front parlour – dusty, shabbily furnished, and disorderly, with a child's broken toys scattered on the floor, and the scent of stale tobacco hanging about the muslin window curtains.

'Look!' said George, pointing to a picture over the mantel-piece.

It was his own portrait, painted in the old dragooning days. A pretty good likeness, representing him in uniform, with his charger in the background.

Perhaps the most animated of men would have been scarcely so wise a comforter as Robert Audley. He did not utter a word to the stricken widower, but quietly seated himself with his back to George, looking out of the open window.

For some time the young man wandered restlessly about the room, looking at and sometimes touching the knick-knacks lying here and there.

Her work-box, with an unfinished piece of work; her album, full of extracts from Byron and Moore, written in his own scrawling hand; some books which he had given her, and a bunch of withered flowers in a vase they had bought in Italy.

'Her portrait used to hang by the side of mine,' he muttered; 'I wonder what they have done with it?'

By-and-by he said, after about half-an-hour's silence –

'I should like to see the woman of the house; I should like to ask her about—'

He broke down, and buried his face in his hands.

Robert summoned the landlady. She was a good-natured, garrulous creature, used to sickness and death, for many of her lodgers came to her to die. She told all the particulars of Mrs. Talboys' last hours; how she had come to Ventnor only a week before her death in the last stage of decline; and how day by day she had gradually but surely sunk under the fatal malady. 'Was the gentleman any relative?' she asked of Robert Audley, as George sobbed aloud.

'Yes, he is the lady's husband.'

'What!' the woman cried; 'him as deserted her so cruel, and left her with her pretty boy upon her poor old father's hands, which Captain Maldon has told me often, with the tears in his poor eyes?'

'I did not desert her,' George cried out; and then he told the history of his three years' struggle.

'Did she speak of me?' he asked; 'did she speak of me at – at – the last?'

'No, she went off as quiet as a lamb. She said very little from the first; but the last day she knew nobody, not even her little boy nor her poor old father, who took on awful. Once she went off wild like, talking about her mother, and about the cruel shame it was to have to die in a strange place, till it was quite pitiful to hear her.'

'Her mother died when she was quite a child,' said George. 'To think that she should remember her and speak of her, but never once of me.'

The woman took him into the little bed-room in which his wife had died. He knelt down by the bed and kissed the pillow tenderly, the landlady crying as he did so.

While he was kneeling, praying perhaps, with his face buried in this humble snow-white pillow, the woman took something from a drawer. She gave it to him when he rose from his knees; it was a long tress of hair wrapped in silver paper.

'I cut this off when she lay in her coffin,' she said, 'poor dear!'

He pressed the soft lock to his lips. 'Yes,' he murmured; 'this is the dear hair that I have kissed so often when her head lay upon my shoulder. But it always had a rippling wave in it then, and now it seems smooth and straight.'

'It changes in illness,' said the landlady. 'If you'd like to see where they have laid her, Mr. Talboys, my little boy shall show you the way to the churchyard.'

So George Talboys and his faithful friend walked to the quiet spot, where beneath a mound of earth, to which the patches of fresh turf hardly adhered, lay that wife of whose welcoming smile George had dreamed so often in the far Antipodes.

Robert left the young man by the side of this new-made grave, and returning in about a quarter of an hour, found that he had not once stirred.

He looked up presently, and said that if there was a stone-mason's anywhere near he should like to give an order.

They very easily found the stonemason, and sitting down amidst the fragmentary litter of the man's yard, George Talboys wrote in pencil this brief inscription for the headstone of his dead wife's grave:–

Sacred to the Memory of

HELEN,

THE BELOVED WIFE OF GEORGE TALBOYS,

Who departed this life

August 24th, 1857, aged 22,

Deeply regretted by her sorrowing Husband.

CHAPTER VI

Anywhere, anywhere out of the world

When they returned to Landsdowne Cottage they found the old man had not yet come in, so they walked down to the beach to look for him. After a brief search they found him, sitting upon a heap of pebbles, reading a newspaper and eating filberts. The little boy was at some distance from his grandfather, digging in the sand with a wooden spade. The crape round the old man's shabby hat, and the child's poor little black frock, went to George's heart. Go where he would he met confirmation of this great grief of his life. His wife was dead.

'Mr. Maldon,' he said, as he approached his father-in-law.

The old man looked up, and, dropping his newspaper, rose from the pebbles with a ceremonious bow. His faded, light hair was tinged with grey; he had a pinched hook nose, watery blue eyes, and an irresolute-looking mouth; he wore his shabby dress with an affectation of foppish gentility; an eye-glass dangled over his closely-buttoned-up waistcoat, and he carried a cane in his ungloved hand.

'Good heavens!' cried George, 'don't you know me?'

Mr. Maldon started and coloured violently, with something of a frightened look, as he recognised his son-in-law.

'My dear boy,' he said, 'I did not; for the first moment I did not; that beard makes such a difference. You find the beard makes a great difference, do you not, sir?' he said, appealing to Robert.

'Great Heaven!' exclaimed George Talboys, 'is this the way

50

you welcome me? I come to England to find my wife dead within a week of my touching land, and you begin to chatter to me about my beard – you, her father!'

'True! true!' muttered the old man, wiping his blood-shot eyes; 'a sad shock, a sad shock, my dear George. If you'd only been here a week earlier!'

'If I had,' cried George, in an outburst of grief and passion, 'I scarcely think that I would have *let* her die. I would have disputed for her with death. I would! I would! O God! why did not the *Argus* go down with every soul on board her before I came to see this day?'

He began to walk up and down the beach, his father-in-law looking helplessly at him, rubbing his feeble eyes with a handkerchief.

'I've a strong notion that that old man didn't treat his daughter too well,' thought Robert, as he watched the half-pay lieutenant. 'He seems, for some reason or other, to be half afraid of George.'

While the agitated young man walked up and down in a fever of regret and despair, the child ran to his grandfather and clung about the tails of his coat.

'Come home, grandpa, come home,' he said. 'I'm tired.'

George Talboys turned at the sound of the babyish voice, and long and earnestly looked at the boy.

He had his father's brown eyes and dark hair.

'My darling! my darling!' said George, taking the child in his arms, 'I am your father, come across the sea to find you. Will you love me?'

The little fellow pushed him away. 'I don't know you,' he said. 'I love grandpa and Mrs. Monks, at Southampton.'

'Georgey has a temper of his own, sir,' said the old man. 'He has been spoiled.'

They walked slowly back to the cottage, and once more George Talboys told the history of that desertion which had seemed so cruel. He told, too, of the twenty thousand pounds banked by him the day before. He had not the heart to ask any questions about the past, and his father-in-law only told him that a few months after his departure they had gone from the place where George left them to live at Southampton, where Helen got a few pupils for the piano, and where they managed pretty well till her health failed, and she fell into the decline of which she died. Like most sad stories, it was a very brief one.

'The boy seems fond of you, Mr. Maldon,' said George, after a pause.

'Yes, yes,' answered the old man, smoothing the child's curling hair, 'yes, Georgey is very fond of his grandfather.'

'Then he had better stop with you. The interest of my money will be about six hundred a year. You can draw a hundred of that for Georgey's education, leaving the rest to accumulate till he is of age. My friend here will be trustee, and if he will undertake the charge, I will appoint him guardian to the boy, allowing him for the present to remain under your care.'

'But why not take care of him yourself, George?' asked Robert Audley.

'Because I shall sail in the very next vessel that leaves Liverpool for Australia. I shall be better in the diggings or the backwoods than ever I could be here. I'm broken for a civilised life from this hour, Bob.'

The old man's weak eyes sparkled as George declared this determination.

'My poor boy, I think you're right,' he said, 'I really think you're right. The change, the wild life, the – the—' He hesitated and broke down, as Robert looked earnestly at him.

'You're in a great hurry to get rid of your son-in-law, I think, Mr. Maldon,' he said gravely.

'Get rid of him, dear boy! Oh, no, no! But for his own sake, my dear sir, for his own sake, you know.'

'I think for his own sake he'd much better stay in England and look after his son,' said Robert.

'But I tell you I can't,' cried George; 'every inch of this accursed ground is hateful to me – I want to run out of it as I would out of a graveyard. I'll go back to town to-night, get that business about the money settled early to-morrow morning, and start for Liverpool without a moment's delay. I shall be better when I've put half the world between me and her grave.'

Before he left the house he stole out to the landlady, and asked some more questions about his dead wife.

'Were they poor?' he asked; 'were they pinched for money while she was ill?'

'Oh, no!' the woman answered; 'though the captain dresses shabby, he has always plenty of sovereigns in his purse. The poor lady wanted for nothing.'

George was relieved at this, though it puzzled him to know where the drunken half-pay lieutenant could have contrived to find money for all the expenses of his daughter's illness.

But he was too thoroughly broken down by the calamity which had befallen him to be able to think much of anything, so he asked no further questions, but walked with his father-in-law and Robert Audley down to the boat by which they were to cross to Portsmouth.

The old man bade Robert a very ceremonious adieu.

'You did not introduce me to your friend, by-the-bye, my dear boy,' he said. George stared at him, muttered something indistinct, and ran down the ladder to the boat before Mr. Maldon could repeat his request. The steamer sped away through the sunset, and the outlines of the island melted in the horizon as they neared the opposite shore.

'To think,' said George, 'that two nights ago at this time I was steaming into Liverpool, full of the hope of clasping her to my heart, and to-night I am going away from her grave!'

The document which appointed Robert Audley as guardian to little George Talboys was drawn up in a solicitor's office the next morning.

'It's a great responsibility,' exclaimed Robert; 'I, guardian to anybody or anything! I, who never in my life could take care of myself!'

'I trust in your noble heart, Bob,' said George, 'I know you will take care of my poor orphan boy, and see that he is well used by his grandfather. I shall only draw enough from George's fortune to take me back to Sydney, and then begin my old work again.'

But it seemed as if George was destined to be himself the guardian of his son; for when he reached Liverpool, he found that a vessel had just sailed, and that there would not be another for a month; so he returned to London, and once more threw himself upon Robert Audley's hospitality.

The barrister received him with open arms; he gave him the room with the birds and flowers, and had a bed put up in his dressing-room for himself. Grief is so selfish that George did not know the sacrifices his friend made for his comfort. He only knew that for him the sun was darkened, and the business of life done. He sat all day long smoking cigars, and staring at the flowers and canaries, chafing for the time to pass that he might be far out at sea.

But, just as the hour was drawing near for the sailing of the vessel, Robert Audley came in one day full of a great scheme. A friend of his, another of those barristers whose last thought is of a brief, was going to St. Petersburg to spend the winter, and wanted Robert to accompany him. Robert would only go on condition that George went too.

For a long time the young man resisted, but when he found that Robert was, in a quiet way, thoroughly determined upon not going without him, he gave in, and consented to join the party. 'What did it matter?' he said. 'One place was the same to him as another, anywhere out of England; what did he care where?'

This was not a very cheerful way of looking at things, but Robert Audley was quite satisfied with having won his consent.

The three young men started under very favourable circumstances, carrying letters of introduction to the most influential inhabitants of the Russian capital.

Before leaving England Robert wrote to his cousin Alicia, telling her of his intended departure with his old friend George Talboys, whom he had lately met for the first time after a lapse of years, and who had just lost his wife.

Alicia's reply came by return of post, and ran thus:–

'MY DEAR ROBERT, – How cruel of you to run away to that horrid St. Petersburg before the hunting season! I have heard that people lose their noses in that disagreeable climate, and as yours is rather a long one, I should advise you to return before the very severe weather sets in. What sort of person is this young Mr. Talboys? If he is very agreeable you may bring him to the Court as soon as you return from your travel. Lady Audley tells me to request you to secure her a set of sables. You are not to consider the price, but to be sure that they are the handsomest that can be obtained. Papa is perfectly absurd about his new wife, and she and I cannot get on together at all; not that she is disagreeable to me, for, as far as that goes, she makes herself agreeable to every one; but she is so irretrievably childish and silly.

'Believe me to be, my dear Robert,

'Your affectionate Cousin,
'ALICIA AUDLEY.'

CHAPTER VII
After a year

The first year of George Talboys' widowhood passed away; the deep band of crape about his hat grew brown and rusty, and as the last burning day of another August faded out, he sat smoking cigars in the quiet chambers in Fig-tree Court, much as he had done the year before, when the horror of his grief was new to him, and every object in life, however trifling or however important, seemed saturated with his one great sorrow.

But the big ex-dragoon had survived his affliction by a twelvemonth, and hard as it may be to have to tell it, he did not look much the worse for it. Heaven knows what inner change may have been worked by that bitter disappointment! Heaven knows what wasted agonies of remorse and self-reproach may not have racked George's honest heart as he lay awake at nights thinking of the wife he had abandoned in the pursuit of a fortune which she never lived to share.

Once, while they were abroad, Robert Audley ventured to congratulate him upon his recovered spirits. He burst into a bitter laugh.

'Do you know, Bob,' he said, 'that when some of our fellows were wounded in India, they came home bringing bullets inside them. They did not talk of them, and they were stout and hearty, and looked as well, perhaps, as you or I; but every change in the weather, however slight, every variation of the atmosphere, however trifling, brought back the old agony of their wounds as sharp as ever they had felt it on the battle-field.

I've had my wound, Bob; I carry the bullet still, and I shall carry it into my coffin.'

The travellers returned from St. Petersburg in the spring, and George again took up his quarters in his old friend's chambers, only leaving them now and then to run down to Southampton and take a look at his little boy. He always went loaded with toys and sweetmeats to give to the child; but, for all this, Georgey would not become very familiar with his papa, and the young man's heart sickened as he began to fancy that even his child was lost to him.

'What can I do?' he thought. 'If I take him away from his grandfather I shall break his heart; if I let him remain he will grow up a stranger to me, and care more for that drunken old hypocrite than for his own father. But then what could an ignorant heavy dragoon like me do with such a child? What could I teach him except to smoke cigars, and idle about all day with his hands in his pockets?'

So the anniversary of that 30th of August, upon which George had seen the advertisement of his wife's death in the *Times* newspaper, came round for the first time, and the young man put off his black clothes and the shabby crape from his hat, and laid his mourning garments in a trunk in which he kept a packet of his wife's letters, and that lock of hair which had been cut from her head after death. Robert Audley had never seen either the letters or the long tress of silky hair; nor, indeed, had George ever mentioned the name of his dead wife after that one day at Ventnor on which he learned the full particulars of her decease.

'I shall write to my cousin Alicia to-day, George,' the young barrister said, upon this very 30th of August. 'Do you know that the day after to-morrow is the 1st of September? I shall write and tell her that we will both run down to the Court for a week's shooting.'

'No, no, Bob: go by yourself; they don't want me, and I'd rather—'

'Bury yourself in Fig-tree Court, with no company but my dogs and canaries! No, George, you shall do nothing of the kind.'

'But I don't care for shooting.'

'And do you suppose *I* care for it?' cried Robert, with charming *naïveté*. 'Why, man, I don't know a partridge from a pigeon, and it might be the 1st of April instead of the 1st of September for aught I care. I never hit a bird in my life, but I have hurt my own shoulder with the weight of my gun. I only go down to Essex for the change of air, the good dinners, and the sight of my uncle's honest, handsome face. Besides, this time I've another inducement, as I want to see this fair-haired paragon, my new aunt. You'll go with me, George?'

'Yes, if you really wish it.'

The quiet form which his grief had taken after its first brief violence left him as submissive as a child to the will of his friend; ready to go anywhere or do anything; never enjoying himself, or originating any enjoyment, but joining in the pleasures of others with a hopeless, quiet, uncomplaining, unobtrusive resignation peculiar to his simple nature. But the return of post brought a letter from Alicia Audley, to say that the two young men could not be received at the Court.

'There are seventeen spare bed-rooms,' wrote the young lady, in an indignant running hand, 'but for all that, my dear Robert, you can't come; for my lady has taken it into her silly head that she is too ill to entertain visitors (there is no more the matter with her than there is with me), and she cannot have gentlemen (great rough men, she says) in the house. Please apologise to your friend Mr. Talboys, and tell him that papa hopes to see you both in the hunting season.'

'My lady's airs and graces shan't keep us out of Essex for all that,' said Robert, as he twisted the letter into a pipe-light for his big meerschaum. 'I'll tell you what we'll do, George; there's a glorious inn at Audley, and plenty of fishing in the neighbourhood: we'll go there and have a week's sport. Fishing is much better than shooting; you've only to lie on a bank and stare at your line; I don't find that you often catch anything, but it's very pleasant.'

He held the twisted letter to the feeble spark of fire glimmering in the grate as he spoke, and then changing his mind, deliberately unfolded it and smoothed the crumpled paper with his hand.

'Poor little Alicia!' he said thoughtfully; 'it's rather hard to treat her letters so cavalierly – I'll keep it;' upon which Mr. Robert Audley put the note back into its envelope, and afterwards thrust it into a pigeon-hole in his office desk marked *Important*. Heaven knows what wonderful documents there were in this particular pigeon-hole, but I do not think it likely to have contained anything of great judicial value. If any one could at that moment have told the young barrister that so simple a thing as his cousin's brief letter would one day come to be a link in that terrible chain of evidence afterwards to be slowly forged in the one only criminal case in which he was ever to be concerned, perhaps Mr. Robert Audley would have lifted his eyebrows a little higher than usual.

So the two young men left London the next day with one portmanteau and a rod and tackle between them, and reached the straggling, old-fashioned, fast-decaying village of Audley in time to order a good dinner at the Sun Inn.

Audley Court was about three-quarters of a mile from the village, lying, as I have said, deep down in a hollow, shut in by luxuriant timber. You could only reach it by a cross road, bordered by trees, and as trimly kept as the avenues in a gentleman's park. It was a dreary place enough, even in all its rustic beauty, for so bright a creature as the late Miss Lucy Graham, but the generous baronet had transformed the interior of the grey old mansion into a little palace for his young wife, and Lady Audley seemed as happy as a child surrounded by new and costly toys.

In her better fortunes, as in her old days of dependence, wherever she went she seemed to take sunshine and gladness with her. In spite of Miss Alicia's undisguised contempt for her step-mother's childishness and frivolity, Lucy was better loved and more admired than the baronet's daughter. That very childishness had a charm which few could resist. The innocence and candour of an infant beamed in Lady Audley's fair face, and shone out of her large and liquid blue eyes. The rosy lips, the delicate nose, the profusion of fair ringlets, all contributed to preserve to her beauty the character of extreme youth and freshness. She owned to twenty years of age, but it was hard to believe her more than seventeen. Her fragile figure, which she loved to dress in heavy velvets and stiff rustling silks, till she looked like a child tricked out for a masquerade, was as girlish as if she had but just left the nursery. All her amusements were childish. She hated reading, or study of any kind, and loved society; rather than be alone she would admit Phœbe Marks into her confidence, and loll on one of the sofas in her luxurious dressing-room, discussing a new costume for some coming dinner party, or sit chattering to the girl, with her jewel box beside her, upon the satin cushions, and Sir Michael's presents spread out in her lap, while she counted and admired her treasures.

She had appeared at several public balls at Chelmsford and Colchester, and was immediately established as the belle of the county. Pleased with her high position and her handsome house; with every caprice gratified, every whim indulged; admired and caressed wherever she went; fond of her generous husband; rich in a noble allowance of pin-money; with no poor relations to worry her with claims upon her purse or patronage, it would have been hard to find in the county of Essex a more fortunate creature than Lucy, Lady Audley.

The two young men loitered over the dinner-table in the private sitting-room at the Sun Inn. The windows were thrown wide open, and the fresh country air blew in upon them as they dined. The weather was lovely; the foliage of the woods touched here and there with faint gleams of the earliest tints of autumn; the yellow corn still standing in some of the fields, in others just falling under the shining sickle; while in the narrow lanes you met great waggons drawn by broad-chested cart horses, carrying home the rich golden store. To any one who has been, during the hot summer months, pent up in London, there is in the first taste of rustic life a kind of sensuous rapture scarcely to be described. George Talboys felt this, and in this he experienced the nearest approach to enjoyment that he had ever known since his wife's death.

The clock struck five as they finished dinner.

'Put on your hat, George,' said Robert Audley; 'they don't dine at the Court till seven; we shall have time to stroll down and see the old place and its inhabitants.'

The landlord, who had come into the room with a bottle of wine, looked up as the young man spoke.

'I beg your pardon, Mr. Audley,' he said, 'but if you want to see your uncle, you'll lose your time by going to the Court just now. Sir Michael and my lady and Miss Alicia have all gone to the races up at Chorley, and they won't be back till nigh upon eight o'clock most likely. They must pass by here to go home.'

Under these circumstances of course it was no use going to the Court, so the two young men strolled through the village and looked at the old church, and then went and reconnoitred the streams in which they were to fish the next day, and by such means beguiled the time till after seven o'clock. At about a quarter past that hour they returned to the inn, and seating themselves in an open window, lit their cigars and looked out at the peaceful prospect.

We hear every day of murders committed in the country. Brutal and treacherous murders; slow, protracted agonies from poisons administered by some kindred hand; sudden and violent deaths by cruel blows, inflicted with a stake cut from some spreading oak, whose very shadow promised – peace. In the county of which I write, I have been shown a meadow in which, on a quiet summer Sunday evening, a young farmer murdered the girl who had loved and trusted him; and yet even now, with the stain of that foul deed upon it, the aspect of the spot is – peace. No crime has ever been committed in the worst rookeries about Seven Dials that has not been also done in the face of that sweet rustic calm which still, in spite of all, we look on with a tender, half-mournful yearning, and associate with – peace.

It was dusk when gigs and chaises, dog-carts and clumsy farmers' phaetons, began to rattle through the village street, and under the windows of the Sun Inn; deeper dusk still when an open carriage and four drew suddenly up beneath the rocking sign-post.

It was Sir Michael Audley's barouche which came to so sudden a stop before the little inn. The harness of one of the leaders had become out of order, and the foremost postilion dismounted to set it right.

'Why, it's my uncle!' cried Robert Audley, as the carriage stopped. "I'll run down and speak to him.'

George lit another cigar, and, sheltered by the window curtains, looked out at the little party. Alicia sat with her back to the horses, and he could perceive, even in the dusk, that she was a handsome brunette; but Lady Audley was seated on the side of the carriage furthest from the inn, and he could see nothing of the fair-haired paragon of whom he had heard so much.

'Why, Robert,' exclaimed Sir Michael, as his nephew emerged from the inn, 'this is a surprise!'

'I have not come to intrude upon you at the Court, my dear uncle,' said the young man, as the baronet shook him by the hand in his own hearty fashion. 'Essex is my native county, you know, and about this time of year I generally have a touch of home sickness; so George and I have come down to the inn for two or three days' fishing.'

'George – George who?'

'George Talboys.'

'What, has he come?' cried Alicia. 'I'm so glad; for I'm dying to see this handsome young widower.'

'Are you, Alicia?' said her cousin. 'Then, egad, I'll run and fetch him, and introduce you to him at once.'

Now, so complete was the dominion which Lady Audley had, in her own childish, unthinking way, obtained over her devoted husband, that it was very rarely that the baronet's eyes were long removed from his wife's pretty face. When Robert, therefore, was about to re-enter the inn, it needed but the faintest elevation of Lucy's eyebrows, with a charming expression of weariness and terror, to make her husband aware that she did not want to be bored by an introduction to Mr. George Talboys.

'Never mind to-night, Bob,' he said. 'My wife is a little tired after our long day's pleasure. Bring your friend to dinner to-morrow, and then he and Alicia can make each other's acquaintance. Come round and speak to Lady Audley, and then we'll drive home.'

My lady was so terribly fatigued that she could only smile sweetly, and hold out a tiny gloved hand to her nephew by marriage.

'You will come and dine with us to-morrow, and bring your interesting friend?' she said, in a low and tired voice. She had been the chief attraction of the race-course, and was wearied out by the exertion of fascinating half the county.

'It's a wonder she didn't treat you to her never-ending laugh,' whispered Alicia, as she leant over the carriage door to bid Robert good night; 'but I dare say she reserves that for your delectation to-morrow. I suppose *you* are fascinated as well as everybody else?' added the young lady rather snappishly.

'She is a lovely creature, certainly,' murmured Robert, with placid admiration.

'Oh, of course! Now, she is the first woman of whom I ever heard you say a civil word, Robert Audley. I'm sorry to find you can only admire wax dolls.'

Poor Alicia had had many skirmishes with her cousin upon that peculiar temperament of his, which, while it enabled him to go through life with perfect content and tacit enjoyment, entirely precluded his feeling one spark of enthusiasm upon any subject whatever.

'As to his ever falling in love,' thought the young lady sometimes, 'the idea is too preposterous. If all the divinities upon earth were ranged before him, waiting for his sultan-ship to throw the handkerchief, he would only lift his eyebrows to the middle of his forehead, and then tell them to scramble for it.'

But, for once in his life, Robert was almost enthusiastic.

'She's the prettiest little creature you ever saw in your life, George,' he cried, when the carriage had driven off and he returned to his friend. 'Such blue eyes, such ringlets, such a ravishing smile, such a fairy-like bonnet – all of a tremble with heartsease and dewy spangles, shining out of a cloud of gauze. George Talboys, I feel like the hero of a French novel; I am falling in love with my aunt.'

The widower only sighed and puffed his cigar fiercely out of the open window. Perhaps he was thinking of that far-away time – little better than five years ago, in fact; but such an age gone by to him – when he first met the woman for whom he had worn crape round his hat three days before. They returned, all those old unforgotten feelings; they came back, with the scene of their birthplace. Again he lounged with his brother officers upon the shabby pier at the shabby watering-place, listening to a dreary band with a cornet that was a note and a half flat. Again he heard the old operatic airs, and again *she* came tripping towards him leaning on her old father's arm, and pretending (with such a charming, delicious, serio-comic pretence) to be listening to the music, and quite unaware of the admiration of half-a-dozen open-mouthed cavalry officers. Again the old fancy came back that she was something too beautiful for earth, or earthly uses, and that to approach her was to walk in a higher atmosphere and to breathe a purer air. And since this she had been his wife, and the mother of his child. She lay in the little churchyard at Ventnor, and only a year ago he had given the order for her tombstone. A few slow, silent tears dropped upon his waistcoat as he thought of these things in the quiet and darkening room.

Lady Audley was so exhausted when she reached home, that she excused herself from the dinner-table, and retired at once to her dressing-room, attended by her maid, Phœbe Marks.

She was a little capricious in her conduct to this maid; sometimes very confidential, sometimes rather reserved; but she was a liberal mistress, and the girl had every reason to be satisfied with her situation.

This evening, in spite of her fatigue, she was in extremely high spirits, and gave an animated account of the races, and the company present at them.

'I am tired to death, though, Phœbe,' she said by-and-by. 'I'm afraid I must look a perfect fright, after a day in the hot sun.'

There were lighted candles on each side of the glass before which Lady Audley was standing unfastening her dress. She looked full at her maid as she spoke, her blue eyes clear and bright, and the rosy, childish lips puckered into an arch smile.

'You are a little pale, my lady,' answered the girl, 'but you look as pretty as ever.'

'That's right, Phœbe,' she said, flinging herself into a chair and throwing back her curls at the maid, who stood, brush in hand, ready to arrange the luxuriant hair for the night. 'Do you know, Phœbe, I have heard some people say you and I are alike?'

'I have heard them say so too, my lady,' said the girl quietly, 'but they must be very stupid to say it, for your ladyship is a beauty, and I'm a poor plain creature.'

'Not at all, Phœbe,' said the little lady superbly; 'you *are* like me, and your features are very nice; it is only colour that you want. My hair is pale yellow shot with gold, and yours is drab; my eyebrows and eyelashes are dark brown, and yours are almost – I scarcely like to say it, but they're almost white, my dear Phœbe; your complexion is sallow, and mine is pink and rosy. Why, with a bottle of hair dye, such as we see advertised in the papers, and a pot of rouge, you'd be as good-looking as I any day, Phœbe.'

She prattled on in this way for a long time, talking of a hundred frivolous subjects, and ridiculing the people she had met at the races for her maid's amusement. Her step-daughter came into the dressing-room to bid her good night, and found the maid and mistress laughing aloud over one of the day's adventures. Alicia, who was never familiar with her servants, withdrew in disgust at my lady's frivolity.

'Go on brushing my hair, Phœbe,' Lady Audley said, every time the girl was about to complete her task; 'I quite enjoy a chat with you.'

At last, just as she had dismissed her maid, she suddenly called her back. 'Phœbe Marks,' she said, 'I want you to do me a favour.'

'Yes, my lady.'

'I want you to go to London by the first train to-morrow morning to execute a little commission for me. You may take a day's holiday afterwards, as I know you have friends in town, and I shall give you a five-pound note if you do what I want, and keep your own counsel about it.'

'Yes, my lady.'

'See that that door is securely shut, and come and sit on this stool at my feet.'

The girl obeyed. Lady Audley smoothed her maid's neutral-tinted hair with her plump, white, and bejewelled hand as she reflected for a few moments.

'And now listen, Phœbe. What I want you to do is very simple.'

It was so simple that it was told in five minutes, and then Lady Audley retired into her bed-room, and curled herself up cosily under the eider-down quilt. She was a chilly little creature, and loved to bury herself in soft wrappings of satin and fur.

'Kiss me, Phœbe,' she said, as the girl arranged the curtains. 'I hear Sir Michael's step in the ante-room; you will meet him as you go out, and you may as well tell him that you are going up by the first train to-morrow morning to get my dress from Madame Frederick for the dinner at Morton Abbey.'

It was late the next morning when Lady Audley went down to breakfast – past ten o'clock. While she was sipping her coffee a servant brought her a sealed packet, and a book for her to sign.

'A telegraphic message!' she cried; for the convenient word telegram had not yet been invented. 'What can be the matter?'

She looked up at her husband with wide-open, terrified eyes, and seemed half afraid to break the seal. The envelope was addressed to Miss Lucy Graham, at Mr. Dawson's, and had been sent on from the village.

'Read it, my darling,' he said, 'and do not be alarmed; it may be nothing of any importance.'

It came from a Mrs. Vincent, the schoolmistress to whom she had referred on entering Mr. Dawson's family. The lady was dangerously ill, and implored her old pupil to go and see her.

'Poor soul! she always meant to leave me her money,' said Lucy, with a mournful smile. 'She has never heard of the change in my fortunes. Dear Sir Michael, I must go to her.'

'To be sure you must, dearest. If she was kind to my poor girl in her adversity, she has a claim upon her prosperity that shall never be forgotten. Put on your bonnet, Lucy; we shall be in time to catch the express.'

'You will go with me?'

'Of course, my darling. Do you suppose I would let you go alone?'

'I was sure you would go with me,' she said thoughtfully. 'Does your friend send any address?'

'No; but she always lived at Crescent Villas, West Brompton; and no doubt she lives there still.'

There was only time for Lady Audley to hurry on her bonnet and shawl before she heard the carriage drive round to the door, and Sir Michael calling to her at the foot of the staircase.

Her suite of rooms, as I have said, opened one out of another, and terminated in an octagon ante-chamber hung with oil paintings. Even in her haste she paused deliberately at the door of this room, double locked it, and dropped the key into her pocket. This door, once locked, cut off all access to my lady's apartments.

CHAPTER VIII
Before the storm

So the dinner at Audley Court was postponed, and Miss Alicia had to wait still longer for an introduction to the handsome young widower, Mr. George Talboys.

I am afraid, if the real truth is to be told, there was, perhaps, something of affectation in the anxiety this young lady expressed to make George's acquaintance; but if poor Alicia for a moment calculated upon arousing any latent spark of jealousy lurking in her cousin's breast by this exhibition of interest, she was not so well acquainted with Robert Audley's disposition as she might have been. Indolent, handsome, and indifferent, the young barrister took life as altogether too absurd a mistake for any one event in its foolish course to be for a moment considered seriously by a sensible man.

His pretty, gipsy-faced cousin might have been over head and ears in love with him, and she might have told him so, in some charming, roundabout, womanly fashion, a hundred times in a day for all the three hundred and sixty-five days in the year; but unless she had waited for some privileged 29th of February, and walked straight up to him, saying, 'Robert, please will you marry me?' I very much doubt if he would ever have discovered the state of her feelings.

Again, had he been in love with her himself, I fancy that the tender passion would, with him, have been so vague and feeble a sentiment that he might have gone down to his grave with a dim sense of some uneasy sensation which might be love or indigestion, and with, beyond this, no knowledge whatever of his state.

So it was not the least use, my poor Alicia, to ride about the lanes round Audley during those three days which the two young men spent in Essex; it was wasted trouble to wear that pretty cavalier hat and plume, and to be always, by the most singular of chances, meeting Robert and his friend. The black curls (nothing like Lady Audley's feathery ringlets, but heavy clustering locks, that clung about your slender brown throat), the red and pouting lips, the nose inclined to be *retroussé*; the dark complexion, with its bright crimson flush, always ready to glance up like a signal light in a dusky sky, when you came suddenly upon your apathetic cousin – all this coquettish, *espiègle*, brunette beauty was thrown away upon the dull eyes of Robert Audley, and you might as well have taken your rest in the cool drawing-room at the Court, instead of working your pretty mare to death under the hot September sun.

Now fishing, except to the devoted disciple of Izaac Walton, is not the most lively of occupations; therefore it is scarcely, perhaps, to be wondered that on the day after Lady Audley's departure, the two young men (one of whom was disabled, by that heart wound which he bore so quietly, from really taking pleasure in anything, and the other of whom looked upon almost all pleasure as a negative kind of trouble) began to grow weary of the shade of the willows overhanging the winding streams about Audley.

'Fig-tree Court is not gay in the long vacation,' said Robert reflectively: 'but I think, upon the whole, it's better than this; at any rate it's near a tobacconist's,' he added, puffing resignedly at an execrable cigar procured from the landlord of the Sun Inn.

George Talboys, who had only consented to the Essex expedition in passive submission to his friend, was by no means inclined to object to their immediate return to London.

'I shall be glad to get back, Bob,' he said, 'for I want to take a run down to Southampton; I haven't seen the little one for upwards of a month.'

He always spoke of his son as 'the little one;' always spoke of him mournfully rather than hopefully. It seemed as if he could take no comfort from the thought of his boy. He accounted for this by saying that he had a fancy that the child would never learn to love him; and worse even than this fancy, a dim presentiment that he would not live to see his little Georgey reach manhood.

'I'm not a romantic man, Bob,' he would say sometimes, 'and I never read a line of poetry in my life that was any more to me than so many words and so much jingle; but a feeling has come over me since my wife's death, that I am like a man standing upon a long low shore, with hideous cliffs frowning down upon him from behind, and the rising tide crawling slowly but surely about his feet. It seems to grow nearer and nearer every day, that black, pitiless tide; not rushing upon me with a great noise and a mighty impetus, but crawling, creeping, stealing, gliding towards me, ready to close in above my head when I am least prepared for the end.'

Robert Audley stared at his friend in silent amazement; and, after a pause of profound deliberation, said solemnly, 'George Talboys, I could understand this if you had been eating heavy suppers. Cold pork, now, especially if underdone, might produce this sort of thing. You want change of air, dear boy; you want the refreshing breezes of Fig-tree Court, and the soothing atmosphere of Fleet Street. Or, stay,' he added suddenly; 'I have it! You've been smoking our friend the landlord's cigars; that accounts for everything.'

They met Alicia Audley on her mare about half-an-hour after they had come to the determination of leaving Essex early the next morning. The young lady was very much surprised and disappointed at hearing her cousin's determination, and for that very reason pretended to take the matter with supreme indifference.

'You are very soon tired of Audley, Robert,' she said carelessly; 'but of course you have no friends here, except your relations at the Court; while in London, no doubt, you have the most delightful society, and—'

'I get good tobacco,' murmured Robert, interrupting his cousin. 'Audley is the dearest old place, but when a man has to smoke dried cabbage leaves, you know, Alicia—'

'Then you really are going to-morrow morning?'

'Positively – by the express that leaves at 10.50.'

'Then Lady Audley will lose an introduction to Mr. Talboys, and Mr. Talboys will lose the chance of seeing the prettiest woman in Essex.'

'Really—' stammered George.

'The prettiest woman in Essex would have a poor chance of getting much admiration out of my friend, George Talboys,' said Robert. 'His heart is at Southampton, where he has a curly-headed little urchin, about as high as his knee, who calls him "the big gentleman," and asks him for sugar-plums.'

'I am going to write to my step-mother by to-night's post,' said Alicia. 'She asked me particularly, in her letter, how long you were going to stop, and whether there was any chance of her being back in time to receive you.'

Miss Audley took a letter from the pocket of her riding-jacket as she spoke – a pretty, fairy-like note, written on shining paper of a peculiar creamy hue.

'She says in her postscript, "Be sure you answer my question about Mr. Audley and his friend, you volatile, forgetful Alicia!"'

'What a pretty hand she writes!' said Robert, as his cousin folded the note.

'Yes, it is pretty, is it not? Look at it, Robert.'

She put the letter into his hand, and he contemplated it

lazily for a few minutes, while Alicia patted the graceful neck of her chestnut mare, which was anxious to be off once more.

'Presently, Atalanta, presently. Give me back my note, Bob.'

'It is the prettiest, most coquettish little hand I ever saw. Do you know, Alicia, I never believed in those fellows who ask you for thirteen postage stamps, and offer to tell you what you have never been able to find out yourself; but upon my word I think that if I had never seen your aunt, I should know what she was like by this slip of paper. Yes, here it all is – the feathery, gold-shot, flaxen curls, the pencilled eyebrows, the tiny straight nose, the winning childish smile, all to be guessed in these few graceful up-strokes and down-strokes. George, look here!'

But absent-minded and gloomy George Talboys had strolled away along the margin of a ditch, and stood striking the bulrushes with his cane, half-a-dozen paces away from Robert and Alicia.

'Never mind,' said the young lady impatiently; for she by no means relished this long disquisition upon my lady's little note. 'Give me the letter, and let me go; it's past eight, and I must answer it by to-night's post. Come, Atalanta! Good-by, Robert – good-by, Mr. Talboys. A pleasant journey to town.'

The chestnut mare cantered briskly through the lane, and Miss Audley was out of sight before those two big bright tears that stood in her eyes for one moment, before her pride sent them back again, rose from her angry heart.

'To have only one cousin in the world,' she cried passionately, 'my nearest relation after papa, and for him to care about as much for me as he would for a dog!'

By the merest of accidents, however, Robert and his friend did not go by the 10.50 express on the following morning, for the young barrister awoke with such a splitting headache, that he asked George to send him a cup of the strongest green tea that had ever been made at the Sun, and to be furthermore so good as to defer their journey until the next day. Of course George assented, and Robert Audley spent the forenoon lying in a darkened room, with a five-days-old Chelmsford paper to entertain himself withal.

'It's nothing but the cigars, George,' he said repeatedly. 'Get me out of the place without my seeing the landlord; for if that man and I meet there will be bloodshed.'

Fortunately for the peace at Audley, it happened to be market-day at Chelmsford; and the worthy landlord had ridden off in his chaise-cart to purchase supplies for his house – amongst other things, perhaps, a fresh stock of those very cigars which had been so fatal in their effect upon Robert.

The young men spent a dull, dawdling, stupid, unprofitable day; and towards dusk Mr. Audley proposed that they should stroll down to the Court, and ask Alicia to take them over the house.

'It will kill a couple of hours you know, George; and it seems a great pity to drag you away from Audley without having shown you the old place, which I give you my honour is very well worth seeing.'

The sun was low in the skies as they took a short cut through the meadows, and crossed a stile into the avenue leading to the archway – a lurid, heavy-looking, ominous sun-set, and a deathly stillness in the air, which frightened the birds that had a mind to sing, and left the field open to a few captious frogs croaking in the ditches. Still as the atmosphere was, the leaves rustled with that sinister, shivering motion which proceeds from no outer cause, but is rather an instinctive shudder of the frail branches, prescient of a coming storm. That stupid clock, which knew no middle course, and always skipped from one hour to the other, pointed to seven as the young men passed under the archway; but, for all that, it was nearer eight.

They found Alicia in the lime-walk, wandering listlessly up and down under the black shadow of the trees, from which every now and then a withered leaf flapped slowly to the ground.

Strange to say, George Talboys, who very seldom observed anything, took particular notice of this place.

'It ought to be an avenue in a churchyard,' he said. 'How peacefully the dead might sleep under this sombre shade! I wish the churchyard at Ventnor was like this.'

They walked on to the ruined well; and Alicia told them some old legend connected with the spot – some gloomy story, such as those always attached to an old house, as if the past were one dark page of sorrow and crime.

'We want to see the house before it is dark, Alicia,' said Robert.

'Then we must be quick,' she answered. 'Come.'

She led the way through an open French window, modernised a few years before, into the library, and thence to the hall.

In the hall they passed my lady's pale-faced maid, who looked furtively under her white eyelashes at the two young men.

They were going up-stairs, when Alicia turned and spoke to the girl.

'After we have been in the drawing-room I should like to show these gentlemen Lady Audley's rooms. Are they in good order, Phœbe?'

'Yes, Miss; but the door of the ante-room is locked, and I fancy that my lady has taken the key to London.'

'Taken the key! Impossible!' cried Alicia.

'Indeed, Miss, I think she has. I cannot find it, and it always used to be in the door.'

'I declare,' said Alicia impatiently, 'that it is not at all unlike my lady to have taken this silly freak into her head. I dare say she was afraid we should go into her rooms, and pry about

75

amongst her pretty dresses, and meddle with her jewellery. It is very provoking, for the best pictures in the house are in that ante-chamber. There is her own portrait, too, unfinished, but wonderfully like.'

'Her portrait!' exclaimed Robert Audley. 'I would give anything to see it, for I have only an imperfect notion of her face. Is there no other way of getting into the room, Alicia?'

'Another way?'

'Yes; is there any door, leading through some of the other rooms, by which we can contrive to get into hers?'

His cousin shook her head, and conducted them into a corridor where there were some family portraits. She showed them a tapestried chamber, the large figures upon the faded canvas looking threatening in the dusky light.

'That fellow with the battle-axe looks as if he wanted to split George's head open,' said Mr. Audley, pointing to a fierce warrior whose uplifted arm appeared above George Talboys' dark hair.

'Come out of this room, Alicia. I believe it's damp, or else haunted. Indeed I believe all ghosts to be the result of damp. You sleep in a damp bed – you awake suddenly in the dead of the night with a cold shiver, and see an old lady in the court costume of George the First's time, sitting at the foot of the bed. The old lady is indigestion, and the cold shiver is a damp sheet.'

There were lighted candles in the drawing-room. No new-fangled lamps had ever made their appearance at Audley Court. Sir Michael's rooms were lighted by honest, thick, yellow-looking wax candles, in massive silver candlesticks, and in sconces against the walls.

There was very little to see in the drawing-room; and George Talboys soon grew tired of staring at the handsome modern furniture, and at a few pictures by some of the Academicians.

'Isn't there a secret passage, or an old oak chest, or something of that kind, somewhere about the place, Alicia?' asked Robert.

'To be sure!' cried Miss Audley; with a vehemence that startled her cousin; 'of course. Why didn't I think of it before? How stupid of me, to be sure!'

'Why stupid?'

'Because, if you don't mind crawling upon your hands and knees, you can see my lady's apartments, for that very passage communicates with her dressing-room. She doesn't know of it herself, I believe. How astonished she'd be if some black-visored burglar, with a dark lantern, were to rise through the floor some night as she sat before her looking-glass, having her hair dressed for a party!'

'Shall we try the secret passage, George?' asked Mr. Audley.

'Yes, if you wish it.'

Alicia led them into the room which had once been her nursery. It was now disused, except on very rare occasions when the house was full of company.

Robert Audley lifted a corner of the carpet, according to his cousin's directions, and disclosed a rudely-cut trap-door in the oak flooring.

'Now listen to me,' said Alicia. 'You must let yourself down by your hands into the passage, which is about four feet high; stoop your head, and walk straight along it till you come to a sharp turn which will take you to the left, and at the extreme end of it you will find a short ladder below a trap-door like this, which you will have to unbolt; that door opens into the flooring of my lady's dressing-room, which is only covered with a square Persian carpet that you can easily manage to raise. You understand me?'

'Perfectly.'

'Then take the light; Mr. Talboys will follow you. I give you twenty minutes for your inspection of the paintings – that is about a minute apiece – and at the end of that time I shall expect to see you return.'

Robert obeyed her implicitly, and George, submissively following his friend, found himself, in five minutes, standing amidst the elegant disorder of Lady Audley's dressing-room.

She had left the house in a hurry on her unlooked-for journey to London, and the whole of her glittering toilette apparatus lay about on the marble dressing-table. The atmosphere of the room was almost oppressive from the rich odours of perfumes in bottles whose gold stoppers had not been replaced. A bunch of hothouse flowers was withering upon a tiny writing-table. Two or three handsome dresses lay in a heap upon the ground, and the open doors of a wardrobe revealed the treasures within. Jewellery, ivory-backed hair-brushes, and exquisite china were scattered here and there about the apartment. George Talboys saw his bearded face and tall gaunt figure reflected in the cheval-glass, and wondered to see how out of place he seemed among all these womanly luxuries.

They went from the dressing-room to the boudoir, and through the boudoir into the ante-chamber, in which there were, as Alicia had said, about twenty valuable paintings besides my lady's portrait.

My lady's portrait stood on an easel covered with a green baize in the centre of the octagonal chamber. It had been a fancy of the artist to paint her standing in this very room, and to make his background a faithful reproduction of the pictured walls. I am afraid the young man belonged to the pre-Raphaelite brotherhood, for he had spent a most unconscionable time upon the accessories of this picture – upon my lady's crispy ringlets and the heavy folds of her crimson velvet dress.

The two young men looked at the paintings on the walls first, leaving this unfinished portrait for a *bonne bouche*.

By this time it was dark, the one candle carried by Robert

only making one bright nucleus of light as he moved about holding it before the pictures one by one. The broad bare window looked out upon the pale sky, tinged with the last cold flicker of the dead twilight. The ivy rustled against the glass with the same ominous shiver as that which agitated every leaf in the garden, prophetic of the storm that was to come.

'There are our friend's eternal white horses,' said Robert, stopping before a Wouvermans. 'Nicholas Poussin – Salvator – ha – hum! Now for the portrait!'

He paused with his hand on the baize, and solemnly addressed his friend.

'George Talboys,' he said, 'we have between us only one wax candle, a very inadequate light with which to look at a painting. Let me, therefore, request that you will suffer us to look at it one at a time: if there is one thing more disagreeable than another, it is to have a person dodging behind your back and peering over your shoulder, when you're trying to see what a picture's made of.'

George fell back immediately. He took no more interest in my lady's picture than in all the other weariness of this troublesome world. He fell back, and leaning his forehead against the window-panes, looked out at the night.

When he turned round he saw that Robert had arranged the easel very conveniently, and that he had seated himself on a chair before it for the purpose of contemplating the painting at his leisure.

He rose as George turned round.

'Now, then, for your turn, Talboys,' he said. 'It's an extra-ordinary picture.'

He took George's place at the window, and George seated himself in the chair before the easel.

Yes; the painter must have been a pre-Raphaelite. No one but a pre-Raphaelite would have painted, hair by hair, those feathery masses of ringlets with every glimmer of gold, and every shadow of pale brown. No one but a pre-Raphaelite would have so exaggerated every attribute of that delicate face as to give a lurid lightness to the blonde complexion, and a strange, sinister light to the deep blue eyes. No one but a pre-Raphaelite could have given to that pretty pouting mouth the hard and almost wicked look it had in the portrait.

It was so like and yet so unlike; it was as if you had burned strange-coloured fires before my lady's face, and by their influence brought out new lines and new expressions never seen in it before. The perfection of feature, the brilliancy of colouring, were there; but I suppose the painter had copied quaint mediæval monstrosities until his brain had grown bewildered, for my lady, in his portrait of her, had something of the aspect of a beautiful fiend.

Her crimson dress, exaggerated like all the rest in this strange picture, hung about her in folds that looked like flames, her fair head peeping out of the lurid mass of colour, as if out of a raging furnace. Indeed, the crimson dress, the sunshine on the face, the red gold gleaming in the yellow hair, the ripe scarlet of the pouting lips, the glowing colours of each accessory of the minutely-painted background, all combined to render the first effect of the painting by no means an agreeable one.

But strange as the picture was, it could not have made any great impression on George Talboys, for he sat before it for about a quarter of an hour without uttering a word – only staring blankly at the painted canvas, with the candlestick grasped in his strong right hand, and his left arm hanging loosely by his side. He sat so long in this attitude, that Robert turned round at last.

'Why, George, I thought you had gone to sleep!'

'I had almost.'

'You've caught a cold from standing in that damp tapestried

room. Mark my words, George Talboys, you've caught a cold; you're as hoarse as a raven. But come along.'

Robert Audley took the candle from his friend's hand, and crept back through the secret passage, followed by George, very quiet, but scarcely more quiet than usual.

They found Alicia in the nursery waiting for them.

'Well?' she said interrogatively.

'We managed it capitally. But I don't like the portrait; there's something odd about it.'

'There is,' said Alicia; 'I've a strange fancy on that point. I think that sometimes a painter is in a manner inspired, and is able to see, through the normal expression of the face, another expression that is equally a part of it, though not to be perceived by common eyes. *We* have never seen my lady look as she does in that picture; but I think that she *could* look so.'

'Alicia,' said Robert Audley imploringly, 'don't be German!'

'But, Robert—'

'Don't be German, Alicia, if you love me. The picture is – the picture; and my lady is – my lady. That's my way of taking things, and I'm not metaphysical; don't unsettle me.'

He repeated this several times with an air of terror perfectly sincere; and then, having borrowed an umbrella in case of being overtaken by the coming storm, left the Court, leading passive George Talboys away with him. The one hand of the stupid old clock had skipped to nine by the time they reached the archway; but before they could pass under its shadow they had to step aside to allow a carriage to dash by them. It was a fly from the village, but Lady Audley's fair face peeped out at the window. Dark as it was, she could see the two figures of the young men black against the dusk.

'Who is that?' she asked, putting out her head. 'Is it the gardener?'

'No, my dear aunt,' said Robert, laughing; 'it is your most dutiful nephew.'

He and George stopped by the archway while the fly drew up at the door, and the surprised servants came out to welcome their master and mistress.

'I think the storm will hold off to-night,' said the baronet, looking up at the sky; 'but we shall certainly have it to-morrow.'

CHAPTER IX
After the storm

Sir Michael was mistaken in his prophecy upon the weather. The storm did not hold off until next day, but burst with terrible fury over the village of Audley about half-an-hour before midnight.

Robert Audley took the thunder and lightning with the same composure with which he accepted all the other ills of life. He lay on a sofa in the sitting-room, ostensibly reading the five-days-old Chelmsford paper, and regaling himself occasionally with a few sips from a large tumbler of cold punch. But the storm had quite a different effect upon George Talboys. His friend was startled when he looked at the young man's white face as he sat opposite the open window listening to the thunder, and staring at the black sky, rent every now and then by forked streaks of steel-blue lightning.

'George,' said Robert, after watching him for some time, 'are you frightened at the lightning?'

'No,' he answered curtly.

'But, my dear fellow, some of the most courageous men have been frightened at it. It is scarcely to be called a fear; it is constitutional. I am sure you are frightened at it.'

'No, I am not.'

'But, George, if you could see yourself, white and haggard, with your great hollow eyes staring out at the sky as if they were fixed upon a ghost. I tell you I know that you are frightened.'

'And I tell you that I am not.'

'George Talboys, you are not only afraid of the lightning, but you are savage with yourself for being afraid, and with me for telling you of your fear.'

'Robert Audley, if you say another word to me I shall knock you down;' having said which, Mr. Talboys strode out of the room, banging the door after him with a violence that shook the house. Those inky clouds which had shut in the sultry earth as if with a roof of hot iron, poured out their blackness in a sudden deluge as George left the room; but if the young man was afraid of the lightning, he certainly was not afraid of the rain; for he walked straight down-stairs to the inn door, and went out into the wet high road. He walked up and down, up and down, in the soaking shower for about twenty minutes, and then, re-entering the inn, strode up to his bed-room.

Robert Audley met him on the landing, with his hair beaten about his white face, and his garments dripping wet.

'Are you going to bed, George?'

'Yes.'

'But you have no candle.'

'I don't want one.'

'But look at your clothes, man! Do you see the wet streaming down your coat-sleeves? What on earth made you go out upon such a night?'

'I am tired, and want to go to bed – don't bother me.'

'You'll take some hot brandy-and-water, George?'

Robert Audley stood in his friend's way as he spoke, anxious to prevent his going to bed in the state he was in; but George pushed him fiercely aside, and striding past him, said, in the same hoarse voice Robert had noticed at the Court –

'Let me alone, Robert Audley, and keep clear of me if you can.'

Robert followed George to his bed-room, but the young man banged the door in his face; so there was nothing for it but to leave Mr. Talboys to himself, to recover his temper as best he might.

'He was irritated at my noticing his terror at the lightning,' thought Robert, as he calmly retired to rest, serenely indifferent to the thunder, which seemed to shake him in his bed, and the lightning playing fitfully round the razors in his open dressing-case.

The storm rolled away from the quiet village of Audley, and when Robert awoke the next morning it was to see bright sunshine, and a peep of cloudless sky between the white curtains of his bed-room window.

It was one of those serene and lovely mornings that sometimes succeed a storm. The birds sung loud and cheerily, the yellow corn uplifted itself in the broad fields, and waved proudly after its sharp tussle with the storm, which had done its best to beat down the heavy ears with cruel wind and driving rain half the night through. The vine-leaves clustering round Robert's window fluttered with a joyous rustling, shaking the rain-drops in diamond showers from every spray and tendril.

Robert Audley found his friend waiting for him at the breakfast-table.

George was very pale, but perfectly tranquil – if anything, indeed, more cheerful than usual.

He shook Robert by the hand with something of that old hearty manner for which he had been distinguished before the one affliction of his life overtook and shipwrecked him.

'Forgive me, Bob,' he said frankly, 'for my surly temper of last night. You were quite correct in your assertion; the thunderstorm *did* upset me. It always had the same effect upon me in my youth.'

'Poor old boy! Shall we go up by the express, or shall we stop here and dine with my uncle to-night?' asked Robert.

'To tell the truth, Bob, I would rather do neither. It's a

glorious morning. Suppose we stroll about all day, take another turn with the rod and line, and go up to town by the train that leaves here at 6.15 in the evening?'

Robert Audley would have assented to a far more disagreeable proposition than this, rather than have taken the trouble to oppose his friend, so the matter was immediately agreed upon; and after they had finished their breakfast, and ordered a four-o'clock dinner, George Talboys took the fishing-rod across his broad shoulders, and strode out of the house with his friend and companion.

But if the equable temperament of Mr. Robert Audley had been undisturbed by the crackling peals of thunder that shook the very foundations of the Sun Inn, it had not been so with the more delicate sensibilities of his uncle's young wife. Lady Audley confessed herself terribly frightened of the lightning. She had her bedstead wheeled into a corner of the room, and with the heavy curtains drawn tightly round her, she lay with her face buried in the pillows, shuddering convulsively at every sound of the tempest without. Sir Michael, whose stout heart had never known a fear, almost trembled for this fragile creature, whom it was his happy privilege to protect and defend. My lady would not consent to undress till nearly three o'clock in the morning, when the last lingering peal of thunder had died away amongst the distant hills. Until that hour she lay in the handsome silk dress in which she had travelled, huddled together, amongst the bed-clothes, only looking up now and then with a scared face to ask if the storm was over.

Towards four o'clock, her husband, who spent the night in watching by her bedside, saw her drop off into a deep sleep, from which she did not awake for nearly five hours.

But she came into the breakfast-room, at half-past nine o'clock, singing a little Scotch melody, her cheeks tinged with as delicate a pink as the pale hue of her muslin morning dress.

Like the birds and the flowers, she seemed to recover her beauty and joyousness in the morning sunshine. She tripped lightly out on to the lawn, gathering a last lingering rosebud here and there, and a sprig or two of geranium, and returning through the dewy grass, warbling long cadences for very happiness of heart, and looking as fresh and radiant as the flowers in her hands. The baronet caught her in his strong arms as she came in through the open window.

'My pretty one,' he said, 'my darling, what happiness to see you your own merry self again! Do you know, Lucy, that once last night, when you looked out through the dark green bed-curtains, with your poor white face, and the purple rims round your hollow eyes, I had almost a difficulty to recognise my little wife in that ghastly, terrified, agonised-looking creature, crying out about the storm. Thank God for the morning sun, which has brought back the rosy cheeks and the bright smile! I hope to Heaven, Lucy, I shall never again see you look as you did last night.'

She stood on tiptoe to kiss him, and was then only tall enough to reach his white beard. She told him, laughing, that she had always been a silly, frightened creature – frightened of dogs, frightened of cattle, frightened of a thunder-storm, frightened of a rough sea. 'Frightened of everything and everybody, but my dear, noble, handsome husband,' she said.

She had found the carpet in her dressing-room disarranged, and had inquired into the mystery of the secret passage. She chid Miss Alicia in a playful, laughing way, for her boldness in introducing two great men into my lady's rooms.

'And they had the audacity to look at my picture, Alicia,' she said, with mock indignation. 'I found the baize thrown on the ground, and a great man's glove on the carpet. Look!'

She held up a thick driving-glove as she spoke. It was George's, which he had dropped while looking at the picture.

'I shall go up to the Sun, and ask those boys to dinner,' Sir

Michael said, as he left the Court upon his morning walk round his farm.

Lady Audley flitted from room to room in the bright September sunshine – now sitting down to the piano to trill out a ballad, or the first page of an Italian bravura, or running with rapid fingers through a brilliant waltz – now hovering about a stand of hothouse flowers, doing amateur gardening with a pair of fairy-like silver-mounted embroidery scissors – now strolling into her dressing-room to talk to Phœbe Marks, and have her curls re-arranged for the third or fourth time; for the ringlets were always getting into disorder, and gave no little trouble to Lady Audley's maid.

My lady seemed, on this particular September day, restless from very joyousness of spirit, and unable to stay long in one place, or occupy herself with one thing.

While Lady Audley amused herself in her own frivolous fashion, the two young men strolled slowly along the margin of a stream until they reached a shady corner where the water was deep and still, and the long branches of the willows trailed into the brook.

George Talboys took the fishing-rod, while Robert stretched himself at full length on a railway rug, and balancing his hat upon his nose as a screen from the sunshine, fell fast asleep.

Those were happy fish in the stream on the banks of which Mr. Talboys was seated. They might have amused themselves to their heart's content with timid nibbles at this gentleman's bait, without in any manner endangering their safety; for George only stared vacantly at the water, holding his rod in a loose, listless hand, and with a strange far-away look in his eyes. As the church clock struck two he threw down his rod, and striding away along the bank, left Robert Audley to enjoy a nap, which, according to that gentleman's habits, was by no means unlikely to last for two or three hours. About a quarter of a mile further on George crossed a rustic bridge, and struck into the meadows which led to Audley Court.

The birds had sung so much all the morning that they had, perhaps, by this time grown tired; the lazy cattle were asleep in the meadows; Sir Michael was still away on his morning's ramble; Miss Alicia had scampered off an hour before upon her chestnut mare; the servants were all at dinner in the back part of the house; and my lady had strolled, book in hand, into the shadowy lime-walk; so the grey old building had never worn a more peaceful aspect than on that bright afternoon when George Talboys walked across the lawn to ring a sonorous peal at the sturdy, iron-bound oak door.

The servant who answered his summons told him that Sir Michael was out, and my lady walking in the lime-tree avenue.

He looked a little disappointed at this intelligence, and muttering something about wishing to see my lady, or going to look for my lady (the servant did not clearly distinguish his words), strode away from the door without leaving either card or message for the family.

It was full an hour and a half after this when Lady Audley returned to the house, not coming from the lime-walk, but from exactly the opposite direction, carrying her open book in her hand, and singing as she came. Alicia had just dismounted from her mare, and stood in the low-arched doorway, with her great Newfoundland dog by her side.

The dog, which had never liked my lady, showed his teeth with a suppressed growl.

'Send that horrid animal away, Alicia,' Lady Audley said impatiently. 'The brute knows that I am frightened of him, and takes advantage of my terror. And yet they call the creatures generous and noble-natured! Bah, Cæsar; I hate you, and you hate me; and if you met me in the dark in some narrow passage you would fly at my throat and strangle me, wouldn't you?'

My lady, safely sheltered behind her step-daughter, shook her yellow curls at the angry animal, and defied him maliciously.

'Do you know, Lady Audley, that Mr. Talboys, the young widower, has been here asking for Sir Michael and for you?'

Lucy Audley lifted her pencilled eyebrows. 'I thought he was coming to dinner,' she said. 'Surely we shall have enough of him then.'

She had a heap of wild autumn flowers in the skirt of her muslin dress. She had come through the fields at the back of the Court, gathering the hedge-row blossoms in her way. She ran lightly up the broad staircase to her own rooms. George's glove lay on her boudoir table. Lady Audley rang the bell violently, and it was answered by Phœbe Marks. 'Take that litter away,' she said sharply. The girl collected the glove and a few withered flowers and torn papers lying on the table into her apron.

'What have you been doing all this morning?' asked my lady. 'Not wasting your time, I hope?'

'No, my lady, I have been altering the blue dress. It is rather dark on this side of the house, so I took it up to my own room, and worked at the window.'

The girl was leaving the room as she spoke, but she turned round and looked at Lady Audley as if waiting for further orders.

Lucy looked up at the same moment, and the eyes of the two women met.

'Phœbe Marks,' said my lady, throwing herself into an easy-chair, and trifling with the wild flowers in her lap, 'you are a good industrious girl, and while I live and am prosperous you shall never want a firm friend or a twenty-pound note.'

CHAPTER X
Missing

When Robert Audley awoke he was surprised to see the fishing-rod lying on the bank, the line trailing idly in the water, and the float bobbing harmlessly up and down in the afternoon sunshine. The young barrister was a long time stretching his arms and legs in various directions to convince himself, by means of such exercise, that he still retained the proper use of those members; then, with a mighty effort, he contrived to rise from the grass, and having deliberately folded his railway rug into a convenient shape for carrying over his shoulder, he strolled away to look for George Talboys.

Once or twice he gave a sleepy shout, scarcely loud enough to scare the birds in the branches above his head, or the trout in the stream at his feet; but receiving no answer, grew tired of the exertion, and dawdled on, yawning as he went, and still looking for George Talboys.

By-and-by he took out his watch, and was surprised to find that it was a quarter past four.

'Why, the selfish beggar must have gone home to his dinner!' he muttered reflectively; 'and yet that isn't much like him, for he seldom remembers even his meals unless I jog his memory.'

Even a good appetite, and the knowledge that his dinner would very likely suffer by this delay, could not quicken Mr. Robert Audley's constitutional dawdle, and by the time he strolled in at the front door of the Sun the clocks were striking five. He so fully expected to find George Talboys waiting for him in the little sitting-room, that the absence of that gentle-man seemed to give the apartment a dreary look, and Robert groaned aloud.

'This is lively!' he said. 'A cold dinner, and nobody to eat it with!'

The landlord of the Sun came himself to apologise for his ruined dishes.

'As fine a pair of ducks, Mr. Audley, as ever you clapped eyes on, but burnt up to a cinder, along of being kep' hot.'

'Never mind the ducks,' Robert said, impatiently; 'where's Mr. Talboys?'

'He ain't been in, sir, since you went out together this morning.'

'What!' cried Robert. 'Why, in Heaven's name, what has the man done with himself?'

He walked to the window and looked out upon the broad white high road. There was a waggon laden with trusses of hay crawling slowly past, the lazy horses and the lazy waggoner dropping their heads with a weary stoop under the afternoon sunshine. There was a flock of sheep straggling about the road, with a dog running himself into a fever in the endeavour to keep them decently together. There were some bricklayers just released from work – a tinker mending some kettles by the road-side; there was a dog-cart dashing down the road, carrying the master of the Audley hounds to his seven-o'clock dinner; there were a dozen common village sights and sounds that mixed themselves up into a cheerful bustle and confusion; but there was no George Talboys.

'Of all the extraordinary things that ever happened to me in the whole course of my life,' said Mr. Robert Audley, 'this is the most miraculous!'

The landlord, still in attendance, opened his eyes as Robert made this remark. What could there be so extraordinary in the simple fact of a gentleman being late for his dinner?

'I shall go and look for him,' said Robert, snatching up his hat and walking straight out of the house.

But the question was where to look for him. He certainly was not by the trout stream, so it was no good going back there in search of him. Robert was standing before the inn, deliberating on what was best to be done, when the landlord came out after him.

'I forgot to tell you, Mr. Audley, as how your uncle called here five minutes after you was gone, and left a message asking of you and the other gentleman to go down to dinner at the Court.'

'Then I shouldn't wonder,' said Robert, 'if George Talboys has gone down to the Court to call upon my uncle. It isn't like him, but it's just possible that he has done it.'

It was six o'clock when Robert knocked at the door of his uncle's house. He did not ask to see any of the family, but inquired at once for his friend.

Yes, the servant told him; Mr. Talboys had been there at two o'clock, or a little after.

'And not since?'

'No, not since.'

Was the man sure that it was at two Mr. Talboys called? Robert asked.

Yes, perfectly sure. He remembered the hour because it was the servants' dinner hour, and he had left the table to open the door to Mr. Talboys.

'Why, what can have become of the man?' thought Robert, as he turned his back upon the Court. 'From two till six – four good hours – and no signs of him!'

If any one had ventured to tell Mr. Robert Audley that he could possibly feel a strong attachment to any creature breathing, that cynical gentleman would have elevated his eyebrows in supreme contempt at the preposterous notion. Yet here he was, flurried and anxious, bewildering his brain by all manner of conjectures about his missing friend, and, false to every attribute of his nature, walking fast.

'I haven't walked fast since I was at Eton,' he murmured, as he hurried across one of Sir Michael's meadows in the direction of the village; 'and the worst of it is that I haven't the most remote idea where I am going.'

He crossed another meadow, and then seating himself upon a stile, rested his elbows upon his knees, buried his face in his hands, and set himself seriously to think the matter out.

'I have it!' he said, after a few minutes' thought; 'the railway-station!' He sprang over the stile, and started off in the direction of the little red-brick building.

There was no train expected for another half hour, and the clerk was taking his tea in an apartment on one side of the office, on the door of which was inscribed, in large white letters, 'Private.'

But Mr. Audley was too much occupied with the one idea of looking for his friend to pay any attention to this warning. He strode at once to the door, and rattling his cane against it, brought the clerk out of his sanctum in a perspiration from hot tea, and with his mouth full of bread and butter.

'Do you remember the gentleman that came down to Audley with me, Smithers?' asked Robert.

'Well, to tell you the real truth, Mr. Audley, I can't say I do. You came by the four o'clock, if you remember, and there's always a many by that train.'

'You don't remember him, then?'

'Not to my knowledge, Sir.'

'That's provoking! I want to know, Smithers, whether he has taken a ticket for London since two o'clock to-day. He's a tall, broad-chested young fellow, with a big brown beard. You couldn't well mistake him.'

'There was four or five gentlemen as took tickets for the 3.30 up,' said the clerk rather vaguely, casting an anxious glance over his shoulder at his wife, who looked by no means pleased at this interruption to the harmony of the tea-table.

'Four or five gentlemen! But did either of them answer to the description of my friend?'

'Well, I think one of them had a beard, sir.'

'A dark brown beard?'

'Well, I don't know but what it was brownish like.'

'Was he dressed in grey?'

'I believe it was grey: a many gents wears grey. He asked for the ticket sharp and short like, and when he'd got it walked straight out on to the platform whistling.'

'That's George!' said Robert. 'Thank you, Smithers: I needn't trouble you any more. It's as clear as daylight,' he muttered, as he left the station, 'he's got one of his gloomy fits on him, and he's gone back to London without saying a word about it. I'll leave Audley myself to-morrow morning; and for to-night – why, I may as well go down to the Court, and make the acquaintance of my uncle's young wife. They don't dine till seven: if I get back across the fields I shall be in time. Bob – otherwise Robert Audley, this sort of thing will never do: you are falling over head and ears in love with your aunt.'

CHAPTER XI

The mark upon my lady's wrist

Robert found Sir Michael and Lady Audley in the drawing-room. My lady was sitting on a music-stool before the grand piano, turning over the leaves of some new music. She twirled round upon this revolving seat, making a rustling with her silk flounces, as Mr. Robert Audley's name was announced; then, leaving the piano, she made her nephew a pretty mock ceremonious curtsey. 'Thank you so much for the sables,' she said, holding out her little fingers, all glittering and twinkling with the diamonds she wore upon them; 'thank you for those beautiful sables. How good it was of you to get them for me!'

Robert had almost forgotten the commission he had executed for Lady Audley during his Russian expedition. His mind was so full of George Talboys that he only acknowledged my lady's gratitude by a bow.

'Would you believe it, Sir Michael?' he said. 'That foolish chum of mine has gone back to London, leaving me in the lurch.'

'Mr. George Talboys returned to town!' exclaimed my lady, lifting her eyebrows.

'What a dreadful catastrophe!' said Alicia maliciously, 'since Pythias, in the person of Mr. Robert Audley, cannot exist for half-an-hour without Damon, commonly known as George Talboys.'

'He's a very good fellow,' Robert said stoutly; 'and to tell the honest truth, I'm rather uneasy about him.'

Uneasy about him! My lady was quite anxious to know why Robert was uneasy about his friend.

'I'll tell you why, Lady Audley,' answered the young barrister. 'George had a bitter blow a year ago in the death of his wife. He has never got over that trouble. He takes life pretty quietly – almost as quietly as I do – but he often talks very strangely, and I sometimes think that one day this grief will get the better of him, and he'll do something rash.'

Mr. Robert Audley spoke vaguely; but all three of his listeners knew that the something rash to which he alluded was that one deed for which there is no repentance.

There was a brief pause, during which Lady Audley arranged her yellow ringlets by the aid of the glass over the console table opposite to her.

'Dear me!' she said, 'this is very strange. I did not think men were capable of these deep and lasting affections. I thought that one pretty face was as good as another pretty face to them, and that when number one with blue eyes and fair hair died, they had only to look out for number two with black eyes and hair, by way of variety.'

'George Talboys is not one of those men. I firmly believe that his wife's death broke his heart.'

'How sad!' murmured Lady Audley. 'It seems almost cruel of Mrs. Talboys to die, and grieve her poor husband so much.'

'Alicia was right; she *is* childish,' thought Robert, as he looked at his aunt's pretty face.

My lady was very charming at the dinner-table; she professed the most bewitching incapacity for carving the pheasant set before her, and called Robert to her assistance.

'I could carve a leg of mutton at Mr. Dawson's,' she said, laughing; 'but a leg of mutton is so easy; and then I used to stand up.'

Sir Michael watched the impression my lady made upon his nephew with a proud delight in her beauty and fascination.

'I am so glad to see my poor little woman in her usual good spirits once more,' he said. 'She was very down-hearted yesterday at a disappointment she met with in London.'

'A disappointment!'

'Yes, Mr. Audley, a very cruel one,' answered my lady. 'I received the other morning a telegraphic message from my dear old friend and schoolmistress, telling me that she was dying, and that if I wanted to see her again I must hasten to her immediately. The telegraphic despatch contained no address, and of course, from that very circumstance, I imagined that she must be living in the house in which I left her three years ago. Sir Michael and I hurried up to town immediately, and drove straight to the old address. The house was occupied by strange people, who could give me no tidings of my friend. It is in a retired place, where there are very few tradespeople about. Sir Michael made inquiries at the few shops there are, but, after taking an immense deal of trouble, could discover nothing whatever likely to lead to the information we wanted. I have no friends in London, and had therefore no one to assist me except my dear, generous husband, who did all in his power, but in vain, to find my friend's new residence.'

'It was very foolish not to send the address in the telegraphic message,' said Robert.

'When people are dying it is not so easy to think of all these things,' murmured my lady, looking reproachfully at Mr. Audley with her soft blue eyes.

In spite of Lady Audley's fascination, and in spite of Robert's very unqualified admiration of her, the barrister could not overcome a vague feeling of uneasiness on this quiet September evening.

As he sat in the deep embrasure of a mullioned window, talking to my lady, his mind wandered away to shady Fig-tree Court, and he thought of poor George Talboys smoking his solitary cigar in the room with the dogs and the canaries. 'I wish I'd never felt any friendliness for the fellow,' he thought. 'I feel like a man who has an only son whose life has gone wrong with him. I wish to Heaven I could give him back his wife, and send him down to Ventnor to finish his days in peace.'

Still my lady's pretty musical prattle ran on as merrily and continuously as the babble of some brook; and still Robert's thoughts wandered, in spite of himself, to George Talboys.

He thought of him hurrying down to Southampton by the mail train to see his boy. He thought of him as he had often seen him, spelling over the shipping advertisements in the *Times*, looking for a vessel to take him back to Australia. Once he thought of him with a shudder, lying cold and stiff at the bottom of some shallow stream, with his dead face turned towards the darkening sky.

Lady Audley noticed his abstraction, and asked him what he was thinking of.

'George Talboys,' he answered abruptly.

She gave a little nervous shudder.

'Upon my word,' she said, 'you make me quite uncomfortable by the way in which you talk of Mr. Talboys. One would think that something extraordinary had happened to him.'

'God forbid! But I cannot help feeling uneasy about him.'

Later in the evening Sir Michael asked for some music, and my lady went to the piano. Robert Audley strolled after her to the instrument to turn over the leaves of her music; but she played from memory, and he was spared the trouble his gallantry would have imposed upon him.

He carried a pair of lighted candles to the piano, and arranged them conveniently for the pretty musician. She struck a few chords, and then wandered into a pensive sonata of Beethoven's. It was one of the many paradoxes in her character, that love of sombre and melancholy melodies, so opposite to her gay, frivolous nature.

Robert Audley lingered by her side, and as he had no occupation in turning over the leaves of her music, he amused himself by watching her jewelled white hands gliding softly over the keys, with the lace sleeves dropping away from her graceful arched wrists. He looked at her pretty fingers one by one; this one glittering with a ruby heart; that encoiled by an emerald serpent; and about them all a starry glitter of diamonds. From the fingers his eyes wandered to the rounded wrists: the broad, flat, gold bracelet upon her right wrist dropped over her hand, as she executed a rapid passage. She stopped abruptly to re-arrange it; but before she could do so, Robert Audley noticed a bruise upon her delicate skin.

'You have hurt your arm, Lady Audley,' he exclaimed.

She hastily replaced the bracelet.

'It is nothing,' she said. 'I am unfortunate in having a skin which the slightest touch bruises.'

She went on playing, but Sir Michael came across the room to look into the matter of the bruise upon his wife's pretty wrist.

'What is it, Lucy?' he asked; 'and how did it happen?'

'How foolish you all are to trouble yourselves about anything so absurd!' said Lady Audley, laughing. 'I am rather absent in mind, and amused myself a few days ago by tying a piece of ribbon round my arm so tightly, that it left a bruise when I removed it.'

'Hum!' thought Robert. 'My lady tells little childish white lies; the bruise is of a more recent date than a few days ago; the skin has only just begun to change colour.'

Sir Michael took the slender wrist in his strong hand.

'Hold the candles, Robert,' he said, 'and let us look at this poor little arm.'

It was not one bruise, but four slender, purple marks, such as might have been made by the four fingers of a powerful hand that had grasped the delicate wrist a shade too roughly. A narrow ribbon, bound tightly, might have left some such marks, it is true, and my lady protested once more that, to the best of her recollection, that must have been how they were made.

Across one of the faint purple marks there was a darker tinge, as if a ring worn on one of these strong and cruel fingers had been ground into the tender flesh.

'I am sure my lady must tell white lies,' thought Robert, 'for I can't believe the story of the ribbon.'

He wished his relations good night and good-by at about half-past ten o'clock; he said that he should run up to London by the first train to look for George, in Fig-tree Court.

'If I don't find him there, I shall go to Southampton,' he said; 'and if I don't find him there—'

'What then?' asked my lady.

'I shall think that something strange has happened.'

Robert Audley felt very low-spirited as he walked slowly home between the shadowy meadows; more low-spirited still when he re-entered the sitting-room at the Sun Inn, where he and George had lounged together, staring out of the window, and smoking their cigars.

'To think,' he said, meditatively, 'that it is possible to care so much for a fellow! But come what may, I'll go up to town after him the first thing to-morrow morning, and sooner than be balked in finding him, I'll go to the very end of the world.'

With Mr. Robert Audley's lymphatic nature, determination was so much the exception, rather than the rule, that when he did for once in his life resolve upon any course of action, he had a certain dogged, iron-like obstinacy that pushed him on to the fulfilment of his purpose.

The lazy bent of his mind, which prevented him from thinking of half-a-dozen things at a time, and not thinking thoroughly of any one of them, as is the manner of your more energetic people, made him remarkably clear-sighted upon any point to which he ever gave his serious attention.

Indeed, after all, though solemn benchers laughed at him, and rising barristers shrugged their shoulders under rustling silk gowns when people spoke of Robert Audley, I doubt if, had he ever taken the trouble to get a brief, he might not have rather surprised the magnates who underrated his abilities.

CHAPTER XII
Still missing

The September sunlight sparkled upon the fountain in the Temple Gardens, when Robert Audley returned to Fig-tree Court early the following morning.

He found the canaries singing in the pretty little room in which George had slept, but the apartment was in the same prim order in which the laundress had arranged it after the departure of the two young men – not a chair displaced, or so much as the lid of a cigar-box lifted, to bespeak the presence of George Talboys. With a last lingering hope he searched upon the mantel-pieces and tables of his rooms, on the chance of finding some letter left by George.

'He may have slept here last night, and started for South-ampton early this morning,' he thought. 'Mrs. Maloney has been here very likely, to make everything tidy after him.'

But as he sat looking lazily round the room, now and then whistling to his delighted canaries, a slipshod foot upon the staircase without bespoke the advent of that very Mrs. Maloney who waited upon the two young men.

No, Mr. Talboys had not come home; she had looked in as early as six o'clock that morning, and found the chambers empty.

Had anything happened to the poor dear gentleman? she asked, seeing Robert Audley's pale face.

He turned round upon her quite savagely at this question.

Happened to him! What should happen to him? They had only parted at two o'clock the day before.

Mrs. Maloney would have related to him the history of a poor dear young engine-driver, who had once lodged with her, and who went out, after eating a hearty dinner, in the best of spirits, to meet with his death from the concussion of an express and a luggage train; but Robert put on his hat again, and walked straight out of the house, before the honest Irishwoman could begin her pitiful story.

It was growing dusk when he reached Southampton. He knew his way to the poor little terrace of houses, in a dull street leading down to the water, where George's father-in-law lived. Little Georgey was playing at the open parlour window as the young man walked down the street.

Perhaps it was this fact, and the dull and silent aspect of the house, which filled Robert Audley's mind with a vague conviction that the man he came to look for was not there. The old man himself opened the door, and the child peeped out of the parlour to look at the strange gentleman.

He was a handsome boy, with his father's brown eyes and dark waving hair, and yet with some latent expression which was not his father's, and which pervaded his whole face, so that although each feature of the child resembled the same feature in George Talboys, the boy was not actually like him.

The old man was delighted to see Robert Audley; he remembered having had the pleasure of meeting him at Ventnor, on the melancholy occasion of— He wiped his watery old eyes by way of conclusion to the sentence. Would Mr. Audley walk in? Robert strode into the little parlour. The furniture was shabby and dingy, and the place reeked with the smell of stale tobacco and brandy-and-water. The boy's broken playthings and the old man's broken clay pipes, and torn, brandy-and-water stained newspapers, were scattered upon the dirty carpet. Little Georgey crept towards the visitor, watching him furtively out of his big brown eyes. Robert took the boy on his knee, and gave him his watch-chain to play with while he talked to the old man.

'I need scarcely ask the question that I came to ask,' he said. 'I was in hopes I should have found your son-in-law here.'

'What! you knew that he was coming to Southampton?'

'Knew that he was coming!' cried Robert, brightening up. 'He *is* here, then?'

'No, he is not here now, but he has been here.'

'When?'

'Late last night; he came by the mail.'

'And left again immediately?'

'He stayed little better than an hour.'

'Good heavens!' said Robert, 'what useless anxiety that man has given me! What can be the meaning of all this?'

'You knew nothing of his intention, then?'

'Of what intention?'

'I mean of his determination to go to Australia.'

'I knew that it was always in his mind more or less, but not more just now than usual.'

'He sails to-night from Liverpool. He came here at one o'clock this morning to have a look at the boy, he said, before he left England, perhaps never to return. He told me he was sick of the world, and that the rough life out there was the only thing to suit him. He stayed an hour, kissed the boy, without awaking him, and left Southampton by the mail that starts at a quarter past two.'

'What can be the meaning of all this?' said Robert. 'What could be his motive for leaving England in this manner, without a word to me, his most intimate friend – without even a change of clothes; for he has left everything at my chambers? It is the most extraordinary proceeding!'

The old man looked very grave. 'Do you know, Mr. Audley,' he said, tapping his forehead significantly, 'I sometimes fancy that Helen's death had a strange effect upon poor George.'

'Pshaw!' cried Robert contemptuously; 'he felt the blow most cruelly, but his brain was as sound as yours or mine.'

'Perhaps he will write to you from Liverpool,' said George's father-in-law. He seemed anxious to smooth over any indignation that Robert might feel at his friend's conduct.

'He ought,' said Robert gravely, 'for we've been good friends from the days when we were together at Eton. It isn't kind of George Talboys to treat me like this.'

But even at the moment that he uttered the reproach a strange thrill of remorse shot through his heart.

'It isn't like him,' he said, 'it isn't like George Talboys.'

Little Georgey caught at the sound. 'That's my name,' he said, 'and my papa's name – the big gentleman's name.'

'Yes, little Georgey, and your papa came last night and kissed you in your sleep. Do you remember?'

'No,' said the boy, shaking his curly little head.

'You must have been very fast asleep, little Georgey, not to see poor papa.'

The child did not answer, but presently, fixing his eyes upon Robert's face, he said abruptly –

'Where's the pretty lady?'

'What pretty lady?'

'The pretty lady that used to come a long while ago.'

'He means his poor mamma,' said the old man.

'No,' cried the boy resolutely, 'not mamma. Mamma was always crying. I didn't like mamma—'

'Hush, little Georgey!'

'But I didn't, and she didn't like me. She was always crying. I mean the pretty lady; the lady that was dressed so fine, and that gave me my gold watch.'

'He means the wife of my old captain – an excellent creature, who took a great fancy to Georgey, and gave him some handsome presents.'

'Where's my gold watch? Let me show the gentleman my gold watch,' cried Georgey.

'It's gone to be cleaned, Georgey,' answered his grandfather.

'It's always going to be cleaned,' said the boy.

'The watch is perfectly safe, I assure you, Mr. Audley,' murmured the old man, apologetically; and taking out a pawnbroker's duplicate, he handed it to Robert.

It was made out in the name of Captain Mortimer: 'Watch, set with diamonds, £11.'

'I'm often hard pressed for a few shillings, Mr. Audley,' said the old man. 'My son-in-law has been very liberal to me; but there are others, there are others, Mr. Audley – and – and – I've not been treated well.' He wiped away some genuine tears as he said this in a pitiful, crying voice. 'Come, Georgey, it's time the brave little man was in bed. Come along with grandpapa. Excuse me for a quarter of an hour, Mr. Audley.'

The boy went very willingly. At the door of the room the old man looked back at his visitor, and said, in the same peevish voice, 'This is a poor place for me to pass my declining years in, Mr. Audley. I've made many sacrifices, and I make them still, but I've not been treated well.'

Left alone in the dusky little sitting-room, Robert Audley folded his arms, and sat absently staring at the floor.

George was gone, then; he might receive some letter of explanation, perhaps, when he returned to London; but the chances were that he would never see his old friend again.

'And to think that I should care so much for the fellow!' he said, lifting his eyebrows to the centre of his forehead.

'The place smells of stale tobacco like a tap-room,' he muttered presently; 'there can be no harm in my smoking a cigar here.'

He took one from the case in his pocket; there was a spark

of fire in the little grate, and he looked about for something to light his cigar with.

A twisted piece of paper lay half burned upon the hearth-rug; he picked it up, and unfolded it, in order to get a better pipe-light by folding it the other way of the paper. As he did so, absently glancing at the pencilled writing upon the fragment of thin paper, a portion of a name caught his eye – a portion of the name that was most in his thoughts. He took the scrap of paper to the window, and examined it by the declining light.

It was part of a telegraphic despatch. The upper portion had been burnt away, but the more important part, the greater part of the message itself, remained.

                  alboys came to   last night, and left by the mail for London, on his way for Liverpool, whence he was to sail for Sydney.

The date and the name and address of the sender of the message had been burnt with the heading. Robert Audley's face blanched to a deathly whiteness. He carefully folded the scrap of paper, and placed it between the leaves of his pocket-book.

'My God!' he said, 'what is the meaning of this? I shall go to Liverpool to-night, and make inquiries there.'

CHAPTER XIII
Troubled dreams

Robert Audley left Southampton by the mail, and let himself into his chambers just as the dawn was creeping cold and grey into the solitary rooms, and the canaries were beginning to rustle their feathers feebly in the early morning.

There were several letters in the box behind the door, but there was none from George Talboys.

The young barrister was worn out by a long day spent in hurrying from place to place. The usual lazy monotony of his life had been broken as it had never been broken before in eight-and-twenty tranquil, easy-going years. His mind was beginning to grow confused upon the point of time. It seemed to him months since he had lost sight of George Talboys. It was so difficult to believe that it was less than forty-eight hours ago that the young man had left him asleep under the willows by the trout stream.

His eyes were painfully weary for want of sleep. He searched about the rooms for some time, looking in all sorts of impossible places for a letter from George Talboys, and then threw himself dressed upon his friend's bed, in the room with the canaries and geraniums.

'I shall wait for to-morrow morning's post,' he said, 'and if that brings no letter from George I shall start for Liverpool without a moment's delay.'

He was thoroughly exhausted, and fell into a heavy sleep – a sleep which was profound without being altogether refreshing, for he was tormented all the time by disagreeable dreams –

dreams which were painful, not from any horror in themselves, but from a vague and wearying sense of their confusion and absurdity.

At one time he was pursuing strange people and entering strange houses in the endeavour to unravel the mystery of the telegraphic despatch; at another time he was in the churchyard at Ventnor, gazing at the headstone George had ordered for the grave of his dead wife. Once in the long rambling mystery of these dreams he went to the grave, and found this headstone gone, and on remonstrating with the stonemason, was told that the man had a reason for removing the inscription, a reason that Robert would some day learn.

He started from his dreams to find there was some one knocking at the outer door of his chambers.

It was a dreary wet morning, the rain beating against the windows, and the canaries twittering dismally to each other – complaining, perhaps, of the bad weather. Robert could not tell how long the person had been knocking. He had heard the sound with his dreams, and when he woke he was only half conscious of outer things.

'It is that stupid Mrs. Maloney, I dare say,' he muttered. 'She may knock again for all I care. Why can't she use her duplicate key, instead of dragging a man out of bed when he's half dead with fatigue?'

The person, whoever it was, did knock again, and then desisted, apparently tired out; but about a minute afterwards a key turned in the door.

'She had her key with her all the time, then,' said Robert. 'I'm very glad I didn't get up.'

The door between the sitting-room and bed-room was half open, and he could see the laundress bustling about, dusting the furniture, and re-arranging things that had never been disarranged.

'Is that you, Mrs. Maloney?' he asked.

'Yes, Sir.'

'Then why, in goodness' name, did you make that row at the door, when you had a key with you all the time?'

'A row at the door, Sir!'

'Yes; that infernal knocking.'

'Sure I never knocked, Misther Audley, but walked straight in with the key—'

'Then who did knock? There's been some one kicking up a row at that door for a quarter of an hour I should think; you must have met him going down-stairs.'

'But I'm rather late this morning, Sir, for I've been in Mr. Martin's rooms first, and I've come straight from the floor above.'

'Then you didn't see any one at the door, or on the stairs?'

'Not a mortal soul, Sir.'

'Was ever anything so provoking?' said Robert. 'To think that I should have let this person go away without ascertaining who he was, or what he wanted! How do I know that it was not some one with a message or a letter from George Talboys?'

'Sure, if it was, Sir, he'll come again,' said Mrs. Maloney, soothingly.

'Yes, of course, if it was anything of consequence, he'll come again,' muttered Robert. The fact was, that from the moment of finding the telegraphic message at Southampton all hope of hearing of George had faded out of his mind. He felt that there was some mystery involved in the disappearance of his friend – some treachery towards himself, or towards George. What if the young man's greedy old father-in-law had tried to separate them on account of the monetary trust lodged in Robert Audley's hands? Or what if, since even in these civilised days all kinds of unsuspected horrors are constantly committed – what if the old man had decoyed George down to Southampton, and made away with him in order to get

III

possession of that £20,000, left in Robert's custody for little Georgey's use?

But neither of these suppositions explained the telegraphic message, and it was the telegraphic message which had filled Robert's mind with a vague sense of alarm. The postman brought no letter from George Talboys, and the person who had knocked at the door of the chambers did not return between seven and nine o'clock, so Robert Audley left Fig-tree Court once more in search of his friend. This time he told the cabman to drive to the Euston Station, and in twenty minutes he was on the platform, making inquiries about the trains.

The Liverpool express had started half-an-hour before he reached the station, and he had to wait an hour and a quarter for a slow train to take him to his destination.

Robert Audley chafed cruelly at this delay. Half-a-dozen vessels might sail for Australia while he roamed up and down the long platform, tumbling over trucks and porters, and swearing at his ill-luck.

He bought the *Times* newspaper, and looked instinctively at the second column, with a morbid interest in the advertisements of people missing – sons, brothers, and husbands who had left their homes, never to return or to be heard of more.

There was one advertisement of a young man who was found drowned somewhere on the Lambeth shore.

What if that should have been George's fate? No; the telegraphic message involved his father-in-law in the fact of his disappearance, and every speculation about him must start from that one point.

It was eight o'clock in the evening when Robert got into Liverpool, too late for anything except to make inquiries as to what vessels had sailed within the last two days for the Antipodes.

An emigrant ship had sailed at four o'clock that afternoon – the *Victoria Regia*, bound for Melbourne.

The result of his inquiries amounted to this – if he wanted to find out who had sailed in the *Victoria Regia*, he must wait till the next morning, and apply for information of that vessel.

Robert Audley was at the office at nine o'clock the next morning, and was the first person after the clerks who entered it.

He met with every civility from the clerk to whom he applied. The young man referred to his books, and running his pen down the list of passengers who had sailed in the *Victoria Regia*, told Robert that there was no one amongst them of the name of Talboys. He pushed his inquiries further. Had any of the passengers entered their names within a short time of the vessel's sailing?

One of the other clerks looked up from his desk as Robert asked this question. Yes, he said, he remembered a young man's coming into the office at half-past three o'clock in the afternoon, and paying his passage-money. His name was the last on the list – Thomas Brown.

Robert Audley shrugged his shoulders. There could have been no possible reason for George's taking a feigned name. He asked the clerk who had last spoken if he could remember the appearance of this Mr. Thomas Brown.

No, the office was crowded at the time; people were running in and out, and he had not taken any particular notice of this last passenger.

Robert thanked them for their civility, and wished them good morning. As he was leaving the office one of the young men called after him.

'Oh, by-the-bye, Sir,' he said, 'I remember one thing about this Mr. Thomas Brown – his arm was in a sling.'

There was nothing more for Robert Audley to do but to return to town. He re-entered his chambers at six o'clock that evening, thoroughly worn out once more with his useless search.

Mrs. Maloney brought him his dinner and a pint of wine from a tavern in the Strand. The evening was raw and chilly, and the laundress had lighted a good fire in the sitting-room grate.

After eating about half a mutton chop, Robert sat with his wine untasted upon the table before him, smoking cigars and staring into the blaze.

'George Talboys never sailed for Australia,' he said, after long and painful reflection. 'If he is alive he is still in England, and if he is dead his body is hidden in some corner of England.'

He sat for hours smoking and thinking – troubled and gloomy thoughts, leaving a dark shadow upon his moody face, which neither the brilliant light of the gas nor the red blaze of the fire could dispel.

Very late in the evening he rose from his chair, pushed away the table, wheeled his desk over to the fire-place, took out a sheet of foolscap, and dipped a pen in the ink.

But after doing this he paused, leaned his forehead upon his hand, and once more relapsed into thought.

'I shall draw up a record of all that has occurred between our going down to Essex and to-night, beginning at the very beginning.'

He drew up this record in short detached sentences, which he numbered as he wrote.

It ran thus:–

'JOURNAL OF FACTS CONNECTED WITH THE DISAPPEARANCE OF GEORGE TALBOYS, INCLUSIVE OF FACTS WHICH HAVE NO APPARENT RELATION TO THAT CIRCUMSTANCE.'

In spite of the troubled state of his mind he was rather inclined to be proud of the official appearance of this heading. He sat for some time looking at it with affection, and with the feather of his pen in his mouth. 'Upon my word,' he said, 'I begin to think that I ought to have pursued my profession, instead of dawdling my life away as I have done.'

He smoked half a cigar before he had got his thoughts in proper train, and then began to write:–

'1. I write to Alicia, proposing to take George down to the Court.

'2. Alicia writes, objecting to the visit on the part of Lady Audley.

'3. We go to Essex in spite of this objection. I see my lady. My lady refuses to be introduced to George that particular evening on the score of fatigue.

'4. Sir Michael invites George and me to dinner for the following evening.

'5. My lady receives a telegraphic despatch the next morning which summons her to London.

'6. Alicia shows me a letter from my lady, in which she requests to be told when I and my friend, Mr. Talboys, mean to leave Essex. To this letter is subjoined a postscript reiterating the above request.

'7. We call at the Court, and ask to see the house. My lady's apartments are locked.

'8. We get at the aforesaid apartments by means of a secret passage, the existence of which is unknown to my lady. In one of the rooms we find her portrait.

'9. George is frightened at the storm. His conduct is exceedingly strange for the rest of the evening.

'10. George quite himself again the following morning. I propose leaving Audley Court immediately; he prefers remaining till the evening.

'11. We go out fishing. George leaves me to go to the Court.

'12. The last positive information I can obtain of him in Essex is at the Court, where the servant says he thinks Mr. Talboys told him he would go and look for my lady in the grounds.

'13. I receive information about him at the station which may, or may not, be correct.

'14. I hear of him positively once more at Southampton, where, according to his father-in-law, he had been for an hour on the previous night.

'15. The telegraphic message.'

When Robert Audley had completed this brief record, which he drew up with great deliberation, and with frequent pauses for reflection, alterations, and erasures, he sat for a long time contemplating the written page.

At last he read it carefully over, stopping at some of the numbered paragraphs, and marking several of them with a pencilled cross; then he folded the sheet of foolscap, went over to a cabinet on the opposite side of the room, unlocked it, and placed the paper in that very pigeon-hole into which he had thrust Alicia's letter – the pigeon-hole marked *Important*.

Having done this, he returned to his easy-chair by the fire, pushed away his desk, and lighted a cigar. 'It's as dark as midnight from first to last,' he said; 'and the clue to the mystery must be found either at Southampton or in Essex. Be it how it may, my mind is made up. I shall first go to Audley Court, and look for George Talboys in a narrow radius.'

CHAPTER XIV

Phœbe's suitor

'Mr. George Talboys. – Any person who has met this gentleman since the 7th inst., or who possesses any information respecting him subsequent to that date, will be liberally rewarded on communicating with A. Z., 14, Chancery Lane.'

Sir Michael Audley read the above advertisement in the second column of the *Times*, as he sat at breakfast with my lady and Alicia two or three days after Robert's return to town.

'Robert's friend has not yet been heard of, then,' said the baronet, after reading the advertisement to his wife and daughter.

'As for that,' replied my lady, 'I cannot help wondering who can be silly enough to advertise for him. The young man was evidently of a restless, roving disposition – a sort of Bamfylde Moore Carew of modern life, whom no attraction could ever keep in one spot.'

Though the advertisement appeared three successive times, the party at the Court attached very little importance to Mr. Talboys' disappearance; and after this one occasion his name was never again mentioned by either Sir Michael, my lady, or Alicia.

Alicia Audley and her pretty step-mother were by no means any better friends after that quiet evening on which the young barrister had dined at the Court.

'She is a vain, frivolous, heartless little coquette,' said Alicia, addressing herself to her Newfoundland dog, Cæsar, who was the sole recipient of the young lady's confidences; 'she is a practised and consummate flirt, Cæsar; and not contented with setting her yellow ringlets and her silly giggle at half the men in Essex, she must needs make that stupid cousin of mine dance attendance upon her. I haven't common patience with her.'

In proof of which last assertion Miss Alicia Audley treated her step-mother with such very palpable impertinence that Sir Michael felt himself called upon to remonstrate with his only daughter.

'The poor little woman is very sensitive, you know, Alicia,' the baronet said gravely, 'and she feels your conduct most acutely.'

'I don't believe it a bit, papa,' answered Alicia stoutly. 'You think her sensitive because she has soft little white hands, and big blue eyes with long lashes, and all manner of affected, fantastical ways, which you stupid men call fascinating. Sensitive! Why, I've seen her do cruel things with those slender white fingers, and laugh at the pain she inflicted. I'm very sorry, papa,' she added, softened a little by her father's look of distress; 'though she has come between us, and robbed poor Alicia of the love of that dear, generous heart, I wish I could like her for your sake; but I can't, I can't, and no more can Cæsar. She came up to him once with her red lips apart, and her little white teeth glistening between them, and stroked his great head with her soft hand; but if I had not had hold of his collar, he would have flown at her throat and strangled her. She may bewitch every man in Essex, but she'd never make friends with my dog.'

'Your dog shall be shot,' answered Sir Michael angrily, 'if his vicious temper ever endangers Lucy.'

The Newfoundland rolled his eyes slowly round in the direction of the speaker, as if he understood every word that had been said. Lady Audley happened to enter the room at this very moment, and the animal cowered down by the side of his mistress with a suppressed growl. There was something in the manner of the dog which was, if anything, more indicative of terror than of fury, incredible as it appears that Cæsar should be frightened of so fragile a creature as Lucy Audley.

Amiable as was my lady's nature, she could not live long at the Court without discovering Alicia's dislike to her. She never alluded to it but once; then, shrugging her graceful white shoulders, she said with a sigh:

'It seems very hard that you cannot love me, Alicia, for I have never been used to make enemies; but since it seems that it must be so, I cannot help it. If we cannot be friends, let us at least be neutral. You won't try to injure me?'

'Injure you!' exclaimed Alicia; 'how should I injure you?'

'You'll not try to deprive me of your father's affection?'

'I may not be as amiable as you are, my lady, and I may not have the same sweet smiles and pretty words for every stranger I meet, but I am not capable of a contemptible meanness; and even if I were, I think you are so secure of my father's love, that nothing but your own act will ever deprive you of it.'

'What a severe creature you are, Alicia!' said my lady, making a little grimace. 'I suppose you mean to infer by all that, that I'm deceitful. Why, I can't help smiling at people, and speaking prettily to them. I know I'm no *better* than the rest of the world, but I can't help it if I'm *pleasanter*. It's constitutional.'

Alicia having thus entirely shut the door upon all intimacy between Lady Audley and herself, and Sir Michael being chiefly occupied in agricultural pursuits and manly sports, which kept him away from home, it was, perhaps, only natural that my lady, being of an eminently social disposition, should find herself thrown a good deal upon her white-eyelashed maid for society.

Phœbe Marks was exactly the sort of girl who is generally

promoted from the post of lady's-maid to that of companion. She had just sufficient education to enable her to understand her mistress when Lucy chose to allow herself to run riot in a species of intellectual tarantella, in which her tongue went mad to the sound of its own rattle, as the Spanish dancer at the noise of his castanets. Phœbe knew enough of the French language to be able to dip into the yellow-paper-covered novels which my lady ordered from the Burlington Arcade, and to discourse with her mistress upon the questionable subjects of those romances. The likeness which the lady's-maid bore to Lucy Audley was, perhaps, a point of sympathy between the two women. It was not to be called a striking likeness; a stranger might have seen them both together, and yet have failed to remark it. But there were certain dim and shadowy lights in which, meeting Phœbe Marks gliding softly through the dark oak passages of the Court, or under the shrouded avenues in the garden, you might have easily mistaken her for my lady.

Sharp October winds were sweeping the leaves from the limes in the long avenue, and driving them in withered heaps with a ghostly rustling noise along the dry gravel walks. The old well must have been half choked up with the leaves that drifted about it, and whirled in eddying circles into its black, broken mouth. On the still bosom of the fish-pond the same withered leaves slowly rotted away, mixing themselves with the tangled weeds that discoloured the surface of the water. All the gardeners Sir Michael could employ could not keep the impress of autumn's destroying hand from the grounds about the Court.

'How I hate this desolate month!' my lady said, as she walked about the garden, shivering beneath her sable mantle. 'Everything dropping to ruin and decay, and the cold flicker of the sun lighting up the ugliness of the earth, as the glare of gas-lamps lights the wrinkles of an old woman. Shall I ever grow old, Phœbe? Will my hair ever drop off as the leaves are falling from those trees, and leave me wan and bare like them? What is to become of me when I grow old?'

She shivered at the thought of this more than she had done at the cold wintry breeze, and muffling herself closely in her fur, walked so fast, that her maid had some difficulty in keeping up with her.

'Do you remember, Phœbe,' she said presently, relaxing her pace, 'do you remember that French story we read – the story of a beautiful woman who committed some crime – I forget what – in the zenith of her power and loveliness, when all Paris drank to her every night, and when the people ran away from the carriage of the king to flock about hers, and get a peep at her face? Do you remember how she kept the secret of what she had done for nearly half a century, spending her old age in her family château, beloved and honoured by all the province, as an uncanonised saint and benefactress to the poor; and how, when her hair was white, and her eyes almost blind with age, the secret was revealed through one of those strange accidents by which such secrets always are revealed in romances, and she was tried, found guilty, and condemned to be burned alive? The king who had worn her colours was dead and gone; the court of which she had been the star had passed away; powerful functionaries and great magistrates, who might perhaps have helped her, were mouldering in their graves; brave young cavaliers, who would have died for her, had fallen upon distant battle-fields; she had lived to see the age to which she had belonged fade like a dream; and she went to the stake, followed only by a few ignorant country people, who forgot all her bounties, and hooted at her for a wicked sorceress.'

'I don't care for such dismal stories, my lady,' said Phœbe Marks with a shudder. 'One has no need to read books to give one the horrors in this dull place.'

Lady Audley shrugged her shoulders and laughed at her maid's candour.

'It is a dull place, Phœbe,' she said, 'though it doesn't do to say so to my dear old husband. Though I am the wife of one of the most influential men in the county, I don't know that I wasn't nearly as well off at Mr. Dawson's; and yet it's something to wear sables that cost sixty guineas, and have a thousand pounds spent on the decorations of one's apartments.'

Treated as a companion by her mistress, in the receipt of the most liberal wages, and with perquisites such as perhaps no lady's-maid ever had before, it was strange that Phœbe Marks should wish to leave her situation; but it was not the less a fact that she was anxious to exchange all the advantages of Audley Court for the very unpromising prospect which awaited her as the wife of her cousin Luke.

The young man had contrived in some manner to associate himself with the improved fortunes of his sweetheart. He had never allowed Phœbe any peace till she obtained for him, by the aid of my lady's interference, a situation as under-groom at the Court.

He never rode out with either Alicia or Sir Michael; but on one of the few occasions upon which my lady mounted the pretty little grey thoroughbred reserved for her use, he contrived to attend her in her ride. He saw enough, in the very first half hour they were out, to discover that, graceful as Lucy Audley might look in her long blue cloth habit, she was a timid horsewoman, and utterly unable to manage the animal she rode.

Lady Audley remonstrated with her maid upon her folly in wishing to marry the uncouth groom.

The two women were seated together over the fire in my lady's dressing-room, the grey sky closing in upon the October afternoon, and the black tracery of ivy darkening the casement windows.

'You surely are not in love with the awkward, ugly creature, are you, Phœbe?' asked my lady sharply.

The girl was sitting on a low stool at her mistress's feet. She did not answer my lady's question immediately, but sat for some time looking vacantly into the red abyss in the hollow fire.

Presently she said, rather as if she had been thinking aloud than answering Lucy's question –

'I don't think I can love him. We have been together from children, and I promised, when I was little better than fifteen, that I'd be his wife. I daren't break that promise now. There have been times when I've made up the very sentence I meant to say to him, telling him that I couldn't keep my faith with him; but the words have died upon my lips, and I've sat looking at him, with a choking sensation in my throat that wouldn't let me speak. I daren't refuse to marry him. I've often watched and watched him, as he has sat slicing away at a hedge-stake with his great clasp-knife, till I have thought that it is just such men as he who have decoyed their sweethearts into lonely places, and murdered them for being false to their word. When he was a boy he was always violent and revengeful. I saw him once take up that very knife in a quarrel with his mother. I tell you, my lady, I must marry him.'

'You silly girl, you shall do nothing of the kind!' answered Lucy. 'You think he'll murder you, do you? Do you think, then, if murder is in him, you would be any safer as his wife? If you thwarted him, or made him jealous; if he wanted to marry another woman, or to get hold of some poor, pitiful bit of money of yours, couldn't he murder you then? I tell you you shan't marry him, Phœbe. In the first place, I hate the man; and, in the next place, I can't afford to part with you. We'll give him a few pounds and send him about his business.'

Phœbe Marks caught my lady's hands in hers, and clasped them convulsively.

'My lady – my good, kind mistress!' she cried vehemently, 'don't try to thwart me in this – don't ask me to thwart him. I tell you I must marry him. You don't know what he is. It will be my ruin, and the ruin of others, if I break my word. I must marry him!'

'Very well, then, Phœbe,' answered her mistress, 'I can't oppose you. There must be some secret at the bottom of all this.'

'There is, my lady,' said the girl, with her face turned away from Lucy.

'I shall be very sorry to lose you; but I have promised to stand your friend in all things. What does your cousin mean to do for a living when you are married?'

'He would like to take a public-house.'

'Then he shall take a public-house, and the sooner he drinks himself to death the better. Sir Michael dines at a bachelor's party at Major Margrave's this evening, and my step-daughter is away with her friends at the Grange. You can bring your cousin into the drawing-room after dinner, and I'll tell him what I mean to do for him.'

'You are very good, my lady,' Phœbe answered with a sigh.

Lady Audley sat in the glow of firelight and wax candles in the luxurious drawing-room; the amber damask cushions of the sofa contrasting with her dark violet velvet dress, and her rippling hair falling about her neck in a golden haze. Everywhere around her were the evidences of wealth and splendour; while in strange contrast to all this, and to her own beauty, the awkward groom stood rubbing his bullet head as my lady explained to him what she meant to do for her confidential maid. Lucy's promises were very liberal, and she had expected that, uncouth as the man was, he would in his own rough manner have expressed his gratitude.

To her surprise he stood staring at the floor without uttering a word in answer to her offer. Phœbe was standing close to his elbow, and seemed distressed at the man's rudeness.

'Tell my lady how thankful you are, Luke,' she said.

'But I'm not so over and above thankful,' answered her lover savagely. 'Fifty pound ain't much to start a public. You'll make it a hundred, my lady.'

'I shall do nothing of the kind,' said Lady Audley, her clear blue eyes flashing with indignation, 'and I wonder at your impertinence in asking it.'

'Oh yes, you will though,' answered Luke, with quiet insolence, that had a hidden meaning. 'You'll make it a hundred, my lady.'

Lady Audley rose from her seat, looked the man steadfastly in the face till his determined gaze sank under hers; then walking straight up to her maid, she said in a high, piercing voice, peculiar to her in moments of intense agitation, 'Phœbe Marks, you have told *this man!*'

The girl fell on her knees at my lady's feet.

'Oh, forgive me, forgive me!' she cried. 'He forced it from me, or I would never, never have told!'

CHAPTER XV
On the watch

Upon a lowering morning late in November, with the yellow fog low upon the flat meadows, and the blinded cattle groping their way through the dim obscurity, and blundering stupidly against black and leafless hedges, or stumbling into ditches, undistinguishable in the hazy atmosphere; with the village church looming brown and dingy through the uncertain light; with every winding path and cottage door, every gable-end and grey old chimney, every village child and straggling cur, seeming strange and weird of aspect in the semi-darkness, Phœbe Marks and her cousin Luke made their way through the churchyard of Audley, and presented themselves before a shivering curate, whose surplice hung in damp folds, soddened by the morning mist, and whose temper was not improved by his having waited five minutes for the bride and bridegroom.

Luke Marks, dressed in his ill-fitting Sunday clothes, looked by no means handsomer than in his every-day apparel; but Phœbe, arrayed in a rustling silk of delicate grey, that had been worn about half-a-dozen times by her mistress, looked, as the few spectators of the ceremony remarked, quite the lady.

A very dim and shadowy lady; vague of outline, and faint of colouring; with eyes, hair, complexion, and dress all melting into such pale and uncertain shades that, in the obscure light of the foggy November morning, a superstitious stranger might have mistaken the bride for the ghost of some other bride, dead and buried in the vaults below the church.

Mr. Luke Marks, the hero of the occasion, thought very little of all this. He had secured the wife of his choice, and the object of his life-long ambition – a public-house. My lady had provided the seventy-five pounds necessary for the purchase of the good-will and fixtures, with the stock of ales and spirits, of a small inn in the centre of a lonely little village, perched on the summit of a hill, and called Mount Stanning. It was not a very pretty house to look at; it had something of a tumble-down, weather-beaten appearance, standing as it did upon high ground, sheltered only by four or five bare and overgrown poplars, that had shot up too rapidly for their strength, and had a blighted forlorn look in consequence. The wind had had its own way with the Castle Inn, and had sometimes made cruel use of its power. It was the wind that battered and bent the low, thatched roofs of out-houses and stables, till they hung over and lurched forward, as a slouched hat hangs over the low forehead of some village ruffian; it was the wind that shook and rattled the wooden shutters before the narrow casements, till they hung broken and dilapidated upon their rusty hinges; it was the wind that overthrew the pigeon-house, and broke the vane that had been impudently set up to tell the movements of its mightiness; it was the wind that made light of any little bit of wooden trellis-work, or creeping plant, or tiny balcony, or any modest decoration whatsoever, and tore and scattered it in its scornful fury; it was the wind that left mossy secretions on the discoloured surface of the plaster walls; it was the wind, in short, that shattered, and ruined, and rent, and trampled upon the tottering pile of buildings, and then flew shrieking off, to riot and glory in its destroying strength. The dispirited proprietor grew tired of his long struggle with this mighty enemy; so the wind was left to work its own will, and the Castle Inn fell slowly to decay. But for all that it suffered without, it was not the less prosperous within doors. Sturdy drovers stopped to drink at the little bar; well-to-do farmers spent their evenings and talked politics in the low, wainscoted parlour, while their horses munched some suspicious mixture of mouldy hay and tolerable beans in the tumble-down stables. Sometimes even the members of the Audley hunt stopped to drink and bait their horses at the Castle Inn; while, on one grand and never-to-be-forgotten occasion, a dinner had been ordered by the master of the hounds for some thirty gentlemen, and the proprietor driven nearly mad by the importance of the demand.

So Luke Marks, who was by no means troubled with an eye for the beautiful, thought himself very fortunate in becoming landlord of the Castle Inn, Mount Stanning.

A chaise-cart was waiting in the fog to convey the bride and bridegroom to their new home; and a few of the simple villagers, who had known Phœbe from a child, were lingering round the churchyard gate to bid her good-by. Her pale eyes were still paler from the tears she had shed, and the red rims which surrounded them. The bridegroom was annoyed at this exhibition of emotion.

'What are you blubbering for, lass?' he said fiercely. 'If you didn't want to marry me, you should have told me so. I ain't going to murder you, am I?'

The lady's-maid shivered as he spoke to her, and dragged her little silk mantle closely round her.

'You're cold in all this here finery,' said Luke, staring at her costly dress with no expression of good-will. 'Why can't women dress according to their station? You won't have no silk gowns out of my pocket, I can tell you.'

He lifted the shivering girl into the chaise, wrapped a rough great-coat about her, and drove off through the yellow fog, followed by a feeble cheer from two or three urchins clustered round the gate.

A new maid was brought from London to replace Phœbe

Marks about the person of my lady – a very showy damsel, who wore a black satin gown, and rose-coloured ribbons in her cap, and complained bitterly of the dulness of Audley Court.

But Christmas brought visitors to the rambling old mansion. A country squire and his fat wife occupied the tapestried chamber; merry girls scampered up and down the long passages, and young men stared out of the latticed windows watching for southerly winds and cloudy skies; there was not an empty stall in the roomy old stables; an extempore forge had been set up in the yard for the shoeing of hunters; yelping dogs made the place noisy with their perpetual clamour; strange servants horded together on the garret storey; and every little casement hidden away under some pointed gable, and every dormer window in the quaint old roof, glimmered upon the winter's night with its separate taper, till, coming suddenly upon Audley Court, the benighted stranger, misled by the light and noise, and bustle of the place, might have easily fallen into young Marlowe's error, and have mistaken the hospitable mansion for a good, old-fashioned inn, such as have faded from this earth since the last mail coach and prancing tits took their last melancholy journey to the knacker's yard.

Amongst other visitors Mr. Robert Audley came down to Essex for the hunting season, with half-a-dozen French novels, a case of cigars, and three pounds of Turkish tobacco in his portmanteau.

The honest young country squires, who talked all breakfast time of Flying Dutchman fillies and Voltigeur colts; of glorious runs of seven hours' hard riding over three counties, and a midnight homeward ride of thirty miles upon their covert hacks; and who ran away from the well-spread table with their mouths full of cold sirloin to look at that off pastern, or that sprained fore-arm, or the colt that had just come back from the veterinary surgeon's, set down Mr. Robert Audley, dawdling

129

over a slice of bread and marmalade, as a person utterly unworthy of any remark whatsoever.

The young barrister had brought a couple of dogs with him; and the country gentleman who gave fifty pounds for a pointer, and travelled a couple of hundred miles to look at a leash of setters before he struck a bargain, laughed aloud at the two miserable curs; one of which had followed Robert Audley through Chancery Lane and half the length of Holborn; while his companion had been taken by the barrister *vi et armis* from a costermonger who was ill-using him. And as Robert furthermore insisted on having these two deplorable animals under his easy-chair in the drawing-room, much to the annoyance of my lady, who, as we know, hated all dogs, the visitors at Audley Court looked upon the baronet's nephew as an inoffensive species of maniac.

During other visits to the Court, Robert Audley had made a feeble show of joining in the sports of the merry assembly. He had jogged across half-a-dozen ploughed fields on a quiet grey pony of Sir Michael's, and drawing up breathless and panting at the door of some farm-house, had expressed his intention of following the hounds no further *that* morning. He had even gone so far as to put on, with great labour, a pair of skates, with a view to taking a turn on the frozen surface of the fish-pond, and had fallen ignominiously at the first attempt, lying placidly extended on the flat of his back until such time as the bystanders should think fit to pick him up. He had occupied the back seat in a dog-cart during a pleasant morning drive, vehemently protesting against being taken up-hill, and requiring the vehicle to be stopped every ten minutes for the re-adjustment of the cushions. But this year he showed no inclination for any of these outdoor amusements. He spent his time entirely in lounging in the drawing-room, and making himself agreeable, after his own lazy fashion, to my lady and Alicia.

Lady Audley received her nephew's attentions in that graceful, half-childish fashion which her admirers found so charming; but Alicia was indignant at the change in her cousin's conduct.

'You were always a poor, spiritless fellow, Bob,' said the young lady, contemptuously, as she bounced into the drawing-room, in her riding habit, after a hunting breakfast, from which Robert had absented himself, preferring a cup of tea in my lady's boudoir; 'but this year I don't know what has come to you. You are good for nothing but to hold a skein of silk or read Tennyson to Lady Audley.'

'My dear, hasty, impetuous Alicia, don't be violent,' said the young man imploringly. 'A conclusion isn't a five-barred gate; and you needn't give your judgment its head, as you give your mare, Atalanta, hers, when you're flying across country at the heels of an unfortunate fox. Lady Audley interests me, and my uncle's county friends do not. Is that a sufficient answer, Alicia?'

Miss Audley gave her head a little scornful toss.

'It's as good an answer as I shall ever get from you, Bob,' she said impatiently; 'but pray amuse yourself in your own way; loll in an easy-chair all day, with those two absurd dogs asleep on your knees; spoil my lady's window-curtains with your cigars; and annoy everybody in the house with your stupid, inanimate countenance.'

Mr. Robert Audley opened his handsome grey eyes to their widest extent at this tirade, and looked helplessly at Miss Alicia.

The young lady was walking up and down the room, slashing the skirt of her habit with her riding-whip. Her eyes sparkled with an angry flash, and a crimson glow burned under her clear brown skin. The young barrister knew very well by these diagnostics that his cousin was in a passion.

'Yes,' she repeated, 'your stupid, inanimate countenance.

Do you know, Robert Audley, that with all your mock amiability, you are brimful of conceit and superciliousness. You look down upon our amusements; you lift up your eyebrows, and shrug your shoulders, and throw yourself back in your chair, and wash your hands of us and our pleasures. You are a selfish, cold-hearted Sybarite—'

'Alicia! Good – gracious – me!'

The morning paper dropped out of his hands, and he sat feebly staring at his assailant.

'Yes, *selfish*, Robert Audley! You take home half-starved dogs, because you like half-starved dogs. You stoop down and pat the head of every good-for-nothing cur in the village street, because you like good-for-nothing curs. You notice little children, and give them halfpence, because it pleases you to do so. But you lift your eyebrows a quarter of a yard when poor Sir Harry Towers tells a stupid story, and stare the poor fellow out of countenance with your lazy insolence. As to your amiability, you would let a man hit you, and say "Thank you" for the blow, rather than take the trouble to hit him again; but you wouldn't go half a mile out of your way to serve your dearest friend. Sir Harry is worth twenty of you, though he *did* write to ask if my ma-a-i-r, Atalanta, had recovered from the sprain. He can't spell, or lift his eyebrows to the roots of his hair; but he would go through fire and water for the girl he loves; while *you*—'

At this very point, when Robert was most prepared to encounter his cousin's violence, and when Miss Alicia seemed about to make her strongest attack, the young lady broke down altogether and burst into tears.

Robert sprang from his easy-chair, upsetting his dogs on the carpet.

'Alicia, my darling, what is it?'

'It's – it's – it's the feather of my hat that got into my eyes,' sobbed his cousin; and before Robert could investigate the truth of this assertion Alicia had darted out of the room.

Mr. Audley was preparing to follow her, when he heard her voice in the courtyard below, amidst the trampling of horses and the clamour of visitors, dogs, and grooms. Sir Harry Towers, the most aristocratic young sportsman in the neighbourhood, had just taken her little foot in his hand as she sprang into her saddle.

'Good heavens!' exclaimed Robert, as he watched the merry party of equestrians until they disappeared under the archway. 'What does all this mean? How charmingly she sits her horse! What a pretty figure, too, and a fine, candid, brown, rosy face; but to fly at a fellow like that, without the least provocation! That's the consequence of letting a girl follow the hounds. She learns to look at everything in life as she does at six feet of timber or a sunk fence; she goes through the world as she goes across country – straight ahead, and over everything. Such a nice girl as she might have been, too, if she'd been brought up in Fig-tree Court! If ever I marry, and have daughters (which remote contingency may Heaven forefend!), they shall be educated in Paper Buildings, take their sole exercise in the Temple Gardens, and they shall never go beyond the gates till they are marriageable, when I will take them straight across Fleet Street to St. Dunstan's Church, and deliver them into the hands of their husbands.'

With such reflections as these did Mr. Robert Audley beguile the time until my lady re-entered the drawing-room, fresh and radiant in her elegant morning costume, her yellow curls glistening with the perfumed waters in which she had bathed, and her velvet-covered sketch-book in her arms. She planted a little easel upon a table by the window, seated herself before it, and began to mix the colours upon her palette, Robert watching her out of his half-closed eyes.

'You are sure my cigar does not annoy you, Lady Audley?'

'Oh no, indeed; I am quite used to the smell of tobacco. Mr. Dawson, the surgeon, smoked all the evening, when I lived in his house.'

'Dawson is a good fellow, isn't he?' Robert asked carelessly.

My lady burst into her pretty gushing laugh.

'The dearest of good creatures,' she said. 'He paid me five-and-twenty pounds a year – only fancy – that made six pounds five a quarter. How well I remember receiving the money – six dingy old sovereigns, and a little heap of untidy, dirty silver, that came straight from the till in the surgery! And then how glad I was to get it; while *now* – I can't help laughing while I think of it – these colours I am using cost a guinea each at Winsor and Newton's – the carmine and ultramarine thirty shillings. I gave Mrs. Dawson one of my silk dresses the other day, and the poor thing kissed me, and the surgeon carried the bundle home under his cloak.'

My lady laughed long and joyously at the thought. Her colours were mixed; she was copying a water-coloured sketch of an impossibly beautiful Italian peasant, in an impossibly Turneresque atmosphere. The sketch was nearly finished, and she had only to put in some critical little touches with the most delicate of her sable pencils. She prepared herself daintily for the work, looking sideways at the painting.

All this time Mr. Robert Audley's eyes were fixed intently on her pretty face.

'It *is* a change,' he said, after so long a pause that my lady might have forgotten what she had been talking of; 'it *is* a change! Some women would do a great deal to accomplish such a change as that.'

Lucy Audley's clear blue eyes dilated as she fixed them suddenly on the young barrister. The winter sunlight, gleaming full upon her face from a side window, lit up the azure of those beautiful eyes, till their colour seemed to flicker and tremble betwixt blue and green, as the opal tints of the sea change upon a summer's day. The small brush fell from her hand, and blotted out the peasant's face under a widening circle of crimson lake.

Robert Audley was tenderly coaxing the crumpled leaf of his cigar with cautious fingers.

'My friend at the corner of Chancery Lane has not given me such good Manillas as usual,' he murmured. 'If ever you smoke, my dear aunt (and I am told that many women take a quiet weed under the rose), be very careful how you choose your cigars.'

My lady drew a long breath, picked up her brush, and laughed aloud at Robert's advice.

'What an eccentric creature you are, Mr. Audley! Do you know that you sometimes puzzle me—'

'Not more than you puzzle me, my dear aunt.'

My lady put away her colours and sketch-book, and seating herself in the deep recess of another window at a considerable distance from Robert Audley, settled herself to a large piece of Berlin-wool work – a piece of embroidery which the Penelopes of ten or twelve years ago were very fond of exercising their ingenuity upon – the Olden Time at Bolton Abbey.

Seated in the embrasure of this window, my lady was separated from Robert Audley by the whole length of the room, and the young man could only catch an occasional glimpse of her fair face, surrounded by its bright aureole of hazy golden hair.

Robert Audley had been a week at the Court, but as yet neither he nor my lady had mentioned the name of George Talboys.

This morning, however, after exhausting the usual topics of conversation, Lady Audley made an inquiry about her nephew's friend – 'that Mr. George – George—' she said, hesitating.

'Talboys,' suggested Robert.

'Yes, to be sure – Mr. George Talboys. Rather a singular name by-the-bye, and certainly, by all accounts, a very singular person. Have you seen him lately?'

'I have not seen him since the 7th of September – the day upon which he left me asleep in the meadows on the other side of the village.'

'Dear me!' exclaimed my lady, 'what a strange young man this Mr. George Talboys must be! Pray tell me all about it.'

Robert told, in a few words, of his visit to Southampton, and his journey to Liverpool, with their different results, my lady listening very attentively.

In order to tell this story to better advantage the young man left his chair, and crossing the room, took up his place opposite to Lady Audley in the embrasure of the window.

'And what do you infer from all this?' asked my lady after a pause.

'It is so great a mystery to me,' he answered, 'that I scarcely dare to draw any conclusion whatever; but in the obscurity I think I can grope my way to two suppositions, which to me seem almost certainties.'

'And they are—'

'First, that George Talboys never went beyond South-ampton. Secondly, that he never went to Southampton at all.'

'But you traced him there. His father-in-law had seen him.'

'I have reason to doubt his father-in-law's integrity.'

'Good gracious me!' cried my lady, piteously. 'What do you mean by all this?'

'Lady Audley,' answered the young man gravely, 'I have never practised as a barrister. I have enrolled myself in the ranks of a profession, the members of which hold solemn responsibilities, and have sacred duties to perform; and I have shrunk from those responsibilities and duties, as I have from all the fatigues of this troublesome life: but we are sometimes forced into the very position we have most avoided, and I have found myself lately compelled to think of these things. Lady Audley, did you ever study the theory of circumstantial evidence?'

'How can you ask a poor little woman about such horrid things?' exclaimed my lady.

'Circumstantial evidence,' continued the young man, as if he scarcely heard Lady Audley's interruption, 'that wonderful fabric which is built out of straws collected at every point of the compass, and which is yet strong enough to hang a man. Upon what infinitesimal trifles may sometimes hang the whole secret of some wicked mystery, inexplicable heretofore to the wisest upon the earth! A scrap of paper; a shred of some torn garment; the button off a coat; a word dropped incautiously from the over-cautious lips of guilt; the fragment of a letter; the shutting or opening of a door; a shadow on a window-blind; the accuracy of a moment; a thousand circumstances so slight as to be forgotten by the criminal, but links of steel in the wonderful chain forged by the science of the detective officer; and lo! the gallows is built up; the solemn bell tolls through the dismal grey of the early morning; the drop creaks under the guilty feet; and the penalty of crime is paid.'

Faint shadows of green and crimson fell upon my lady's face from the painted escutcheons in the mullioned window by which she sat; but every trace of the natural colour of that face had faded out, leaving it a ghastly ashen grey.

Sitting quietly in her chair, her head fallen back upon the amber damask cushions, and her little hands lying powerless in her lap, Lady Audley had fainted away.

'The radius grows narrower day by day,' said Robert Audley. 'George Talboys never reached Southampton.'

CHAPTER XVI

Robert Audley gets his congé

The Christmas week was over, and one by one the country visitors dropped away from Audley Court. The fat squire and his wife abandoned the grey, tapestried chamber, and left the black-browed warriors looming from the wall to scowl upon and threaten new guests, or to glare vengefully upon vacancy. The merry girls on the second storey packed, or caused to be packed, their trunks and imperials, and tumbled gauze ball-dresses were taken home that had been brought fresh to Audley. Blundering old family chariots, with horses whose untrimmed fetlocks told of rougher work than even country roads, were brought round to the broad space before the grim oak door, and laden with chaotic heaps of womanly luggage. Pretty rosy faces peeped out of the carriage windows to smile the last farewell upon the group at the hall door, as the vehicle rattled and rumbled under the ivied archway. Sir Michael was in request everywhere. Shaking hands with the young sportsmen; kissing the rosy-cheeked girls; sometimes even embracing portly matrons who came to thank him for their pleasant visit; everywhere genial, hospitable, generous, happy, and beloved, the baronet hurried from room to room, from the hall to the stables, from the stables to the courtyard, from the courtyard to the arched gateway, to speed the parting guest.

My lady's yellow curls flashed hither and thither like wandering gleams of sunshine on these busy days of farewell. Her great blue eyes had a pretty mournful look, in charming unison with the soft pressure of her little hand, and that friendly, though perhaps rather stereotyped speech, in which she told her visitors how she was *so* sorry to lose them, and how she didn't know what she should do till they came once more to enliven the Court by their charming society.

But however sorry my lady might be to lose her visitors, there was at least one guest whose society she was not deprived of. Robert Audley showed no intention whatever of leaving his uncle's house. He had no professional duties, he said; Fig-tree Court was delightfully shady in hot weather, but there was a sharp corner round which the wind came in the winter months, armed with avenging rheumatisms and influenzas. Everybody was so good to him at the Court, that really he had no inclination to hurry away.

Sir Michael had but one answer to this: 'Stay, my dear boy; stay, my dear Bob, as long as ever you like. I have no son, and you stand to me in the place of one. Make yourself agreeable to Lucy, and make the Court your home as long as you live.'

To which Robert would merely reply by grasping his uncle's hand vehemently, and muttering something about 'a jolly old prince.'

It was to be observed that there was sometimes a certain vague sadness in the young man's tone when he called Sir Michael 'a jolly old prince;' some shadow of affectionate regret that brought a mist into Robert's eyes, as he sat in a corner of the room looking thoughtfully at the white-bearded baronet.

Before the last of the young sportsmen departed, Sir Harry Towers demanded and obtained an interview with Miss Alicia Audley in the oak library – an interview in which considerable emotion was displayed by the stalwart young fox-hunter; so much emotion, indeed, and of such a genuine and honest character, that Alicia fairly broke down as she told him that she should for ever esteem and respect him for his true and noble heart, but that he must never, never, never, unless he wished to cause her the most cruel distress, ask more from her than this esteem and respect.

Sir Harry left the library by the French window opening into the pond-garden. He strolled into that very lime-walk which George Talboys had compared to an avenue in a church-yard, and under the leafless trees fought the battle of his brave young heart.

'What a fool I am to feel it like this!' he cried, stamping his foot upon the frosty ground. 'I always knew it would be so; I always knew that she was a hundred times too good for me. God bless her! How nobly and tenderly she spoke; how beautiful she looked with the crimson blushes under her brown skin, and the tears in her big grey eyes – almost as handsome as the day she took the sunk fence, and let me put the brush in her hat as we rode home! God bless her! I can get over anything as long as she doesn't care for that sneaking lawyer. But I couldn't stand that.'

That sneaking lawyer, by which appellation Sir Harry alluded to Mr. Robert Audley, was standing in the hall, looking at a map of the midland counties, when Alicia came out of the library, with red eyes, after her interview with the fox-hunting baronet.

Robert, who was short-sighted, had his eyes within half an inch of the surface of the map as the young lady approached him.

'Yes,' he said, 'Norwich *is* in Norfolk, and that fool, young Vincent, said it was in Herefordshire. Ha, Alicia, is that you?'

He turned round so as to intercept Miss Audley on her way to the staircase.

'Yes,' replied his cousin curtly, trying to pass him.

'Alicia, you've been crying?'

The young lady did not condescend to reply.

'You've been crying, Alicia. Sir Harry Towers, of Towers Park, in the county of Herts, has been making you an offer of his hand, eh?'

'Have you been listening at the door, Mr. Audley?'

'I have not, Miss Audley. On principle I object to listen, and in practice I believe it to be a very troublesome proceeding; but I am a barrister, Miss Alicia, and able to draw a conclusion by induction. Do you know what inductive evidence is, Miss Audley?'

'No,' replied Alicia, looking at her cousin as a handsome young panther might look at its daring tormentor.

'I thought not. I dare say Sir Harry would ask if it was a new kind of horse-ball. I knew by induction that the baronet was going to make you an offer; first, because he came down-stairs with his hair parted on the wrong side, and his face as pale as the table-cloth; secondly, because he couldn't eat any breakfast, and let his coffee go the wrong way; and, thirdly, because he asked for an interview with you before he left the Court. Well, how's it to be, Alicia? Do you marry the baronet, and is poor Cousin Bob to be best man at the wedding?'

'Sir Harry Towers is a noble-hearted young man,' said Alicia, still trying to pass her cousin.

'But do we accept him – yes or no? Are we to be Lady Towers, with a superb estate in Hertfordshire, summer quarters for our hunters, and a drag with outriders to drive us across to papa's place in Essex? Is it to be so, Alicia, or not?'

'What is that to you, Mr. Robert Audley?' cried Alicia passionately. 'What do *you* care what becomes of me, and whom I marry? If I married a chimney-sweep, you'd only lift up your eyebrows and say, "Bless my soul, she was always eccentric." I have refused Sir Harry Towers; but when I think of his generous and unselfish affection, and compare it with the heartless, lazy, selfish, supercilious indifference of other men, I've a good mind to run after him, and tell him—'

'That you'll retract, and be my Lady Towers?'

'Yes.'

'Then don't, Alicia, don't,' said Robert Audley, grasping his cousin's slender little wrist, and leading her upstairs. 'Come into the drawing-room with me, Alicia, my poor little cousin; my charming, impetuous, alarming little cousin. Sit down here in this mullioned window, and let us talk seriously, and leave off quarrelling, if we can.'

The cousins had the drawing-room all to themselves. Sir Michael was out, my lady in her own apartments, and poor Sir Harry Towers walking up and down upon the gravel walk, darkened with the flickering shadows of the leafless branches in the cold winter sunshine.

'My poor little Alicia,' said Robert, as tenderly as if he had been addressing some spoiled child, 'do you suppose that because people don't wear vinegar tops, or part their hair on the wrong side, or conduct themselves altogether after the manner of well-meaning maniacs, by way of proving the vehemence of their passion – do you suppose because of this, Alicia Audley, that they may not be just as sensible of the merits of a dear little, warm-hearted, and affectionate girl as ever their neighbours can be? Life is such a very troublesome matter, when all is said and done, that it's as well even to take its blessings quietly. I don't make a great howling because I can get good cigars one door from the corner of Chancery Lane, and have a dear, good girl for my cousin: but I am not the less grateful to Providence that it is so.'

Alicia opened her grey eyes to their widest extent, looking her cousin full in the face with a bewildered stare. Robert had picked up the ugliest and leanest of his attendant curs, and was placidly stroking the animal's ears.

'Is this all you have to say to me, Robert?' Miss Audley asked, meekly.

'Well, yes, I think so,' replied her cousin, after considerable deliberation. 'I fancy that what I wanted to say was this – don't marry the fox-hunting baronet, if you like anybody else better; for if you'll only be patient, and take life easily, and try and reform yourself of banging doors, bouncing in and out of rooms, talking of the stables, and riding across country, I've no doubt the person you prefer will make you a very excellent husband.'

'Thank you, cousin,' said Miss Audley, crimsoning with bright indignant blushes up to the roots of her waving brown hair; 'but as you may not know the person I prefer, I think you had better not take upon yourself to answer for him.'

Robert pulled the dog's ears thoughtfully for some moments.

'No, to be sure,' he said, after a pause. 'Of course, if I don't know him – but I thought I did.'

'*Did you!*' exclaimed Alicia; and opening the door with a violence that made her cousin shiver, she bounced out of the drawing-room.

'I only said I thought I knew him,' Robert called after her; and then, as he sank into an easy-chair, he murmured thoughtfully, 'Such a nice girl, too, if she didn't bounce!'

So poor Sir Harry Towers rode away from Audley Court, looking very crestfallen and dismal.

He had very little pleasure now in returning to the stately mansion hidden among sheltering oaks and venerable beeches. The square, red-brick house gleaming at the end of a long arcade of leafless trees was to be for ever desolate, he thought, since Alicia would not come to be its mistress.

A hundred improvements planned and thought of were dismissed from his mind as useless now. The hunter that Jim the trainer was breaking in for a lady; the two pointer pups that were being reared for the next shooting season; the big black retriever that would have carried Alicia's parasol; the pavilion in the garden, disused since his mother's death, but which he had meant to have restored for Miss Audley – all these things were now so much vanity and vexation of spirit.

'What's the good of being rich, if one has no one to help spend one's money?' said the young baronet. 'One only grows a selfish beggar, and takes to drinking too much port. It's a hard thing that a girl can refuse a true heart and such stables as we've got at the park. It unsettles a man somehow.'

Indeed, this unlooked-for rejection had very much unsettled the few ideas which made up the small sum of the young baronet's mind.

He had been desperately in love with Alicia ever since the last hunting season, when he had met her at a county ball. His passion, cherished through the slow monotony of a summer, had broken out afresh in the merry winter months, and the young man's *mauvaise honte* alone had delayed the offer of his hand. But he had never for a moment supposed that he would be refused; he was so used to the adulation of mothers who had daughters to marry, and of even the daughters themselves; he had been so accustomed to feel himself the leading personage in an assembly, although half the wits of the age had been there, and he could only say, 'Haw, to be sure!' and 'By Jove!'; he had been so spoiled by the flatteries of bright eyes that had looked, or seemed to look, the brighter when he drew near, that without being possessed of one shadow of personal vanity, he had yet come to think that he had only to make an offer to the prettiest girl in Essex, to behold himself immediately accepted.

'Yes,' he would say complacently to some admiring satellite, 'I know I'm a good match, and I know what makes the gals so civil. They're very pretty, and they're very friendly to a fellow; but I don't care about 'em. They're all alike – they can only drop their eyes and say, "Lor, Sir Harry, and why do you call that curly black dog a retriever?" or, "Oh, Sir Harry, and did the poor mare really sprain her pastern shoulder-blade?" I haven't got much brains myself, I know,' the baronet would add deprecatingly; 'and I don't want a strong-minded woman, who writes books and wears green spectacles; but, hang it! I like a girl who knows what she's talking about.'

So when Alicia said 'No,' or rather, made that pretty speech about esteem and respect, which well-bred young ladies substitute for the obnoxious monosyllable, Sir Harry Towers felt that the whole fabric of the future he had built up so complacently was shivered into a heap of dingy ruins.

Sir Michael grasped him warmly by the hand just before the young man mounted his horse in the courtyard.

'I'm very sorry, Towers,' he said. 'You're as good a fellow as ever breathed, and would have made my girl an excellent husband; but you know there's a cousin, and I think that—'

'Don't say that, Sir Michael,' interposed the fox-hunter energetically. 'I can get over anything but that. A fellow whose hand upon the curb weighs half a ton (why, he pulled the Cavalier's mouth to pieces, Sir, the day you let him ride the horse); a fellow who turns his collars down, and eats bread and marmalade! No, no, Sir Michael; it's a queer world, but I can't think that of Miss Audley. There must be some one in the background, Sir: it can't be the cousin.'

Sir Michael shook his head as the rejected suitor rode away.

'I don't know about that,' he muttered. 'Bob's a good lad, and the girl might do worse; but he hangs back, as if he didn't care for her. There's some mystery – there's some mystery!'

The old baronet said this in that semi-thoughtful tone with which we speak of other people's affairs. The shadows of the early winter twilight, gathering thickest under the low oak ceiling of the hall, and the quaint curve of the arched doorway, fell darkly round his handsome head; but the light of his declining life, his beautiful and beloved young wife, was near him, and he could see no shadows when she was by.

She came skipping through the hall to meet him, and shaking her golden ringlets, buried her bright head on her husband's breast.

'So the last of our visitors is gone, dear, and we're all alone,' she said. 'Isn't that nice?'

'Yes, darling,' he answered fondly, stroking her bright hair.

'Except Mr. Robert Audley. How long is that nephew of yours going to stay here?'

'As long as he likes, my pet; he's always welcome,' said the baronet; and then, as if remembering himself, he added tenderly, 'but not unless his visit is agreeable to you, darling; not if his lazy habits, or his smoking, or his dogs, or anything about him, is displeasing to you.'

Lady Audley pursed up her rosy lips, and looked thoughtfully at the ground.

'It isn't that,' she said hesitatingly. 'Mr. Audley is a very agreeable young man, and a very honourable young man; but you know, Sir Michael, I'm rather a young aunt for such a nephew, and—'

'And what, Lucy?' asked the baronet, fiercely.

'Poor Alicia is rather jealous of any attention Mr. Audley pays me, and – and – I think it would be better for her happiness if your nephew were to bring his visit to a close.'

'He shall go to-night, Lucy!' exclaimed Sir Michael. 'I've been a blind, neglectful fool not to have thought of this before. My lovely little darling, it was scarcely just to Bob to expose the poor lad to your fascinations. I know him to be as good and true-hearted a fellow as ever breathed, but – but – he shall go to-night.'

'But you won't be too abrupt, dear! You won't be rude?'

'Rude! No, Lucy. I left him smoking in the lime-walk. I'll go and tell him that he must get out of the house in an hour.'

So in that leafless avenue, under whose gloomy shade George Talboys had stood on that thunderous evening before the day of his disappearance, Sir Michael Audley told his nephew that the Court was no home for him, and that my lady was too young and pretty to accept the attentions of a handsome nephew of eight-and-twenty.

Robert only shrugged his shoulders and elevated his thick black eyebrows, as Sir Michael delicately hinted all this.

'I *have* been attentive to my lady,' he said. 'She interests me – strongly, strangely interests me;' and then, with a change in his voice, and an emotion not common to him, he turned to the baronet, and grasping his hand, exclaimed – 'God forbid, my dear uncle, that I should ever bring trouble upon such a noble heart as yours! God forbid that the lightest shadow of dishonour should ever fall upon your honoured head – least of all through any agency of mine!'

The young man uttered these few words in a broken and disjointed fashion in which Sir Michael had never heard him speak before, and then, turning away his head, fairly broke down.

He left the Court that night, but he did not go far. Instead of taking the evening train for London, he went straight up to the little village of Mount Stanning, and walking into the neatly-kept inn, asked Phœbe Marks if he could be accommodated with apartments.

CHAPTER XVII
At the Castle Inn

The little sitting-room into which Phœbe Marks ushered the baronet's nephew was situated on the ground floor, and only separated by a lath-and-plaster partition from the little bar-parlour occupied by the innkeeper and his wife.

It seemed as though the wise architect who had superintended the building of the Castle Inn had taken especial care that nothing but the frailest and most flimsy material should be employed in its construction, and that the wind, having a special fancy for this unprotected spot, should have full play for the indulgence of its caprices.

To this end pitiful woodwork had been used instead of solid masonry; rickety ceilings had been propped up by fragile rafters, and beams that threatened on every stormy night to fall upon the heads of those beneath them; doors whose speciality was never to be shut, yet always to be banging; windows constructed with a peculiar view to letting in the draught when they were closed, and keeping out the air when they were open. The hand of genius had devised this lonely country inn; and there was not an inch of woodwork, or a trowelful of plaster employed in all the rickety construction, that did not offer its own peculiar weak point to every assault of its indefatigable foe.

Robert looked about him with a feeble smile of resignation.

It was a change, decidedly, from the luxurious comforts of Audley Court, and it was rather a strange fancy of the young barrister to prefer loitering at this dreary village hostelry, to returning to his snug chambers in Fig-tree Court.

But he had brought his Lares and Penates with him, in the shape of his German pipe, his tobacco canister, half-a-dozen French novels, and his two ill-conditioned canine favourites, who sat shivering before the smoky little fire, barking shortly and sharply now and then, by way of hinting for some slight refreshment.

While Mr. Robert Audley contemplated his new quarters, Phœbe Marks summoned a little village lad who was in the habit of running errands for her, and taking him into the kitchen, gave him a tiny note, carefully folded and sealed.

'You know Audley Court?'

'Yes, Mum.'

'If you'll run there with this letter to-night, and see that it's put safely into Lady Audley's hands, I'll give you a shilling.'

'Yes, Mum.'

'You understand? Ask to see my lady; you can say you've a message – not a note, mind – but a message from Phœbe Marks; and when you see her give this into her own hand.'

'Yes, Mum.'

'You won't forget?'

'No, Mum.'

'Then be off with you.'

The boy waited for no second bidding, but in another moment was scudding along the hilly high road, down the sharp descent that led to Audley.

Phœbe Marks went to the window, and looked out at the black figure of the lad hurrying through the dusky winter evening.

'If there's any bad meaning in his coming here,' she thought, 'my lady will know of it in time, at any rate.'

Phœbe herself brought the neatly-arranged tea-tray; and the little covered dish of ham and eggs which had been prepared for this unlooked-for visitor. Her pale hair was as smoothly braided, and her light grey dress fitted as precisely, as of old. The same neutral tints pervaded her person and her dress; no showy rose-coloured ribbons or rustling silk gown proclaimed the well-to-do inn-keeper's wife. Phœbe Marks was a person who never lost her individuality. Silent and self-contained, she seemed to hold herself within herself, and take no colour from the outer world.

Robert looked at her thoughtfully as she spread the cloth, and drew the table nearer to the fire-place.

'That,' he thought, 'is a woman who could keep a secret.'

The dogs looked rather suspiciously at the quiet figure of Mrs. Marks gliding softly about the room, from the teapot to the caddy, and from the caddy to the kettle singing on the hob.

'Will you pour out my tea for me, Mrs. Marks?' said Robert, seating himself in a horsehair-covered arm-chair, which fitted him as tightly in every direction as if he had been measured for it.

'You have come straight from the Court, Sir?' said Phœbe, as she handed Robert the sugar-basin.

'Yes; I only left my uncle's an hour ago.'

'And my lady, Sir, was she quite well?'

'Yes, quite well.'

'As gay and light-hearted as ever, Sir?'

'As gay and light-hearted as ever.'

Phœbe retired respectfully after having given Mr. Audley his tea, but as she stood with her hand upon the lock of the door he spoke again.

'You knew Lady Audley when she was Miss Lucy Graham, did you not?' he asked.

'Yes, Sir. I lived at Mrs. Dawson's when my lady was governess there.'

'Indeed! Was she long in the surgeon's family?'

'A year and a half, Sir.'

'And she came from London?'

'Yes, Sir.'

'And she was an orphan, I believe?'

'Yes, Sir.'

'Always as cheerful as she is now?'

'Always, Sir.'

Robert emptied his teacup and handed it to Mrs. Marks. Their eyes met – a lazy look in his, and an active, searching glance in hers.

'This woman would be good in a witness-box,' he thought; 'it would take a clever lawyer to bother her in a cross-examination.'

He finished his second cup of tea, pushed away his plate, fed his dogs, and lighted his pipe, while Phœbe carried off the tea-tray.

The wind came whistling up across the frosty open country, and through the leafless woods, and rattled fiercely at the window-frames.

'There's a triangular draught from those two windows and the door that scarcely adds to the comfort of this apartment,' murmured Robert; 'and there certainly are pleasanter sensations than that of standing up to one's knees in cold water.'

He poked the fire, patted his dogs, put on his great-coat, rolled a rickety old sofa close to the hearth, wrapped his legs in his railway rug, and stretching himself at full length upon the narrow horsehair cushion, smoked his pipe, and watched the bluish-grey wreaths curling slowly upwards to the dingy ceiling.

'No,' he murmured again; 'that is a woman who can keep a secret. A counsel for the prosecution would get very little out of her.'

I have said that the bar-parlour was only separated from the sitting-room occupied by Robert by a lath-and-plaster partition. The young barrister could hear the two or three village tradesmen and a couple of farmers laughing and talking round the bar, while Luke Marks served them from his stock of liquors.

Very often he could even hear their words, especially the landlord's, for he spoke in a coarse, loud voice, and had a more boastful manner than any of his customers.

'The man is a fool,' said Robert, as he laid down his pipe. 'I'll go and talk to him by-and-by.'

He waited till the few visitors to the Castle had dropped away one by one, and, when Luke Marks had bolted the front door upon the last of his customers, he strolled quietly into the bar-parlour where the landlord was seated with his wife.

Phœbe was busy at a little table, upon which stood a prim workbox, with every reel of cotton and glistening steel bodkin in its appointed place. She was darning the coarse grey stockings that adorned her husband's awkward feet, but she did her work as daintily as if they had been my lady's delicate silken hose.

I say that she took no colour from external things, and that the vague air of refinement that pervaded her nature, clung to her as closely in the society of her boorish husband at the Castle Inn, as in Lady Audley's fairy boudoir at the Court.

She looked up suddenly as Robert entered the bar-parlour. There was some shade of vexation in her pale grey eyes, which changed to an expression of anxiety – nay, rather, of almost terror – as she glanced from Mr. Audley to Luke Marks.

'I have come in for a few minutes' chat before I go to bed,' said Robert, settling himself very comfortably before the cheerful fire. 'Would you object to a cigar, Mrs. Marks? I mean, of course, to my smoking one,' he added, explanatorily.

'Not at all, Sir.'

'It would be a good 'un her objectin' to a bit o' bacca,' growled Mr. Marks, 'when me and the customers smokes all day.'

Robert lighted his cigar with a gilt-paper match of Phœbe's

making that adorned the chimney-piece, and took half-a-dozen reflective puffs before he spoke.

'I want you to tell me all about Mount Stanning, Mr. Marks,' he said presently.

'Then that's pretty soon told,' replied Luke, with a harsh, grating laugh. 'Of all the dull holes as ever a man set foot in, this is about the dullest. Not that the business don't pay pretty tidy; I don't complain of that; but I should ha' liked a public at Chelmsford, or Brentwood, or Romford, or some place where there's a bit of life in the streets; and I might have had it,' he added, discontentedly, 'if folks hadn't been so precious stingy.'

As her husband muttered this complaint in a grumbling under-tone, Phœbe looked up from her work and spoke to him.

'We forgot the brewhouse door, Luke,' she said. 'Will you come with me and help me put up the bar?'

'The brewhouse door can bide for to-night,' said Mr. Marks; 'I ain't agoin' to move now I've seated myself for a comfortable smoke.'

He took a long clay pipe from a corner of the fender as he spoke, and began to fill it deliberately.

'I don't feel easy about that brewhouse door, Luke,' remonstrated his wife; 'there are always tramps about, and they can get in easily when the bar isn't up.'

'Go and put the bar up yourself, then, can't you!' answered Mr. Marks.

'It's too heavy for me to lift.'

'Then let it bide, if you're too fine a lady to see to it yourself. You're very anxious all of a sudden about this here brewhouse door. I suppose you don't want me to open my mouth to this gent, that's about it. Oh, you needn't frown at me to stop my speaking! You're always putting in your tongue and clipping off my words before I've half said 'em; but I won't stand it. Do you hear? I won't stand it!'

Phœbe Marks shrugged her shoulders, folded her work, shut her workbox, and crossing her hands in her lap, sat with her grey eyes fixed upon her husband's bull-like face.

'Then you don't particularly care to live at Mount Stanning?' said Robert, politely, as if anxious to change the conversation.

'No, I don't,' answered Luke; 'and I don't care who knows it; and, as I said before, if folks hadn't been so precious stingy, I might have had a public in a thrivin' market town, instead of this tumble-down old place, where a man has his hair blowed off his head on a windy day. What's fifty pound, or what's a hundred pound—?'

'Luke! Luke!'

'No, you're not agoin' to stop my mouth with all your "Luke, Lukes!"' answered Mr. Marks, to his wife's remonstrance. 'I say again, what's a hundred pound?'

'No,' answered Robert Audley, speaking with wonderful distinctness, and addressing his words to Luke Marks, but fixing his eyes upon Phœbe's anxious face. 'What, indeed, is a hundred pounds to a man possessed of the power which you hold, or rather which your wife holds, over the person in question?'

Phœbe's face, at all times almost colourless, seemed scarcely capable of growing paler; but as her eyelids dropped under Robert Audley's searching glance, a visible change came over the pallid hues of her complexion.

'A quarter to twelve,' said Robert, looking at his watch. 'Late hours for such a quiet village as Mount Stanning. Good night, my worthy host. Good night, Mrs. Marks. You needn't send me my shaving water till nine o'clock to-morrow morning.'

CHAPTER XVIII

Robert receives a visitor whom he had scarcely expected

Eleven o'clock struck the next morning, and found Mr. Robert Audley still lounging over the well-ordered little breakfast-table, with one of his dogs at each side of his arm-chair, regarding him with watchful eyes and opened mouth, awaiting the expected morsel of ham or toast. Robert had a county paper on his knees, and made a feeble effort now and then to read the first page, which was filled with advertisements of farming stock, quack medicines, and other interesting matter.

The weather had changed, and the snow, which had for the last few days been looming blackly in the frosty sky, fell in great feathery flakes against the windows, and lay piled in the little bit of garden ground without.

The long, lonely road leading towards Audley seemed untrodden by a footstep, as Robert looked out at the wintry landscape.

'Lively,' he said, 'for a man used to the fascinations of Temple Bar!'

As he watched the snow-flakes falling every moment thicker and faster upon the lonely road, he was surprised by seeing a brougham driving slowly up the hill.

'I wonder what unhappy wretch has too restless a spirit to stop at home on such a morning as this,' he muttered, as he returned to the arm-chair by the fire.

He had only reseated himself a few minutes when Phœbe Marks entered the room to announce Lady Audley.

'Lady Audley! Pray beg her to come in,' said Robert; and

then, as Phœbe left the room to usher in this unexpected visitor, he muttered between his teeth –

'A false move, my lady, and one I never looked for from you.'

Lucy Audley was radiant on this cold and snowy January morning. Other people's noses are rudely assailed by the sharp fingers of the grim ice-king, but not my lady's; other people's lips turn pale and blue with the chilling influence of the bitter weather, but my lady's pretty little rosebud of a mouth retained its brightest colouring and cheeriest freshness.

She was wrapped in the very sables which Robert Audley had brought from Russia, and carried a muff that the young man thought seemed almost as big as herself.

She looked a childish, helpless, babyfied little creature; and Robert watched her with some touch of pity in his eyes, as she came up to the hearth by which he was standing, and warmed her tiny gloved hands at the blaze.

'What a morning, Mr. Audley,' she said, 'what a morning!'

'Yes, indeed! Why did you come out in such weather, Lady Audley?'

'Because I wished to see you – particularly.'

'Indeed!'

'Yes,' said my lady, with an air of considerable embarrassment, playing with the button of her glove, and almost wrenching it off in her restlessness – 'yes, Mr. Audley, I felt that you had not been well treated; that – that you had, in short, reason to complain; and that an apology was due to you.'

'I do not wish for any apology, Lady Audley.'

'But you are entitled to one,' answered my lady, quietly. 'Why, my dear Robert, should we be so very ceremonious towards each other? You were very comfortable at Audley; we were very glad to have you there; but my dear, silly husband must needs take it into his foolish head that it is dangerous for his poor little wife's peace of mind to have a nephew of eight or nine-and-twenty smoking his cigars in her boudoir, and, behold! our pleasant little family circle is broken up.'

Lucy Audley spoke with that peculiar childish vivacity which seemed so natural to her. Robert looked down almost sadly at her bright, animated face.

'Lady Audley,' he said, 'Heaven forbid that either you or I should ever bring grief or dishonour upon my uncle's generous heart! Better, perhaps, that I should be out of the house – better, perhaps, that I had never entered it!'

My lady had been looking at the fire while her nephew spoke, but at his last words she lifted her head suddenly, and looked him full in the face with a wondering expression – an earnest, questioning gaze, whose full meaning the young barrister understood.

'Oh, pray do not be alarmed, Lady Audley,' he said gravely. 'You have no sentimental nonsense, no silly infatuation, borrowed from Balzac, or Dumas *fils*, to fear from me. The benchers of the Inner Temple will tell you that Robert Audley is troubled with none of the epidemics whose outward signs are turn-down collars and Byronic neckties. I say that I wish I had never entered my uncle's house during the last year; but I say it with a far more solemn meaning than any sentimental one.'

My lady shrugged her shoulders.

'If you insist on talking in enigmas, Mr. Audley,' she said, 'you must forgive a poor little woman if she declines to answer them.'

Robert made no reply to this speech.

'But tell me,' said my lady, with an entire change of tone, 'what could have induced you to come up to this dismal place?'

'Curiosity.'

'Curiosity!'

'Yes; I felt an interest in that bull-necked man, with the dark red hair and wicked grey eyes. A dangerous man, my lady – a man in whose power I should not like to be.'

A sudden change came over Lady Audley's face; the pretty roseate flush faded out from her cheeks, and left them waxen white, and angry flashes lightened in her blue eyes.

'What have I done to you, Robert Audley,' she cried passionately – 'what have I done to you, that you should hate me so?'

He answered her very gravely –

'I had a friend, Lady Audley, whom I loved very dearly, and since I have lost him I fear that my feelings towards other people are strangely embittered.'

'You mean – the Mr. Talboys who went to Australia?'

'Yes, I mean the Mr. Talboys, who I was told set out for Liverpool with the idea of going to Australia.'

'And you do not believe in his having sailed for Australia?'

'I do not.'

'But why not?'

'Forgive me, Lady Audley, if I decline to answer that question.'

'As you please,' she said carelessly.

'A week after my friend disappeared,' continued Robert, 'I posted an advertisement to the Sydney and Melbourne papers, calling upon him, if he was in either city when the advertisement appeared, to write and tell me of his whereabouts, and also calling on any one who had met him, either in the colonies or on the voyage out, to give me any information respecting him. George Talboys left Essex, or disappeared from Essex, on the 6th of September last. I ought to receive some answer to this advertisement by the end of this month. To-day is the 27th: the time draws very near.'

'And if you receive no answer?' asked Lady Audley.

'If I receive no answer I shall think that my fears have been not unfounded, and I shall do my best to act.'

'What do you mean by that?'

'Ah, Lady Audley, you remind me how very powerless I am in this matter. My friend might have been made away with in this very inn, stabbed to death upon this hearth-stone on which I now stand, and I might stay here for a twelvemonth, and go away at the last as ignorant of his fate as if I had never crossed the threshold. What do we know of the mysteries that may hang about the houses we enter? If I were to go to-morrow into that common-place, plebeian, eight-roomed house in which Maria Manning and her husband murdered their guest, I should have no awful prescience of that bygone horror. Foul deeds have been done under the most hospitable roofs, terrible crimes have been committed amid the fairest scenes, and have left no trace upon the spot where they were done. I do not believe in mandrake, or in blood-stains that no time can efface. I believe rather that we may walk unconsciously in an atmosphere of crime, and breathe none the less freely. I believe that we may look into the smiling face of a murderer, and admire its tranquil beauty.'

My lady laughed at Robert's earnestness.

'You seem to have quite a taste for discussing these horrible subjects,' she said, rather scornfully; 'you ought to have been a detective police officer.'

'I sometimes think I should have been a good one.'

'Why?'

'Because I am patient.'

'But to return to Mr. George Talboys, whom we lost sight of in your eloquent discussion. What if you receive no answer to your advertisements?'

'I shall then consider myself justified in concluding that my friend is dead.'

'Yes, and then—?'

'I shall examine the effects he left at my chambers.'

'Indeed! and what are they? Coats, waistcoats, varnished

boots, and meerschaum pipes, I suppose,' said Lady Audley, laughing.

'No; letters – letters from his friends, his old school-fellows, his father, his brother-officers.'

'Yes?'

'Letters, too, from his wife.'

My lady was silent for some few moments, looking thoughtfully at the fire.

'Have you ever seen any of the letters written by the late Mrs. Talboys?' she asked presently.

'Never. Poor soul! her letters are not likely to throw much light upon my friend's fate. I dare say she wrote the usual womanly scrawl. There are very few who write so charming and uncommon a hand as yours, Lady Audley.'

'Ah, you know my hand of course.'

'Yes, I know it very well indeed.'

My lady warmed her hands once more, and then taking up the big muff which she had laid aside upon a chair, prepared to take her departure.

'You have refused to accept my apology, Mr. Audley,' she said; 'but I trust you are not the less assured of my feelings towards you.'

'Perfectly assured, Lady Audley.'

'Then good-by, and let me recommend you not to stay long in this miserable draughty place, if you do not wish to take rheumatism back to Fig-tree Court.'

'I shall return to town to-morrow morning to see after my letters.'

'Then, once more, good-by.'

She held out her hand; he took it loosely in his own. It seemed such a feeble little hand that he might have crushed it in his strong grasp, had he chosen to be so pitiless.

He attended her to her carriage, and watched it as it drove

off, not towards Audley, but in the direction of Brentwood, which was about six miles from Mount Stanning.

About an hour and a half after this, as Robert stood at the door of the inn, smoking a cigar and watching the snow falling in the whitened fields opposite, he saw the brougham drive back, empty this time, to the door of the inn.

'Have you taken Lady Audley back to the Court?' he said to the coachman, who had stopped to call for a mug of hot spiced ale.

'No, Sir; I've just come from the Brentwood station. My lady started for London by the 12.40 train.'

'For town?'

'Yes, Sir.'

'My lady gone to London!' said Robert, as he returned to the little sitting-room. 'Then I'll follow her by the next train; and if I'm not very much mistaken, I know where to find her.'

He packed his portmanteau, paid his bill, which was carefully receipted by Phœbe Marks, fastened his dogs together with a couple of leathern collars and a chain, and stepped into the rumbling fly kept at the Castle Inn for the convenience of Mount Stanning. He caught an express that left Brentwood at three o'clock, and settled himself comfortably in a corner of an empty first-class carriage, coiled up in a couple of huge railway rugs, and smoking a cigar in mild defiance of the authorities. 'The Company may make as many bye-laws as they please,' he murmured, 'but I shall take the liberty of enjoying my cheroot as long as I've half-a-crown left to give the guard.'

CHAPTER XIX
The blacksmith's mistake

It was exactly five minutes past four as Mr. Robert Audley stepped out upon the platform at Shoreditch, and waited placidly until such time as his dogs and his portmanteau should be delivered up to the attendant porter who had called his cab, and undertaken the general conduct of his affairs, with that disinterested courtesy which does such infinite credit to a class of servitors who are forbidden to accept the tribute of a grateful public. Robert Audley waited with consummate patience for a considerable time; but as the express was generally a long train, and as there were a great many passengers from Norfolk carrying guns and pointers, and other paraphernalia of a critical description, it took a long while to make matters agreeable to all claimants, and even the barrister's seraphic indifference to mundane affairs nearly gave way.

'Perhaps, when that gentleman who is making such a noise about a pointer with liver-coloured spots, has discovered the particular pointer and spots that he wants – which happy combination of events scarcely seems likely to arrive – they'll give me my luggage and let me go. The designing wretches knew at a glance that I was born to be imposed upon; and that if they were to trample the life out of me upon this very platform, I should never have the spirit to bring an action against the Company.' Suddenly an idea seemed to strike him, and he left the porter to struggle for the custody of his goods, and walked round to the other side of the station.

He had heard a bell ring, and, looking at the clock, had

remembered that the down-train for Colchester started at this time. He had learned what it was to have an honest purpose since the disappearance of George Talboys; and he reached the opposite platform in time to see the passengers take their seats.

There was one lady who had evidently only just arrived at the station; for she hurried on to the platform at the very moment that Robert approached the train, and almost ran against that gentleman in her haste and excitement.

'I beg your pardon—' she began, ceremoniously; then raising her eyes from Mr. Audley's waistcoat, which was about on a level with her pretty face, she exclaimed, 'Robert! You in London already?'

'Yes, Lady Audley; you were quite right, the Castle Inn is a dismal place, and—'

'You got tired of it – I knew you would. Please open the carriage-door for me: the train will start in two minutes.'

Robert Audley was looking at his uncle's wife with rather a puzzled expression of countenance.

'What does it mean?' he thought. 'She is altogether a different being to the wretched, helpless creature who dropped her mask for a moment, and looked at me with her own pitiful face, in the little room at Mount Stanning, four hours ago. What has happened to cause the change?'

He opened the door for her while he thought this, and helped her to settle herself in her seat, spreading her furs over her knees, and arranging the huge velvet mantle in which her slender little figure was almost hidden.

'Thank you very much; how good you are to me!' she said, as he did this. 'You will think me very foolish to travel upon such a day, without my dear darling's knowledge too; but I went up to town to settle a very terrific milliner's bill, which I did not wish my best of husbands to see; for indulgent as he is, he might think me extravagant; and I cannot bear to suffer even in his thoughts.'

'Heaven forbid that you ever should, Lady Audley,' Robert said, gravely.

She looked at him for a moment with a smile, which had something defiant in its brightness.

'Heaven forbid it, indeed,' she murmured. 'I don't think I ever shall.'

The second bell rang, and the train moved as she spoke. The last Robert Audley saw of her was that bright defiant smile.

'Whatever object brought her to London has been successfully accomplished,' he thought. 'Has she baffled me by some piece of womanly jugglery? Am I never to get any nearer to the truth; but am I to be tormented all my life by vague doubts, and wretched suspicions, which may grow upon me till I become a monomaniac? Why did she come to London?'

He was still mentally asking himself this question as he ascended the stairs in Fig-tree Court, with one of his dogs under each arm, and his railway rugs over his shoulder.

He found his chambers in their accustomed order. The geraniums had been carefully tended, and the canaries had retired for the night under cover of a square of green baize, testifying to the care of honest Mrs. Maloney. Robert cast a hurried glance round the sitting-room; then setting down the dogs upon the hearth-rug, he walked straight into the little inner chamber which served as his dressing-room.

It was in this room that he kept disused portmanteaus, battered japanned cases, and other lumber; and it was in this room that George Talboys had left his luggage. Robert lifted a portmanteau from the top of a large trunk, and kneeling down before it with a lighted candle in his hand, carefully examined the lock.

To all appearance it was exactly in the same condition in which George had left it when he laid his mourning garments aside and placed them in this shabby repository, with all other memorials of his dead wife. Robert brushed his coat sleeve across the worn leather-covered lid, upon which the initials G. T. were inscribed with big brass-headed nails; but Mrs. Maloney, the laundress, must have been the most precise of housewives, for neither the portmanteau nor the trunk was dusty.

Mr. Audley despatched a boy to fetch his Irish attendant, and paced up and down his sitting-room, waiting anxiously for her arrival.

She came in about ten minutes, and, after expressing her delight in the return of 'the masther,' humbly awaited his orders.

'I only sent for you to ask if anybody has been here; that is to say, if anybody has applied to you for the key of my rooms to-day – any lady?'

'Lady? No, indeed, yer honour; there's been no lady for the kay; barrin' it's the blacksmith yer honour manes.'

'The blacksmith!'

'Yes; the blacksmith your honour ordered to come to-day.'

'I order a blacksmith!' exclaimed Robert. 'I left a bottle of French brandy in the cupboard,' he thought, 'and Mrs. M. has been evidently enjoying herself.'

'Sure, and the blacksmith your honour tould to see to the locks,' replied Mrs. Maloney. 'It's him that lives down in one of the little streets by the bridge,' she added, giving a very lucid description of the man's whereabouts.

Robert lifted his eyebrows in mute despair.

'If you'll sit down and compose yourself, Mrs. M.,' he said – he abbreviated her name thus on principle, for the avoidance of unnecessary labour – 'perhaps we shall be able by-and-by to understand each other. You say a blacksmith has been here?'

'Sure and I did, Sir.'

'To-day?'

'Quite correct, Sir.'

Step by step Mr. Audley elicited the following information. A locksmith had called upon Mrs. Maloney that afternoon at three o'clock, and had asked for the key of Mr. Audley's chambers, in order that he might look to the locks of the doors, which he stated were all out of repair. He declared that he was acting upon Mr. Audley's own orders, conveyed to him by a letter from the country, where the gentleman was spending his Christmas. Mrs. Maloney, believing in the truth of this statement, had admitted the man to the chambers, where he stayed about half-an-hour.

'But you were with him while he examined the locks, I suppose?' Mr. Audley asked.

'Sure I was, Sir, in and out, as you may say, all the time; for I've been cleaning the stairs this afternoon, and I took the opporchunity to begin my scouring while the man was at work.'

'Oh, you were in and out all the time. If you *could* conveniently give me a plain answer, Mrs. M., I should be glad to know what was the longest time that you were *out* while the locksmith was in my chambers?'

But Mrs. Maloney could not give a plain answer. It might have been ten minutes; though she didn't think it was as much. It might have been a quarter of an hour; but she was sure it wasn't more. It didn't *seem* to her more than five minutes; but 'thim stairrs, your honour—' and here she rambled off into a disquisition upon the scouring of stairs in general, and the stairs outside Robert's chambers in particular.

Mr. Audley sighed the weary sigh of mournful resignation.

'Never mind, Mrs. M.,' he said; 'the locksmith had plenty of time to do anything he wanted to do, I dare say, without your being any the wiser.'

Mrs. Maloney stared at her employer with mingled surprise and alarm.

'Sure, there wasn't anythin' for him to stale, your honour, barrin' the birrds and the geranums, and—'

'No, no, I understand. There, that'll do, Mrs. M. Tell me where the man lives, and I'll go and see him.'

'But you'll have a bit of dinner first, Sir?'

'I'll go and see the locksmith before I have my dinner.'

He took up his hat as he announced his determination, and walked towards the door.

'The man's address, Mrs. M.?'

The Irishwoman directed him to a small street at the back of St. Bride's Church, and thither Mr. Robert Audley quietly strolled, through the miry slush which simple Londoners call *snow*.

He found the locksmith, and, at the sacrifice of the crown of his hat, contrived to enter the low narrow doorway of a little open shop. A jet of gas was flaring in the unglazed window, and there was a very merry party in the little room behind the shop; but no one responded to Robert's 'Hulloa!' The reason of this was sufficiently obvious. This merry party was so much absorbed in its own merriment as to be deaf to all common-place summonses from the outer world; and it was only when Robert, advancing further into the cavernous little shop, made so bold as to open the half-glass door which separated him from the merry-makers, that he succeeded in obtaining their attention.

A very jovial picture of the Teniers school was presented to Mr. Robert Audley upon the opening of this door.

The locksmith, with his wife and family, and two or three droppers-in of the female sex, were clustered about a table, which was adorned by two bottles: not vulgar bottles of that colourless extract of the juniper berry, much affected by the masses; but of *bonâ fide* port and sherry – fiercely strong sherry, which left a fiery taste in the mouth; nut-brown sherry – rather unnaturally brown, if anything – and fine old port; no sickly vintage, faded and thin from excessive age; but a rich, full-bodied wine, sweet and substantial, and high coloured.

The locksmith was speaking as Robert Audley opened the door.

'And with that,' he said, 'she walked off, as graceful as you please.'

The whole party was thrown into confusion by the appearance of Mr. Audley; but it was to be observed that the locksmith was more embarrassed than his companions. He set down his glass so hurriedly, that he spilt his wine, and wiped his mouth nervously with the back of his dirty hand.

'You called at my chambers to-day,' Robert said, quietly. 'Don't let me disturb you, ladies.' This to the droppers-in. 'You called at my chambers to-day, Mr. White,' and—'

The man interrupted him.

'I hope, sir, you'll be so good as to look over the mistake,' he stammered. 'I'm sure, sir, I'm very sorry it should have occurred. I was sent for to another gentleman's chambers, Mr. Aulwin, in Garden Court; and the name slipped my memory; and havin' done odd jobs before for you, I thought it must be you as wanted me to-day; and I called at Mrs. Maloney's for the key accordin'; but directly I see the locks in your chambers, I says to myself, "the gentleman's locks ain't out of order; the gentleman don't want all his locks repaired."'

'But you stayed half-an-hour.'

'Yes, Sir; for there was *one* lock out of order – the door nighest the staircase – and I took it off and cleaned it, and put it on again. I won't charge you nothin' for the job, and I hope as you'll be so good as to look over the mistake as has occurred, which I've been in business thirteen year come July, and—'

'Nothing of this kind ever happened before, I suppose,' said Robert, gravely. 'No, it's altogether a singular kind of business, not likely to come about every day. You've been enjoying yourself this evening, I see, Mr. White. You've done a good stroke of work to-day, I'll wager – made a lucky hit, and you're what you call "standing treat," eh?'

Robert Audley looked straight into the man's dingy face as he spoke. The locksmith was not a bad-looking fellow, and there was nothing that he need have been ashamed of in his face, except the dirt, and that, as Hamlet's mother says, 'is common;' but in spite of this, Mr. White's eyelids dropped under the young barrister's calm scrutiny, and he stammered out some apologetic sort of speech about his 'missus,' and his missus's neighbours, and port wine and sherry wine, with as much confusion as if he, an honest mechanic in a free country, were called upon to excuse himself to Mr. Robert Audley for being caught in the act of enjoying himself in his own parlour.

Robert cut him short with a careless nod.

'Pray don't apologise,' he said; 'I like to see people enjoy themselves. Good night, Mr. White – good night, ladies.'

He lifted his hat to 'the missus,' and the missus's neighbours, who were much fascinated by his easy manner and his handsome face, and left the shop.

'And so,' he muttered to himself as he went back to his chambers, '"with that she walked off as graceful as you please." Who was it that walked off ? and what was the story which the locksmith was telling when I interrupted him at that sentence? Oh, George Talboys, George Talboys, am I ever to come any nearer to the secret of your fate? Am I coming nearer to it now, slowly but surely? Is the radius to grow narrower day by day, until it draws a dark circle round the home of those I love? How is it all to end?'

He sighed wearily as he walked slowly back across the flagged quadrangles in the Temple to his own solitary chambers.

Mrs. Maloney had prepared for him that bachelor's dinner which, however excellent and nutritious in itself, has no claim to the special charm of novelty. She had cooked for him a mutton chop, which was soddening itself between two plates upon the little table near the fire.

Robert Audley sighed as he sat down to the familiar meal; remembering his uncle's cook with a fond, regretful sorrow.

'Her cutlets à la Maintenon made mutton seem more than mutton; a sublimated meat that could scarcely have grown upon any mundane sheep,' he murmured, sentimentally, 'and Mrs. Maloney's chops are apt to be tough; but such is life – what does it matter?'

He pushed away his plate impatiently after eating a few mouthfuls.

'I have never eaten a good dinner at this table since I lost George Talboys,' he said. 'The place seems as gloomy as if the poor fellow had died in the next room, and had never been taken away to be buried. How long ago that September afternoon appears as I look back at it – that September afternoon upon which I parted with him alive and well; and lost him as suddenly and unaccountably as if a trap-door had opened in the solid earth, and let him through to the Antipodes!'

END OF VOL. I.

VOLUME II

CHAPTER I

The writing in the book

Mr. Audley rose from the dinner-table and walked over to the cabinet in which he kept the document he had drawn up relating to George Talboys. He unlocked the doors of this cabinet, took the paper from the pigeon-hole marked *Important*, and seated himself at his desk to write. He added several paragraphs to those in the document, numbering the fresh paragraphs as carefully as he had numbered the old ones.

'Heaven help us all,' he muttered once; 'is this paper, with which no attorney has had any hand, to be my first brief?'

He wrote for about half-an-hour, then replaced the document in the pigeon-hole, and locked the cabinet. When he had done this, he took a candle in his hand, and went into the room in which were his own portmanteaus and the trunk belonging to George Talboys.

He took a bunch of keys from his pocket, and tried them one by one. The lock of the shabby old trunk was a common one, and at the fifth trial the key turned easily.

'There'd be no need for any one to break open such a lock as this,' muttered Robert, as he lifted the lid of the trunk.

He slowly emptied it of its contents, taking out each article separately, and laying it carefully upon a chair by his side. He handled the things with a respectful tenderness, as if he had been lifting the dead body of his lost friend. One by one he laid the neatly folded mourning garments on the chair. He found old meerschaum pipes, and soiled, crumpled gloves that had once been fresh from the Parisian maker; old play bills, whose biggest letters spelled the names of actors who were dead and gone; old perfume bottles, fragrant with essences, whose fashion had passed away; neat little parcels of letters, each carefully labelled with the name of the writer; fragments of old newspapers; and a little heap of shabby dilapidated books, each of which tumbled into as many pieces as a pack of cards in Robert's incautious hand. But amongst all the mass of worthless litter, each scrap of which had once had its separate purpose, Robert Audley looked in vain for that which he sought – the packet of letters written to the missing man by his dead wife, Helen Talboys. He had heard George allude more than once to the existence of these letters. He had seen him once sorting the faded papers with a reverent hand; and he had seen him replace them, carefully tied together with a faded ribbon which had once been Helen's, amongst the mourning garments in the trunk. Whether he had afterwards removed them, or whether they had been removed since his disappearance by some other hand, it was not easy to say; but they were gone.

Robert Audley sighed wearily as he replaced the things in the empty box, one by one, as he had taken them out. He stopped with the little heap of tattered books in his hand, and hesitated for a moment.

'I will keep these out,' he muttered: 'there may be something to help me in one of them.'

George's library was no very brilliant collection of literature. There was an old Greek Testament and the Eton Latin Grammar; a French pamphlet on the cavalry sword exercise; an odd volume of *Tom Jones*, with one half of its stiff leather cover hanging to it by a thread; Byron's *Don Juan*, printed in a murderous type, which must have been invented for the special advantage of oculists and opticians; and a fat book in a faded gilt and crimson cover.

Robert Audley locked the trunk and took the books under his arm. Mrs. Maloney was clearing away the remains of his repast when he returned to his sitting-room. He put the books aside on a little table in a corner of the fire-place, and waited patiently while the laundress finished her work. He was in no humour even for his meerschaum consoler; the yellow-papered fictions on the shelves above his head seemed stale and profitless – he opened a volume of Balzac, but his uncle's wife's golden curls danced and trembled in a glittering haze, alike upon the metaphysical diablerie of the *Peau de Chagrin*, and the hideous social horrors of *Cousine Bette*. The volume dropped from his hand, and he sat wearily watching Mrs. Maloney as she swept up the ashes on the hearth, replenished the fire, drew the dark damask curtains, supplied the simple wants of the canaries, and put on her bonnet in the disused clerk's office, prior to bidding her employer good night. As the door closed upon the Irishwoman, he rose impatiently from his chair, and paced up and down the room.

'Why do I go on with this,' he said, 'when I know that it is leading me, step by step, day by day, hour by hour, nearer to that conclusion which of all others I should avoid? Am I tied to a wheel, and must I go with its every revolution, let it take me where it will? Or can I sit down here to-night and say, I have done my duty to my missing friend; I have searched for him patiently, but I have searched in vain? Should I be justified in doing this? Should I be justified in letting the chain which I have slowly put together, link by link, drop at this point, or must I go on adding fresh links to that fatal chain until the last rivet drops into its place and the circle is complete? I think and believe that I shall never see my friend's face again; and that no exertion of mine can ever be of any benefit to him. In plainer, crueller words, I believe him to be dead. Am I bound to discover how and where he died? or being, as I think, on the road to that discovery, shall I do a wrong to the memory of George Talboys by turning back or stopping still? What am I to do? What am I to do?'

He rested his elbows on his knees and buried his face in his hands. The one purpose which had slowly grown up in his careless nature until it had become powerful enough to work a change in that very nature, made him what he had never been before – a Christian; conscious of his own weakness; anxious to keep to the strict line of duty; fearful to swerve from the conscientious discharge of the strange task that had been forced upon him; and reliant on a stronger hand than his own to point the way which he was to go. Perhaps he uttered his first thoroughly earnest prayer that night, seated by his lonely fireside, thinking of George Talboys. When he raised his head from that long and silent reverie, his eyes had a bright, determined glance, and every feature in his face seemed to wear a new expression.

'Justice to the dead first,' he said, 'mercy to the living afterwards.'

He wheeled his easy-chair to the table, trimmed the lamp, and settled himself to the examination of the books.

He took them up one by one, and looked carefully through them, first looking at the page on which the name of the owner is ordinarily written; and then searching for any scrap of paper which might have been left within the leaves. On the first page of the Eton Latin Grammar the name of Master Talboys was written in a prim scholastic hand; the French pamphlet had a careless G. T. scrawled on the cover in pencil, in George's big, slovenly calligraphy; the *Tom Jones* had evidently been bought at a book-stall, and bore an inscription, dated March 14th, 1788, setting forth that the work was a tribute of respect to Mr. Thomas Scrowton, from his obedient servant, James Anderley; the *Don Juan* and the Testament were blank. Robert Audley breathed more freely: he had arrived at the last but one of the books without any result whatever, and there only remained the fat gilt-and-crimson-bound volume to be examined before his task was finished.

It was an annual of the year 1845. The copper-plate engravings of lovely ladies who had flourished in that day were yellow and spotted with mildew; the costumes grotesque and outlandish; the simpering beauties faded and common-place. Even the little clusters of verses (in which the poet's feeble candle shed its sickly light upon the obscurities of the artist's meaning) had an old-fashioned twang; like music on a lyre whose strings are slackened by the damps of time. Robert Audley did not stop to read any of these mild productions. He ran rapidly through the leaves, looking for any scrap of writing or fragment of a letter which might have been used to mark a place. He found nothing but a bright ring of golden hair, of that glittering hue which is so rarely seen except upon the head of a child – a sunny lock which curled as naturally as the tendril of a vine; and was very opposite in texture, if not different in hue, to the soft, smooth tress which the landlady at Ventnor had given to George Talboys after his wife's death. Robert Audley suspended his examination of the book, and folded this yellow lock in a sheet of letter-paper, which he sealed with his signet-ring, and laid aside, with the memorandum about George Talboys and Alicia's letter, in the pigeon-hole marked *Important*. He was going to replace the fat annual amongst the other books, when he discovered that the two blank leaves at the beginning were stuck together. He was so determined to prosecute his search to the very uttermost, that he took the trouble to part these leaves with the sharp end of his paper-knife; and he was rewarded for his perseverance by finding an inscription upon one of them. This inscription was in three parts and in three different hands. The first paragraph was dated as far back as the year in which the annual had been published, and set forth that the book was the property of a certain Miss Elizabeth Ann Bince who had obtained the precious volume as a reward for habits of order, and for obedience to the authorities of Camford-house Seminary, Torquay. The second paragraph was dated five years later, and was in the handwriting of Miss Bince herself, who presented the book as a mark of undying affection and unfading esteem (Miss Bince was evidently of a romantic temperament) to her beloved friend Helen Maldon. The third paragraph was dated September, 1853, and was in the hand of Helen Maldon, who gave the annual to George Talboys; and it was at the sight of this third paragraph that Mr. Robert Audley's face changed from its natural hue to a sickly, leaden pallor.

'I thought it would be so,' said the young man, shutting the book with a weary sigh. 'God knows I was prepared for the worst, and the worst has come. I can understand all now. My next visit must be to Southampton. I must place the boy in better hands.'

CHAPTER II
Mrs. Plowson

Amongst the packet of letters which Robert Audley had found in George's trunk, there was one labelled with the name of the missing man's father – the father, who had never been too indulgent a friend to his only son, and who had gladly availed himself of the excuse afforded by George's imprudent marriage to abandon the young man to his own resources. Robert Audley had never seen Mr. Harcourt Talboys; but George's careless talk of his father had given his friend some notion of that gentleman's character. He had written to Mr. Talboys immediately after the disappearance of George, carefully wording his letter, which vaguely hinted at the writer's fear of some foul play in the mysterious business; and after the lapse of several weeks, he had received a formal epistle, in which Mr. Harcourt Talboys expressly declared that he had washed his hands of all responsibility in his son George's affairs upon the young man's wedding-day; and that his absurd disappearance was only in character with his preposterous marriage. The writer of this fatherly letter added in a postscript that if Mr. George Talboys had any low design of alarming his friends by this pretended disappearance, and thereby playing on their feelings with a view to pecuniary advantage, he was most egregiously deceived in the character of those persons with whom he had to deal.

Robert Audley had answered this letter by a few indignant lines, informing Mr. Talboys that his son was scarcely likely to hide himself for the furtherance of any deep-laid design on the pockets of his relatives, as he had left twenty thousand pounds in his bankers' hands at the time of his disappearance. After despatching this letter, Robert had abandoned all thought of assistance from the man who, in the natural course of things, should have been most interested in George's fate; but now that he found himself advancing every day some step nearer to the end that lay so darkly before him, his mind reverted to this heartlessly indifferent Mr. Harcourt Talboys.

'I will run into Dorsetshire after I leave Southampton,' he said, 'and see this man. If *he* is content to let his son's fate rest a dark and cruel mystery to all who knew him – if he is content to go down to his grave uncertain to the last of this poor fellow's end – why should I try to unravel the tangled skein, to fit the pieces of the terrible puzzle, and gather together the stray fragments which when collected may make such a hideous whole? I will go to him and lay my darkest doubts freely before him. It will be for him to say what I am to do.'

Robert Audley started by an early express for Southampton. The snow lay thick and white upon the pleasant country through which he went; and the young barrister had wrapped himself in so many comforters and railway rugs as to appear a perambulating mass of woollen goods rather than a living member of a learned profession. He looked gloomily out of the misty window, opaque with the breath of himself and an elderly Indian officer, who was his only companion, and watched the fleeting landscape, which had a certain phantom-like appearance in its shroud of snow. He wrapped himself in the vast folds of his railway rug with a peevish shiver, and felt inclined to quarrel with the destiny which compelled him to travel by an early train upon a pitiless winter's day.

'Who would have thought that I could have grown so fond of the fellow,' he muttered, 'or feel so lonely without him? I've a comfortable little fortune in the three per cents.; I'm heir-presumptive to my uncle's title; and I know of a certain dear little girl, who, as I think, would do her best to make me happy; but I declare that I would freely give up all and stand penniless in the world to-morrow, if this mystery could be satisfactorily cleared away, and George Talboys could stand by my side.'

He reached Southampton between eleven and twelve o'clock, and walked across the platform, with the snow drifting in his face, towards the pier and the lower end of the town. The clock of St. Michael's Church was striking twelve as he crossed the quaint old square in which that edifice stands, and groped his way through the narrow streets leading down to the water.

Mr. Maldon had established his slovenly household gods in one of those dreary thoroughfares which speculative builders love to raise upon some miserable fragment of waste ground hanging to the skirts of a prosperous town. Brigsome's Terrace was perhaps one of the most dismal blocks of building that was ever composed of brick and mortar since the first mason plied his trowel and the first architect drew his plan. The builder who had speculated in the ten dreary eight-roomed prison-houses had hung himself behind the parlour door of an adjacent tavern while the carcases were yet unfinished. The man who had bought the brick and mortar skeletons had gone through the Bankruptcy Court while the paper-hangers were still busy in Brigsome's Terrace, and had whitewashed his ceilings and himself simultaneously. Ill-luck and insolvency clung to the wretched habitations. The bailiff and the broker's man were as well known as the butcher and the baker to the noisy children who played upon the waste ground in front of the parlour windows. Solvent tenants were disturbed at unhallowed hours by the noise of ghostly furniture vans creeping stealthily away in the moonless night. Insolvent tenants openly defied the collector of the water-rate from their eight-roomed strongholds, and existed for weeks without any visible means of procuring that necessary fluid.

Robert Audley looked about him with a shudder as he turned from the water-side into this poverty-stricken locality. A child's funeral was leaving one of the houses as he approached, and he thought with a thrill of horror that if the little coffin had held George's son, he would have been in some measure responsible for the boy's death.

'The poor child shall not sleep another night in this wretched hovel,' he thought, as he knocked at the door of Mr. Maldon's house. 'He is the legacy of my lost friend, and it shall be my business to secure his safety.'

A slipshod servant girl opened the door and looked at Mr. Audley rather suspiciously as she asked him, very much through her nose, what he pleased to want. The door of the little sitting-room was ajar, and Robert could hear the clattering of knives and forks and the childish voice of little George prattling gaily. He told the servant that he had come from London, that he wanted to see Master Talboys, and that he would announce himself; and walking past her, without further ceremony, he opened the door of the parlour. The girl stared at him aghast as he did this; and, as if struck by some sudden conviction, threw her apron over her head and ran out into the snow. She darted across the waste ground, plunged into a narrow alley, and never drew breath till she found herself upon the threshold of a certain tavern called the Coach and Horses, and much affected by Mr. Maldon. The lieutenant's faithful retainer had taken Robert Audley for some new and determined collector of poor's rates – rejecting that gentleman's account of himself as an artful fiction devised for the destruction of parochial defaulters – and had hurried off to give her master timely warning of the enemy's approach.

When Robert entered the sitting-room he was surprised to

find little George seated opposite to a woman who was doing the honours of a shabby repast, spread upon a dirty tablecloth, and flanked by a pewter beer measure. The woman rose as Robert entered, and curtsied very humbly to the young barrister. She looked about fifty years of age, and was dressed in rusty widow's weeds. Her complexion was insipidly fair, and the two smooth bands of hair beneath her cap were of that sunless flaxen hue which generally accompanies pink cheeks and white eyelashes. She had been a rustic beauty perhaps in her time, but her features, although tolerably regular in their shape, had a mean pinched look, as if they had been made too small for her face. This defect was peculiarly noticeable in her mouth, which was an obvious misfit for the set of teeth it contained. She smiled as she curtsied to Mr. Robert Audley, and her smile, which laid bare the greater part of this set of square, hungry-looking teeth, by no means added to the beauty of her personal appearance.

'Mr. Maldon is not at home, Sir,' she said, with insinuating civility; 'but if it's for the water-rate, he requested me to say that—'

She was interrupted by little George Talboys, who scrambled down from the high chair upon which he had been perched, and ran to Robert Audley.

'I know you,' he said; 'you came to Ventnor with the big gentleman, and you came here once, and you gave me some money, and I gave it to granpa to take care of, and granpa kept it, and he always does.'

Robert Audley took the boy in his arms, and carried him to a little table in the window.

'Stand there, Georgey,' he said, 'I want to have a good look at you.'

He turned the boy's face to the light, and pushed the brown curls off his forehead with both hands.

'You're growing more like your father every day, Georgey;

and you're growing quite a man, too,' he said; 'would you like to go to school?'

'Oh, yes, please, I should like it very much,' the boy answered, eagerly. 'I went to school at Miss Pevins's once – day-school, you know – round the corner in the next street; but I caught the measles, and granpa wouldn't let me go any more, for fear I should catch the measles again; and granpa won't let me play with the little boys in the street, because they're rude boys; he said blackguard boys; but he said I mustn't say blackguard boys, because it's naughty. He says damn and devil, but he says he may because he's old. I shall say damn and devil when I'm old; and I should like to go to school, please, and I can go to-day, if you like; Mrs. Plowson will get my frocks ready, won't you, Mrs. Plowson?'

'Certainly, Master Georgey, if your grandpapa wishes it,' the woman answered, looking rather uneasily at Mr. Robert Audley.

'What on earth is the matter with this woman?' thought Robert, as he turned from the boy to the fair-haired widow, who was edging herself slowly towards the table upon which little George Talboys stood talking to his guardian. 'Does she still take me for a tax-collector with inimical intentions towards these wretched goods and chattels; or can the cause of her fidgety manner lie deeper still? That's scarcely likely though; for whatever secrets Lieutenant Maldon may have, it's not very probable that this woman has any knowledge of them.'

Mrs. Plowson had edged herself close to the little table by this time, and was making a stealthy descent upon the boy, when Robert turned sharply round.

'What are you going to do with the child?' he said.

'I was only going to take him away to wash his pretty face, Sir, and smooth his hair,' answered the woman, in the same insinuating tone in which she had spoken of the water-rate. 'You don't see him to any advantage, Sir, while his precious face is dirty. I won't be five minutes making him as neat as a new pin.'

She had her long thin arms about the boy as she spoke, and she was evidently going to carry him off bodily, when Robert stopped her.

'I'd rather see him as he is, thank you,' he said. 'My time in Southampton isn't very long, and I want to hear all that the little man can tell me.'

The little man crept closer to Robert, and looked confidingly into the barrister's grey eyes.

'I like you very much,' he said. 'I was frightened of you when you came before, because I was shy. I am not shy now – I am nearly six years old.'

Robert patted the boy's head encouragingly, but he was not looking at little George; he was watching the fair-haired widow, who had moved to the window, and was looking out at the patch of waste ground.

'You're rather fidgety about some one, ma'am, I'm afraid,' said Robert.

She coloured violently as the barrister made this remark, and answered him in a confused manner.

'I was looking for Mr. Maldon, Sir,' she said; 'he'll be so disappointed if he doesn't see you.'

'You know who I am, then?'

'No, Sir, but—'

The boy interrupted her by dragging a little jewelled watch from his bosom and showing it to Robert.

'This is the watch the pretty lady gave me,' he said. 'I've got it now – but I haven't had it long, because the jeweller who cleans it is an idle man, granpa says, and always keeps it such a long time; and granpa says it will have to be cleaned again, because of the taxes. He always takes it to be cleaned when there's taxes – but he says, if he were to lose it, the pretty lady would give me another. Do you know the pretty lady?'

'No, Georgey; but tell me all about her.'

Mrs. Plowson made another descent upon the boy. She was armed with a pocket-handkerchief this time, and displayed great anxiety about the state of little George's nose, but Robert warded off the dreaded weapon, and drew the child away from his tormentor.

'The boy will do very well, ma'am,' he said, 'if you'll be good enough to let him alone for five minutes. Now, Georgey, suppose you sit on my knee, and tell me all about the pretty lady.'

The child clambered from the table on to Mr. Audley's knees, assisting his descent by a very unceremonious manipulation of his guardian's coat collar.

'I'll tell you all about the pretty lady,' he said, 'because I like you very much. Granpa told me not to tell anybody, but I'll tell you, you know, because I like you, and because you're going to take me to school. The pretty lady came here one night – long ago – oh, so long ago,' said the boy, shaking his head, with a face whose solemnity was expressive of some prodigious lapse of time. 'She came when I was not nearly so big as I am now – and she came at night – after I'd gone to bed, and she came up into my room, and sat upon the bed, and cried – and she left the watch under my pillow, and she— Why do you make faces at me, Mrs. Plowson? I may tell this gentleman,' Georgey added, suddenly addressing the widow, who was standing behind Robert's shoulder.

Mrs. Plowson mumbled some confused apology to the effect that she was afraid Master George was troublesome.

'Suppose you wait till I say so, ma'am, before you stop the little fellow's mouth,' said Robert Audley, sharply. 'A suspicious person might think, from your manner, that Mr. Maldon and you had some conspiracy between you, and that you were afraid of what the boy's talk may let slip.'

He rose from his chair, and looked full at Mrs. Plowson as

he said this. The fair-haired widow's face was as white as her cap when she tried to answer him, and her pale lips were so dry that she was obliged to wet them with her tongue before the words would come.

The little boy relieved her embarrassment.

'Don't be cross, Mrs. Plowson,' he said. 'Mrs. Plowson is very kind to me. Mrs. Plowson is Matilda's mother. You didn't know Matilda. Poor Matilda was always crying; she was ill, she—'

The boy was stopped by the sudden appearance of Mr. Maldon, who stood on the threshold of the parlour-door, staring at Robert Audley with a half-drunken, half-terrified aspect, scarcely consistent with the dignity of a retired naval officer. The servant girl, breathless and panting, stood close behind her master. Early in the day though it was, the old man's speech was thick and confused, as he addressed himself fiercely to Mrs. Plowson.

'You're a prett' creature to call yoursel' sensible woman!' he said. 'Why don't you take th' chile 'way, er wash 's face? D'yer want to ruin me? D'yer want to 'stroy me? Take th' chile 'way! Mr. Audley, Sir, I'm ver' glad to see yer; ver 'appy to 'ceive yer in m' humbl' 'bode,' the old man added, with tipsy politeness, dropping into a chair as he spoke, and trying to look steadily at his unexpected visitor.

'Whatever this man's secrets are,' thought Robert, as Mrs. Plowson hustled little George Talboys out of the room, 'that woman has no unimportant share of them. Whatever the mystery may be, it grows darker and thicker at every step; but I try in vain to draw back or to stop short upon the road, for a stronger hand than my own is pointing the way to my lost friend's unknown grave.'

CHAPTER III
Little Georgey leaves his old home

'I am going to take your grandson away with me, Mr. Maldon,' Robert said, gravely, as Mrs. Plowson retired with her young charge.

The old man's drunken imbecility was slowly clearing away, like the heavy mists of a London fog, through which the feeble sunshine struggles dimly to appear. The very uncertain radiance of Lieutenant Maldon's intellect took a considerable time in piercing the hazy vapours of rum and water; but the flickering light at last faintly glimmered athwart the clouds, and the old man screwed his poor wits to the sticking-point.

'Yes, yes,' he said, feebly; 'take the boy away from his poor old grandfather. I always thought so.'

'You always thought that I should take him away?' asked Robert, scrutinising the half-drunken countenance with a searching glance. 'Why did you think so, Mr. Maldon?'

The fogs of intoxication got the better of the light of sobriety for a moment, and the lieutenant answered vaguely:

'Thought so? – 'cause I thought so.'

Meeting the young barrister's impatient frown, he made another effort, and the light glimmered again.

'Because I thought you or his father would fetch 'm away.'

'When I was last in this house, Mr. Maldon, you told me that George Talboys had sailed for Australia.'

'Yes, yes – I know, I know,' the old man answered, confusedly, shuffling his scanty limp grey hairs with his two wandering hands – 'I know; but he might have come back – mightn't he? He was restless, and – and – queer in his mind, perhaps, sometimes. He might have come back.'

He repeated this two or three times, in feeble, muttering tones; groping about on the littered mantel-piece for a dirty-looking clay-pipe, and filling and lighting it with hands that trembled violently.

Robert Audley watched those poor withered, tremulous fingers dropping shreds of tobacco upon the hearth-rug, and scarcely able to kindle a lucifer for their unsteadiness. Then walking once or twice up and down the little room, he left the old man to take a few puffs from the great consoler.

Presently he turned suddenly upon the half-pay lieutenant with a dark solemnity in his handsome face.

'Mr. Maldon,' he said, slowly, watching the effect of every syllable as he spoke, 'George Talboys never sailed for Australia – that I know. More than this, he never came to Southampton; and the lie you told me on the 8th of last September was dictated to you by the telegraphic message which you received on that day.'

The dirty clay-pipe dropped from the tremulous hand, and shivered against the iron fender, but the old man made no effort to find a fresh one; he sat trembling in every limb, and looking, Heaven knows how piteously, at Robert Audley.

'The lie was dictated to you, and you repeated your lesson. But you no more saw George Talboys here on the 7th of September than I see him in this room now. You thought you had burnt the telegraphic message, but you had only burnt a part of it – the remainder is in my possession.'

Lieutenant Maldon was quite sober now.

'What have I done?' he murmured, helplessly. 'O, my God! what have I done?'

'At two o'clock on the 7th of September last,' continued the pitiless, accusing voice, 'George Talboys was seen, alive and well, at a house in Essex.'

Robert paused to see the effect of these words. They had produced no change in the old man. He still sat trembling from head to foot, and staring with the fixed and stolid gaze of some helpless wretch, whose every sense is gradually becoming numbed by terror.

'At two o'clock on that day,' repeated Robert Audley, 'my poor friend was seen, alive and well, at—, at the house of which I speak. From that hour to this I have never been able to hear that he has been seen by any living creature. I have taken such steps as *must* have resulted in procuring the information of his whereabouts, were he alive. I have done this patiently and carefully – at first, even hopefully. Now I know that he is dead.'

Robert Audley had been prepared to witness some considerable agitation in the old man's manner, but he was not prepared for the terrible anguish, the ghastly terror, which convulsed Mr. Maldon's haggard face as he uttered the last word.

'No, no, no, no,' reiterated the lieutenant, in a shrill, half-screaming voice; 'no, no! For God's sake, don't say that! Don't think it – don't let *me* think it – don't let me dream of it! Not dead – anything but dead! Hiding away, perhaps – bribed to keep out of the way, perhaps; but not dead – not dead – not dead!'

He cried these words aloud, like one beside himself; beating his hands upon his grey head, and rocking backwards and forwards in his chair. His feeble hands trembled no longer – they were strengthened by some convulsive force that gave them a new power.

'I believe,' said Robert, in the same solemn, relentless voice, 'that my friend never left Essex; and I believe that he died on the 7th of September last.'

The wretched old man, still beating his hands amongst his thin grey hair, slid from his chair to the ground, and grovelled at Robert's feet.

'Oh! no, no – for God's sake, no!' he shrieked hoarsely. 'No! you don't know what you say – you don't know what you ask me to think – you don't know what your words mean!'

'I know their weight and value only too well – as well as I see you do, Mr. Maldon. God help us!'

'Oh, what am I doing? what am I doing?' muttered the old man, feebly; then raising himself from the ground with an effort, he drew himself to his full height, and said, in a manner which was new to him, and which was not without a certain dignity of its own – that dignity which must always be attached to unutterable misery, in whatever form it may appear – he said, gravely:–

'You have no right to come here and terrify a man who has been drinking; and who is not quite himself. You have no right to do it, Mr. Audley. Even the – the officer, Sir, who – who—' He did not stammer, but his lips trembled so violently that his words seemed to be shaken into pieces by their motion. 'The officer, I repeat, sir, who arrests a – a thief, or a—' He stopped to wipe his lips, and to still them if he could by doing so, which he could not. 'A thief – or a murderer—' His voice died suddenly away upon the last word, and it was only by the motion of those trembling lips that Robert knew what he meant. 'Gives him warning, Sir, fair warning, that he may say nothing which shall commit himself – or – or – other people. The – the – law, Sir, has that amount of mercy for a – a – suspected criminal. But you, Sir, you – you come to my house, and you come at a time when – when – contrary to my usual habits – which, as people will tell you, are sober – you come, and perceiving that I am not quite myself – you take – the – opportunity to – terrify me – and it is not right, sir – it is—'

Whatever he would have said died away into inarticulate gasps which seemed to choke him, and sinking into a chair, he dropped his face upon the table and wept aloud. Perhaps in all the dismal scenes of domestic misery which had been

191

acted in those spare and dreary houses – in all the petty miseries, the burning shames, the cruel sorrows, the bitter disgraces which own poverty for their common father – there had never been such a scene as this. An old man hiding his face from the light of day, and sobbing aloud in his wretchedness. Robert Audley contemplated the painful picture with a hopeless and pitying face.

'If I had known this,' he thought, 'I might have spared him. It would have been better, perhaps, to have spared him.'

The shabby room, the dirt, the confusion, the figure of the old man, with his grey head upon the soiled tablecloth, amid the muddled *débris* of a wretched dinner, grew blurred before the sight of Robert Audley as he thought of another man, as old as this one, but, ah, how widely different in every other quality! who might come by-and-by to feel the same, or even a worse anguish, and to shed, perhaps, yet bitterer tears. The moment in which the tears rose to his eyes and dimmed the piteous scene before him, was long enough to take him back to Essex and to show him the image of his uncle, stricken by agony and shame.

'Why do I go on with this?' he thought; 'how pitiless I am, and how relentlessly I am carried on. It is not myself; it is the hand which is beckoning me further and further upon the dark road whose end I dare not dream of.'

He thought this, and a hundred times more than this, while the old man sat with his face still hidden, wrestling with his anguish, but without power to keep it down.

'Mr. Maldon,' Robert Audley said, after a pause, 'I do not ask you to forgive me for what I have brought upon you, for the feeling is strong within me that it must have come to you sooner or later – if not through me, through some one else. There are—' He stopped for a moment, hesitating. The sobbing did not cease; it was sometimes low, sometimes loud, bursting out with fresh violence, or dying away for an instant, but never ceasing. 'There are some things which, as people say, cannot be hidden. I think there is truth in that common saying which had its origin in that old worldly wisdom which people gathered from experience and not from books. If – if I were content to let my friend rest in his hidden grave, it is but likely that some stranger, who had never heard the name of George Talboys, might fall by the remotest accident upon the secret of his death. To-morrow, perhaps; or ten years hence; or in another generation, when the – the hand that wronged him is as cold as his own. If I *could* let the matter rest; if – if I could leave England for ever, and purposely fly from the possibility of ever coming across another clue to the secret, I would do it – I would gladly, thankfully do it – but I *cannot*! A hand which is stronger than my own beckons me on. I wish to take no base advantage of you, less than of all other people; but I must go on; I must go on. If there is any warning you would give to any one, give it. If the secret towards which I am travelling day by day, hour by hour, involves any one in whom you have an interest; let that person fly before I come to the end. Let them leave this country; let them leave all who know them – all whose peace their wickedness has endangered; let them go away – they shall not be pursued. But if they slight your warning – if they try to hold their present position in defiance of what it will be in your power to tell them – let them beware of me, for when the hour comes, I swear that I will not spare them.'

The old man looked up for the first time, and wiped his wrinkled face upon a ragged silk handkerchief.

'I declare to you that I do not understand you,' he said. 'I solemnly declare to you that I cannot understand; and I do not believe that George Talboys is dead.'

'I would give ten years of my own life if I could see him alive,' answered Robert, sadly. 'I am sorry for you, Mr. Maldon – I am sorry for all of us.'

'I do not believe that my son-in-law is dead,' said the lieutenant; 'I do not believe that the poor lad is dead.'

He endeavoured in a feeble manner to show to Robert Audley that his wild outburst of anguish had been caused by his grief for the loss of George Talboys; but the pretence was miserably shallow.

Mrs. Plowson re-entered the room, leading little Georgey, whose face shone with that brilliant polish which yellow soap and friction can produce upon the human countenance.

'Dear heart alive!' exclaimed Mrs. Plowson, 'what has the poor old gentleman been taking on about? We could hear him in the passage, sobbin' awful.'

Little George crept up to his grandfather and smoothed the wet and wrinkled face with his pudgy hand.

'Don't cry, gran'pa,' he said, 'don't cry. You shall have my watch to be cleaned, and the kind jeweller shall lend you the money to pay the taxman while he cleans the watch – I don't mind, gran'pa. Let's go to the jeweller – the jeweller in High Street, you know, with golden balls painted upon his door, to show that he comes from Lombar – Lombarshire,' said the boy, making a dash at the name. 'Come, gran'pa.'

The little fellow took the jewelled toy from his bosom and made for the door, proud of being possessed of a talisman which he had seen so often made useful.

'There are wolves at Southampton,' he said, with rather a triumphant nod to Robert Audley. 'My gran'pa says when he takes my watch that he does it to keep the wolf from the door. Are there wolves where you live?'

The young barrister did not answer the child's question, but stopped him as he was dragging his grandfather towards the door.

'Your grandpapa does not want the watch to-day, Georgey,' he said, gravely.

'Why is he sorry, then?' asked Georgey, naïvely; 'when he

wants the watch he is always sorry, and beats his poor forehead
so' – the boy stopped to pantomime with his small fists – 'and
says that she – the pretty lady, I think, he means – uses him
very hard, and that he can't keep the wolf from the door; and
then I say, "Gran'pa, have the watch;" and then he takes me
in his arms and says, "Oh, my blessed angel! how can I rob
my blessed angel?" and then he cries, but not like to-day – not
loud, you know; only tears running down his poor cheeks;
not so that you could hear him in the passage.'

Painful as the child's prattle was to Robert Audley, it seemed
a relief to the old man. He did not hear the boy's talk, but
walked two or three times up and down the little room and
smoothed his rumpled hair and suffered his cravat to be
arranged by Mrs. Plowson, who seemed very anxious to find
out the cause of his agitation.

'Poor dear old gentleman,' she said, looking at Robert.
'What has happened to upset him so?'

'His son-in-law is dead,' answered Mr. Audley, fixing his
eyes upon Mrs. Plowson's sympathetic face. 'He died within
a year and a half after the death of Helen Talboys, who lies
buried in Ventnor churchyard.'

The face into which he was looking changed very slightly;
but the eyes that had been looking at his shifted away as he
spoke, and once more Mrs. Plowson was obliged to moisten
her white lips with her tongue before she answered him.

'Poor Mr. Talboys dead!' she said; 'that is bad news indeed, sir.'

Little George looked wistfully up at his guardian's face as
this was said.

'Who's dead?' he said. 'George Talboys is my name. Who's
dead?'

'Another person whose name is Talboys, Georgey.'

'Poor person! Will he go to the pit-hole?'

The boy had that common notion of death which is generally imparted to children by their wise elders, and which

always leads the infant mind to the open grave, but rarely carries it any higher.

'I should like to *see* him put in the pit-hole,' Georgey remarked, after a pause. He had attended several infant funerals in the neighbourhood, and was considered valuable as a mourner on account of his interesting appearance. He had come, therefore, to look upon the ceremony of interment as a solemn festivity; in which cake and wine and a carriage drive were the leading features.

'You have no objection to my taking Georgey away with me, Mr. Maldon?' asked Robert Audley.

The old man's agitation had very much subsided by this time. He had found another pipe stuck behind the tawdry frame of the looking-glass, and was trying to light it with a bit of twisted newspaper.

'You do not object, Mr. Maldon?'

'No, Sir – no, Sir; you are his guardian, and you have a right to take him where you please. He has been a very great comfort to me in my lonely old age; but I have been prepared to lose him. I – I – may not have always done my duty to him, Sir, in – in the way of schooling and – and boots. The number of boots which boys of his age wear out, sir, is not easily realised by the mind of a young man like yourself; he has been kept away from school, perhaps, sometimes, and has occasionally worn shabby boots when our funds have got low; but he has not been unkindly treated. No, sir; if you were to question him for a week, I don't think you'd hear that his poor old grandfather ever said a harsh word to him.'

Upon this, Georgey, perceiving the distress of his old protector, set up a terrible howl, and declared that he would never leave him.

'Mr. Maldon,' said Robert Audley, with a tone which was half-mournful, half-compassionate, 'when I looked at my position last night, I did not believe that I could ever come to think it more painful than I thought it then. I can only say – God have mercy upon us all. I feel it my duty to take the child away; but I shall take him straight from your house to the best school in Southampton; and I give you my honour that I will extort nothing from his innocent simplicity which can in any manner – I mean,' he said, breaking off abruptly, 'I mean this – I will not seek to come one step nearer the secret through him. I – I am not a detective officer, and I do not think that the most accomplished detective would like to get his information from a child.'

The old man did not answer; he sat with his face shaded by his hand, and with his extinguished pipe between the listless fingers of the other.

'Take the boy away, Mrs. Plowson,' he said, after a pause; 'take him away and put his things on. He is going with Mr. Audley.'

'Which I do say that it's not kind of the gentleman to take his poor grandpa's pet away,' Mrs. Plowson exclaimed, suddenly, with respectful indignation.

'Hush, Mrs. Plowson,' the old man answered, piteously; 'Mr. Audley is the best judge. I – I – haven't many years to live; I shan't trouble anybody long.'

The tears oozed slowly through the dirty fingers with which he shaded his bloodshot eyes as he said this.

'God knows, I never injured your friend, Sir,' he said by-and-by, when Mrs. Plowson and Georgey had returned, 'nor ever wished him any ill. He was a good son-in-law to me – better than many a son. I never did him any wilful wrong, Sir. I – I spent his money, perhaps, but I am sorry for it – I am very sorry for it now. But I don't believe he is dead – no, sir, no, I don't believe it!' exclaimed the old man, dropping his hand from his eyes, and looking with new energy at Robert Audley. 'I – I don't believe it, Sir! How – how should he be dead?'

Robert did not answer this eager questioning. He shook his head mournfully, and walking to the little window looked out across a row of straggling geraniums at the dreary patch of waste ground on which the children were at play.

Mrs. Plowson returned with little Georgey muffled in a coat and comforter, and Robert took the boy's hand.

'Say good-by to your grandpapa, Georgey.'

The little fellow sprang towards the old man, and clinging about him, kissed the dirty tears from his faded cheeks.

'Don't be sorry for me, grandpa,' he said; 'I am going to school to learn to be a clever man, and I shall come home to see you and Mrs. Plowson, shan't I?' he added, turning to Robert.

'Yes, my dear, by-and-by.'

'Take him away, Sir – take him away,' cried Mr. Maldon; 'you are breaking my heart.'

The little fellow trotted away contentedly at Robert's side. He was very well pleased at the idea of going to school, though he had been happy enough with his drunken old grandfather, who had always displayed a maudlin affection for the pretty child, and had done his best to spoil Georgey, by letting him have his own way in everything; in consequence of which indulgence Master Talboys had acquired a taste for late hours, hot suppers of the most indigestible nature, and sips of rum and water from his grandfather's glass.

He communicated his sentiments upon many subjects to Robert Audley, as they walked to the Dolphin Hotel; but the barrister did not encourage him to talk.

It was no very difficult matter to find a good school in such a place as Southampton. Robert Audley was directed to a pretty house between the Bar and the Avenue, and leaving Georgey to the care of a good-natured waiter, who seemed to have nothing to do but to look out of the window, and whisk invisible dust off the brightly polished tables, the barrister walked up the High Street, towards Mr. Marchmont's academy for young gentlemen.

He found Mr. Marchmont a very sensible man, and he met a file of orderly looking young gentlemen walking townwards under the escort of a couple of ushers as he entered the house.

He told the schoolmaster that little George Talboys had been left in his charge by a dear friend, who had sailed for Australia some months before, and whom he believed to be dead. He confided him to Mr. Marchmont's especial care, and he further requested that no visitors should be admitted to see the boy, unless accredited by a letter from himself. Having arranged the matter in a very few business-like words, he returned to the hotel to fetch Georgey.

He found the little man on intimate terms with the idle waiter, who had been directing Master Georgey's attention to the different objects of interest in the High Street.

Poor Robert had about as much notion of the requirements of a child as he had of those of a white elephant. He had catered for silkworms, guinea-pigs, dormice, canary birds, and dogs, without number, during his boyhood, but he had never been called upon to provide for a young person of five years old.

He looked back five-and-twenty years, and tried to remember his own diet at the age of five.

'I've a vague recollection of getting a good deal of bread and milk and boiled mutton,' he thought; 'and I've another vague recollection of not liking them. I wonder if this boy likes bread and milk and boiled mutton.'

He stood pulling his thick moustache and staring thoughtfully at the child for some minutes before he could get any further.

'I dare say you're hungry, Georgey,' he said, at last.

The boy nodded, and the waiter whisked some more invisible dust from the table, as a preparatory step towards laying a cloth.

'Perhaps you'd like some lunch?' Mr. Audley suggested, still pulling his moustache.

The boy burst out laughing.

'Lunch!' he cried. 'Why, it's afternoon, and I've had my dinner.'

Robert Audley felt himself brought to a standstill. What refreshment could he possibly provide for a boy who called it afternoon at three o'clock?

'You shall have some bread and milk, Georgey,' he said, presently. 'Waiter, bread and milk, and a pint of hock.'

Master Talboys made a wry face.

'I never have bread and milk,' he said; 'I don't like it. I like what grandpa calls something savoury. I should like a veal cutlet. Grandpa told me he dined here once, and the veal cutlets were lovely, grandpa said. Please, may I have a veal cutlet, with egg and bread-crumb, you know, and some lemon-juice, you know?' he added to the waiter. 'Grandpa knows the cook here. The cook's such a nice gentleman, and once gave me a shilling, when grandpa brought me here. The cook wears better clothes than grandpa – better than yours even,' said Master Georgey, pointing to Robert's rough great-coat with a depreciatory nod.

Robert Audley stared aghast. How was he to deal with this epicure of five years old, who rejected bread and milk and asked for veal cutlets?

'I'll tell you what I'll do with you, little Georgey,' he exclaimed, after a pause – *'I'll give you a dinner.'*

The waiter nodded briskly.

'Upon my word, sir,' he said, approvingly, 'I think the little gentleman will know how to eat it.'

'I'll give you a dinner, Georgey,' repeated Robert – 'a little Julienne, some stewed eels, a dish of cutlets, a bird, and a pudding. What do you say to that, Georgey?'

'I don't think the young gentleman will object to it when

he sees it, Sir,' said the waiter. 'Eels, Julienne, cutlets, bird, pudding – I'll go and tell the cook, Sir. What time, Sir?'

'Well, we'll say six, and Master Georgey will get to his new school by bedtime. You can contrive to amuse the child for this afternoon, I dare say. I have some business to settle, and shan't be able to take him out. I shall sleep here to-night. Good-by, Georgey; take care of yourself, and try and get your appetite in order against six o'clock.'

Robert Audley left the boy in charge of the idle waiter, and strolled down to the water-side, choosing that lonely bank which leads away under the mouldering walls of the town towards the little villages beside the narrowing river.

He had purposely avoided the society of the child, and he walked through the light drifting snow till the early darkness closed upon him.

He went back to the town, and made inquiries at the station about the trains for Dorsetshire.

'I shall start early to-morrow morning,' he thought, 'and see George's father before night-fall. I will tell him all – all but the interest which I take in – in the suspected person, and he shall decide what is next to be done.'

Master Georgey did very good justice to the dinner which Robert had ordered. He drank Bass's pale ale to an extent which considerably alarmed his entertainer, and enjoyed himself amazingly, showing an appreciation of roast pheasant and bread-sauce which was beyond his years. At eight o'clock a fly was brought out for his accommodation, and he departed in the highest spirits, with a sovereign in his pocket, and a letter from Robert to Mr. Marchmont, enclosing a cheque for the young gentleman's outfit.

'I'm glad I'm going to have new clothes,' he said, as he bade Robert good-by; 'for Mrs. Plowson has mended the old ones ever so many times. She can have them now for Billy.'

'Who's Billy?' Robert asked, laughing at the boy's chatter.

'Billy is poor Matilda's little brother. He's a common boy, you know. Matilda was common, but she—'

But the flyman smacking his whip at this moment, the old horse jogged off, and Robert Audley heard no more of Matilda.

CHAPTER IV
Coming to a standstill

Mr. Harcourt Talboys lived in a prim, square, red-brick mansion, within a mile of a little village called Grange Heath, in Dorsetshire. The prim, square, red-brick mansion stood in the centre of prim, square grounds, scarcely large enough to be called a park, too large to be called anything else – so neither the house nor the grounds had any name, and the estate was simply designated Squire Talboys'.

Perhaps Mr. Harcourt Talboys was the very last person in this world with whom it was possible to associate the homely, hearty, rural, old English title of squire. He neither hunted nor farmed. He had never worn crimson-pink, or top-boots in his life. A southerly wind and a cloudy sky were matters of supreme indifference to him so long as they did not in any way interfere with his own prim comforts; and he only cared for the state of the crops insomuch as it involved the hazard of certain rents which he received for the farms upon his estate. He was a man of about fifty years of age, tall, straight, bony, and angular, with a square, pale face, light grey eyes, and scanty dark hair, brushed from either ear across a bald crown, and thus imparting to his physiognomy some faint resemblance to that of a terrier – a sharp, uncompromising, hard-headed terrier – a terrier not to be taken in by the cleverest dog-stealer who ever distinguished himself in his profession.

Nobody ever remembered getting upon what is popularly called the blind side of Harcourt Talboys. He was like his own square-built, northern-fronted, shelterless house. There were no shady nooks in his character into which one could creep for shelter from his hard daylight. He was all daylight. He looked at everything in the same broad glare of intellectual sunlight, and would see no softening shadows that might alter the sharp outlines of cruel facts, subduing them to beauty. I do not know if I express what I mean, when I say that there were no curves in his character – that his mind ran in straight lines, never diverging to the right or the left to round off their pitiless angles. With him right was right and wrong was wrong. He had never in his merciless, conscientious life admitted the idea that circumstance might mitigate the blackness of wrong or weaken the force of right. He had cast off his only son because his only son had disobeyed him, and he was ready to cast off his only daughter at five minutes' notice for the same reason.

If this square-built, hard-headed man could be possessed of such a weakness as vanity, he was certainly vain of his hardness. He was vain of that inflexible squareness of intellect which made him the disagreeable creature that he was. He was vain of that unwavering obstinacy which no influence of love or pity had been ever known to bend from its remorseless purpose. He was vain of the negative force of a nature which had never known the weakness of the affections, or the strength which may be born of that very weakness.

If he had regretted his son's marriage, and the breach, of his own making, between himself and George, his vanity had been more powerful than his regret, and had enabled him to conceal it. Indeed, unlikely as it appears at the first glance that such a man as this could have been vain, I have little doubt that vanity was the centre from which radiated all the disagreeable lines in the character of Mr. Harcourt Talboys. I dare say Junius Brutus was vain, and enjoyed the approval of awe-stricken Rome when he ordered his son off for execution. Harcourt Talboys would have sent poor George from his presence between the reversed fasces of the lictors, and grimly relished his own agony. Heaven only knows how bitterly this hard man may have felt the separation between himself and his only son, or how much the more terrible the anguish might have been made by that unflinching self-conceit which concealed the torture.

'My son did me an unpardonable wrong by marrying the daughter of a drunken pauper,' Mr. Talboys would answer to any one who had the temerity to speak to him about George, 'and from that hour I had no longer a son. I wish him no ill. He is simply dead to me. I am sorry for him, as I am sorry for his mother who died nineteen years ago. If you talk to me of him as you would talk of the dead, I shall be ready to hear you. If you speak of him as you would speak of the living, I must decline to listen.'

I believe that Harcourt Talboys hugged himself upon the gloomy Roman grandeur of this speech, and that he would have liked to have worn a toga, and wrapped himself sternly in its folds, as he turned his back upon poor George's intercessor. George never in his own person made any effort to soften his father's verdict. He knew his father well enough to know that the case was hopeless.

'If I write to him, he will fold my letter with the envelope inside, and indorse it with my name and the date of its arrival,' the young man would say, 'and call everybody in the house to witness that it has not moved him to one softening recollection or one pitiful thought. He will stick to his resolution to his dying day. I dare say, if the truth were known, he is glad that his only son has offended him and given him the opportunity of parading his Roman virtues.'

George had answered his wife thus when she and her father had urged him to ask assistance from Harcourt Talboys.

'No, my darling,' he would say conclusively. 'It is very hard, perhaps, to be poor, but we will bear it. We won't go with pitiful faces to the stern father, and ask him to give us food and shelter, only to be refused in long Johnsonian sentences, and made a classical example of for the benefit of the neighbourhood. No, my pretty one; it is easy to starve, but it is difficult to stoop.'

Perhaps poor Mrs. George did not agree very heartily to the first of these two propositions. She had no great fancy for starving, and she whimpered pitifully when the pretty pint bottles of champagne, with Cliquot's and Moet's brands upon their corks, were exchanged for sixpenny ale, procured by a slipshod attendant from the nearest beershop. George had been obliged to carry his own burden and lend a helping hand with that of his wife, who had no idea of keeping her regrets or disappointments a secret.

'I thought dragoons were always rich,' she used to say, peevishly. 'Girls always want to marry dragoons; and tradespeople always want to serve dragoons; and hotel-keepers to entertain dragoons; and theatrical managers to be patronised by dragoons. Who could have ever expected that a dragoon would drink sixpenny ale, smoke horrid bird's-eye tobacco, and let his wife wear a shabby bonnet?'

If there were any selfish feeling displayed in such speeches as these, George Talboys had never discovered it. He had loved and believed in his wife from the first to the last hour of his brief married life. The love that is not blind is perhaps only a spurious divinity after all; for when Cupid takes the fillet from his eyes it is a fatally certain indication that he is preparing to spread his wings for a flight. George never forgot the hour in which he had first been bewitched by Lieutenant Maldon's pretty daughter, and however she might have changed, the image which had charmed him then, unchanged and unchanging represented her in his heart.

Robert Audley left Southampton by a train which started before daybreak, and reached Wareham station early in the day. He hired a vehicle at Wareham to take him over to Grange Heath.

The snow had hardened upon the ground, and the day was clear and frosty, every object in the landscape standing in sharp outline against the cold blue sky. The horses' hoofs clattered upon the ice-bound road, the iron shoes striking on ground that was almost as iron as themselves. The wintry day bore some resemblance to the man to whom Robert was going. Like him, it was sharp, frigid, and uncompromising; like him, it was merciless to distress, and impregnable to the softening power of sunshine. It would accept no sunshine but such January radiance as would light up the bleak, bare country without brightening it; and thus resembled Harcourt Talboys, who took the sternest side of every truth, and declared loudly to the disbelieving world that there never had been, and never could be, any other side.

Robert Audley's heart sank within him as the shabby hired vehicle stopped at a stern-looking barred fence, and the driver dismounted to open a broad iron gate, which swung back with a clanking noise and was caught by a great iron tooth planted in the ground, which snapped at the lowest bar of the gate, as if it wanted to bite.

This iron gate opened into a scanty plantation of straight-limbed fir-trees that grew in rows and shook their sturdy winter foliage defiantly in the very teeth of the frosty breeze. A straight, gravelled carriage-drive ran between these straight trees across a smoothly-kept lawn to a square red-brick mansion, every window of which winked and glittered in the January sunlight, as if it had been that moment cleaned by some indefatigable house-maid.

I don't know whether Junius Brutus was a nuisance in his own house, but amongst other of his Roman virtues,

Mr. Talboys owned an extreme aversion to disorder, and was the terror of every domestic in his establishment.

The windows winked and the flight of stone steps glared in the sunlight, the prim garden walks were so freshly gravelled that they gave a sandy, gingery aspect to the place, reminding one unpleasantly of red hair. The lawn was chiefly ornamented with dark, wintry shrubs of a funereal aspect, which grew in beds that looked like problems in algebra; and the flight of stone steps leading to the square half-glass door of the hall was adorned with dark-green wooden tubs containing the same sturdy evergreens.

'If the man is anything like his house,' Robert thought, 'I don't wonder that poor George and he parted.'

At the end of a scanty avenue the carriage-drive turned a sharp corner (it would have been made to describe a curve in any other man's grounds) and ran before the lower windows of the house. The flyman dismounted at the steps, ascended them, and rang a brass-handled bell, which flew back to its socket with an angry metallic snap, as if it had been insulted by the plebeian touch of the man's hand.

A man in black trousers and a striped linen jacket, which was evidently fresh from the hands of the laundress, opened the door. Mr. Talboys was at home. Would the gentleman send in his card?

Robert waited in the hall while his card was taken to the master of the house.

The hall was large, lofty, and paved with stone. The panels of the oaken wainscot shone with the same uncompromising polish which was on every object within and without the red-brick mansion.

Some people are so weak-minded as to affect pictures and statues. Mr. Harcourt Talboys was far too practical to indulge in any such foolish fancies. A barometer and an umbrella-stand were the only adornments of his entrance-hall.

Robert Audley looked at these while his name was being submitted to George's father.

The linen-jacketed servant returned presently. He was a spare, pale-faced man of almost forty, and had the appearance of having outlived every emotion to which humanity is subject.

'If you will step this way, Sir,' he said, 'Mr. Talboys will see you, although he is at breakfast. He begged me to state that he had imagined that everybody in Dorsetshire was acquainted with his breakfast-hour.'

This was intended as a stately reproof to Mr. Robert Audley. It had, however, very small effect upon the young barrister. He merely lifted his eyebrows in placid deprecation of himself and everybody else.

'I don't belong to Dorsetshire,' he said. 'Mr. Talboys might have known that, if he'd done me the honour to exercise his powers of ratiocination. Drive on, my friend.'

The emotionless man looked at Robert Audley with the vacant stare of unmitigated horror, and opening one of the heavy oak doors, led the way into a large dining-room furnished with the severe simplicity of an apartment which is meant to be ate in, but never lived in; and at the top of a table which would have accommodated eighteen persons, Robert beheld Mr. Harcourt Talboys.

Mr. Talboys was robed in a dressing-gown of grey cloth, fastened about his waist with a girdle. It was a severe-looking garment, and was perhaps the nearest approach to a toga to be obtained within the range of modern costume. He wore a buff waistcoat, a stiffly starched cambric cravat, and a faultless shirt collar. The cold grey of his dressing-gown was almost the same as the cold grey of his eyes, and the pale buff of his waistcoat was the pale buff of his complexion.

Robert Audley had not expected to find Harcourt Talboys at all like George in manners or disposition, but he had expected to see some family likeness between the father and the son. There was none. It would have been impossible to imagine any one more unlike George than the author of his existence. Robert scarcely wondered at the cruel letter he had received from Mr. Talboys when he saw the writer of it. Such a man could scarcely have written otherwise.

There was a second person in the large room, towards whom Robert glanced after saluting Harcourt Talboys, doubtful how to proceed. This second person was a lady, who sat at the last of a range of four windows, employed with some needlework, the kind which is generally called plain work, and with a large wicker basket, filled with calicoes and flannels, standing by her.

The whole length of the room divided this lady from Robert, but he could see that she was young, and that she was like George Talboys.

'His sister!' he thought in that one moment during which he ventured to glance away from the master of the house towards the female figure at the window. 'His sister, no doubt. He was fond of her, I know. Surely, she is not utterly indifferent as to his fate?'

The lady half rose from her seat, letting her work, which was large and awkward, fall from her lap as she did so, and dropping a reel of cotton, which rolled away upon the polished oaken flooring beyond the margin of the Turkey carpet.

'Sit down, Clara,' said the hard voice of Mr. Talboys.

That gentleman did not appear to address his daughter, nor had his face been turned towards her when she rose. It seemed as if he had known it by some social magnetism peculiar to himself; it seemed, as his servants were apt disrespectfully to observe, as if he had eyes in the back of his head.

'Sit down, Clara,' he repeated, 'and keep your cotton in your workbox.'

The lady blushed at this reproof, and stooped to look for

the cotton. Mr. Robert Audley, who was unabashed by the stern presence of the master of the house, knelt on the carpet, found the reel, and restored it to its owner; Harcourt Talboys staring at the proceeding with an expression of supreme astonishment.

'Perhaps, Mr. —, Mr. Robert Audley!' he said, looking at the card which he held between his finger and thumb, 'perhaps when you have finished looking for reels of cotton, you will be good enough to tell me to what I owe the honour of this visit?'

He waved his well-shaped hand with a gesture which might have been admired in the stately John Kemble; and the servant understanding the gesture, brought forward a ponderous red morocco chair.

The proceeding was so slow and solemn that Robert had at first thought that something extraordinary was about to be done; but the truth dawned upon him at last, and he dropped into the massive chair.

'You may remain, Wilson,' said Mr. Talboys, as the servant was about to withdraw; 'Mr. Audley would perhaps like coffee.'

Robert had eaten nothing that morning, but he glanced at the long expanse of dreary table-cloth, the silver tea and coffee equipage, the stiff splendour, and the very little appearance of any substantial entertainment, and he declined Mr. Talboys' invitation.

'Mr. Audley will not take coffee, Wilson,' said the master of the house. 'You may go.'

The man bowed and retired, opening and shutting the door as cautiously as if he were taking a liberty in doing it at all, or as if the respect due to Mr. Talboys demanded his walking straight through the oaken panel like a ghost in a German story.

Mr. Harcourt Talboys sat with his grey eyes fixed severely

on his visitor, his elbows on the red morocco arms of his chair, and his finger-tips joined. It was the attitude in which, had he been Junius Brutus, he would have sat at the trial of his son. Had Robert Audley been easily to be embarrassed, Mr. Talboys might have succeeded in making him feel so: as he would have sat with perfect tranquillity upon an open gunpowder barrel lighting his cigar, he was not at all disturbed upon this occasion. The father's dignity seemed a very small thing to him when he thought of the possible causes of the son's disappearance.

'I wrote to you some time since, Mr. Talboys,' he said quietly, when he saw that he was expected to open the conversation.

Harcourt Talboys bowed. He knew that it was of his lost son that Robert came to speak. Heaven grant that his icy stoicism was the paltry affectation of a vain man, rather than the utter heartlessness which Robert thought it. He bowed across his finger-tips at his visitor. The trial had begun, and Junius Brutus was enjoying himself.

'I received your communication, Mr. Audley,' he said. 'It is indorsed amongst other business letters: it was duly answered.'

'That letter concerned your son.'

There was a little rustling noise at the window where the lady sat, as Robert said this: he looked at her almost instantaneously, but she did not seem to have stirred. She was not working, but she was perfectly quiet.

'She's as heartless as her father, I expect, though she is like George,' thought Mr. Audley.

'Your letter concerned the person who was once my son, perhaps, sir,' said Harcourt Talboys; 'I must ask you to remember that I have no longer a son.'

'You have no reason to remind me of that, Mr. Talboys,' answered Robert, gravely; 'I remember it only too well. I have fatal reason to believe that you have no longer a son. I have bitter cause to think that he is dead.'

It may be that Mr. Talboys' complexion faded to a paler shade of buff as Robert said this; but he only elevated his bristling grey eyebrows and shook his head gently.

'No,' he said, 'no, I assure you, no.'

'I believe that George Talboys died in the month of September.'

The girl who had been addressed as Clara sat with her work primly folded upon her lap, and her hands lying clasped together on her work, and never stirred when Robert spoke of his friend's death. He could not distinctly see her face, for she was seated at some distance from him, and with her back to the window.

'No, no, I assure you,' repeated Mr. Talboys, 'you labour under a sad mistake.'

'You believe that I am mistaken in thinking your son dead?' asked Robert.

'Most certainly,' replied Mr. Talboys, with a smile, expressive of the serenity of wisdom. 'Most certainly, my dear sir. The disappearance was a very clever trick, no doubt, but it was not sufficiently clever to deceive me. You must permit me to understand this matter a little better than you, Mr. Audley, and you must also permit me to assure you of three things. In the first place, your friend is not dead. In the second place, he is keeping out of the way for the purpose of alarming me, of trifling with my feelings as a – as a man who was once his father, and of ultimately obtaining my forgiveness. In the third place, he will not obtain that forgiveness, however long he may please to keep out of the way; and he would therefore act wisely by returning to his ordinary residence and avocations without delay.'

'Then you imagine him to purposely hide himself from all who know him, for the purpose of—?'

'For the purpose of influencing *me*,' exclaimed Mr. Talboys, who, taking a stand upon his own vanity, traced every event in life from that one centre, and resolutely declined to look at it from any other point of view. 'For the purpose of influencing me. He knew the inflexibility of my character; to a certain degree he was acquainted with me, and he knew that all ordinary attempts at softening my decision, or moving me from the fixed purpose of my life, would fail. He therefore tried extraordinary means; he has kept out of the way in order to alarm me; and when after due time he discovers that he has not alarmed me, he will return to his old haunts. When he does so,' said Mr. Talboys, rising to sublimity, 'I will forgive him. Yes, Sir, I will forgive him. I shall say to him: You have attempted to deceive me, and I have shown you that I am not to be deceived; you have tried to frighten me, and I have convinced you that I am not to be frightened; you did not believe in my generosity, I will show you that I can be generous.'

Harcourt Talboys delivered himself of these superb periods with a studied manner, that showed they had been carefully composed long ago.

Robert Audley sighed as he heard them.

'Heaven grant that you may have an opportunity of saying this to your son, sir,' he answered sadly. 'I am very glad to find that you are willing to forgive him, but I fear that you will never see him again upon this earth. I have a great deal to say to you upon this – this sad subject, Mr. Talboys; but I would rather say it to you alone,' he added, glancing at the lady in the window.

'My daughter knows my ideas upon this subject, Mr. Audley,' said Harcourt Talboys; 'there is no reason why she should not hear all you have to say. Miss Clara Talboys, Mr. Robert Audley,' he added, waving his hand majestically.

The young lady bent her head in recognition of Robert's bow.

'Let her hear it,' he thought. 'If she has so little feeling as to show no emotion upon such a subject, let her hear the worst I have to tell.'

There was a few minutes' pause, during which Robert took some papers from his pocket; amongst them the document which he had written immediately after George's disappearance.

'I shall require all your attention, Mr. Talboys,' he said, 'for that which I have to disclose to you is of a very painful nature. Your son was my very dear friend – dear to me for many reasons. Perhaps most of all dear, because I had known him and been with him through the great trouble of his life; and because he stood comparatively alone in the world – cast off by you, who should have been his best friend, bereft of the only woman he had ever loved.'

'The daughter of a drunken pauper,' Mr. Talboys remarked, parenthetically.

'Had he died in his bed, as I sometimes thought he would,' continued Robert Audley, 'of a broken heart, I should have mourned for him very sincerely, even though I had closed his eyes with my own hands, and had seen him laid in his quiet resting-place. I should have grieved for my old school-fellow, and for the companion who had been dear to me. But the grief would have been a very small one compared to that which I feel now, believing, as I do only too firmly, that my poor friend has been murdered.'

'Murdered!'

The father and daughter simultaneously repeated the horrible word. The father's face changed to a ghastly duskiness of hue; the daughter's face dropped upon her clasped hands, and was never lifted again throughout the interview.

'Mr. Audley, you are mad!' exclaimed Harcourt Talboys; 'you are mad, or else you are commissioned by your friend to play upon my feelings. I protest against this proceeding as a conspiracy, and I – I revoke my intended forgiveness of the person who was once my son.'

He was himself again as he said this. The blow had been a sharp one, but its effect had been momentary.

'It is far from my wish to alarm you unnecessarily, Sir,' answered Robert. 'Heaven grant that you may be right and I wrong. I pray for it, but I cannot think it – I cannot even hope it. I come to you for advice. I will state to you plainly and dispassionately the circumstances which have aroused my suspicions. If you say those suspicions are foolish and unfounded, I am ready to submit to your better judgment. I will leave England; and I abandon my search for the evidence wanting to – to confirm my fears. If you say go on, I will go on.'

Nothing could be more gratifying to the vanity of Mr. Harcourt Talboys than this appeal. He declared himself ready to listen to all that Robert might have to say, and ready to assist him to the uttermost of his power.

He laid some stress upon this last assurance, deprecating the value of his advice with an affectation that was as transparent as his vanity itself.

Robert Audley drew his chair nearer to that of Mr. Talboys, and commenced a minutely-detailed account of all that had happened to George from the time of his arrival in England to the hour of his disappearance, as well as all that had occurred since his disappearance in any way touching upon that particular subject. Harcourt Talboys listened with demonstrative attention, now and then interrupting the speaker to ask some magisterial kind of question. Clara Talboys never once lifted her face from her clasped hands.

The hands of the clock pointed to a quarter past eleven when Robert began his story. The clock struck twelve as he finished.

He had carefully suppressed the names of his uncle and his uncle's wife, in relating the circumstances in which they had been concerned.

'Now, Sir,' he said, when the story had been told, 'I await your decision. You have heard my reasons for coming to this terrible conclusion. In what manner do those reasons influence you?'

'They do not in any way turn me from my previous opinion,' answered Mr. Harcourt Talboys, with the unreasoning pride of an obstinate man. 'I still think, as I thought before, that my son is alive, and that his disappearance is a conspiracy against myself. I decline to become the victim of that conspiracy.'

'And you tell me to stop?' asked Robert, solemnly.

'I tell you only this:– If you go on, you go on for your own satisfaction, not for mine. I see nothing in what you have told me to alarm me for the safety of – your friend.'

'So be it, then!' exclaimed Robert, suddenly; 'from this moment I wash my hands of this business. From this moment the purpose of my life shall be to forget it.'

He rose as he spoke, and took his hat from the table on which he had placed it. He looked at Clara Talboys. Her attitude had never changed since she had dropped her face upon her hands. 'Good morning, Mr. Talboys,' he said gravely. 'God grant that you are right. God grant that I am wrong. But I fear a day will come when you will have reason to regret your apathy respecting the untimely fate of your only son.'

He bowed gravely to Mr. Harcourt Talboys and to the lady, whose face was hidden by her hands.

He lingered for a moment looking at Miss Talboys, thinking that she would look up, that she would make some sign, or show some desire to detain him.

Mr. Talboys rang for the emotionless servant, who led Robert off to the hall door with the solemnity of manner which would have been in perfect keeping had he been leading him to execution.

'She is like her father,' thought Mr. Audley, as he glanced

for the last time at the drooping head. 'Poor George, you had need of one friend in this world, for you have had very few to love you.'

CHAPTER V
Clara

Robert Audley found the driver asleep upon the box of his lumbering vehicle. He had been entertained with beer of so hard a nature, as to induce temporary strangulation in the daring imbiber thereof, and he was very glad to welcome the return of his fare. The old white horse, who looked as if he had been foaled in the year in which the carriage had been built, and seemed, like the carriage, to have outlived the fashion, was as fast asleep as his master, and woke up with a jerk as Robert came down the stony flight of steps, attended by his executioner, who waited respectfully till Mr. Audley had entered the vehicle and been turned off.

The horse, roused by a smack of his driver's whip, and a shake of the shabby reins, crawled off in a semi-somnambulent state, and Robert, with his hat very much over his eyes, thought of his missing friend.

He had played in these stiff gardens, and under these dreary firs, years ago, perhaps – if it were possible for the most frolicsome youth to be playful within the range of Mr. Harcourt Talboys' hard grey eyes. He had played beneath these dark trees, perhaps, with the sister who had heard of his fate to-day without a tear. Robert Audley looked at the rigid primness of the orderly grounds, wondering how George could have grown up in such a place to be the frank, generous, careless friend whom he had known. How was it that with his father perpetually before his eyes, he had not grown up after the father's disagreeable model, to be a nuisance to his fellow-men? How was it? Because we have Some One higher than our parents to thank for the souls which make us great or small; and because, while family noses and family chins may descend in orderly sequence from father to son, from grandsire to grandchild, as the fashion of the fading flowers of one year are reproduced in the budding blossoms of the next, the spirit, more subtle than the wind which blows among those flowers, independent of all earthly rule, owns no order but the harmonious Law of God.

'Thank God!' thought Robert Audley – 'thank God! it is over. My poor friend must rest in his unknown grave; and I shall not be the means of bringing disgrace upon those I love. It will come, perhaps, sooner or later, but it will not come through me. The crisis is past, and I am free.'

He felt an unutterable relief in this thought. His generous nature revolted at the office into which he had found himself drawn – the office of spy, the collector of damning facts that led on to horrible deductions.

He drew a long breath – a sigh of relief at his release. It was all over now.

The fly was crawling out of the gate of the plantation as he thought this, and he stood up in the vehicle to look back at the dreary fir-trees, the gravel paths, the smooth grass, and the great desolate-looking, red-brick mansion.

He was startled by the appearance of a woman running, almost flying, along the carriage-drive by which he had come, and waving a handkerchief in her uplifted hand.

He stared at this singular apparition for some moments in silent wonder, before he was able to reduce his stupefaction into words.

'Is it *me* the flying female wants?' he exclaimed at last. 'You'd better stop, perhaps,' he added to the flyman. 'It is an age of eccentricity, an abnormal era of the world's history. She may want me. Very likely I left my pocket-handkerchief behind me, and Mr. Talboys has sent this person with it. Perhaps I'd better get out and go and meet her. It's civil to send my handkerchief.'

Mr. Robert Audley deliberately descended from the fly, and walked slowly towards the hurrying female figure, which gained upon him rapidly.

He was rather short-sighted, and it was not until she came very near to him that he saw who she was.

'Good heavens!' he exclaimed, 'it's Miss Talboys.'

It was Miss Talboys, flushed and breathless, with a woollen shawl over her head.

Robert Audley now saw her face clearly for the first time, and he saw that she was very handsome. She had brown eyes, like George's, a pale complexion (she had been flushed when she approached him, but the colour faded away as she recovered her breath), regular features, and a mobility of expression which bore record of every change of feeling. He saw all this in a few moments, and he wondered only the more at the stoicism of her manner during his interview with Mr. Talboys. There were no tears in her eyes, but they were bright with a feverish lustre – terribly bright and dry – and he could see that her lips trembled as she spoke to him.

'Miss Talboys,' he said, 'what can I? – why—'

She interrupted him suddenly, catching at his wrist with her disengaged hand – she was holding her shawl in the other.

'Oh, let me speak to you,' she cried – 'let me speak to you, or I shall go mad. I heard it all. I believe what you believe; and I shall go mad unless I can do something – something towards avenging his death.'

For a few moments Robert Audley was too much bewildered to answer her. Of all things possible upon earth he had least expected to behold her thus.

'Take my arm, Miss Talboys,' he said. 'Pray calm yourself. Let us walk a little way back towards the house, and talk quietly. I would not have spoken as I did before you, had I known—'

'Had you known that I loved my brother,' she said quickly. 'How should you know that I loved him! How should any one think that I loved him, when I have never had power to win him a welcome beneath that roof, or a kindly word from his father? How should I dare to betray my love for him in that house, when I knew that even a sister's affection would be turned to his disadvantage? You do not know my father, Mr. Audley. I do. I knew that to intercede for George would have been to ruin his cause. I knew that to leave matters in my father's hands, and to trust to time, was my only chance of ever seeing that dear brother again. And I waited – waited patiently, always hoping for the best; for I knew that my father loved his only son. I see your contemptuous smile, Mr. Audley, and I dare say it is difficult for a stranger to believe that underneath his affected stoicism, my father conceals some degree of affection for his children – no very warm attachment perhaps, for he has always ruled his life by the strict law of duty. Stop,' she said, suddenly, laying her hand upon his arm, and looking back through the straight avenue of pines; 'I ran out of the house by the backway. Papa must not see me talking to you, Mr. Audley, and he must not see the fly standing at the gate. Will you go into the high road and tell the man to drive on a little way? I will come out of the plantation by a little gate further on, and meet you in the road.'

'But you will catch cold, Miss Talboys,' remonstrated Robert, looking at her anxiously, for he saw that she was trembling. 'You are shivering now.'

'Not with cold,' she answered. 'I am thinking of my brother George. If you have any pity for the only sister of your lost friend, do what I ask you, Mr. Audley. I must speak to you – I must speak to you – calmly, if I can.'

She put her hand to her head as if trying to collect her

thoughts, and then pointed to the gate. Robert bowed and left her. He told the man to drive slowly towards the station, and walked on by the side of the tarred fence surrounding Mr. Talboys' grounds. About a hundred yards beyond the principal entrance he came to a little wooden gate in the fence, and waited at it for Miss Talboys.

She joined him presently, with her shawl still over her head, and her eyes still bright and tearless.

'Will you walk with me inside the plantation?' she said. 'We might be observed on the high road.'

He bowed, passed through the gate, and shut it behind him.

When she took his offered arm he found that she was still trembling – trembling very violently.

'Pray, pray calm yourself, Miss Talboys,' he said: 'I may have been deceived in the opinion which I have formed; I may—'

'No, no, no,' she exclaimed, 'you are not deceived. My brother has been murdered. Tell me the name of that woman – the woman whom you suspect of being concerned in his disappearance – in his murder.'

'That I cannot do until—'

'Until when?'

'Until I know that she is guilty.'

'You told my father that you would abandon all idea of discovering the truth – that you would rest satisfied to leave my brother's fate a horrible mystery never to be solved upon this earth; but you will not do so, Mr. Audley – you will not be false to the memory of your friend. You will see vengeance done upon those who have destroyed him. You will do this, will you not?'

A gloomy shadow spread itself like a dark veil over Robert Audley's handsome face.

He remembered what he had said the day before at Southampton –

'A hand that is stronger than my own is beckoning me onward upon the dark road.'

A quarter of an hour before, he had believed that all was over, and that he was released from the dreadful duty of discovering the secret of George's death. Now this girl, this apparently passionless girl, had found a voice, and was urging him on towards his fate.

'If you knew what misery to me may be involved in discovering the truth, Miss Talboys,' he said, 'you would scarcely ask me to pursue this business any further.'

'But I do ask you,' she answered, with suppressed passion – 'I do ask you. I ask you to avenge my brother's untimely death. Will you do so? Yes or no?'

'What if I answer no?'

'Then I will do it myself!' she exclaimed, looking at him with her bright brown eyes. 'I myself will follow up the clue to this mystery; I will find this woman – yes, though you refuse to tell me in what part of England my brother disappeared. I will travel from one end of the world to the other to find the secret of his fate, if you refuse to find it for me. I am of age; my own mistress; rich, for I have money left me by one of my aunts; I shall be able to employ those who will help me in my search, and I will make it to their interest to serve me well. Choose between the two alternatives, Mr. Audley. Shall you or I find my brother's murderer?'

He looked in her face, and saw that her resolution was the fruit of no transient womanish enthusiasm, which would give way under the iron hand of difficulty. Her beautiful features, naturally statuesque in their noble outlines, seemed transformed into marble by the rigidity of her expression. The face in which he looked was the face of a woman whom death only could turn from her purpose.

'I have grown up in an atmosphere of suppression,' she said, quietly; 'I have stifled and dwarfed the natural feelings of

224

my heart, until they have become unnatural in their intensity; I have been allowed neither friends nor lovers. My mother died when I was very young. My father has always been to me what you saw him to-day. I have had no one but my brother. All the love that my heart can hold has been centred upon him. Do you wonder, then, that when I hear that his young life has been ended by the hand of treachery, that I wish to see vengeance done upon the traitor? Oh, my God,' she cried, suddenly clasping her hands and looking up at the cold winter sky, 'lead me to the murderer of my brother, and let mine be the hand to avenge his untimely death!'

Robert Audley stood looking at her with awe-stricken admiration. Her beauty was elevated into sublimity by the intensity of her suppressed passion. She was different to all other women that he had ever seen. His cousin was pretty, his uncle's wife was lovely, but Clara Talboys was beautiful. Niobe's face, sublimated by sorrow, could scarcely have been more purely classical than hers. Even her dress, puritan in its grey simplicity, became her beauty better than a more beautiful dress would have become a less beautiful woman.

'Miss Talboys,' said Robert, after a pause, 'your brother shall not be unavenged. He shall not be forgotten. I do not think that any professional aid which you could procure would lead you as surely to the secret of this mystery as I can lead you, if you are patient and trust me.'

'I will trust you,' she answered, 'for I see that you will help me.'

'I believe that it is my destiny to do so,' he said, solemnly.

In the whole course of his conversation with Harcourt Talboys, Robert Audley had carefully avoided making any deductions from the circumstances which he had submitted to George's father. He had simply told the story of the missing man's life, from the hour of his arriving in London to that of his disappearance: but he saw that Clara Talboys had arrived at the same conclusion as himself, and that it was tacitly understood between them.

'Have you any letters of your brother's, Miss Talboys?' he asked.

'Two. One written soon after his marriage; the other written at Liverpool, the night before he sailed for Australia.'

'Will you let me see them?'

'Yes, I will send them to you, if you will give me your address. You will write to me from time to time, will you not? to tell me whether you are approaching the truth. I shall be obliged to act secretly here, but I am going to leave home in two or three months, and I shall be perfectly free then to act as I please.'

'You are not going to leave England?' Robert asked.

'Oh no! I am only going to pay a long-promised visit to some friends in Essex.'

Robert started so violently, as Clara Talboys said this, that she looked suddenly at his face. The agitation visible there betrayed a part of his secret.

'My brother George disappeared in Essex,' she said.

He could not contradict her.

'I am sorry you have discovered so much,' he replied. 'My position becomes every day more complicated, every day more painful. Good-by.'

She gave him her hand mechanically when he held out his, but it was colder than marble, and it lay listlessly in his own, and fell like a log at her side when he released it.

'Pray lose no time in returning to the house,' he said, earnestly. 'I fear you will suffer from this morning's work.'

'Suffer!' she exclaimed, scornfully. 'You talk to me of suffering, when the only creature in this world who ever loved me has been taken from it in the bloom of youth. What can there be for me henceforth but suffering? What is the cold to me?' she said, flinging back her shawl and baring her beautiful head to the bitter wind. 'I would walk from here to London barefoot through the snow, and never stop by the way, if I could bring him back to life. What would I not do to bring him back? What would I not do?'

The words broke from her in a wail of passionate sorrow; and clasping her hands before her face, she wept for the first time that day. The violence of her sobs shook her slender frame, and she was obliged to lean against the trunk of a tree for support.

Robert looked at her with a tender compassion in his face; she was so like the friend whom he had loved and lost, that it was impossible for him to think of her as a stranger; impossible to remember that they had met that morning for the first time.

'Pray, pray be calm,' he said; 'hope even against hope. We may both be deceived, your brother may still live.'

'Oh! if it were so,' she murmured, passionately; 'if it could be so.'

'Let us try and hope that it may be so.'

'No,' she answered, looking at him through her tears, 'let us hope for nothing but revenge. Good-by, Mr. Audley. Stop; your address.'

He gave her a card, which she put into the pocket of her dress.

'I will send you George's letters,' she said; 'they may help you. Good-by.'

She left him half-bewildered by the passionate energy of her manner, and the noble beauty of her face. He watched her as she disappeared amongst the straight trunks of the fir-trees, and then walked slowly out of the plantation.

'Heaven help those who stand between me and the secret,' he thought, 'for they will be sacrificed to the memory of George Talboys.'

CHAPTER VI
George's letters

Robert Audley did not return to Southampton, but took a ticket for the first up-train that left Wareham, and reached Waterloo Bridge an hour or two after dark. The snow, which had been hard and crisp in Dorsetshire, was a black and greasy slush in the Waterloo Road, thawed by the lamps of the gin-palaces and the flaring gas in the butchers' shops.

Robert Audley shrugged his shoulders as he looked at the dingy streets through which the Hansom carried him, the cabman choosing – with that delicious instinct which seems innate in the drivers of hackney vehicles – all those dark and hideous thoroughfares utterly unknown to the ordinary pedestrian.

'What a pleasant thing life is,' thought the barrister. 'What an unspeakable boon – what an overpowering blessing! Let any man make a calculation of his existence, substracting the hours in which he has been *thoroughly* happy – really and entirely at his ease, without one *arrière pensée* to mar his enjoyment – without the most infinitesimal cloud to over-shadow the brightness of his horizon. Let him do this, and surely he will laugh in utter bitterness of soul when he sets down the sum of his felicity, and discovers the pitiful smallness of the amount. He will have enjoyed himself for a week or ten days in thirty years perhaps. In thirty years of dull December, and blustering March, and showery April, and dark November weather, there may have been seven or eight glorious August days through which the sun has blazed in cloudless radiance, and the summer breezes have breathed perpetual balm. How fondly we recollect these solitary days of pleasure, and hope for their recurrence, and try to plan the circumstances that made them bright; and arrange, and predestinate, and diplomatise with fate for a renewal of the remembered joy. As if any joy could ever be built up out of such and such constituent parts! As if happiness were not essentially accidental – a bright and wandering bird, utterly irregular in its migration; with us one summer's day, and for ever gone from us on the next! Look at marriages, for instance,' mused Robert, who was as meditative in the jolting vehicle for whose occupation he was to pay sixpence a mile, as if he had been riding a mustang on the wide loneliness of the prairies. 'Look at marriages! Who is to say which shall be the one judicious selection out of the nine hundred and ninety-nine mistakes? Who shall decide from the first aspect of the slimy creature, which is to be the one eel out of the colossal bag of snakes? That girl on the kerbstone yonder, waiting to cross the street when my chariot shall have passed, may be the one woman out of every female creature in this vast universe who could make me a happy man. Yet I pass her by – bespatter her with the mud from my wheels, in my helpless ignorance, in my blind submission to the awful hand of fatality. If that girl, Clara Talboys, had been five minutes later, I should have left Dorsetshire, thinking her cold, hard, and unwomanly, and should have gone to my grave with that mistake part and parcel of my mind. I took her for a stately and heartless automaton; I know her now to be a noble and beautiful woman. What an incalculable difference this may make in my life! When I left that house, I went out into the winter day with the determination of abandoning all further thought of the secret of George's death. I see her, and she forces me onward upon the loathsome path – the crooked by-way of watchfulness and suspicion. How can I say to this sister of my dead friend, "I believe that your brother has been murdered! I believe that I know by whom, but I will take no step to set my doubts at rest, or to confirm my fears"? I cannot say this. This woman knows half my secret; she will soon possess herself of the rest, and then – and then—'

The cab stopped in the midst of Robert Audley's meditation, and he had to pay the cabman, and submit to all the dreary mechanism of life, which is the same whether we are glad or sorry – whether we are to be married or hung, elevated to the woolsack or disbarred by our brother benchers on some mysterious technical tangle of wrong-doing, which is a social enigma to those outside the Middle Temple.

We are apt to be angry with this cruel hardness in our life – this unflinching regularity in the smaller wheels and meaner mechanism of the human machine, which knows no stoppage or cessation, though the mainspring be for ever broken, and the hands pointing to purposeless figures upon a shattered dial.

Who has not felt, in the first madness of sorrow, an un-reasoning rage against the mute propriety of chairs and tables, the stiff squareness of Turkey carpets, the unbending obstinacy of the outward apparatus of existence? We want to root up gigantic trees in a primeval forest, and to tear their huge branches asunder in our convulsive grasp; and the utmost that we can do for the relief of our passion is to knock over an easy-chair, or smash a few shillings'-worth of Mr. Copeland's manufacture.

Mad-houses are large and only too numerous; yet surely it is strange they are not larger, when we think of how many helpless wretches must beat their brains against this hopeless persistency of the orderly outward world, as compared with the storm and tempest, the riot and confusion within: – when we remember how many minds must tremble upon the nar-row boundary between reason and unreason, mad to-day and sane to-morrow, mad yesterday and sane to-day.

Robert had directed the cabman to drop him at the corner of Chancery Lane, and he ascended the brilliantly-lighted staircase leading to the dining saloon of *The London*, and seated himself at one of the snug tables with a confused sense of emptiness and weariness, rather than any agreeable sensation of healthy hunger. He had come to the luxurious eating-house to dine, because it was absolutely necessary to eat something somewhere, and a great deal easier to get a very good dinner from Mr. Sawyer, than a very bad one from Mrs. Maloney, whose mind ran in one narrow channel of chops and steaks, only variable by small creeks and outlets in the way of 'briled sole' or 'biled mack'*rill*.' The solicitous waiter tried in vain to rouse poor Robert to a proper sense of the solemnity of the dinner question. He muttered something to the effect that the man might bring him anything he liked, and the friendly waiter, who knew Robert as a frequent guest at the little tables, went back to his master with a doleful face to say that Mr. Audley from Fig-tree Court was evidently out of spirits. Robert ate his dinner, and drank a pint of Moselle; but he had poor appreciation for the excellence of the viands or the delicate fragrance of the wine. The mental monologue still went on, and the young philosopher of the modern school was arguing the favourite modern question of the nothingness of everything and the folly of taking too much trouble to walk upon a road that led nowhere, or to compass a work that meant nothing.

'I accept the dominion of that pale girl, with the statuesque features and the calm brown eyes,' he thought. 'I recognise the power of a mind superior to my own, and I yield to it, and bow down to it. I've been acting for myself, and thinking for myself, for the last few months, and I'm tired of the unnatural business. I've been false to the leading principle of my life, and I've suffered for my folly. I found two grey hairs in my head the week before last, and an impertinent crow has planted a delicate impression of his foot under my right eye. Yes, I'm getting old upon the right side; and why – why should it be so?'

He pushed away his plate, and lifted his eyebrows, staring at the crumbs upon the glistening damask, as he pondered the question –

'What the devil am I doing in this *galère*?' he asked. 'But I am in it, and I can't get out of it; so I'd better submit myself to the brown-eyed girl, and do what she tells me, patiently and faithfully. What a wonderful solution to life's enigma there is in petticoat government! A man might lie in the sunshine and eat lotuses, and fancy it "always afternoon," if his wife would let him! But she won't, bless her impulsive heart and active mind! She knows better than that. Whoever heard of a woman taking life as it ought to be taken? Instead of supporting it as an unavoidable nuisance, only redeemable by its brevity, she goes through it as if it were a pageant or a procession. She dresses for it, and simpers, and grins, and gesticulates for it. She pushes her neighbours, and struggles for a good place in the dismal march; she elbows, and writhes, and tramples, and prances, to the one end of making the most of the misery. She gets up early and sits up late, and is loud, and restless, and noisy, and unpitying. She drags her husband on to the woolsack, or pushes him into Parliament. She drives him full butt at the dear, lazy machinery of government; and knocks and buffets him about the wheels, and cranks, and screws, and pulleys; until somebody, for quiet's sake, makes him something that she wanted him to be made. That's why incompetent men sometimes sit in high places, and interpose their poor muddled intellects between the things to be done and the people that can do them, making universal confusion in the helpless innocence of well-placed incapacity. The square men in the round holes are pushed into them by their wives. The Eastern potentate who declared that women were at the bottom of all mischief, should have gone a little further and seen why it is so. It is because women are *never lazy*. They don't know what it is to be quiet. They are Semiramides, and Cleopatras, and Joan of Arcs, Queen Elizabeths, and Catharine the Seconds, and they riot in battle, and murder, and clamour, and desperation. If they can't agitate the universe and play at ball with hemispheres, they'll make mountains of warfare and vexation out of domestic molehills; and social storms in household teacups. Forbid them to hold forth upon the freedom of nations and the wrongs of mankind, and they'll quarrel with Mrs. Jones about the shape of a mantle or the character of a small maid-servant. To call them the weaker sex is to utter a hideous mockery. They are the stronger sex, the noisier, the more persevering, the most self-assertive sex. They want freedom of opinion, variety of occupation, do they? Let them have it. Let them be lawyers, doctors, preachers, teachers, soldiers, legislators – anything they like – but let them be quiet – if they can.'

Mr. Audley pushed his hands through the thick luxuriance of his straight brown hair, and uplifted the dark mass in his despair.

'I hate women,' he thought savagely. 'They're bold, brazen, abominable creatures, invented for the annoyance and destruction of their superiors. Look at this business of poor George's! It's all woman's work from one end to the other. He marries a woman, and his father casts him off, penniless and professionless. He hears of the woman's death and he breaks his heart – his good, honest, manly heart, worth a million of the treacherous lumps of self-interest and mercenary calculation which beat in women's breasts. He goes to a woman's house and he is never seen alive again. And now I find myself driven into a corner by another woman, of whose existence I had never thought until this day. And – and then,' mused Mr. Audley, rather irreverently, 'there's Alicia, too; *she's* another nuisance. She'd like me to marry her, I know: and she'll make me do it, I dare say, before she's done with me. But I'd much rather not; though she is a dear, bouncing, generous thing, bless her poor little heart.'

Robert paid his bill and rewarded the waiter liberally. The young barrister was very willing to distribute his comfortable little income amongst the people who served him, for he carried his indifference to all things in the universe, even to the matter of pounds, shillings, and pence. Perhaps he was rather exceptional in this, as you may frequently find that the philosopher who calls life an empty delusion is pretty sharp in the investment of his moneys; and recognises the tangible nature of India Bonds, Spanish Certificates, and Egyptian Scrip – as contrasted with the painful uncertainty of an Ego or a non-Ego in metaphysics.

The snug rooms in Fig-tree Court seemed dreary in their orderly quiet to Robert Audley upon this particular evening. He had no inclination for his French novels, though there was a packet of uncut romances, comic and sentimental, ordered a month before, waiting his pleasure upon one of the tables. He took his favourite meerschaum and dropped into his favourite chair with a sigh.

'It's comfortable, but it seems so d—d lonely to-night. If poor George were sitting opposite to me, or – or even George's sister – she's very like him – existence might be a little more endurable. But when a fellow has lived by himself for eight or ten years he begins to be bad company.'

He burst out laughing presently, as he finished his first pipe.

'The idea of my thinking of George's sister,' he thought; 'what a preposterous idiot I am.'

The next day's post brought him a letter in a firm but feminine hand, which was strange to him. He found the little packet lying on his breakfast-table, beside the warm French roll wrapped in a napkin by Mrs. Maloney's careful but rather dirty hands. He contemplated the envelope for some minutes before opening it – not in any wonder as to his correspondent, for the letter bore the postmark of Grange Heath, and he knew that there was only one person who was likely to write to him from that obscure village; but in that lazy dreaminess which was a part of his character.

'From Clara Talboys,' he murmured slowly, as he looked critically at the clearly-shaped letters of his name and address. 'Yes, from Clara Talboys, most decidedly; I recognise a feminine resemblance to poor George's hand; neater than his, and more decided than his, but very like, very like.'

He turned the letter over and examined the seal, which bore his friend's familiar crest.

'I wonder what she says to me!' he thought. 'It's a long letter, I dare say; she's the kind of woman who would write a long letter – a letter that will urge me on, drive me forward, wrench me out of myself, I've no doubt. But that can't be helped – so here goes!'

He tore open the envelope with a sigh of resignation. It contained nothing but George's two letters, and a few words written on the flap:– 'I send the letters; please preserve and return them. – C. T.'

The letter written from Liverpool told nothing of the writer's life, except his sudden determination of starting for a new world, to redeem the fortunes that had been ruined in the old. The letter written almost immediately after George's marriage contained a full description of his wife – such a description as a man could only write within three weeks of a love-match – a description in which every feature was minutely catalogued, every grace of form or beauty of expression fondly dwelt upon, every charm of manner lovingly depicted.

Robert Audley read the letter three times before he laid it down.

'If George could have known for what purpose this description would serve when he wrote it,' thought the young barrister, 'surely his hand would have fallen paralysed by horror, and powerless to shape one syllable of these tender words.'

CHAPTER VII
Retrograde investigation

The dreary London January dragged its dull length slowly out. The last slender records of Christmas time were swept away, and Robert Audley still lingered in town – still spent his lonely evenings in his quiet sitting-room in Fig-tree Court – still wandered listlessly in the Temple Gardens on sunny mornings, absently listening to the children's babble, idly watching their play. He had many friends among the inhabitants of the quaint old buildings round him; he had other friends far away in pleasant country places, whose spare bed-rooms were always at Bob's service, whose cheerful firesides had snugly luxurious chairs specially allotted to him. But he seemed to have lost all taste for companionship, all sympathy with the pleasures and occupations of his class, since the disappearance of George Talboys. Elderly benchers indulged in facetious observations upon the young man's pale face and moody manner. They suggested the probability of some unhappy attachment, some feminine ill-usage as the secret cause of the change. They told him to be of good cheer, and invited him to supper-parties, at which 'lovely woman, with all her faults, God bless her,' was drunk by gentlemen who shed tears as they proposed the toast, and were maudlin and unhappy in their cups towards the close of the entertainment. Robert had no inclination for the wine-bibbing and the punch-making. The one idea of his life had become his master. He was the bonden slave of one gloomy thought – one horrible presentiment. A dark cloud was brooding over his uncle's house, and it was his hand which was to give the signal for the thunder-clap and the tempest that were to ruin that noble life.

'If she would only take warning and run away,' he said to himself sometimes. 'Heaven knows, I have given her a fair chance. Why doesn't she take it, and run away?'

He heard sometimes from Sir Michael, sometimes from Alicia. The young lady's letters rarely contained more than a few curt lines, informing him that her papa was well; and that Lady Audley was in very high spirits, amusing herself in her usual frivolous manner, and with her usual disregard for other people.

A letter from Mr. Marchmont, the Southampton school-master, informed Robert that little Georgey was going on very well, but that he was behind-hand in his education, and had not yet passed the intellectual Rubicon of words of two syllables. Captain Maldon had called to see his grandson, but that privilege had been withheld from him, in accordance with Mr. Audley's instructions. The old man had furthermore sent a parcel of pastry and sweetmeats to the little boy, which had also been rejected on the ground of indigestible and bilious tendencies in the edibles.

Towards the close of February, Robert received a letter from his cousin Alicia which hurried him one step further forward towards his destiny, by causing him to return to the house from which he had been in a manner exiled at the instigation of his uncle's wife.

'Papa is very ill,' Alicia wrote; 'not dangerously ill, thank God; but confined to his room by an attack of low fever which has succeeded a violent cold. Come and see him, Robert, if you have any regard for your nearest relations. He has spoken about you several times; and I know he will be glad to have you with him. Come at once, but say nothing about this letter.

'From your affectionate cousin,
'ALICIA.'

A sick and deadly terror chilled Robert Audley's heart as he read this letter – a vague yet hideous fear, which he dared not shape into any definite form.

'Have I done right?' he thought, in the first agony of this new horror – 'have I done right to tamper with justice; and to keep the secret of my doubts, in the hope that I was shielding those I love from sorrow and disgrace? What shall I do if I find him ill; very ill; dying perhaps; dying upon *her* breast? What shall I do?'

One course was clear before him; and the first step of that course, a rapid journey to Audley Court. He packed his portmanteau; jumped into a cab; and reached the railway-station within an hour of his receipt of Alicia's letter, which had come by the afternoon post.

The dim village lights flickered faintly through the growing dusk when Robert reached Audley. He left his portmanteau with the station-master, and walked at a leisurely pace through the quiet lanes that led away to the still loneliness of the Court. The over-arching trees stretched their leafless branches above his head, bare and weird in the dusky light. A low moaning wind swept across the flat meadow-land, and tossed those rugged branches hither and thither against the dark grey sky. They looked like the ghostly arms of shrunken and withered giants beckoning Robert to his uncle's house. They looked like threatening phantoms in the chill winter twilight, gesticulating to him to hasten upon his journey. The long avenue, so bright and pleasant when the perfumed limes scattered their light bloom upon the pathway, and the dog-rose leaves floated on the summer air, was terribly bleak and desolate in the cheerless interregnum that divides the homely joys of Christmas from the pale blush of coming spring – a dead pause in the year, in which Nature seems to lie in a tranced sleep, awaiting the wondrous signal for the budding of the tree, and the bursting of the flower.

A mournful presentiment crept into Robert Audley's heart as he drew nearer to his uncle's house. Every changing outline in the landscape was familiar to him; every bend of the trees; every caprice of the untrammelled branches; every undulation in the bare hawthorn hedge, broken by dwarf horse-chestnuts, stunted willows, blackberry and hazel bushes.

Sir Michael had been a second father to the young man, a generous and noble friend, a grave and earnest adviser; and perhaps the strongest sentiment of Robert's heart was his love for the grey-bearded baronet. But the grateful affection was so much a part of himself, that it seldom found an outlet in words; and a stranger would never have fathomed the strength of feeling which lay, a deep and powerful current, beneath the stagnant surface of the barrister's character.

'What would become of this place if my uncle were to die?' he thought, as he drew nearer to the ivied archway, and the still waterpools, coldly grey in the twilight. 'Would other people live in the old house, and sit under the low oak ceilings in the homely familiar rooms?'

That wonderful faculty of association, so interwoven with the inmost fibres of even the hardest nature, filled the young man's breast with a prophetic pain as he remembered that, however long or late, the day must come on which the oaken shutters would be closed for awhile, and the sunshine shut out of the house he loved. It was painful to him even to remember this; as it must always be painful to think of the narrow lease which the greatest upon this earth can ever hold of its grandeurs. Is it so wonderful that some wayfarers drop asleep under the hedges; scarcely caring to toil onward on a journey that leads to no abiding habitation? Is it wonderful that there have been quietists in the world ever since Christ's religion was first preached upon earth? Is it strange that there is patient endurance and tranquil resignation, calm expectation of that which is to come on the further shore of the dark-flowing river? Is it not rather to be wondered that anybody should ever care to be great for greatness' sake; for any other reason than pure conscientiousness; the simple fidelity of the servant who fears to lay his talent by in a napkin, knowing that indifference is near akin to dishonesty? If Robert Audley had lived in the time of Thomas à Kempis, he would very likely have built himself a narrow hermitage amid some forest loneliness, and spent his life in tranquil imitation of the reputed author of *The Imitation*. As it was, Fig-tree Court was a pleasant hermitage in its way, and for breviaries and Books of Hours, I am ashamed to say the young barrister substituted Paul de Kock and Dumas *fils*. But his sins were of so simply negative an order, that it would have been very easy for him to have abandoned them for negative virtues.

Only one solitary light was visible in the long irregular range of windows facing the archway, as Robert passed under the gloomy shade of the rustling ivy, restless in the chill moaning of the wind. He recognised that lighted window as the large oriel in his uncle's room. When last he had looked at the old house it had been gay with visitors, every window glittering like a low star in the dusk; now, dark and silent, it faced the winter's night like some dismal baronial habitation, deep in a woodland solitude.

The man who opened the door to the unlooked-for visitor brightened as he recognised his master's nephew.

'Sir Michael will be cheered up a bit, sir, by the sight of you,' he said, as he ushered Robert Audley into the fire-lit library, which seemed desolate by reason of the baronet's easy-chair standing empty on the broad hearth-rug. 'Shall I bring you some dinner here, Sir, before you go upstairs?' the servant asked. 'My lady and Miss Audley have dined early during my master's illness, but I can bring you anything you would please to take, Sir.'

'I'll take nothing until I have seen my uncle,' Robert

answered, hurriedly; 'that is to say, if I can see him at once. He is not too ill to receive me, I suppose?' he added, anxiously.

'Oh, no, sir – not too ill; only a little low, sir. This way, if you please.'

He conducted Robert up the short flight of shallow oaken stairs to the octagon chamber in which George Talboys had sat so long five months before, staring absently at my lady's portrait. The picture was finished now, and hung in the post of honour opposite the window, amidst Claudes, Poussins, and Wouvermans, whose less brilliant hues were killed by the vivid colouring of the modern artist. The bright face looked out of that tangled glitter of golden hair, in which the pre-Raphaelites delight, with a mocking smile, as Robert paused for a moment to glance at the well-remembered picture. Two or three moments afterwards he had passed through my lady's boudoir and dressing-room, and stood upon the threshold of Sir Michael's room. The baronet lay in a quiet sleep, his arm lying outside the bed, and his strong hand clasped in his young wife's delicate fingers. Alicia sat in a low chair beside the broad open hearth, on which the huge logs burned fiercely in the frosty atmosphere. The interior of this luxurious bed-chamber might have made a striking picture for an artist's pencil. The massive furniture, dark and sombre, yet broken up and relieved here and there by scraps of gilding, and masses of glowing colour; the elegance of every detail, in which wealth was subservient to purity of taste; and last, but greatest in importance, the graceful figures of the two women and the noble form of the old man would have formed a worthy study for any painter.

Lucy Audley, with her disordered hair in a pale haze of yellow gold about her thoughtful face, the flowing lines of her soft muslin dressing-gown falling in straight folds to her feet, and clasped at the waist by a narrow circlet of agate links, might have served as a model for a mediæval saint, in one of the tiny chapels hidden away in the nooks and corners of a grey old cathedral, unchanged by Reformation or Cromwell; and what saintly martyr of the Middle Ages could have borne a holier aspect than the man whose grey beard lay upon the dark silken coverlet of the stately bed?

Robert paused upon the threshold, fearful of awaking his uncle. The two ladies had heard his step, cautious though he had been, and lifted their heads to look at him. My lady's face, quietly watching the sick man, had worn an anxious earnestness which made it only more beautiful; but the same face, recognising Robert Audley, faded from its delicate brightness, and looked scared and wan in the lamplight.

'Mr. Audley!' she cried, in a faint tremulous voice.

'Hush!' whispered Alicia, with a warning gesture; 'you will wake papa. How good of you to come, Robert,' she added, in the same whispered tones, beckoning to her cousin to take an empty chair near the bed.

The young man seated himself in the indicated seat at the bottom of the bed, and opposite to my lady, who sat close beside the pillows. He looked long and earnestly at the face of the sleeper; still longer, still more earnestly at the face of Lady Audley, which was slowly recovering its natural hues.

'He has not been very ill, has he?' Robert asked, in the same key as that in which Alicia had spoken.

My lady answered the question.

'Oh, no, not dangerously ill,' she said, without taking her eyes from her husband's face; 'but still we have been anxious, very, very anxious.'

Robert never relaxed his scrutiny of that pale face.

'She shall look at me,' he thought; 'I will make her meet my eyes, and I will read her as I have read her before. She shall know how useless her artifices are with me.'

He paused for a few minutes before he spoke again. The regular breathing of the sleeper, the ticking of a gold hunting-watch suspended at the head of the bed, and the crackling of the burning logs, were the only sounds that broke the stillness.

'I have no doubt you have been anxious, Lady Audley,' Robert said, after a pause, fixing my lady's eyes as they wandered furtively to his face. 'There is no one to whom my uncle's life can be of more value than to you. Your happiness, your prosperity, your *safety* depend alike upon his existence.'

The whisper in which he uttered these words was too low to reach the other side of the room where Alicia sat.

Lucy Audley's eyes met those of the speaker with some gleam of triumph in their light.

'I know that,' she said. 'Those who strike me must strike through him.'

She pointed to the sleeper as she spoke, still looking at Robert Audley. She defied him with her blue eyes, their brightness intensified by the triumph in their glance. She defied him with her quiet smile – a smile of fatal beauty, full of lurking significance and mysterious meaning – the smile which the artist had exaggerated in his portrait of Sir Michael's wife.

Robert turned away from the lovely face, and shaded his eyes with his hand; putting a barrier between my lady and himself; a screen which baffled her penetration and provoked her curiosity. Was he still watching her, or was he thinking? and of what was he thinking?

Robert Audley had been seated at the bedside for upwards of an hour before his uncle woke. The baronet was delighted at his nephew's coming.

'It was very good of you to come to me, Bob,' he said. 'I have been thinking of you a good deal since I've been ill. You and Lucy must be good friends, you know, Bob; and you must learn to think of her as your aunt, Sir; though she is young and beautiful; and – and – and – you understand, eh?'

Robert grasped his uncle's hand, but he looked down gravely as he answered –

'I do understand you, Sir,' he said quietly; 'and I give

you my word of honour that I am steeled against my lady's fascinations. She knows that as well as I do.'

Lucy Audley made a little grimace with her pretty lips.

'Bah, you silly Robert,' she exclaimed; 'you take everything *au sérieux*. If I thought you were rather too young for a nephew, it was only in my fear of other people's foolish gossip; not from any—'

She hesitated for a moment, and escaped any conclusion to her sentence by the timely intervention of Mr. Dawson, her late employer, who entered the room upon his evening visit while she was speaking.

He felt the patient's pulse; asked two or three questions; pronounced the baronet to be steadily improving; exchanged a few common-place remarks with Alicia and Lady Audley; and prepared to leave the room. Robert rose and accompanied him to the door.

'I will light you to the staircase,' he said, taking a candle from one of the tables, and lighting it at the lamp.

'No, no, Mr. Audley, pray do not trouble yourself,' expostulated the surgeon; 'I know my way very well indeed.'

Robert insisted; and the two men left the room together. As they entered the octagon ante-chamber, the barrister paused and shut the door behind him.

'Will you see that the other door is closed, Mr. Dawson?' he said, pointing to that which opened upon the staircase. 'I wish to have a few moments' private conversation with you.'

'With much pleasure,' replied the surgeon, complying with Robert's request; 'but if you are at all alarmed about your uncle, Mr. Audley, I can set your mind at rest. There is no occasion for the least uneasiness. Had his illness been at all serious, I should have telegraphed immediately for the family physician.'

'I am sure that you would have done your duty, Sir,' answered Robert, gravely. 'But I am not going to speak of my

245

uncle. I wish to ask you two or three questions about another person.'

'Indeed.'

'The person who once lived in your family as Miss Lucy Graham; the person who is now Lady Audley.'

Mr. Dawson looked up with an expression of surprise upon his quiet face.

'Pardon me, Mr. Audley,' he answered; 'you can scarcely expect me to answer any questions about your uncle's wife, without Sir Michael's express permission. I can understand no motive which can prompt you to ask such questions – no worthy motive, at least.' He looked severely at the young man, as much as to say, 'You have been falling in love with your uncle's pretty wife, Sir, and you want to make me a go-between in some treacherous flirtation; but it won't do, Sir; it won't do.'

'I always respected the lady as Miss Graham, Sir,' he said, 'and I esteem her doubly as Lady Audley – not on account of her altered position, but because she is the wife of one of the noblest men in Christendom.'

'You cannot respect my uncle or my uncle's honour more sincerely than I do,' answered Robert. 'I have no unworthy motive for the questions I am about to ask; and you *must* answer them.'

'*Must!*' echoed Mr. Dawson, indignantly.

'Yes; you are my uncle's friend. It was at your house he met the woman who is now his wife. She called herself an orphan, I believe, and enlisted his pity as well as his admiration in her behalf. She told him that she stood alone in the world, did she not? – without friends or relatives. That was all I could ever learn of her antecedents.'

'What reason have you to wish to know more?' asked the surgeon.

'A very terrible reason,' answered Robert Audley. 'For some

months past I have struggled with doubts and suspicions which have embittered my life. They have grown stronger every day; and they will not be set at rest by the common-place sophistries and the shallow arguments with which men try to deceive themselves, rather than believe that which of all things upon earth they most fear to believe. I do not think that the woman who bears my uncle's name is worthy to be his wife. I may wrong her. Heaven grant that it is so. But if I do, the fatal chain of circumstantial evidence never yet linked itself so closely about an innocent person. I wish to set my doubts at rest, or – or to confirm my fears. There is but one manner in which I can do this. I must trace the life of my uncle's wife backwards, minutely and carefully, from this night to a period of six years ago. This is the twenty-fourth of February, fifty-nine. I want to know every record of her life between to-night and the February of the year fifty-three.'

'And your motive is a worthy one?'

'Yes, I wish to clear her from a very dreadful suspicion.'

'Which exists only in your mind?'

'And in the mind of one other person.'

'May I ask who that person is?'

'No, Mr. Dawson,' answered Robert, decisively; 'I cannot reveal anything more than what I have already told you. I am a very irresolute, vacillating man in most things. In this matter I am compelled to be decided. I repeat once more that I *must* know the history of Lucy Graham's life. If you refuse to help me to the small extent in your power, I will find others who will help me. Painful as it would be to me, I will ask my uncle for the information which you would withhold, rather than be baffled in the first step of my investigation.'

Mr. Dawson was silent for some minutes.

'I cannot express how much you have astonished and alarmed me, Mr. Audley,' he said. 'I can tell you so little about Lady Audley's antecedents, that it would be mere obstinacy to withhold the small amount of information I possess. I have always considered your uncle's wife one of the most amiable of women. I *cannot* bring myself to think her otherwise. It would be an uprooting of one of the strongest convictions of my life, were I compelled to think her otherwise. You wish to follow her life backwards from the present hour to the year fifty-three?'

'I do.'

'She was married to your uncle last June twelvemonth, in the midsummer of fifty-seven. She had lived in my house a little more than thirteen months. She became a member of my household upon the fourteenth of May, in the year fifty-six.'

'And she came to you—?'

'From a school at Brompton; a school kept by a lady of the name of Vincent. It was Mrs. Vincent's strong recommendation that induced me to receive Miss Graham into my family without any more especial knowledge of her antecedents.'

'Did you see this Mrs. Vincent?'

'I did not. I advertised for a governess, and Miss Graham answered my advertisement. In her letter she referred me to Mrs. Vincent, the proprietress of a school in which she was then residing as junior teacher. My time is always so fully occupied, that I was glad to escape the necessity of a day's loss in going from Audley to London to inquire about the young lady's qualifications. I looked for Mrs. Vincent's name in the *Directory*, found it, concluded that she was a responsible person, and wrote to her. Her reply was perfectly satisfactory: – Miss Lucy Graham was assiduous and conscientious; as well as fully qualified for the situation I offered. I accepted this reference, and I had no cause to regret what may have been an indiscretion. And now, Mr. Audley, I have told you all that I have the power to tell.'

'Will you be so kind as to give me the address of this Mrs. Vincent?' asked Robert, taking out his pocket-book.

'Certainly. She was then living at No. 9, Crescent Villas, Brompton.'

'Ah, to be sure,' muttered Mr. Audley, a recollection of last September flashing suddenly back upon him as the surgeon spoke. 'Crescent Villas – yes, I have heard the address before, from Lady Audley herself. This Mrs. Vincent telegraphed to my uncle's wife early in last September. She was ill – dying, I believe – and sent for my lady; but had removed from her old house and was not to be found.'

'Indeed! I never heard Lady Audley mention the circumstance.'

'Perhaps not. It occurred while I was down here. Thank you, Mr. Dawson, for the information which you have so kindly and honestly given me. It takes me back two and a half years in the history of my lady's life; but I have still a blank of three years to fill up, before I can exonerate her from my terrible suspicion. Good evening.'

Robert shook hands with the surgeon and returned to his uncle's room. He had been away about a quarter of an hour. Sir Michael had fallen asleep once more, and my lady's loving hands had lowered the heavy curtains and shaded the lamp by the bedside. Alicia and her father's wife were taking tea in Lady Audley's boudoir, the room next to the ante-chamber in which Robert and Mr. Dawson had been seated.

Lucy Audley looked up from her occupation amongst the fragile china cups, and watched Robert rather anxiously, as he walked softly to his uncle's room, and back again to the boudoir. She looked very pretty and innocent, seated behind the graceful group of delicate opal china and glittering silver. Surely a pretty woman never looks prettier than when making tea. The most feminine and most domestic of all occupations imparts a magic harmony to her every movement, a witchery to her every glance. The floating mists from the boiling liquid in which she infuses the soothing herbs, whose secrets are known to her alone, envelop her in a cloud of scented vapour, through which she seems a social fairy, weaving potent spells with Gunpowder and Bohea. At the tea-table she reigns omnipotent, unapproachable. What do men know of the mysterious beverage? Read how poor Hazlitt made his tea, and shudder at the dreadful barbarism. How clumsily the wretched creatures attempt to assist the witch president of the tea-tray; how hopelessly they hold the kettle, how continually they imperil the frail cups and saucers, or the taper hands of the priestess. To do away with the tea-table is to rob woman of her legitimate empire. To send a couple of hulking men about amongst your visitors, distributing a mixture made in the housekeeper's room, is to reduce the most social and friendly of ceremonies to a formal giving out of rations. Better the pretty influence of the teacups and saucers gracefully wielded in a woman's hand, than all the inappropriate power snatched at the point of the pen from the unwilling sterner sex. Imagine all the women of England elevated to the high level of masculine intellectuality; superior to crinoline; above pearl powder and Mrs. Rachael Levison; above taking the pains to be pretty; above making themselves agreeable; above tea-tables, and that cruelly scandalous and rather satirical gossip which even strong men delight in; and what a dreary, utilitarian, ugly life the sterner sex must lead.

My lady was by no means strong-minded. The starry diamond upon her white fingers flashed hither and thither amongst the tea-things, and she bent her pretty head over the marvellous Indian tea-caddy of sandal-wood and silver, with as much earnestness as if life held no higher purpose than the infusion of Bohea.

'You'll take a cup of tea with us, Mr. Audley?' she asked, pausing with the teapot in her hand to look up at Robert, who was standing near the door.

'If you please.'

'But you have not dined, perhaps? Shall I ring and tell them to bring you something a little more substantial than biscuits and transparent bread-and-butter?'

'No, thank you, Lady Audley. I took some lunch before I left town. I'll trouble you for nothing but a cup of tea.'

He seated himself at the little table and looked across it at his cousin Alicia, who sat with a book in her lap, and had the air of being very much absorbed by its pages. The bright brunette complexion had lost its glowing crimson, and the animation of the young lady's manner was suppressed – on account of her father's illness, no doubt, Robert thought.

'Alicia, my dear,' the barrister said, after a very leisurely contemplation of his cousin, 'you're not looking well.'

Miss Audley shrugged her shoulders, but did not condescend to lift her eyes from her book.

'Perhaps not,' she answered, contemptuously. 'What does it matter? I'm growing a philosopher of your school, Robert Audley. What does it matter? Who cares whether I am well or ill?'

'What a spitfire she is,' thought the barrister. He always knew his cousin was angry with him when she addressed him as 'Robert Audley.'

'You needn't pitch into a fellow because he asks you a civil question, Alicia,' he said, reproachfully. 'As to nobody caring about your health, that's nonsense. *I* care.' Miss Audley looked up with a bright smile. 'Sir Harry Towers cares.' Miss Audley returned to her book with a frown.

'What are you reading there, Alicia?' Robert asked, after a pause, during which he had sat thoughtfully stirring his tea.

'*Changes and Chances.*'

'A novel?'

'Yes.'

'Who is it by?'

'The author of *Follies and Faults*,' answered Alicia, still pursuing her study of the romance upon her lap.

'Is it interesting?'

Miss Audley pursed up her mouth, and shrugged her shoulders.

'Not particularly,' she said.

'Then I think you might have better manners than to read it while your first cousin is sitting opposite you,' observed Mr. Audley, with some gravity, 'especially as he has only come to pay you a flying visit, and will be off to-morrow morning.'

'To-morrow morning!' exclaimed my lady, looking up suddenly.

Though the look of joy upon Lady Audley's face was as brief as a flash of lightning on a summer sky, it was not unperceived by Robert.

'Yes,' he said, 'I shall be obliged to run up to London to-morrow on business, but I shall return the next day, if you will allow me, Lady Audley, and stay here till my uncle recovers.'

'But you are not seriously alarmed about him, are you?' asked my lady, anxiously. 'You do not think him very ill?'

'No,' answered Robert. 'Thank Heaven, I think there is not the slightest cause for apprehension.'

My lady sat silent for a few moments, looking at the empty teacups with a prettily thoughtful face – a face grave with the innocent seriousness of a musing child.

'But you were closeted such a long time with Mr. Dawson just now,' she said, after this brief pause – 'I was quite alarmed at the length of your conversation. Were you talking of Sir Michael all the time?'

'No; not all the time.'

My lady looked down at the teacups once more.

'Why, what could you find to say to Mr. Dawson, or he to say to you?' she asked, after another pause. 'You are almost strangers to each other.'

'Suppose Mr. Dawson wished to consult me about some law business.'

'Was it that?' cried Lady Audley, eagerly.

'It would be rather unprofessional to tell you if it were so, my lady,' answered Robert, gravely.

My lady bit her lip, and relapsed into silence. Alicia threw down her book, and watched her cousin's pre-occupied face. He talked to her now and then for a few minutes, but it was evidently an effort to him to arouse himself from his reverie.

'Upon my word, Robert Audley, you are a very agreeable companion,' exclaimed Alicia at length, her rather limited stock of patience quite exhausted by two or three of these abortive attempts at conversation. 'Perhaps the next time you come to the Court, you will be good enough to bring your *mind* with you. By your present inanimate appearance, I should imagine that you had left your intellect, such as it is, somewhere in the Temple. You were never one of the liveliest of people, but latterly you have really grown almost unendurable. I suppose you are in love, Mr. Audley, and are thinking of the honoured object of your affections.'

He was thinking of Clara Talboys' uplifted face, sublime in its unutterable grief; of her impassioned words, still ringing in his ears as clearly as when they were first spoken. Again he saw her looking at him with her bright brown eyes. Again he heard that solemn question, 'Shall you or I find my brother's murderer?' And he was in Essex; in the little village from which he firmly believed George Talboys had never departed. He was on the spot at which all record of his friend's life ended as suddenly as a story ends when the reader shuts the book. And could he withdraw now from the investigation in which he found himself involved? Could he stop now? For any consideration? No; a thousand times no! Not with the image of that grief-stricken face imprinted on his mind. Not with the accents of that earnest appeal ringing on his ear.

CHAPTER VIII
So far and no farther

Robert left Audley the next morning by an early train, and reached Shoreditch a little after nine o'clock. He did not return to his chambers, but called a cab and drove straight to Crescent Villas, West Brompton. He knew that he should fail in finding the lady he went to seek at this address, as his uncle had failed a few months before, but he thought it possible to obtain some clue to the schoolmistress's new residence, in spite of Sir Michael's ill success.

'Mrs. Vincent was in a dying state, according to the telegraphic message,' Robert thought. 'If I do find her, I shall at least succeed in discovering whether that message was genuine.'

He found Crescent Villas after some difficulty. The houses were large, but they lay half embedded amongst the chaos of brick and mortar rising around them. New terraces, new streets, new squares led away into hopeless masses of stone and plaster on every side. The roads were sticky with damp clay, which clogged the wheels of the cab and buried the fetlocks of the horse. The desolation of desolations – that awful aspect of incompleteness and discomfort which pervades a new and unfinished neighbourhood – had set its dismal seal upon the surrounding streets which had arisen about and entrenched Crescent Villas; and Robert wasted forty minutes by his own watch, and an hour and a quarter according to the cabman's reckoning, in driving up and down uninhabited streets and terraces, trying to find the Villas: whose chimney-pots were frowning down upon him, black and venerable, amid groves of virgin plaster, undimmed by time or smoke.

But having at last succeeded in reaching his destination, Mr. Audley alighted from the cab, directed the driver to wait for him at a certain corner, and set out upon his voyage of discovery.

'If I were a distinguished Q. C., I could not do this sort of thing,' he thought; 'my time would be worth a guinea or so a minute, and I should be retained in the great case of Hoggs v. Boggs, going forward this very day before a special jury at Westminster Hall. As it is, I can afford to be patient.'

He inquired for Mrs. Vincent at the number which Mr. Dawson had given him. The maid who opened the door had never heard that lady's name: but after going to inquire of her mistress, she returned to tell Robert that Mrs. Vincent had lived there, but that she had left two months before the present occupants had entered the house, 'and missus has been here fifteen months,' the girl added, explanatorily.

'But you cannot tell me where she went on leaving here?' Robert asked, despondingly.

'No, Sir; missus says she believes the lady failed, and that she left sudden like, and didn't want her address to be known in the neighbourhood.'

Mr. Audley felt himself at a standstill once more. If Mrs. Vincent had left the place in debt, she had no doubt scrupulously concealed her whereabouts. There was little hope, then, of learning her address from any of the tradespeople; and yet, on the other hand, it was just possible that some of her sharpest creditors might have made it their business to discover the defaulter's retreat.

He looked about him for the nearest shops, and found a baker's, a stationer's, and a fruiterer's, a few paces from the crescent. Three empty-looking, pretentious shops, with plate-glass windows, and a hopeless air of gentility.

He stopped at the baker's, who called himself a pastrycook and confectioner, and exhibited some specimens of petrified sponge-cake in glass bottles, and some highly-glazed tarts, covered with green gauze.

'She *must* have bought bread,' Robert thought, as he deliberated before the baker's shop; 'and she is likely to have bought it at the handiest place. I'll try the baker.'

The baker was standing behind his counter, disputing the items of a bill with a shabby-genteel young woman. He did not trouble himself to attend to Robert Audley till he had settled the dispute, but he looked up as he was receipting the bill, and asked the barrister what he pleased to want.

'Can you tell me the address of a Mrs. Vincent, who lived at No. 9, Crescent Villas, a year and a half ago?' Mr. Audley inquired, mildly.

'No, I can't,' answered the baker, growing very red in the face, and speaking in an unnecessarily loud voice; 'and what's more, I wish I could. That lady owes me upwards of eleven pound for bread, and it's rather more than I can afford to lose. If anybody can tell me where she lives, I shall be much obliged to 'em for so doing.'

Robert Audley shrugged his shoulders, and wished the man good morning. He felt that his discovery of the lady's whereabouts would involve more trouble than he had expected. He might have looked for Mrs. Vincent's name in the *Post Office Directory*, but he thought it scarcely likely that a lady who was on such uncomfortable terms with her creditors would afford them so easy a means of ascertaining her residence.

'If the baker can't find her, how should *I* find her?' he thought, despairingly. 'If a resolute, sanguine, active, and energetic creature, such as the baker, fail to achieve this business, how can a lymphatic wretch like me hope to accomplish it? Where the baker has been defeated, what preposterous folly it would be for me to try to succeed.'

Mr. Audley abandoned himself to these gloomy reflections as he walked slowly back towards the corner at which he had left the cab. About half-way between the baker's shop and this corner, he was arrested by hearing a woman's step close at his side, and a woman's voice asking him to stop. He turned and found himself face to face with the shabbily-dressed woman whom he had left settling her account with the baker.

'Eh, what?' he asked, vaguely. 'Can I do anything for you, ma'am? Does Mrs. Vincent owe *you* money, too?'

'Yes, Sir,' the woman answered, with a semi-genteel manner which corresponded with the shabby gentility of her dress; 'Mrs. Vincent is in my debt; but it isn't that, Sir. I – I want to know, please, what your business may be with her – because – because—'

'You can give me her address if you choose, ma'am? That's what you mean to say, isn't it?'

The woman hesitated a little, looking rather suspiciously at Robert.

'You're not connected with – with the tally business, are you, Sir?' she asked, after considering Mr. Audley's personal appearance for a few moments.

'The *what*, ma'am?' cried the young barrister, staring aghast at his questioner.

'I'm sure I beg your pardon, Sir,' exclaimed the little woman, seeing that she had made some very awful mistake. 'I thought you might have been, you know. Some of the gentlemen who collect for the tally-shops do dress so very handsome, and I know Mrs. Vincent owes a good deal of money.'

Robert Audley laid his hand upon the speaker's arm.

'My dear madam,' he said, 'I want to know nothing of Mrs. Vincent's affairs. So far from being concerned in what you call *the tally business*, I have not the remotest idea of what you mean by that expression. You may mean a political conspiracy; you may mean some new species of taxes. Mrs. Vincent does not owe *me* any money, however badly she may stand with that awful-looking baker. I never saw her in my life; but I wish to see her to-day for the simple purpose of asking her a few very plain questions about a young lady who once resided in her house. If you know where Mrs. Vincent lives, and will give me her address, you will be doing me a great favour.'

He took out his card-case and handed a card to the woman, who examined the slip of pasteboard anxiously before she spoke again.

'I'm sure you look and speak like a gentleman, Sir,' she said, after a brief pause, 'and I hope you will excuse me if I've seemed mistrustful like; but poor Mrs. Vincent has had dreadful difficulties, and I'm the only person hereabouts that she's trusted with her addresses. I'm a dressmaker, Sir, and I've worked for her for upwards of six years, and though she doesn't pay me regular, you know, Sir, she gives me a little money on account now and then, and I get on as well as I can. I may tell you where she lives, then, Sir? You haven't deceived me, have you?'

'On my honour, no.'

'Well, then, Sir,' said the dressmaker, dropping her voice as if she thought the pavement beneath her feet, or the iron railings before the houses by her side, might have ears to hear her, 'it's Acacia Cottage, Peckham Grove. I took a dress there yesterday for Mrs. Vincent.'

'Thank you,' said Robert, writing the address in his pocket-book. 'I am very much obliged to you, and you may rely upon it, Mrs. Vincent shall not suffer any inconvenience through me.'

He lifted his hat, bowed to the little dressmaker, and turned back to the cab.

'I have beaten the baker at any rate,' he thought. 'Now for the second stage, travelling backwards, in my lady's life.'

The drive from Brompton to the Peckham Road was a very long one, and between Crescent Villas and Acacia Cottage

Robert Audley had ample leisure for reflection. He thought of his uncle, lying weak and ill in the oak-room at Audley Court. He thought of the beautiful blue eyes watching Sir Michael's slumbers; the soft white hands, tending on his waking wants; the low, musical voice soothing his loneliness; cheering and consoling his declining years. What a pleasant picture it might have been, had he been able to look upon it ignorantly, seeing no more than others saw, looking no farther than a stranger could look. But with the black cloud which he saw, or fancied he saw, brooding over it, what an arch mockery, what a diabolical delusion it seemed!

Peckham Grove – pleasant enough in the summer-time – has rather a dismal aspect upon a dull February day, when the trees are bare and leafless, and the little gardens desolate. Acacia Cottage bore small token of the fitness of its nomenclature, and faced the road with its stuccoed walls, sheltered only by a couple of tall attenuated poplars. But it announced that it was Acacia Cottage by means of a small brass-plate upon one of the gate-posts, which was sufficient indication for the sharp-sighted cabman, who dropped Mr. Audley upon the pavement before the little gate.

Acacia Cottage was much lower in the social scale than Crescent Villas, and the small maid-servant who came to the low wooden gate and parleyed with Mr. Audley, was evidently well used to the encounter of relentless creditors across the same feeble barricade.

She murmured the familiar domestic fiction of uncertainty regarding her mistress's whereabouts; and told Robert that if he would please to state his name and business, she would go and see if Mrs. Vincent was at home.

Mr. Audley produced a card, and wrote in pencil under his own name – 'A connection of the late Miss Graham.'

He directed the small servant to carry this card to her mistress, and quietly awaited the result.

The servant returned in about five minutes with the key of the gate. Her mistress was at home, she told Robert as she admitted him, and would be happy to see the gentleman.

The square parlour into which Robert was ushered bore in every scrap of ornament, in every article of furniture, the unmistakeable stamp of that species of poverty which is most comfortless, because it is never stationary. The mechanic who furnishes his tiny sitting-room with half-a-dozen cane chairs, a Pembroke table, a Dutch clock, a tiny looking-glass, a crockery shepherd and shepherdess, and a set of gaudily-japanned iron tea-trays, makes the most of his limited possessions, and generally contrives to get some degree of comfort out of them; but the lady who loses the handsome furniture of the house she is compelled to abandon and encamps in some smaller habitation with the shabby remainder – bought in by some merciful friend at the sale of her effects – carries with her an aspect of genteel desolation and tawdry misery not easily to be paralleled in wretchedness by any other phase which poverty can assume.

The room which Robert Audley surveyed was furnished with the shabbier scraps snatched from the ruin which had overtaken the imprudent schoolmistress in Crescent Villas. A cottage piano; a chiffonier, six sizes too large for the room, and dismally gorgeous in gilded mouldings that were chipped and broken; and a slim-legged card-table, placed in the post of honour, formed the principal pieces of furniture. A threadbare patch of Brussels carpet covered the centre of the room, and formed an oasis of roses and lilies upon a desert of faded green drugget. Knitted curtains shaded the windows, in which hung wire baskets of horrible-looking plants of the cactus species, that grew downwards like some demented class of vegetation, whose prickly and spider-like members had a fancy for standing on their heads.

The green-baize-covered card-table was adorned with

gaudily-bound annuals or books of beauty, placed at right angles; but Robert Audley did not avail himself of these literary distractions. He seated himself upon one of the rickety chairs, and waited patiently for the advent of the schoolmistress. He could hear the hum of half-a-dozen voices in a room near him, and the jingling harmonies of a set of variations to *Deh Conte*, upon a piano whose every wire was evidently in the last stage of attenuation.

He had waited for about a quarter of an hour, when the door was opened, and a lady, very much dressed, and with the setting sunlight of faded beauty upon her face, entered the room.

'Mr. Audley, I presume,' she said, motioning to Robert to reseat himself, and placing herself in an easy-chair opposite to him. 'You will pardon me, I hope, for detaining you so long; my duties—'

'It is I who should apologise for intruding upon you,' Robert answered, politely; 'but my motive for calling upon you is a very serious one, and must plead my excuse. You remember the lady whose name I wrote upon my card?'

'Perfectly.'

'May I ask how much you know of that lady's history since her departure from your house?'

'Very little. In point of fact, scarcely anything at all. Miss Graham, I believe, obtained a situation in the family of a surgeon resident in Essex. Indeed, it was I who recommended her to that gentleman. I have never heard from her since she left me.'

'But you have communicated with her?' Robert asked, eagerly.

'No, indeed.'

Mr. Audley was silent for a few moments, the shadow of gloomy thoughts gathering darkly on his face.

'May I ask if you sent a telegraphic despatch to Miss Graham early in last September, stating that you were dangerously ill, and that you wished to see her?'

Mrs. Vincent smiled at her visitor's question.

'I had no occasion to send such a message,' she said. 'I have never been seriously ill in my life.'

Robert Audley paused before he asked any further questions, and scrawled a few pencilled words in his note-book.

'If I ask you a few straightforward questions about Miss Lucy Graham, madam,' he said, 'will you do me the favour to answer them without asking my motive for making such inquiries?'

'Most certainly,' replied Mrs. Vincent. 'I know nothing to Miss Graham's disadvantage, and have no justification for making a mystery of the little I do know.'

'Then will you tell me at what date the young lady first came to you?'

Mrs. Vincent smiled and shook her head. She had a pretty smile – the frank smile of a woman who has been admired, and who has too long felt the certainty of being able to please, to be utterly subjugated by any worldly misfortune.

'It's not the least use to ask me, Mr. Audley,' she said. 'I'm the most careless creature in the world; I never did, and never could remember dates, though I do all in my power to impress upon my girls how important it is for their future welfare that they should know when William the Conqueror began to reign, and all that kind of thing. But I haven't the remotest idea when Miss Graham came to me, although I know it was ages ago, for it was the very summer I had my peach-coloured silk. But we must consult Tonks – Tonks is sure to be right.'

Robert Audley wondered who or what Tonks could be; a diary, perhaps, or a memorandum-book – some obscure rival of Letsome.

Mrs. Vincent rang the bell, which was answered by the maid-servant who had admitted Robert.

'Ask Miss Tonks to come to me,' she said, 'I want to see her particularly.'

In less than five minutes Miss Tonks made her appearance. She was wintry and rather frost-bitten in aspect, and seemed to bring cold air in the scanty folds of her sombre merino dress. She was no age in particular, and looked as if she had never been younger, and would never grow older, but would remain for ever working backwards and forwards in her narrow groove, like some self-feeding machine for the instruction of young ladies.

'Tonks, my dear,' said Mrs. Vincent, without ceremony, 'this gentleman is a relative of Miss Graham's. Do you remember how long it is since she came to us at Crescent Villas?'

'She came in August, 1854,' answered Miss Tonks; 'I think it was the eighteenth of August, but I'm not quite sure that it wasn't the seventeenth. I know it was on a Tuesday.'

'Thank you, Tonks; you are a most invaluable darling,' exclaimed Mrs. Vincent, with her sweetest smile. It was, perhaps, because of the invaluable nature of Miss Tonks's services that she had received no remuneration whatever from her employer for the last three or four years. Mrs. Vincent might have hesitated to pay her from very contempt for the pitiful nature of the stipend as compared with the merits of the teacher.

'Is there anything else that Tonks or I can tell you, Mr. Audley?' asked the schoolmistress. 'Tonks has a far better memory than I have.'

'Can you tell me where Miss Graham came from when she entered your household?' Robert inquired.

'Not very precisely,' answered Mrs. Vincent. 'I have a vague notion that Miss Graham said something about coming from the sea-side, but she didn't say where, or if she did I have forgotten it. Tonks, did Miss Graham tell you where she came from?'

'Oh, no!' replied Miss Tonks, shaking her grim little head significantly. 'Miss Graham told me nothing; she was too clever for that. She knew how to keep her own secrets, in spite of her innocent ways and her curly hair,' Miss Tonks added, spitefully.

'You think she had secrets, then?' Robert asked, rather eagerly.

'I know she had,' replied Miss Tonks with frosty decision; 'all manner of secrets. *I* wouldn't have engaged such a person as junior teacher in a respectable school, without so much as one word of recommendation from any living creature.'

'You had no reference, then, from Miss Graham?' asked Robert, addressing Mrs. Vincent.

'No,' the lady answered with some little embarrassment; 'I waived that. Miss Graham waived the question of salary; I could not do less than waive the question of reference. She had quarrelled with her papa, she told me, and she wanted to find a home away from all the people she had ever known. She wished to keep herself quite separate from these people. She had endured so much, she said, young as she was, and she wanted to escape from her troubles. How could I press her for a reference under these circumstances? especially when I saw that she was a perfect lady? You know that Lucy Graham was a perfect lady, Tonks, and it is very unkind of you to say such cruel things about my taking her without a reference.'

'When people make favourites, they are apt to be deceived by them,' Miss Tonks answered, with icy sententiousness, and with no very perceptible relevance to the point in discussion.

'I never made her a favourite, you jealous Tonks,' Mrs. Vincent answered, reproachfully. 'I never said she was as useful as you, dear. You know I never did.'

'Oh, no!' replied Miss Tonks, with a chilling accent, 'you never said she was *useful*. She was only ornamental; a person to be shown off to visitors, and to play fantasias on the drawing-room piano.'

'Then you can give me no clue to Miss Graham's previous history?' Robert asked, looking from the schoolmistress to her teacher. He saw very clearly that Miss Tonks bore an envious grudge against Lucy Graham – a grudge which even the lapse of time had not healed.

'If this woman knows anything to my lady's detriment, she will tell it,' he thought. 'She will tell it only too willingly.'

But Miss Tonks appeared to know nothing whatever; except that Miss Graham had sometimes declared herself an ill-used creature, deceived by the baseness of mankind, and the victim of unmerited sufferings in the way of poverty and deprivation. Beyond this, Miss Tonks could tell nothing; and although she made the most of what she did know, Robert very soon sounded the depth of her small stock of information.

'I have only one more question to ask,' he said at last. 'It is this. Did Miss Graham leave any books or knick-knacks, or any kind of property whatever behind her, when she left your establishment?'

'Not to my knowledge,' Mrs. Vincent replied.

'Yes,' cried Miss Tonks, sharply. 'She did leave something. She left a box. It's up-stairs in my room. I've got an old bonnet in it. Would you like to see the box?' she asked, addressing Robert.

'If you will be so good as to allow me,' he answered, 'I should very much like to see it.'

'I'll fetch it down,' said Miss Tonks. 'It's not very big.'

She ran out of the room before Mr. Audley had time to utter any polite remonstrance.

'How pitiless these women are to each other,' he thought, while the teacher was absent. 'This one knows intuitively that there is some danger to the other lurking beneath my questions. She sniffs the coming trouble to her fellow female creature, and rejoices in it, and would take any pains to help me. What a world it is, and how these women take life out of our hands. Helen Maldon, Lady Audley, Clara Talboys, and now Miss Tonks – all womankind from beginning to end.'

Miss Tonks re-entered while the young barrister was meditating upon the infamy of her sex. She carried a dilapidated paper-covered bonnet-box, which she submitted to Robert's inspection.

Mr. Audley knelt down to examine the scraps of railway labels and addresses which were pasted here and there upon the box. It had been battered upon a great many different lines of railway, and had evidently travelled considerably. Many of the labels had been torn off, but fragments of some of them remained, and upon one yellow scrap of paper Robert read the letters TURI.

'The box has been to Italy,' he thought. 'Those are the first four letters of the word Turin, and the label is a foreign one.'

The only direction which had not been either defaced or torn away was the last, which bore the name of Miss Graham, passenger to London. Looking very closely at this label, Mr. Audley discovered that it had been pasted over another.

'Will you be so good as to let me have a little water and a piece of sponge?' he said. 'I want to get off this upper label. Believe me that I am justified in what I am doing.'

Miss Tonks ran out of the room, and returned immediately with a basin of water and a sponge.

'Shall I take off the label?' she asked.

'No, thank you,' Robert answered, coldly. 'I can do it very well myself.'

He damped the upper label several times before he could loosen the edges of the paper; but after two or three careful attempts, the moistened surface peeled off without injury to the underneath address.

Miss Tonks could not contrive to read this address across Robert's shoulder, though she exhibited considerable dexterity in her endeavours to accomplish that object.

Mr. Audley repeated his operations upon the lower label, which he removed from the box, and placed very carefully between two blank leaves of his pocket-book.

'I need intrude upon you no longer, ladies,' he said, when he had done this. 'I am extremely obliged to you for having afforded me all the information in your power. I wish you good morning.'

Mrs. Vincent smiled and bowed, murmuring some complacent conventionality about the delight she had felt in Mr. Audley's visit. Miss Tonks, more observant, stared at the white change which had come over the young man's face since he had removed the upper label from the box.

Robert walked slowly away from Acacia Cottage. 'If that which I have found to-day is no evidence for a jury,' he thought, 'it is surely enough to convince my uncle that he has married a designing and infamous woman.'

CHAPTER IX
Beginning at the other end

Robert Audley walked slowly through the leafless grove, under the bare and shadowless trees in the grey February atmosphere, thinking as he went of the discovery he had just made.

'I have that in my pocket-book,' he pondered, 'which forms the connecting link between the woman whose death George Talboys read of in the *Times* newspaper and the woman who rules in my uncle's house. The history of Lucy Graham ends abruptly on the threshold of Mrs. Vincent's school. She entered that establishment in August, 1854. The schoolmistress and her assistant can tell me this, but they cannot tell me whence she came. They cannot give me one clue to the secrets of her life from the day of her birth until the day she entered that house. I can go no further in this backward investigation of my lady's antecedents. What am I to do, then, if I mean to keep my promise to Clara Talboys?'

He walked on for a few paces revolving this question in his mind, with a darker shadow than the shadows of the gathering winter twilight on his face, and a heavy oppression of mingled sorrow and dread weighing down his heart.

'My duty is clear enough,' he thought – 'not the less clear because it is painful – not the less clear because it leads me step by step, carrying ruin and desolation with me, to the home I love. I must begin at the other end – I must begin at the other end, and discover the history of Helen Talboys from the hour of George's departure until the day of the funeral in the churchyard at Ventnor.'

Mr. Audley hailed a passing Hansom, and drove back to his chambers.

He reached Fig-tree Court in time to write a few lines to Miss Talboys, and to post his letter at St. Martin's-le-Grand before six o'clock.

'It will save me a day,' he thought, as he drove to the General Post Office with this brief epistle.

He had written to Clara Talboys to inquire the name of the little seaport town in which George had met Captain Maldon and his daughter; for in spite of the intimacy between the two young men, Robert Audley knew very few particulars of his friend's brief married life.

From the hour in which George Talboys had read the announcement of his wife's death in the columns of the *Times*, he had avoided all mention of the tender history which had been so cruelly broken, the familiar record which had been so darkly blotted out.

There was so much that was painful in that brief story! There was such bitter self-reproach involved in the recollection of that desertion which must have seemed so cruel to her who waited and watched at home! Robert Audley comprehended this, and he did not wonder at his friend's silence. The sorrowful story had been tacitly avoided by both, and Robert was as ignorant of the unhappy history of this one year in his schoolfellow's life as if they had never lived together in friendly companionship in those snug Temple chambers.

The letter, written to Miss Talboys by her brother George within a month of his marriage, was dated Harrogate. It was at Harrogate, therefore, Robert concluded, the young couple spent their honeymoon.

Robert Audley had requested Clara Talboys to telegraph an answer to his question, in order to avoid the loss of a day in the accomplishment of the investigation he had promised to perform.

The telegraphic answer reached Fig-tree Court before twelve o'clock the next day.

The name of the seaport town was Wildernsea, Yorkshire.

Within an hour of the receipt of this message Mr. Audley arrived at the King's Cross station, and took his ticket for Wildernsea by an express train that started at a quarter before two.

The shrieking engine bore him on the dreary northward journey, whirling him over desert wastes of flat meadow-land and bare corn-fields, faintly tinted with fresh sprouting green. This northern road was strange and unfamiliar to the young barrister, and the wide expanse of the wintry landscape chilled him by its aspect of bare loneliness. The knowledge of the purpose of his journey blighted every object upon which his absent glances fixed themselves for a moment; only to wander wearily away; only to turn inwards upon that far darker picture always presenting itself to his anxious mind.

It was dark when the train reached the Hull terminus; but Mr. Audley's journey was not ended. Amidst a crowd of porters and scattered heaps of that incongruous and hetero-geneous luggage with which travellers encumber themselves, he was led, bewildered and half asleep, to another train, which was to convey him along the branch line that swept past Wildernsea, and skirted the border of the German Ocean.

Half-an-hour after leaving Hull, Robert felt the briny fresh-ness of the sea upon the breeze that blew in at the open window of the carriage, and an hour afterwards the train stopped at a melancholy station, built amid a sandy desert, and inhabited by two or three gloomy officials, one of whom rang a terrific peal upon a harshly clanging bell as the train approached.

Mr. Audley was the only passenger who alighted at the dismal station. The train swept on to gayer scenes before the barrister had time to collect his scattered senses, or to pick up the portmanteau, which had been discovered with some difficulty amid a black cavern of luggage, only illuminated by one lantern.

'I wonder whether settlers in the back-woods of America feel as solitary and strange as I feel to-night?' he thought, as he stared hopelessly about him in the darkness.

He called to one of the officials, and pointed to his portmanteau.

'Will you carry that to the nearest hotel for me?' he asked – 'that is to say, if I can get a good bed there.'

The man laughed as he shouldered the portmanteau.

'You could get thirty beds, I dare say, Sir, if you wanted 'em,' he said. 'We ain't over busy at Wildernsea at this time o' year. This way, Sir.'

The porter opened a wooden door in the station wall, and Robert Audley found himself upon a wide bowling-green of smooth grass, which surrounded a huge square building that loomed darkly on him through the winter's night, its black solidity only relieved by two lighted windows, far apart from each other, and glimmering redly like beacons on the darkness.

'This is the Victoria Hotel, sir,' said the porter. 'You wouldn't believe the crowds of company we have down here in the summer.'

In the face of the bare grass-plat, the tenantless wooden alcoves, and the dark windows of the hotel, it was indeed rather difficult to imagine that the place was ever gay with merry people taking pleasure in the bright summer weather; but Robert Audley declared himself willing to believe anything the porter pleased to tell him, and followed his guide meekly to a little door at the side of the big hotel, which led into a comfortable bar, where the humbler classes of summer visitors were accommodated with such refreshments as they pleased to pay for, without running the gauntlet of the prim, white-waistcoated waiters on guard at the principal entrance.

But there were very few attendants retained at the hotel in

this bleak February season, and it was the landlord himself who ushered Robert into a dreary wilderness of polished mahogany tables and horsehair-cushioned chairs, which he called the coffee room.

Mr. Audley seated himself close to the wide steel fender, and stretched his cramped legs upon the hearth-rug, while the landlord drove the poker into the vast pile of coal, and sent a ruddy blaze roaring upward through the chimney.

'If you would prefer a private room, sir—' the man began.

'No, thank you,' said Robert, indifferently; 'this room seems quite private enough just now. If you will order me a mutton chop and a pint of sherry, I shall be obliged.'

'Certainly, Sir.'

'And I shall be still more obliged if you will favour me with a few minutes' conversation before you do so.'

'With very great pleasure, sir,' the landlord answered, good-naturedly. 'We see so very little company at this season of the year, that we are only too glad to oblige those gentlemen who do visit us. Any information which I can afford you respecting the neighbourhood of Wildernsea and its attractions,' added the landlord, unconsciously quoting a small hand-book of the watering place which he sold in the bar, 'I shall be most happy to—'

'But I don't want to know anything about the neighbourhood of Wildernsea,' interrupted Robert, with a feeble protest against the landlord's volubility. 'I want to ask you a few questions about some people who once lived here.'

The landlord bowed and smiled, with an air which implied his readiness to recite the biographies of all the inhabitants of the little seaport, if required by Mr. Audley to do so.

'How many years have you lived here?' Robert asked, taking his memorandum-book from his pocket. 'Will it annoy you if I make notes of your replies to my questions?'

'Not at all, Sir,' replied the landlord, with a pompous

enjoyment of the air of solemnity and importance which pervaded this business. 'Any information which I can afford that is likely to be of ultimate value—'

'Yes, thank you,' Robert murmured, interrupting the flow of words. 'You have lived here—'

'Six years, Sir.'

'Since the year fifty-three?'

'Since November in the year fifty-two, Sir. I was in business in Hull prior to that time. This house was only completed in the October before I entered it.'

'Do you remember a lieutenant in the navy, on half-pay I believe at that time, called Maldon?'

'Captain Maldon, Sir?'

'Yes, commonly called Captain Maldon. I see you do remember him.'

'Yes, sir. Captain Maldon was one of our best customers. He used to spend his evenings in this very room, though the walls were damp at that time, and we weren't able to paper the place for nearly a twelvemonth afterwards. His daughter married a young officer that came here with his regiment at Christmas time in fifty-two. They were married here, Sir, and they travelled on the Continent for six months, and came back here again. But the gentleman ran away to Australia, and left the lady, a week or two after her baby was born. The business made quite a sensation in Wildernsea, Sir, and Mrs. – Mrs. – I forget the name—'

'Mrs. Talboys,' suggested Robert.

'To be sure, Sir, Mrs. Talboys. Mrs. Talboys was very much pitied by the Wildernsea folks, Sir, I was going to say, for she was very pretty, and had such nice winning ways, that she was a favourite with everybody who knew her.'

'Can you tell me how long Mr. Maldon and his daughter remained at Wildernsea after Mr. Talboys left them?' Robert asked.

'Well – no, Sir,' answered the landlord, after a few moments' deliberation. 'I can't say exactly how long it was. I know Mr. Maldon used to sit here in this very parlour, and tell people how badly his daughter had been treated, and how he'd been deceived by a young man he'd put so much confidence in; but I can't say how long it was before he left Wildernsea. But Mrs. Barkamb could tell you, Sir,' added the landlord, briskly.

'Mrs. Barkamb?'

'Yes, Mrs. Barkamb is the person who owns No. 17, North Cottages, the house in which Mr. Maldon and his daughter lived. She's a nice, civil-spoken, motherly woman, Sir, and I'm sure she'll tell you anything you may want to know.'

'Thank you, I will call upon Mrs. Barkamb to-morrow. Stay – one more question. Should you recognise Mrs. Talboys if you were to see her?'

'Certainly, Sir. As sure as I should recognise one of my own daughters.'

Robert Audley wrote Mrs. Barkamb's address in his pocket-book, ate his solitary dinner, drank a couple of glasses of sherry, smoked a cigar, and then retired to the apartment in which a fire had been lighted for his comfort.

He soon fell asleep, worn out with the fatigue of hurrying from place to place during the last two days; but his slumber was not a heavy one, and he heard the disconsolate moaning of the wind upon the sandy wastes, and the long waves rolling in monotonously upon the flat shore. Mingling with these dismal sounds, the melancholy thoughts engendered by his joyless journey repeated themselves in ever-varying succession in the chaos of his slumbering brain, and made themselves into visions of things that never had been and never could be upon this earth; but which had some vague relation to real events, remembered by the sleeper.

In those troublesome dreams he saw Audley Court, rooted up from amidst the green pastures and the shady hedgerows of Essex, standing bare and unprotected upon that desolate northern shore, threatened by the rapid rising of a boisterous sea, whose waves seemed gathering upward to descend and crush the house he loved. As the hurrying waves rolled nearer and nearer to the stately mansion, the sleeper saw a pale, starry face looking out of the silvery foam, and knew that it was my lady, transformed into a mermaid, beckoning his uncle to destruction. Beyond that rising sea great masses of cloud, blacker than the blackest ink, more dense than the darkest night, lowered upon the dreamer's eye; but as he looked at the dismal horizon the storm clouds slowly parted, and from a narrow rent in the darkness a ray of light streamed out upon the hideous waves, which slowly, very slowly, receded, leaving the old mansion safe and firmly rooted on the shore.

Robert awoke with the memory of this dream in his mind, and a sensation of physical relief, as if some heavy weight, which had oppressed him all the night, had been lifted from his breast.

He fell asleep again, and did not wake until the broad winter sunlight shone upon the window-blind, and the shrill voice of the chambermaid at his door announced that it was half-past eight o'clock. At a quarter before ten he had left the Victoria Hotel, and was making his way along the lonely platform in front of a row of shadowless houses that faced the sea.

This row of hard, uncompromising, square-built habitations stretched away to the little harbour, in which two or three merchant vessels and a couple of colliers were anchored. Beyond the harbour there loomed, grey and cold upon the wintry horizon, a dismal barrack, parted from the Wildernsea houses by a narrow creek, spanned by an iron draw-bridge. The scarlet coat of the sentinel who walked backwards and forwards between two cannons, placed at remote angles before the barrack wall, was the only scrap of colour that relieved the neutral-tinted picture of the grey stone houses and the leaden sea.

On one side of the harbour a long stone pier stretched out far away into the cruel loneliness of the sea, as if built for the especial accommodation of some modern Timon, too misanthropical to be satisfied even by the solitude of Wildernsea, and anxious to get still further away from his fellow-creatures.

It was on that pier George Talboys had first met his wife, under the yellow glory of a sunny sky, and to the music of a braying band. It was there that the young cornet had first yielded to that sweet delusion, that fatal infatuation which had exercised so dark an influence upon his after-life.

Robert looked savagely at the solitary watering place – the shabby seaport.

'It is such a place as this,' he thought, 'that works a strong man's ruin. He comes here, heart whole and happy, with no better experience of woman than is to be learnt at a flower-show or in a ball-room; with no more familiar knowledge of the creature than he has of the far-away satellites of the remoter planets; with a vague notion that she is a whirling teetotum in pink or blue gauze, or a graceful automaton for the display of milliners' manufacture. He comes to some place of this kind, and the universe is suddenly narrowed into about half-a-dozen acres; the mighty scheme of creation is crushed into a bandbox. The far-away creatures whom he had seen floating about him, beautiful and indistinct, are brought under his very nose; and before he has time to recover from his bewilderment, hey, presto! the witchcraft has begun: the magic circle is drawn around him, the spells are at work, the whole formula of sorcery is in full play, and the victim is as powerless to escape as the marble-legged prince in the Eastern story.'

Ruminating in this wise, Robert Audley reached the house to which he had been directed as the residence of Mrs. Barkamb. He was admitted immediately by a prim, elderly servant, who ushered him into a sitting-room as prim and elderly-looking as herself. Mrs. Barkamb, a comfortable matron of about sixty years of age, was sitting in an arm-chair before a bright handful of fire in the shining grate. An elderly terrier, whose black-and-tan coat was thickly sprinkled with grey, reposed in Mrs. Barkamb's lap. Every object in the quiet sitting-room had an elderly aspect; an aspect of simple comfort and precision, which is the evidence of outward repose.

'I should like to live here,' Robert thought, 'and watch the grey sea slowly rolling over the grey sand under the still grey sky. I should like to live here, and tell the beads upon my rosary, and repent and rest.'

He seated himself in the arm-chair opposite Mrs. Barkamb, at that lady's invitation, and placed his hat upon the ground. The elderly terrier descended from his mistress's lap to bark at and otherwise take objection to this hat.

'You were wishing, I suppose, Sir, to take one – be quiet, Dash – one of the cottages,' suggested Mrs. Barkamb, whose mind ran in one narrow groove, and whose life during the last twenty years had been an unvarying round of house-letting.

Robert Audley explained the purpose of his visit.

'I come to ask one simple question,' he said, in conclusion. 'I wish to discover the exact date of Mrs. Talboys' departure from Wildernsea. The proprietor of the Victoria Hotel informed me that you were the most likely person to afford me that information.'

Mrs. Barkamb deliberated for some moments.

'I can give you the date of Captain Maldon's departure,' she said, 'for he left No. 17 considerably in my debt, and I have the whole business in black and white; but with regard to Mrs. Talboys—'

Mrs. Barkamb paused for a few moments before resuming.

'You are aware that Mrs. Talboys left rather abruptly?' she asked.

'I was not aware of that fact.'

'Indeed! Yes, she left abruptly, poor little woman! She tried to support herself after her husband's desertion by giving music lessons; she was a very brilliant pianist, and succeeded pretty well, I believe. But I suppose her father took her money from her, and spent it in public-houses. However that might be, they had a very serious misunderstanding one night; and the next morning Mrs. Talboys left Wildernsea, leaving her little boy, who was out at nurse in the neighbourhood.'

'But you cannot tell me the date of her departure?'

'I'm afraid not,' answered Mrs. Barkamb; 'and yet, stay. Captain Maldon wrote to me upon the day his daughter left. He was in very great distress, poor old gentleman, and he always came to me in his troubles. If I could find that letter, it might be dated, you know – mightn't it, now?'

Mr. Audley said that it was only probable the letter was dated.

Mrs. Barkamb retired to a table in the window on which stood an old-fashioned mahogany desk lined with green baize, and suffering from a plethora of documents, which oozed out of it in every direction. Letters, receipts, bills, inventories, and tax-papers were mingled in hopeless confusion; and amongst these Mrs. Barkamb set to work to search for Captain Maldon's letter.

Mr. Audley waited very patiently, watching the grey clouds sailing across the grey sky, the grey vessels gliding past upon the grey sea.

After about ten minutes' search, and a great deal of rustling, crackling, folding and unfolding of the papers, Mrs. Barkamb uttered an exclamation of triumph.

'I've got the letter,' she said; 'and there's a note inside it from Mrs. Talboys.'

Robert Audley's pale face flushed a vivid crimson as he stretched out his hand to receive the papers.

'The person who stole Helen Maldon's love-letters from George's trunk in my chambers might have spared themselves the trouble,' he thought.

The letter from the old lieutenant was not long, but almost every other word was underscored.

> 'My generous friend,' the writer began—
> [Mr. Maldon had tried the lady's generosity pretty severely during his residence in her house, rarely paying his rent until threatened with the intruding presence of the broker's man.]
> 'I am in the depths of despair. My daughter has left me! You may imagine my feelings! We had a few words last night upon the subject of money matters, which subject has always been a disagreeable one between us, and on rising this morning I found that I was deserted! The enclosed from Helen was waiting for me on the parlour table.
>
>> 'Yours in distraction and despair,
>>> 'HENRY MALDON.
>
> 'North Cottages,
>   August 16th, 1854.'

The note from Mrs. Talboys was still more brief. It began abruptly thus:–

> 'I am weary of my life here, and wish, if I can, to find a new one. I go out into the world, dissevered from every link which binds me to the hateful past, to seek another home and another fortune. Forgive me if I have been fretful, capricious, changeable. You should forgive me, for you know why I have been so. You know the secret which is the key to my life.
>
>> 'HELEN TALBOYS.'

These lines were written in a hand that Robert Audley knew only too well.

He sat for a long time pondering silently over the letter written by Helen Talboys.

What was the meaning of those two last sentences – 'You should forgive me, for you know *why* I have been so. You know the *secret* which is the key to my life'?

He wearied his brain in endeavouring to find a clue to the signification of those two sentences. He could remember nothing, nor could he imagine anything that would throw a light upon their meaning. The date of Helen's departure, according to Mr. Maldon's letter, was the 16th of August, 1854. Miss Tonks had declared that Lucy Graham entered the school at Crescent Villas upon the 17th or 18th of August in the same year. Between the departure of Helen Talboys from the Yorkshire watering place, and the arrival of Lucy Graham at the Brompton school, not more than eight-and-forty hours could have elapsed. This made a very small link in the chain of circumstantial evidence, perhaps; but it was a link, nevertheless, and it fitted neatly into its place.

'Did Mr. Maldon hear from his daughter after she had left Wildernsea?' Robert asked.

'Well, I believe he did hear from her,' Mrs. Barkamb answered; 'but I didn't see much of the old gentleman after that August. I was obliged to sell him up in November, poor fellow, for he owed me fifteen months' rent; and it was only by selling his poor little bits of furniture that I could get him out of my place. We parted very good friends, in spite of my sending in the brokers; and the old gentleman went to London with the child, who was scarcely a twelvemonth old.'

Mrs. Barkamb had nothing more to tell, and Robert had no further questions to ask. He requested permission to retain the two letters written by the lieutenant and his daughter, and left the house with them in his pocket-book.

He walked straight back to the hotel, where he called for a time-table. An express for London left Wildernsea at a

281

quarter-past one. Robert sent his portmanteau to the station, paid his bill, and walked up and down the stone terrace fronting the sea, waiting for the starting of the train.

'I have traced the histories of Lucy Graham and Helen Talboys to a vanishing point,' he thought; 'my next business is to discover the history of the woman who lies buried in Ventnor churchyard.'

CHAPTER X
Hidden in the grave

Upon his return from Wildernsea, Robert Audley found a letter from his cousin, Alicia, awaiting him at his chambers.

> 'Papa is much better,' the young lady wrote, 'and is very
> anxious to have you at the Court. For some inexplicable reason,
> my step-mother has taken it into her head that your presence is
> extremely desirable, and worries me with her frivolous questions
> about your movements. So pray come without delay, and set these
> people at rest. Your affectionate cousin,   A. A.'

'So my lady is anxious to know my movements,' thought Robert Audley, as he sat brooding and smoking by his lonely fireside. 'She is anxious; and she questions her step-daughter in that pretty, childlike manner which has such a bewitching air of innocent frivolity. Poor little creature; poor unhappy little golden-haired sinner; the battle between us seems terribly unfair. Why doesn't she run away while there is still time? I have given her fair warning, I have shown her my cards, and worked openly enough in this business, Heaven knows. Why doesn't she run away?'

He repeated this question again and again as he filled and emptied his meerschaum, surrounding himself with the blue vapour from his pipe until he looked like some modern magician, seated in his laboratory.

'Why doesn't she run away? I would bring no needless shame upon that house, of all other houses upon this wide earth. I would only do my duty to my missing friend, and to that brave and generous man who has pledged his faith to a worthless woman. Heaven knows I have no wish to punish. Heaven knows I was never born to be the avenger of guilt or the persecutor of the guilty. I only wish to do my duty. I will give her one more warning, a full and fair one and then—'

His thoughts wandered away to that gloomy prospect in which he saw no gleam of brightness to relieve the dull, black obscurity that encompassed the future, shutting in his pathway on every side, and spreading a dense curtain around and about him, which Hope was powerless to penetrate. He was for ever haunted by the vision of his uncle's anguish, for ever tortured by the thought of that ruin and desolation, which, being brought about by his instrumentality, would seem in a manner his handiwork. But amid all, and through all, Clara Talboys, with an imperious gesture, beckoned him onwards to her brother's unknown grave.

'Shall I go down to Southampton,' he thought, 'and endeavour to discover the history of the woman who died at Ventnor? Shall I work underground, bribing the paltry assistants in that foul conspiracy, until I find my way to the thrice guilty principal? No! not till I have tried other means of discovering the truth. Shall I go to that miserable old man, and charge him with his share in the shameful trick which I believe to have been played upon my poor friend? No; I will not torture that terror-stricken wretch as I tortured him a few weeks ago. I will go straight to the arch conspirator, and will tear away the beautiful veil under which she hides her wickedness, and will wring from her the secret of my friend's fate and banish her for ever from the house which her presence has polluted.'

He started early the next morning for Essex, and reached Audley before eleven o'clock.

Early as it was, my lady was out. She had gone to Chelmsford upon a shopping expedition with her step-daughter. She had several calls to make in the neighbourhood of the town, and was not likely to return until dinner-time. Sir Michael's health was very much improved, and he would come downstairs in the afternoon. Would Mr. Audley go to his uncle's room?

No: Robert had no wish to meet that generous kinsman. What could he say to him? How could he smooth the way to the trouble that was to come? – how soften the cruel blow of the great grief that was preparing for that noble and trusting heart?

'If I could forgive her the wrong done to my friend,' Robert thought, 'I should still abhor her for the misery her guilt must bring upon the man who has believed in her.'

He told his uncle's servant that he would stroll into the village, and return before dinner. He walked slowly away from the Court, wandering across the meadows between his uncle's house and the village, purposeless and indifferent, with the great trouble and perplexity of his life stamped upon his face and reflected in his manner.

'I will go into the churchyard,' he thought, 'and stare at the tombstones. There is nothing I can do that will make me more gloomy than I am.'

He was in those very meadows through which he had hurried from Audley Court to the station upon the September day in which George Talboys had disappeared. He looked at the pathway by which he had gone upon that day, and remembered his unaccustomed hurry, and the vague feeling of terror which had taken possession of him immediately upon losing sight of his friend.

'Why did that unaccountable terror seize upon me?' he thought. 'Why was it that I saw some strange mystery in my friend's disappearance? Was it a monition or a monomania? What if I am wrong after all? What if this chain of evidence which I have constructed link by link is woven out of my own folly? What if this edifice of horror and suspicion is a mere collection of crochets – the nervous fancies of a hypochondriacal bachelor? Mr. Harcourt Talboys sees no meaning in the events out of which I have created a horrible mystery. I lay the separate links of the chain before him, and he cannot recognise their fitness. He is unable to put them together. Oh, my God, if it should be in myself all this time that the misery lies; if—' He smiled bitterly, and shook his head. 'I have the handwriting in my pocket-book which is the evidence of the conspiracy,' he thought. 'It remains for me to discover the darker half of my lady's secret.'

He avoided the village, still keeping to the meadows. The church lay a little way back from the straggling High Street, and a rough wooden gate opened from the churchyard into a broad meadow, that was bordered by a running stream, and sloped down into a grassy valley dotted by groups of cattle.

Robert slowly ascended the narrow hill-side pathway leading up to the gate in the churchyard. The quiet dulness of the lonely landscape harmonised with his own gloom. The solitary figure of an old man hobbling towards a stile at the further end of the wide meadow was the only human creature visible upon the area over which the young barrister looked. The smoke slowly ascending from the scattered houses in the long High Street was the only evidence of human life. The slow progress of the hands of the old clock in the church steeple was the only token by which a traveller could perceive that the sluggish course of rural time had not come to a full stop in the village of Audley.

Yes, there was one other sign. As Robert opened the gate of the churchyard, and strolled listlessly into the little enclosure, he became aware of the solemn music of an organ, audible through a half-open window in the steeple.

He stopped and listened to the slow harmonies of a dreamy

melody that sounded like an extempore composition of an accomplished player.

'Who would have believed that Audley church could boast such an organ?' thought Robert. 'When last I was here, the national schoolmaster used to accompany his children by a primitive performance of common chords. I didn't think the old organ had such music in it.'

He lingered at the gate, not caring to break the lazy spell woven about him by the monotonous melancholy of the organist's performance. The tones of the instrument, now swelling to their fullest power, now sinking to a low, whispering softness, floated towards him upon the misty winter atmosphere, and had a soothing influence, that seemed to comfort him in his trouble.

He closed the gate softly, and crossed the little patch of gravel before the door of the church. This door had been left ajar – by the organist, perhaps. Robert Audley pushed it open, and walked into the square porch, from which a flight of narrow stone steps wound upwards to the organ-loft and the belfry. Mr. Audley took off his hat, and opened the door between the porch and the body of the church. He stepped softly into the holy edifice, which had a damp, mouldy smell upon week-days. He walked down the narrow aisle to the altar-rails, and from that point of observation took a survey of the church. The little gallery was exactly opposite to him, but the scanty green curtains before the organ were closely drawn, and he could not get a glimpse of the player.

The music still rolled on. The organist had wandered into a melody of Mendelssohn's, a strain whose dreamy sadness went straight to Robert's heart. He loitered in the nooks and corners of the church, examining the dilapidated memorials of the well-nigh forgotten dead, and listening to this music.

'If my poor friend, George Talboys, had died in my arms, and I had buried him in this quiet church, in one of the vaults over which I tread to-day, how much anguish of mind, vacillation, and torment I might have escaped,' thought Robert Audley, as he read the faded inscriptions upon tablets of discoloured marble: 'I should have known his fate – I should have known his fate! Ah, how much there would have been in that. It is this miserable uncertainty, this horrible suspicion, which has poisoned my very life.'

He looked at his watch.

'Half-past one,' he muttered. 'I shall have to wait four or five dreary hours before my lady comes home from her morning calls. Her morning calls – her pretty visits of ceremony or friendliness. Good heavens! what an actress this woman is. What an arch trickster – what an all-accomplished deceiver. But she shall play her pretty comedy no longer under my uncle's roof. I have diplomatised long enough. She has refused to accept an indirect warning. To-night I will speak plainly.'

The music of the organ ceased, and Robert heard the closing of the instrument.

'I'll have a look at this new organist,' he thought, 'who can afford to bury his talents at Audley, and play Mendelssohn's finest fugues for a stipend of sixteen pounds a-year.' He lingered in the porch, waiting for the organist to descend the awkward little staircase. In the weary trouble of his mind, and with the prospect of getting through the five hours in the best way he could, Mr. Audley was glad to cultivate any diversion of thought, however idle. He therefore freely indulged his curiosity about the new organist.

The first person who appeared upon the steep stone steps was a boy in corduroy trousers and a dark linen smock-frock, who shambled down the stairs with a good deal of unnecessary clatter of his hobnailed shoes, and who was red in the face from the exertion of blowing the bellows of the old organ. Close behind this boy came a young lady, very plainly dressed in a black silk gown and a large grey shawl, who started and turned pale at the sight of Mr. Audley.

This young lady was Clara Talboys.

Of all people in the world she was the last whom Robert either expected or wished to see. She had told him that she was going to pay a visit to some friends who lived in Essex; but the county is a wide one, and the village of Audley one of the most obscure and least frequented spots in the whole of its extent. That the sister of his lost friend should be here – here where she could watch his every action, and from those actions deduce the secret workings of his mind, tracing his doubts home to their object – made a complication of his difficulties that he could never have anticipated. It brought him back to that consciousness of his own helplessness, in which he had exclaimed –

'A hand that is stronger than my own is beckoning me onward on the dark road that leads to my lost friend's unknown grave.'

Clara Talboys was the first to speak.

'You are surprised to see me here, Mr. Audley,' she said.

'Very much surprised.'

'I told you that I was coming to Essex. I left home the day before yesterday. I was leaving home when I received your telegraphic message. The friend with whom I am staying is Mrs. Martyn, the wife of the new rector of Mount Stanning. I came down this morning to see the village and church, and as Mrs. Martyn had to pay a visit to the schools with the curate and his wife, I stopped here and amused myself by trying the old organ. I was not aware till I came here that there was a village called Audley. The place takes its name from your family, I suppose?'

'I believe so,' Robert answered, wondering at the lady's calmness, in contradistinction to his own embarrassment. 'I have a vague recollection of hearing the story of some ancestor who was called Audley of Audley in the reign of Edward the

Fourth. The tomb inside the rails near the altar belongs to one of the knights of Audley, but I have never taken the trouble to remember his achievements. Are you going to wait here for your friends, Miss Talboys?'

'Yes; they are to return here for me after they have finished their rounds.'

'And you go back to Mount Stanning with them this afternoon?'

'Yes.'

Robert stood with his hat in his hand looking absently out at the tombstones and the low wall of the churchyard. Clara Talboys watched his pale face, haggard under the deepening shadow that had rested upon it so long.

'You have been ill since I saw you last, Mr. Audley,' she said, in a low voice, that had the same melodious sadness as the notes of the old organ under her touch.

'No, I have not been ill; I have been only harassed, wearied by a hundred doubts and perplexities.'

He was thinking as he spoke to her – 'How much does she guess? how much does she suspect?'

He had told the story of George's disappearance and of his own suspicions, suppressing only the names of those concerned in the mystery; but what if this girl should fathom the slender disguise, and discover for herself that which he had chosen to withhold?

Her grave eyes were fixed upon his face, and he knew that she was trying to read the innermost secrets of his mind.

'What am I in her hands?' he thought. 'What am I in the hands of this woman, who has my lost friend's face and the manner of Pallas Athene? She reads my pitiful, vacillating soul, and plucks the thoughts out of my heart with the magic of her solemn brown eyes. How unequal the fight must be between us, and how can I ever hope to conquer against the strength of her beauty and her wisdom?'

Mr. Audley was clearing his throat preparatory to bidding his beautiful companion good morning, and making his escape from the thraldom of her presence into the lonely meadow outside the churchyard, when Clara Talboys arrested him by speaking upon that very subject which he was most anxious to avoid.

'You promised to write to me, Mr. Audley,' she said, 'if you made any discovery which carried you nearer to the mystery of my brother's disappearance. You have not written to me, and I imagine, therefore, that you have discovered nothing.'

Robert Audley was silent for some moments. How could he answer this direct question?

'The chain of circumstantial evidence which unites the mystery of your brother's fate with the person whom I suspect,' he said, after a pause, 'is formed of very slight links. I think that I have added another link to that chain since I saw you in Dorsetshire.'

'And you refuse to tell me what it is that you have discovered.'

'Only until I have discovered more.'

'I thought from your message that you were going to Wildernsea.'

'I have been there.'

'Indeed! It was there that you made some discovery, then?'

'It was,' answered Robert. 'You must remember, Miss Talboys, that the sole ground upon which my suspicions rest is the identity of two individuals who have no apparent connection – the identity of a person who is supposed to be dead with one who is living. The conspiracy of which I believe your brother to have been the victim hinges upon this. If his wife, Helen Talboys, died when the papers recorded her death – if the woman who lies buried in Ventnor churchyard was indeed the woman whose name is inscribed on the headstone of the grave – I have no case, I have no clue to the mystery of your brother's fate. I am about to put this to the test. I believe that I am now in a position to play a bold game, and I believe that I shall soon arrive at the truth.'

He spoke in a low voice, and with a solemn emphasis that betrayed the intensity of his feeling. Miss Talboys stretched out her ungloved hand, and laid it in his own. The cold touch of that slender hand sent a shivering thrill through his frame.

'You will not suffer my brother's fate to remain a mystery, Mr. Audley,' she said quietly. 'I know that you will do your duty to your friend.'

The rector's wife and her two companions entered the churchyard as Clara Talboys said this. Robert Audley pressed the hand that rested in his own, and raised it to his lips.

'I am a lazy, good-for-nothing fellow, Miss Talboys,' he said; 'but if I could restore your brother George to life and happiness, I should care very little for any sacrifice of my own feeling. I fear that the most I can do is to fathom the secret of his fate; and in doing that I must sacrifice those who are dearer to me than myself.'

He put on his hat and hurried away through the gateway leading into the field as Mrs. Martyn came up to the porch.

'Who is that handsome young man I caught *tête-à-tête* with you, Clara?' she asked, laughing.

'He is a Mr. Audley, a friend of my poor brother's.'

'Indeed! He is some relation of Sir Michael Audley, I suppose?'

'Sir Michael Audley!'

'Yes, my dear; the most important personage in the parish of Audley. But we'll call at the Court in a day or two, and you shall see the baronet and his pretty young wife.'

'His young wife!' repeated Clara Talboys, looking earnestly at her friend. 'Has Sir Michael Audley lately married?'

'Yes. He was a widower for sixteen years, and married a penniless young governess about a year and a half ago. The story is quite romantic, and Lady Audley is considered the belle of the county. But come, my dear Clara, the pony is tired of waiting for us, and we've a long drive before dinner.'

Clara Talboys took her seat in the little basket-carriage which was waiting at the principal gate of the churchyard in the care of the boy who had blown the organ-bellows. Mrs. Martyn shook the reins, and the sturdy chestnut cob trotted off in the direction of Mount Stanning.

'Will you tell me more about this Lady Audley, Fanny?' Miss Talboys said, after a long pause. 'I want to know all about her. Have you heard her maiden name?'

'Yes; she was a Miss Graham.'

'And she is very pretty?'

'Yes, very, very pretty. Rather a childish beauty though, with large clear blue eyes, and pale golden ringlets, that fall in a feathery shower over her throat and shoulders.'

Clara Talboys was silent. She did not ask any further questions about my lady.

She was thinking of a passage in that letter which George had written to her during his honeymoon – a passage in which he said: 'My childish little wife is watching me as I write this. Ah! how I wish you could see her, Clara! Her eyes are as blue and as clear as the skies on a bright summer's day, and her hair falls about her face like the pale golden halo you see round the head of a Madonna in an Italian picture.'

CHAPTER XI

In the lime-walk

Robert Audley was loitering upon the broad grass-plat in front of the Court as the carriage containing my lady and Alicia drove under the archway, and drew up at the low turret door. Mr. Audley presented himself in time to hand the ladies out of the vehicle.

My lady looked very pretty in a delicate blue bonnet and the sables which her nephew had bought for her at St. Petersburg. She seemed very well pleased to see Robert, and smiled most bewitchingly as she gave him her exquisitely gloved little hand.

'So you have come back to us, truant?' she said, laughing. 'And now that you have returned, we shall keep you prisoner. We won't let him run away again, will we, Alicia?'

Miss Audley gave her head a scornful toss, that shook the heavy curls under her cavalier hat.

'I have nothing to do with the movements of so erratic an individual,' she said. 'Since Robert Audley has taken it into his head to conduct himself like some ghost-haunted hero in a German story, I have given up attempting to understand him.'

Mr. Audley looked at his cousin with an expression of serio-comic perplexity. 'She's a nice girl,' he thought, 'but she's a nuisance. I don't know how it is, but she seems more a nuisance than she used to be.'

He pulled his mustachios reflectively as he considered this question. His mind wandered away for a few moments from the great trouble of his life to dwell upon this minor perplexity.

'She's a dear girl,' he thought; 'a generous-hearted, bouncing, noble English lassie, and yet—' He lost himself in a quagmire of doubt and difficulty. There was some hitch in his mind which he could not understand; some change in himself, beyond the change made in him by his anxiety about George Talboys, which mystified and bewildered him.

'And pray where have you been wandering during the last day or two, Mr. Audley?' asked my lady, as she lingered with her step-daughter upon the threshold of the turret door, waiting until Robert should be pleased to stand aside and allow them to pass. The young man started as she asked this question and looked up at her suddenly. Something in the aspect of her bright young beauty, something in the childish innocence of her expression, seemed to smite him to the heart, and his face grew pale as he looked at her.

'I have been – in Yorkshire,' he said; 'at the little watering place where my poor friend George Talboys lived at the time of his marriage.'

The white change in my lady's face was the only sign of her having heard these words. She smiled, a faint, sickly smile, and tried to pass her husband's nephew.

'I must dress for dinner,' she said. 'I am going to a dinner-party, Mr. Audley; please let me go in.'

'I must ask you to spare me half-an-hour, Lady Audley,' Robert answered, in a low voice. 'I came down to Essex on purpose to speak to you.'

'What about?' asked my lady.

She had recovered herself from any shock which she might have sustained a few moments before, and it was in her usual manner that she asked this question. Her face expressed the mingled bewilderment and curiosity of a puzzled child, rather than the serious surprise of a woman.

'What can you want to talk to me about, Mr. Audley?' she repeated.

'I will tell you when we are alone,' Robert said, glancing at his cousin, who stood a little way behind my lady, watching this confidential little dialogue.

'He is in love with my step-mother's wax-doll beauty,' thought Alicia, 'and it is for her sake he has become such a disconsolate object. He's just the sort of person to fall in love with his aunt.'

Miss Audley walked away to the grass-plat, turning her back upon Robert and my lady.

'The absurd creature turned as white as a sheet when he saw her,' she thought. 'So he can be in love, after all. That slow lump of torpidity he calls his heart can beat, I suppose, once in a quarter of a century: but it seems that nothing but a blue-eyed wax-doll can set it going. I should have given him up long ago if I'd known that his ideal of beauty was to be found in a toy-shop.'

Poor Alicia crossed the grass-plat and disappeared upon the opposite side of the quadrangle, where there was a Gothic gate that communicated with the stables. I am sorry to say that Sir Michael Audley's daughter went to seek consolation from her dog Cæsar and her chestnut mare Atalanta, whose loose box the young lady was in the habit of visiting every day.

'Will you come into the lime-walk, Lady Audley?' said Robert, as his cousin left the garden. 'I wish to talk to you without fear of interruption or observation. I think we could choose no safer place than that. Will you come there with me?'

'If you please,' answered my lady. Mr. Audley could see that she was trembling, and that she glanced from side to side, as if looking for some outlet by which she might escape him.

'You are shivering, Lady Audley,' he said.

'Yes, I am very cold. I would rather speak to you some other day, please. Let it be to-morrow, if you will. I have to dress for dinner, and I want to see Sir Michael; I have not seen him since ten o'clock this morning. Please let it be to-morrow.'

There was a painful piteousness in her tone. Heaven knows how painful to Robert's heart. Heaven knows what horrible images arose in his mind as he looked down at that fair young face and thought of the task that lay before him.

'I *must* speak to you, Lady Audley,' he said. 'If I am cruel, it is you who have made me cruel. You might have escaped this ordeal. You might have avoided me. I gave you fair warning. But you have chosen to defy me, and it is your own folly which is to blame if I no longer spare you. Come with me. I tell you again I must speak to you.'

There was a cold determination in his tone which silenced my lady's objections. She followed him submissively to the little iron gate which communicated with the long garden behind the house – the garden in which a little rustic wooden bridge led across the quiet fish-pond into the lime-walk.

The early winter twilight was closing in, and the intricate tracery of the leafless branches that overarched the lonely pathway looked black against the cold grey of the evening sky. The lime-walk seemed like some cloister in this uncertain light.

'Why do you bring me to this horrible place to frighten me out of my poor wits?' cried my lady, peevishly. 'You ought to know how nervous I am.'

'You are nervous, my lady?'

'Yes, dreadfully nervous. I am worth a fortune to poor Mr. Dawson. He is always sending me camphor, and sal volatile, and red lavender, and all kinds of abominable mixtures, but he can't cure me.'

'Do you remember what Macbeth tells his physician, my lady?' asked Robert, gravely. 'Mr. Dawson may be very much more clever than the Scottish leech; but I doubt if even *he* can minister to the mind that is diseased.'

'Who said that my mind was diseased?' exclaimed Lady Audley.

'I say so, my lady,' answered Robert. 'You tell me that you are nervous, and that all the medicines your doctor can prescribe are only so much physic that might as well be thrown to the dogs. Let me be the physician to strike to the root of your malady, Lady Audley. Heaven knows that I wish to be merciful – that I would spare you as far as it is in my power to spare you in doing justice to others – but justice must be done. Shall I tell you why you are nervous in this house, my lady?'

'If you can,' she answered, with a little laugh.

'Because for you this house is haunted.'

'Haunted?'

'Yes, haunted by the ghost of George Talboys.'

Robert Audley heard my lady's quickened breathing; he fancied he could almost hear the loud beating of her heart as she walked by his side, shivering now and then, and with her sable cloak wrapped tightly round her.

'What do you mean?' she cried suddenly, after a pause of some moments. 'Why do you torment me about this George Talboys, who happens to have taken it into his head to keep out of your way for a few months? Are you going mad, Mr. Audley, and do you select me as the victim of your monomania? What is George Talboys to me that you should worry me about him?'

'He was a stranger to you, my lady, was he not?'

'Of course!' answered Lady Audley. 'What should he be but a stranger?'

'Shall I tell you the story of my friend's disappearance as I read that story, my lady?' asked Robert.

'No,' cried Lady Audley; 'I wish to know nothing of your friend. If he is dead I am sorry for him. If he lives, I have no wish either to see him or to hear of him. Let me go in to see my husband, if you please, Mr. Audley; unless you wish to detain me in this gloomy place until I catch my death of cold.'

'I wish to detain you until you have heard what I have to say, Lady Audley,' answered Robert, resolutely. 'I will detain you no longer than is necessary; and when you have heard me, you shall choose your own course of action.'

'Very well, then; pray lose no time in saying what you have to say,' replied my lady, carelessly. 'I promise to attend very patiently.'

'When my friend, George Talboys returned to England,' Robert began gravely, 'the thought which was uppermost in his mind was the thought of his wife.'

'Whom he had deserted,' said my lady quickly. 'At least,' she added, more deliberately, 'I remember your telling us something to that effect when you first told us your friend's story.'

Robert Audley did not notice this interruption.

'The thought that was uppermost in his mind was the thought of his wife,' he repeated. 'His fairest hope in the future was the hope of making her happy, and lavishing upon her the fortune which he had won by the force of his own strong arm in the gold-fields of Australia. I saw him within a few hours of his reaching England, and I was a witness of the joyful pride with which he looked forward to his reunion with his wife. I was also a witness of the blow which struck him to the very heart – which changed him from the man he had been, to a creature as unlike that former self as one human being can be unlike another. The blow which made that cruel change was the announcement of his wife's death in the *Times* newspaper. I now believe that that announcement was a black and bitter lie.'

'Indeed!' said my lady; 'and what reason could any one have for announcing the death of Mrs. Talboys, if Mrs. Talboys had been alive?'

'The lady herself might have had a reason,' Robert answered, quietly.

'What reason?'

'How if she had taken advantage of George's absence to win a richer husband? How if she had married again, and wished to throw my poor friend off the scent by this false announcement?'

Lady Audley shrugged her shoulders.

'Your suppositions are rather ridiculous, Mr. Audley,' she said; 'it is to be hoped that you have some reasonable grounds for them.'

'I have examined a file of each of the newspapers published in Chelmsford and Colchester,' continued Robert, without replying to my lady's last observation, 'and I find in one of the Colchester papers, dated July the 2nd, 1857, a brief paragraph amongst numerous miscellaneous scraps of information copied from other newspapers, to the effect that a Mr. George Talboys, an English gentleman, had arrived at Sydney from the gold-fields, carrying with him nuggets and gold-dust to the amount of twenty thousand pounds, and that he had realised his property and sailed for Liverpool in the fast-sailing clipper *Argus*. This is a very small fact of course, Lady Audley, but it is enough to prove that any person residing in Essex in the July of the year fifty-seven, was likely to become aware of George Talboys' return from Australia. Do you follow me?'

'Not very clearly,' said my lady. 'What have the Essex papers to do with the death of Mrs. Talboys?'

'We will come to that by-and-by, Lady Audley. I say that I believe the announcement in the *Times* to have been a false announcement, and a part of the conspiracy which was carried out by Helen Talboys and Lieutenant Maldon against my poor friend.'

'A conspiracy!'

'Yes, a conspiracy concocted by an artful woman, who had speculated upon the chances of her husband's death, and had secured a splendid position at the risk of committing a crime;

a bold woman, my lady, who thought to play her comedy out to the end without fear of detection; a wicked woman, who did not care what misery she might inflict upon the honest heart of the man she betrayed; but a foolish woman, who looked at life as a game of chance, in which the best player was likely to hold the winning cards, forgetting that there is a Providence above the pitiful speculators, and that wicked secrets are never permitted to remain long hidden. If this woman of whom I speak had never been guilty of any blacker sin than the publication of that lying announcement in the *Times* newspaper, I should still hold her as the most detestable and despicable of her sex – the most pitiless and calculating of human creatures. That cruel lie was a base and cowardly blow in the dark; it was the treacherous dagger-thrust of an infamous assassin.'

'But how do you know that the announcement was a false one?' asked my lady. 'You told us that you had been to Ventnor with Mr. Talboys to see his wife's grave. Who was it who died at Ventnor if it was not Mrs. Talboys?'

'Ah, Lady Audley,' said Robert, 'that is a question which only two or three people can answer, and one or other of those persons shall answer it to me before very long. I tell you, my lady, that I am determined to unravel the mystery of George Talboys' death. Do you think I am to be put off by feminine prevarication – by womanly trickery? No! Link by link I have put together the chain of evidence, which wants but a link here and there to be complete in its terrible strength. Do you think I will suffer myself to be baffled? Do you think I shall fail to discover those missing links? No, Lady Audley, I shall not fail, for *I know where to look for them!* There is a fair-haired woman at Southampton – a woman called Plowson, who has some share in the secrets of the father of my friend's wife. I have an idea that she can help me to discover the history of the woman who lies buried in Ventnor churchyard, and I will spare no trouble in making that discovery; unless—'

'Unless what?' asked my lady, eagerly.

'Unless the woman I wish to save from degradation and punishment accepts the mercy I offer her, and takes warning while there is still time.'

My lady shrugged her graceful shoulders, and flashed bright defiance out of her blue eyes.

'She would be a very foolish woman if she suffered herself to be influenced by any such absurdity,' she said. 'You are hypochondriacal, Mr. Audley, and you must take camphor, or red lavender, or sal volatile. What can be more ridiculous than this idea which you have taken into your head? You lose your friend George Talboys in rather a mysterious manner – that is to say, that gentleman chooses to leave England without giving you due notice. What of that? You confess that he became an altered man after his wife's death. He grew eccentric and misanthropical; he affected an utter indifference as to what became of him. What more likely, then, that he grew tired of the monotony of civilised life, and ran away to those savage gold-fields to find a distraction for his grief? It is rather a romantic story, but by no means an uncommon one. But you are not satisfied with this simple interpretation of your friend's disappearance, and you build up some absurd theory of a conspiracy which has no existence except in your own over-heated brain. Helen Talboys is dead. The *Times* newspaper declares she is dead. Her own father tells you that she is dead. The headstone of the grave in Ventnor churchyard bears record of her death. By what right,' cried my lady, her voice rising to that shrill and piercing tone peculiar to her when affected by any intense agitation – 'by what right, Mr. Audley, do you come to me and torment me about George Talboys – by what right do you dare to say that his wife is still alive?'

'By the right of circumstantial evidence, Lady Audley,'

answered Robert – 'by the right of that circumstantial evidence which will sometimes fix the guilt of a man's murder upon that person who, on the first hearing of the case, seems of all other men the most unlikely to be guilty.'

'What circumstantial evidence?'

'The evidence of time and place. The evidence of handwriting. When Helen Talboys left her father's house at Wildernsea, she left a letter behind her – a letter in which she declared that she was weary of her old life, and that she wished to seek a new home and a new fortune. That letter is in my possession.'

'Indeed.'

'Shall I tell you *whose* handwriting resembles that of Helen Talboys so closely, that the most dexterous expert could perceive no distinction between the two?'

'A resemblance between the handwriting of two women is no very uncommon circumstance now-a-days,' replied my lady, carelessly. 'I could show you the calligraphies of half-a-dozen of my female correspondents, and defy you to discover any great differences in them.'

'But what if the handwriting is a very uncommon one, presenting marked peculiarities by which it may be recognised among a hundred?'

'Why, in that case the coincidence is rather curious,' answered my lady; 'but it is nothing more than a coincidence. You cannot deny the fact of Helen Talboys' death on the ground that her handwriting resembles that of some surviving person.'

'But if a series of such coincidences lead up to the same point,' said Robert. 'Helen Talboys left her father's house, according to the declaration in her own handwriting, because she was weary of her old life, and wished to begin a new one. Do you know what I infer from this?'

My lady shrugged her shoulders.

'I have not the least idea,' she said: 'and as you have detained me in this gloomy place nearly half-an-hour, I must beg that you will release me, and let me go and dress for dinner.'

'No, Lady Audley,' answered Robert, with a cold sternness that was so strange to him as to transform him into another creature – a pitiless embodiment of justice, a cruel instrument of retribution – 'no, Lady Audley,' he repeated, 'I have told you that womanly prevarication will not help you; I tell you now that defiance will not serve you. I have dealt fairly with you, and have given you fair warning. I gave you indirect notice of your danger two months ago.'

'What do you mean?' asked my lady, suddenly.

'You did not choose to take that warning, Lady Audley,' pursued Robert, 'and the time has come in which I must speak very plainly to you. Do you think the gifts which you have played against fortune are to hold you exempt from retribution? No, my lady, your youth and beauty, your grace and refinement, only make the horrible secret of your life more horrible. I tell you that the evidence against you wants only one link to be strong enough for your condemnation, and that link shall be added. Helen Talboys never returned to her father's house. When she deserted that poor old father, she went away from his humble shelter with the declared intention of washing her hands of that old life. What do people generally do when they wish to begin a new existence – to start for a second time in the race of life, free from the encumbrances that had fettered their first journey? *They change their names*, Lady Audley. Helen Talboys deserted her infant son – she went away from Wildernsea with the predetermination of sinking her identity. She disappeared as Helen Talboys upon the 16th of August, 1854, and upon the 17th of that month she reappeared as Lucy Graham, the friendless girl who undertook a profitless duty in consideration of a home in which she was asked no questions.'

'You are mad, Mr. Audley!' cried my lady. 'You are mad,

and my husband shall protect me from your insolence. What if this Helen Talboys ran away from her home upon one day, and I entered my employer's house upon the next, what does that prove?'

'By itself, very little,' replied Robert Audley; 'but with the help of other evidence—'

'What evidence?'

'The evidence of two labels, pasted one over the other, upon a box left by you in the possession of Mrs. Vincent, the upper label bearing the name of Miss Graham, the lower that of Mrs. George Talboys.'

My lady was silent. Robert Audley could not see her face in the dusk, but he could see that her two small hands were clasped convulsively over her heart, and he knew that the shot had gone home to its mark.

'God help her, poor, wretched creature,' he thought. 'She knows now that she is lost. I wonder if the judges of the land feel as I do now, when they put on the black cap and pass sentence of death upon some poor, shivering wretch who has never done them any wrong. Do they feel a heroic fervour of virtuous indignation, or do they suffer this dull anguish which gnaws my vitals as I talk to this helpless woman?'

He walked by my lady's side, silently, for some minutes. They had been pacing up and down the dim avenue, and they were now drawing near the leafless shrubbery at one end of the lime-walk – the shrubbery in which the ruined well sheltered its unheeded decay among the tangled masses of briery underwood.

A winding pathway, neglected and half choked with weeds, led towards this well. Robert left the lime-walk, and struck into this pathway. There was more light in the shrubbery than in the avenue, and Mr. Audley wished to see my lady's face.

He did not speak until they reached the patch of rank grass beside the well. The massive brickwork had fallen away here

305

and there, and loose fragments of masonry lay buried amidst weeds and briers. The heavy posts which had supported the wooden roller still remained, but the iron spindle had been dragged from its socket, and lay a few paces from the well, rusty, discoloured, and forgotten.

Robert Audley leant against one of the moss-grown posts and looked down at my lady's face, very pale in the chill winter twilight. The moon had newly risen, a feebly luminous crescent in the grey heavens, and a faint, ghostly light mingled with the misty shadows of the declining day. My lady's face seemed like that face which Robert Audley had seen in his dreams looking out of the white foam flakes on the green sea waves, and luring his uncle to destruction.

'Those two labels are in my possession, Lady Audley,' he resumed. 'I took them from the box left by you at Crescent Villas. I took them in the presence of Mrs. Vincent and Miss Tonks. Have you any proof to offer against this evidence? You say to me, "I am Lucy Graham, and I have nothing whatever to do with Helen Talboys." In that case, you can produce witnesses who will declare your antecedents. Where had you been living prior to your appearance at Crescent Villas? You must have friends, relations, connections, who can come forward to prove as much as this for you. If you were the most desolate creature upon this earth, you would be able to point to some one who could identify you with the past.'

'Yes,' cried my lady, 'if I were placed in a criminal dock, I could, no doubt, bring forward witnesses to refute your absurd accusation. But I am not in a criminal dock, Mr. Audley, and I do not choose to do anything but laugh at your ridiculous folly. I tell you that you are mad! If you please to say that Helen Talboys is not dead, and that I am Helen Talboys, you may do so. If you choose to go wandering about to the places in which I have lived, and to the places in which this Mrs. Talboys has lived, you must follow the bent of your own inclination; but I would warn you that such fancies have sometimes conducted people, as apparently sane as yourself, to the life-long imprisonment of a private lunatic asylum.'

Robert Audley started, and recoiled a few paces among the weeds and brushwood as my lady said this.

'She would be capable of any new crime to shield her from the consequences of the old one,' he thought. 'She would be capable of using her influence with my uncle to place me in a mad-house.'

I do not say that Robert Audley was a coward, but I will admit that a shiver of horror, something akin to fear, chilled him to the heart, as he remembered the horrible things that have been done by women, since that day upon which Eve was created to be Adam's companion and help-meet in the garden of Eden. What if this woman's hellish power of dissimulation should be stronger than the truth, and crush him? She had not spared George Talboys when he had stood in her way, and menaced her with a certain peril; would she spare him who threatened her with a far greater danger? Are women merciful, or loving, or kind in proportion to their beauty and their grace? Was there not a certain Monsieur Mazers de Latude, who had the bad fortune to offend the all-accomplished Madame de Pompadour, who expiated his youthful indiscretion by a life-long imprisonment; who twice escaped from prison, to be twice cast back into captivity; who, trusting in the tardy generosity of his beautiful foe, betrayed himself to an implacable fiend? Robert Audley looked at the pale face of the woman standing by his side: that fair and beautiful face, illumined by starry blue eyes, that had a strange and surely a dangerous light in them; and remembering a hundred stories of womanly perfidy, shuddered as he thought how unequal the struggle might be between himself and his uncle's wife.

'I have shown her my cards,' he thought, 'but she has kept

hers hidden from me. The mask that she wears is not to be plucked away. My uncle would rather think me mad than believe her guilty.'

The pale face of Clara Talboys – that grave and earnest face so different in its character to my lady's fragile beauty – arose before him.

'What a coward I am to think of myself or my own danger,' he thought. 'The more I see of this woman, the more reason I have to dread her influence upon others; the more reason to wish her far away from this house.'

He looked about him in the dusky obscurity. The lonely garden was as quiet as some solitary graveyard, walled in and hidden away from the world of the living.

'It was somewhere in this garden that she met George Talboys upon the day of his disappearance,' he thought. 'I wonder where it was they met; I wonder where it was that he looked into her cruel face, and taxed her with her falsehood.'

My lady, with her little hand resting lightly upon the opposite post to that against which Robert leant, toyed with her pretty foot amongst the long weeds, but kept a furtive watch upon her enemy's face.

'It is to be a duel to the death, then, my lady,' said Robert Audley, solemnly. 'You refuse to accept my warning. You refuse to run away and repent of your wickedness in some foreign place, far from the generous gentleman you have deceived and fooled by your false witcheries. You choose to remain here and defy me.'

'I do,' answered Lady Audley, lifting her head, and looking full at the young barrister. 'It is no fault of mine if my husband's nephew goes mad, and chooses me for the victim of his monomania.'

'So be it, then, my lady,' answered Robert. 'My friend George Talboys was last seen entering these gardens by the little iron gate at which we came in to-night. He was last heard inquiring for you. He was seen to enter these gardens, but he was never seen to leave them. I do not believe that he ever did leave them. I believe that he met with his death within the boundary of these grounds; and that his body lies hidden below some quiet water, or in some forgotten corner of this place. I will have such a search made as shall level that house to the earth, and root up every tree in these gardens, rather than I will fail in finding the grave of my murdered friend.'

Lucy Audley uttered a long, low, wailing cry, and threw up her arms above her head with a wild gesture of despair, but she made no answer to the ghastly charge of her accuser. Her arms slowly dropped, and she stood staring at Robert Audley, her white face gleaming through the dusk, her blue eyes glittering and dilated.

'You shall never live to do this,' she said. '*I will kill you first.* Why have you tormented me so? Why could you not let me alone? What harm had I ever done *you* that you should make yourself my persecutor, and dog my steps, and watch my looks, and play the spy upon me? Do you want to drive me mad? Do you know what it is to wrestle with a madwoman? No,' cried my lady, with a laugh, 'you do not, or you would never—'

She stopped abruptly, and drew herself suddenly to her fullest height. It was the same action which Robert had seen in the old half-drunken lieutenant; and it had that same dignity – the sublimity of extreme misery.

'Go away, Mr. Audley,' she said. 'You are mad, I tell you; you are mad.'

'I am going, my lady,' answered Robert, quietly. 'I would have condoned your crimes out of pity to your wretchedness. You have refused to accept my mercy. I wished to have pity upon the living. I shall henceforth only remember my duty to the dead.'

He walked away from the lonely well under the shadow of

the limes. My lady followed him slowly down that long, gloomy avenue, and across the rustic bridge to the iron gate. As he passed through the gate, Alicia came out of a little half-glass door that opened from an oak-panelled breakfast-room at one angle of the house, and met her cousin upon the threshold of the gateway.

'I have been looking for you everywhere, Robert,' she said. 'Papa has come down to the library, and I am sure he will be glad to see you.'

The young man started at the sound of his cousin's fresh young voice. 'Good heavens!' he thought, 'can these two women be of the same clay? Can this frank, generous-hearted girl, who cannot conceal any impulse of her innocent nature, be of the same flesh and blood as that wretched creature whose shadow falls upon the path beside me?'

He looked from his cousin to Lady Audley, who stood near the gateway, waiting for him to stand aside and let her pass him.

'I don't know what has come to your cousin, my dear Alicia,' said my lady. 'He is so absent-minded and eccentric, as to be quite beyond my comprehension.'

'Indeed,' exclaimed Miss Audley; 'and yet I should imagine, from the length of your *tête-à-tête*, that you had made some effort to understand him.'

'Oh, yes,' said Robert, quietly, 'my lady and I understand each other very well; but as it is growing late I will wish you good evening, ladies. I shall sleep to-night at Mount Stanning, as I have some business to attend to up there, and I will come down and see my uncle to-morrow.'

'What, Robert!' cried Alicia, 'you surely won't go away without seeing papa?'

'Yes, my dear,' answered the young man. 'I am a little disturbed by some disagreeable business in which I am very much concerned, and I would rather not see my uncle. Good night, Alicia. I will come or write to-morrow.'

He pressed his cousin's hand, bowed to Lady Audley, and walked away under the black shadows of the archway, and out into the quiet avenue beyond the Court.

My lady and Alicia stood watching him until he was out of sight.

'What in goodness' name is the matter with my cousin Robert?' exclaimed Miss Audley, impatiently, as the barrister disappeared. 'What does he mean by these absurd goings-on? Some disagreeable business that disturbs him, indeed! I suppose the unhappy creature has had a brief forced upon him by some evil-starred attorney, and is sinking into a state of imbecility from a dim consciousness of his own incompetence.'

'Have you ever studied your cousin's character, Alicia?' asked my lady, very seriously, after a pause.

'Studied his character! No, Lady Audley. Why should I study his character?' said Alicia. 'There is very little study required to convince anybody that he is a lazy, selfish Sybarite, who cares for nothing in the world except his own ease and comfort.'

'But have you never thought him eccentric?'

'Eccentric!' repeated Alicia, pursing up her red lips and shrugging her shoulders. 'Well, yes – I believe that is the excuse generally made for such people. I suppose Bob *is* eccentric.'

'I have never heard you speak of his father and mother,' said my lady, thoughtfully. 'Do you remember them?'

'I never saw his mother. She was a Miss Dalrymple, a very dashing girl, who ran away with my uncle, and lost a very handsome fortune in consequence. She died at Nice when poor Bob was five years old.'

'Did you ever hear anything particular about her?'

'How do you mean, "particular"?' asked Alicia.

'Did you ever hear that she was eccentric – what people call "odd"?'

'Oh, no,' said Alicia, laughing. 'My aunt was a very reasonable woman, I believe, though she did marry for love. But you must remember that she died before I was born, and I have not, therefore, felt very much curiosity about her.'

'But you recollect your uncle, I suppose?'

'My uncle Robert?' said Alicia. 'Oh, yes, I remember him very well indeed.'

'Was *he* eccentric – I mean to say, peculiar in his habits, like your cousin?'

'Yes, I believe Robert inherits all his absurdities from his father. My uncle expressed the same indifference for his fellow-creatures as my cousin; but as he was a good husband, an affectionate father, and a kind master, nobody ever challenged his opinions.'

'But he *was* eccentric?'

'Yes; I suppose he was generally thought a little eccentric.'

'Ah,' said my lady gravely, 'I thought as much. Do you know, Alicia, that madness is more often transmitted from father to son than from father to daughter, and from mother to daughter than from mother to son? Your cousin Robert Audley is a very handsome young man, and I believe a very good-hearted young man; but he must be watched, Alicia, for he is *mad*!'

'Mad!' cried Miss Audley, indignantly; 'you are dreaming, my lady, or – or – you are trying to frighten me,' added the young lady, with considerable alarm.

'I only wish to put you on your guard, Alicia,' answered my lady. 'Mr. Audley may be as you say, merely eccentric; but he has talked to me this evening in a manner that has filled me with absolute terror, and I believe that he is going mad. I shall speak very seriously to Sir Michael this very night.'

'Speak to papa!' exclaimed Alicia; 'you surely won't distress papa by suggesting such a possibility!'

'I shall only put him on his guard, my dear Alicia.'

'But he'll never believe you,' said Miss Audley; 'he will laugh at such an idea.'

'No, Alicia; he will believe anything that I tell him,' answered my lady, with a quiet smile.

CHAPTER XII
Preparing the ground

Lady Audley went from the garden to the library, a pleasant oak-panelled homely apartment in which Sir Michael liked to sit reading or writing, or arranging the business of his estate with his steward, a stalwart countryman, half agriculturist, half lawyer, who rented a small farm a few miles from the Court.

The baronet was seated in a capacious easy-chair near the hearth. The bright blaze of the fire rose and fell, flashing now upon the polished prominences of the black-oak bookcase, now upon the gold and scarlet bindings of the books; sometimes glimmering upon the Athenian helmet of a marble Pallas, sometimes lighting up the forehead of Sir Robert Peel.

The lamp upon the reading-table had not yet been lighted, and Sir Michael sat in the firelight waiting for the coming of his young wife.

It is impossible for me ever to tell the purity of his generous love – it is impossible to describe that affection which was as tender as the love of a young mother for her first-born, as brave and chivalrous as the heroic passion of a Bayard for his liege mistress.

The door opened while he was thinking of this fondly-loved wife, and looking up, the baronet saw the slender form standing in the doorway.

'Why, my darling!' he exclaimed, as my lady closed the door behind her, and came towards his chair, 'I have been thinking of you, and waiting for you for an hour. Where have you been, and what have you been doing?'

My lady, standing in the shadow rather than in the light, paused a few moments before replying to this question.

'I have been to Chelmsford,' she said, 'shopping; and—'

She hesitated – twisting her bonnet-strings in her thin white fingers with an air of pretty embarrassment.

'And what, my dear,' asked the baronet – 'what have you been doing since you came from Chelmsford? I heard a carriage stop at the door an hour ago. It was yours, was it not?'

'Yes, I came home an hour ago,' answered my lady, with the same air of embarrassment.

'And what have you been doing since you came home?'

Sir Michael Audley asked this question with a slightly reproachful accent. His young wife's presence made the sunshine of his life, and though he could not bear to chain her to his side, it grieved him to think that she could willingly remain unnecessarily absent from him frittering away her time in some childish talk or frivolous occupation.

'What have you been doing since you came home, my dear?' he repeated. 'What has kept you so long away from me?'

'I have been talking – to – Mr. Robert Audley.'

She still twisted her bonnet-strings round and round her fingers. She still spoke with the same air of embarrassment.

'Robert!' exclaimed the baronet; 'is Robert here?'

'He was here a little while ago.'

'And is here still, I suppose?'

'No, he has gone away.'

'Gone away!' cried Sir Michael. 'What do you mean, my darling?'

'I mean that your nephew came to the Court this afternoon. Alicia and I found him idling about the gardens. He stayed here till about a quarter of an hour ago talking to me, and then he hurried off, without a word of explanation, except, indeed, some ridiculous excuse about business at Mount Stanning.'

'Business at Mount Stanning! Why, what business can he possibly have in that out-of-the-way place? He has gone to sleep at Mount Stanning, then, I suppose?'

'Yes, I think he said something to that effect.'

'Upon my word,' exclaimed the baronet, 'I think that boy is half mad.'

My lady's face was so much in shadow, that Sir Michael Audley was unaware of the bright change that came over its sickly pallor as he made this very common-place observation. A triumphant smile illumined Lucy Audley's countenance, a smile that plainly said, 'It is coming – it is coming; I can twist him which way I like. I can put black before him, and if I say it is white, he will believe me.'

But Sir Michael Audley, in declaring that his nephew's wits were disordered, merely uttered that common-place ejaculation which is well known to have very little meaning. The baronet had, it is true, no very great estimate of Robert's faculty for the business of this every-day life. He was in the habit of looking upon his nephew as a good-natured nonentity – a man whose heart had been amply stocked by liberal nature with all the best things the generous goddess had to bestow, but whose brain had been somewhat overlooked in the distribution of intellectual gifts. Sir Michael Audley made that mistake which is very commonly made by easy-going, well-to-do observers, who have no occasion to look below the surface. He mistook laziness for incapacity. He thought because his nephew was idle, he must necessarily be stupid. He concluded that if Robert did not distinguish himself it was because he could not.

He forgot the mute inglorious Miltons who die voiceless and inarticulate for want of that dogged perseverance, that blind courage, which the poet must possess before he can find a publisher; he forgot the Cromwells, who see the noble vessel – political economy – floundering upon a sea of confusion, and going down in a tempest of noisy bewilderment, and who yet are powerless to get at the helm, forbidden even to send out a life-boat to the sinking ship. Surely it is a mistake to judge of what a man can do by that which he has done.

The world's Valhalla is a close borough, and perhaps the greatest men may be those who perish silently far away from the sacred portal. Perhaps the purest and brightest spirits are those who shrink from the turmoil of the race-course – the tumult and confusion of the struggle. The game of life is something like the game of *écarté*, and it may be that the best cards are sometimes left in the pack.

My lady threw off her bonnet, and seated herself upon a velvet-covered footstool at Sir Michael's feet. There was nothing studied or affected in this girlish action. It was so natural to Lucy Audley to be childish, that no one would have wished to see her otherwise. It would have seemed as foolish to expect dignified reserve or womanly gravity from this amber-haired syren, as to wish for rich basses in the clear treble of a skylark's song.

She sat with her pale face turned away from the firelight, and with her hands locked together upon the arm of her husband's easy-chair. They were very restless, these slender white hands. My lady twisted the jewelled fingers in and out of each other, as she talked to her husband.

'I wanted to come to you, you know, dear,' she said – 'I wanted to come to you directly I got home, but Mr. Audley insisted upon my stopping to talk to him.'

'But what about, my love?' asked the baronet. 'What could Robert have to say to you?'

My lady did not answer this question. Her fair head dropped upon her husband's knee, her rippling yellow curls fell over her face.

Sir Michael lifted that beautiful head with his strong hands, and raised my lady's face. The fire-light shining on that pale face lit up the large, soft blue eyes which were drowned in tears.

'Lucy, Lucy!' cried the baronet, 'what is the meaning of this? My love, my love, what has happened to distress you in this manner?'

Lady Audley tried to speak, but the words died away inarticulately upon her trembling lips. A choking sensation in her throat seemed to strangle those false and plausible words, her only armour against her enemies. She could not speak. The agony she had endured silently in the dismal lime-walk had grown too strong for her, and she broke into a tempest of hysterical sobbing. It was no simulated grief that shook her slender frame, and tore at her like some ravenous beast that would have rent her piecemeal with its horrible strength. It was a storm of real anguish and terror, of remorse and misery. It was the one wild outcry, in which the woman's feebler nature got the better of the syren's art.

It was not thus that she had meant to fight her terrible duel with Robert Audley. These were not the weapons which she had intended to use; but perhaps no artifice which she could have devised would have served her so well as this one outburst of natural grief. It shook her husband to the very soul. It bewildered and terrified him. It reduced the strong intellect of the man to helpless confusion and perplexity. It struck at the one weak point in a good man's nature. It appealed straight to Sir Michael Audley's affection for his wife.

Ah, Heaven help a strong man's tender weakness for the woman he loves. Heaven pity him when the guilty creature has deceived him and comes with her tears and lamentations to throw herself at his feet in self-abandonment and remorse, torturing him with the sight of her agony, rending *his* heart with her sobs, lacerating *his* breast with her groans. Multiplying her own sufferings into a great anguish for him to bear, multiplying them by twenty-fold, multiplying them in the ratio of a brave man's capacity for endurance. Heaven forgive him if, maddened by that cruel agony, the balance wavers for a moment, and he is ready to forgive *anything*, ready to take this wretched one to the shelter of his breast, and to pardon that which the stern voice of manly honour urges must not be pardoned. Pity him, pity him. The wife's worst remorse when she stands without the threshold of the home she may never enter more is not equal to the agony of the husband who closes the portal on that familiar and entreating face. The anguish of the mother who may never look again upon her children is less than the torment of the father who has to say to those children, 'My little ones, you are henceforth motherless.'

Sir Michael Audley rose from his chair, trembling with indignation, and ready to do immediate battle with the person who had caused his wife's grief.

'Lucy,' he said, 'Lucy, I insist upon your telling me what and who has distressed you. I insist upon it. Whoever has annoyed you shall answer to me for your grief. Come, my love, tell me directly what it is.'

He reseated himself and bent over the drooping figure at his feet, calming his own agitation in his desire to soothe his wife's distress.

'Tell me what it is, my dear,' he whispered, tenderly.

The sharp paroxysm had passed away, and my lady looked up: a glittering light shone through the tears in her eyes, and the lines about her pretty rosy mouth, those hard and cruel lines which Robert Audley had observed in the pre-Raphaelite portrait, were plainly visible in the firelight.

'I am very silly,' she said; 'but really he has made me quite hysterical.'

'Who – who has made you hysterical?'

'Your nephew – Mr. Robert Audley.'

'Robert!' cried the baronet. 'Lucy, what do you mean?'

'I told you that Mr. Audley insisted upon my going into the lime-walk, dear,' said my lady. 'He wanted to talk to me, he said, and I went, and he said such horrible things that—'

'What horrible things, Lucy?'

Lady Audley shuddered and clung with convulsive fingers to the strong hand that had rested caressingly upon her shoulder.

'What did he say, Lucy?'

'Oh, my dear love, how can I tell you?' cried my lady. 'I know that I shall distress you – or you will laugh at me, and then—'

'Laugh at you? no, Lucy.'

Lady Audley was silent for a moment. She sat looking straight before her into the fire, with her fingers still locked about her husband's hand.

'My dear,' she said, slowly, hesitating now and then between her words, as if she almost shrank from uttering them, 'have you ever – I am so afraid of vexing you – or – have you ever thought Mr. Audley – a little—'

'A little what, my darling?'

'A little out of his mind,' faltered Lady Audley.

'Out of his mind!' cried Sir Michael. 'My dear girl, what are you thinking of?'

'You said just now, dear, that you thought he was half mad.'

'Did I, my love?' said the baronet, laughing. 'I don't remember saying it, and it was a mere *façon de parler*, that meant nothing whatever. Robert may be a little eccentric – a little stupid, perhaps – he mayn't be overburdened with wits, but I don't think he has brains enough for madness. I believe it's generally your great intellects that get out of order.'

'But madness is sometimes hereditary,' said my lady. 'Mr. Audley may have inherited—'

'He has inherited no madness from his father's family,' interrupted Sir Michael. 'The Audleys have never peopled private lunatic asylums or fee'd mad doctors.'

'Nor from his mother's family?'

'Not to my knowledge.'

'People generally keep these things a secret,' said my lady, gravely. 'There may have been madness in your sister-in-law's family.'

'I don't think so, my dear,' replied Sir Michael. 'But, Lucy, tell me what, in Heaven's name, has put this idea into your head?'

'I have been trying to account for your nephew's conduct. I can account for it in no other manner. If you had heard the things he said to me to-night, Sir Michael, you too might have thought him mad.'

'But what did he say, Lucy?'

'I can scarcely tell you. You can see how much he has stupified and bewildered me. I believe he has lived too long alone in those solitary Temple chambers. Perhaps he reads too much, or smokes too much. You know that some physicians declare madness to be a mere illness of the brain – an illness to which any one is subject, and which may be produced by given causes, and cured by given means.'

Lady Audley's eyes were still fixed upon the burning coals in the wide grate. She spoke as if she had been discussing a subject that she had often heard discussed before. She spoke as if her mind had almost wandered away from the thought of her husband's nephew to the wider question of madness in the abstract.

'Why should he not be mad?' resumed my lady. 'People are insane for years and years before their insanity is found out. *They* know that they are mad, but they know how to keep their secret; and, perhaps they may sometimes keep it till they die. Sometimes a paroxysm seizes them, and in an evil hour they betray themselves. They commit a crime, perhaps. The horrible temptation of opportunity assails them, the knife is in their hand, and the unconscious victim by their side. They may conquer the restless demon and go away, and die innocent of any violent deed; but they may yield to the horrible temptation – the frightful, passionate, hungry craving for violence and horror. They sometimes yield, and are lost.'

Lady Audley's voice rose as she argued this dreadful question. The hysterical excitement from which she had only just recovered had left its effects upon her, but she controlled herself, and her tone grew calmer as she resumed:–

'Robert Audley is mad,' she said, decisively. 'What is one of the strongest diagnostics of madness – what is the first appalling sign of mental aberration? The mind becomes stationary; the brain stagnates; the even current of the mind is interrupted; the thinking power of the brain resolves itself into a monotone. As the waters of a tideless pool putrefy by reason of their stagnation, the mind becomes turbid and corrupt through lack of action; and perpetual reflection upon one subject resolves itself into monomania. Robert Audley is a monomaniac. The disappearance of his friend, George Talboys, grieved and bewildered him. He dwelt upon this one idea until he lost the power of thinking of anything else. The one idea looked at perpetually became distorted to his mental vision. Repeat the commonest word in the English language twenty times, and before the twentieth repetition you will have begun to wonder whether the word which you repeat is really the word you mean to utter. Robert Audley has thought of his friend's disappearance until the one idea has done its fatal and unhealthy work. He looks at a common event with a vision that is diseased, and he distorts it into a gloomy horror engendered of his own monomania. If you do not want to make me as mad as he is, you must never let me see him again. He declared to-night that George Talboys was murdered in this place, and that he will root up every tree in the gardens, and pull down every brick in the house, in his search for—'

My lady paused. The words died away upon her lips.

She had exhausted herself by the strange energy with which she had spoken. She had been transformed from a frivolous childish beauty into a woman, strong to argue her own cause and plead her own defence.

'Pull down this house!' cried the baronet. 'George Talboys murdered at Audley Court! Did Robert say this, Lucy?'

'He said something of that kind – something that frightened me very much.'

'Then he must be mad,' said Sir Michael, gravely. 'I'm bewildered by what you tell me. Did he really say this, Lucy, or did you misunderstand him?'

'I – I – don't think I did,' faltered my lady. 'You saw how frightened I was when I first came in. I should not have been so much agitated if he hadn't said something horrible.'

Lady Audley had availed herself of the very strongest argument by which she could help her cause.

'To be sure, my darling, to be sure,' answered the baronet. 'What could have put such a horrible fancy into the unhappy boy's head? This Mr. Talboys – a perfect stranger to all of us – murdered, at Audley Court! I'll go to Mount Stanning to-night, and see Robert. I have known him ever since he was a baby, and I cannot be deceived in him. If there is really anything wrong, he will not be able to conceal it from me.'

My lady shrugged her shoulders.

'That is rather an open question,' she said. 'It is generally a stranger who is the first to observe any psychological peculiarity.'

The big words sounded strange from my lady's rosy lips; but her newly-adopted wisdom had a certain quaint prettiness about it, which bewildered her husband.

'But you must not go to Mount Stanning, my dear darling,' she said, tenderly. 'Remember that you are under strict orders to stay in-doors until the weather is milder, and the sun shines upon this cruel ice-bound country.'

Sir Michael Audley sank back into his capacious chair with a sigh of resignation.

'That's true, Lucy,' he said; 'we must obey Mr. Dawson. I suppose Robert will come to see me to-morrow.'

'Yes, dear. I think he said he would.'

'Then we must wait till to-morrow, my darling. I can't believe that there really is anything wrong with the poor boy – I can't believe it, Lucy.'

'Then how do you account for his extraordinary delusion about this Mr. Talboys?' asked my lady.

Sir Michael shook his head.

'I don't know, Lucy – I don't know,' he answered. 'It is always so difficult to believe that any one of the calamities that continually befall our fellow-men will ever happen to us. I can't believe that my nephew's mind is impaired – I can't believe it. I – I'll get him to stop here, Lucy, and I'll watch him closely. I tell you, my love, if there is anything wrong I am sure to find it out. I can't be mistaken in a young man who has always been the same to me as my own son. But, my darling, why were you so frightened by Robert's wild talk? It could not affect you.'

My lady sighed piteously.

'You must think me very strong-minded, Sir Michael,' she said with rather an injured air, 'if you imagine I can hear of these sort of things indifferently. I know I shall never be able to see Mr. Audley again.'

'And you shall not, my dear – you shall not.'

'You said just now you would have him here,' murmured Lady Audley.

'But I will not, my darling girl, if his presence annoys you. Good heavens, Lucy, can you imagine for a moment that I have any higher wish than to promote your happiness? I will consult some London physician about Robert, and let him discover if there really is anything the matter with my poor brother's only son. *You* shall not be annoyed, Lucy.'

324

'You must think me very unkind, dear,' said my lady, 'and I know I *ought* not to be annoyed by the poor fellow; but he really seems to have taken some absurd notion into his head about me.'

'About *you*, Lucy!' cried Sir Michael.

'Yes, dear. He seems to connect me in some vague manner – which I cannot quite understand – with the disappearance of this Mr. Talboys.'

'Impossible, Lucy. You must have misunderstood him.'

'I don't think so.'

'Then he must be mad,' said the baronet – 'he must be mad. I will wait till he goes back to town, and then send some one to his chambers to talk to him. Good heavens, what a mysterious business this is!'

'I fear I have distressed you, darling,' murmured Lady Audley.

'Yes, my dear, I am very much distressed by what you have told me; but you were quite right to talk to me frankly about this dreadful business. I must think it over, dearest, and try and decide what is best to be done.'

My lady rose from the low ottoman on which she had been seated. The fire had burned down, and there was only a faint glow of red light in the room. Lucy Audley bent over her husband's chair, and put her lips to his broad forehead.

'How good you have always been to me, dear,' she whispered softly. 'You would never let any one influence you against me, would you, my darling?'

'Influence me against you?' repeated the baronet. 'No, my love.'

'Because you know, dear,' pursued my lady, 'there are wicked people as well as mad people in the world, and there may be some persons to whose interest it would be to injure me.'

'They had better not try it then, my dear,' answered Sir Michael; 'they would find themselves in rather a dangerous position if they did.'

Lady Audley laughed aloud, with a gay, triumphant, silvery peal of laughter that vibrated through the quiet room.

'My own dear darling,' she said, 'I know you love me. And now I must run away, dear, for it's past seven o'clock. I was engaged to dine at Mrs. Montford's, but I must send a groom with a message of apology, for Mr. Audley has made me quite unfit for company. I shall stay at home, and nurse you, dear. You'll go to bed very early, won't you, and take great care of yourself?'

'Yes, dear.'

My lady tripped out of the room to give her orders about the message which was to be carried to the house at which she was to have dined. She paused for a moment as she closed the library door – she paused, and laid her hand upon her breast to check the rapid throbbing of her heart.

'I have been afraid of you, Mr. Robert Audley,' she thought, 'but perhaps the time may come in which you will have cause to be afraid of me.'

CHAPTER XIII
Phœbe's petition

The division between Lady Audley and her step-daughter had not become any narrower in the two months which had elapsed since the pleasant Christmas holiday time had been kept at Audley Court. There was no open warfare between the two women; there was only an armed neutrality, broken every now and then by brief feminine skirmishes and transient wordy tempests. I am sorry to say that Alicia would very much have preferred a hearty pitched battle to this silent and undemonstrative disunion; but it was not very easy to quarrel with my lady. She had soft answers for the turning away of wrath. She could smile bewitchingly at her step-daughter's open petulance, and laugh merrily at the young lady's ill-temper. Perhaps had she been less amiable, had she been indeed more like Alicia in disposition, the two ladies might have expended their enmity in one tremendous quarrel, and might ever afterwards have been affectionate and friendly. But Lucy Audley would not make war. She carried forward the sum of her dislike, and put it out at a steady rate of interest, until the breach between her step-daughter and herself, widening a little every day, became a great gulf utterly impassable by olive-branch-bearing doves, from either side of the abyss. There can be no reconciliation where there is no open warfare. There must be a battle, a brave boisterous battle, with pennants waving and cannon roaring, before there can be peaceful treaties and enthusiastic shaking of hands. Perhaps the union between France and England owes its greatest force to the recollection of bygone conquest and defeat. We have hated each other and licked each other and *had it out*, as the common phrase goes, and we can afford now to fall into each other's arms and vow eternal friendship and everlasting brotherhood. Let us hope that when Northern Yankeydom has decimated and been decimated, blustering Jonathan may fling himself upon his Southern brother's breast, forgiving and forgiven.

Alicia Audley and her father's pretty wife had plenty of room for the comfortable indulgence of their dislike in the spacious old mansion. My lady had her own apartments, as we know – luxurious chambers, in which all conceivable elegancies had been gathered for the comfort of their occupant. Alicia had her own rooms in another part of the large house. She had her favourite mare, her Newfoundland dog, and her drawing materials, and she made herself tolerably happy. She was not very happy, this frank, generous-hearted girl, for it was scarcely possible that she could be altogether at ease in the constrained atmosphere of the Court. Her father was changed – that dear father, over whom she had once reigned supreme with the boundless authority of a spoiled child, had accepted another ruler and submitted to a new dynasty. Little by little my lady's pretty power made itself felt in that narrow household, and Alicia saw her father gradually lured across the gulf that divided Lady Audley from her step-daughter, until he stood at last quite upon the other side of the abyss, and looked coldly upon his only child across that widening chasm.

Alicia felt that he was lost to her. My lady's beaming smiles, my lady's winning words, my lady's radiant glances and bewitching graces had done their work of enchantment, and Sir Michael had grown to look upon his daughter as a somewhat wilful and capricious young person who had behaved with determined unkindness to the wife he loved.

Poor Alicia saw all this, and bore her burden as well as she could. It seemed very hard to be a handsome grey-eyed heiress, with dogs and horses and servants at her command, and yet to be so much alone in the world as to know of not one friendly ear into which she might pour her sorrows.

'If Bob was good for anything, I could have told him how unhappy I am,' thought Miss Audley; 'but I may just as well tell Cæsar my troubles, for any consolation I should get from my cousin Robert.'

Sir Michael Audley obeyed his pretty nurse, and went to bed at a little after nine o'clock upon this bleak March evening. Perhaps the baronet's bed-room was about the pleasantest retreat that an invalid could have chosen in such cold and cheerless weather. The dark-green velvet curtains were drawn before the windows and about the ponderous bed. The wood fire burned redly upon the broad hearth. The reading-lamp was lighted upon a delicious little table close to Sir Michael's pillow, and a heap of magazines and newspapers had been arranged by my lady's own fair hands for the pleasure of the invalid.

Lady Audley sat by the bedside for about ten minutes talking to her husband, talking very seriously, about this strange and awful question – Robert Audley's lunacy; but at the end of that time she rose and bade him goodnight. She lowered the green silk shade before the reading-lamp, adjusting it carefully for the repose of the baronet's eyes.

'I shall leave you, dear,' she said. 'If you can sleep, so much the better. If you wish to read, the books and papers are close to you. I will leave the doors between the rooms open, and I shall hear your voice if you call me.'

Lady Audley went through her dressing-room into the boudoir, where she had sat with her husband since dinner.

Every evidence of womanly refinement was visible in the elegant chamber. My lady's piano was open, covered with scattered sheets of music and exquisitely-bound collections of scenas and fantasias which no master need have disdained to study. My lady's easel stood near the window, bearing witness to my lady's artistic talent, in the shape of a water-coloured sketch of the Court and gardens. My lady's fairy-like embroideries of lace and muslin, rainbow-hued silks, and delicately-tinted wools littered the luxurious apartment; while the looking-glasses, cunningly placed at angles and opposite corners by an artistic upholsterer, multiplied my lady's image, and in that image reflected the most beautiful object in the enchanted chamber.

Amid all this lamplight, gilding, colour, wealth, and beauty, Lucy Audley sat down on a low seat by the fire to think.

If Mr. Holman Hunt could have peeped into the pretty boudoir, I think the picture would have been photographed upon his brain to be reproduced by-and-by upon a bishop's half-length for the glorification of the pre-Raphaelite brotherhood. My lady in that half-recumbent attitude, with her elbow resting on one knee, and her perfect chin supported by her hand, the rich folds of drapery falling away in long undulating lines from the exquisite outline of her figure, and the luminous rose-coloured fire-light enveloping her in a soft haze, only broken by the golden glitter of her yellow hair. Beautiful in herself, but made bewilderingly beautiful by the gorgeous surroundings which adorn the shrine of her loveliness. Drinking-cups of gold and ivory, chiselled by Benvenuto Cellini; cabinets of buhl and porcelain, bearing the cipher of Austrian Maria Antoinette, amid devices of rosebuds and true lover's knots, birds and butterflies, cupidons and shepherdesses, goddesses, courtiers, cottagers and milkmaids; statuettes of Parian marble and biscuit china; gilded baskets of hothouse flowers; fantastical caskets of Indian filagree work; fragile teacups of turquoise china, adorned by medallion miniatures of Louis the Great and Louis the Well-beloved, Louise de la Vallière, and Jeanne Marie du Barry; cabinet pictures and gilded mirrors, shimmering satin and diaphanous lace; all that gold can buy or art devise had been gathered together for the beautification of this quiet chamber in which my lady sat listening to the moaning of the shrill March wind and the flapping of the ivy leaves against the casements, and looking into the red chasms in the burning coals.

I should be preaching a very stale sermon, and harping upon a very familiar moral, if I were to seize this opportunity of declaiming against art and beauty, because my lady was more wretched in this elegant apartment than many a half-starved sempstress in her dreary garret. She was wretched by reason of a wound which lay too deep for the possibility of any solace from such plasters as wealth and luxury; but her wretchedness was of an abnormal nature, and I can see no occasion for seizing upon the fact of her misery as an argument in favour of poverty and discomfort as opposed to opulence. The Benvenuto Cellini carvings and the Sèvres porcelain could not give her happiness because she had passed out of their region. She was no longer innocent, and the pleasure we take in art and loveliness, being an innocent pleasure, had passed beyond her reach. Six or seven years before, she would have been happy in the possession of this little Aladdin's palace; but she had wandered out of the circle of careless pleasure-seeking creatures, she had strayed far away into a desolate labyrinth of guilt and treachery, terror and crime, and all the treasures that had been collected for her could have given her no pleasure but one, the pleasure of flinging them into a heap beneath her feet, and trampling upon them and destroying them in her cruel despair.

There were some things that would have inspired her with an awful joy, a horrible rejoicing. If Robert Audley, her pitiless enemy, her unrelenting pursuer, had lain dead in the adjoining chamber, she would have exulted over his bier.

What pleasure could have remained for Lucretia Borgia

331

and Catherine de' Medici, when the dreadful boundary line between innocence and guilt was passed, and the lost creatures stood upon the lonely outer side? Only horrible vengeful joys, and treacherous delights were left for these miserable women. With what disdainful bitterness they must have watched the frivolous vanities, the petty deceptions, the paltry sins of ordinary offenders. Perhaps they took a horrible pride in the enormity of their wickedness; in this 'divinity of Hell,' which made them greatest amongst sinful creatures.

My lady, brooding by the fire in her lonely chamber, with her large, clear blue eyes fixed upon the yawning gulfs of lurid crimson in the burning coals, may have thought of many things very far away from the terribly silent struggle in which she was engaged. She may have thought of long-ago years of childish innocence, childish follies and selfishnesses, or frivolous feminine sins that had weighed very lightly upon her conscience. Perhaps in that retrospective reverie she recalled the early time in which she had first looked in the glass and discovered that she was beautiful: that fatal early time in which she had first begun to look upon her loveliness as a right divine, a boundless possession which was to be a set-off against all girlish short-comings, a counter-balance of every youthful sin. Did she remember the day in which that fairy dower of beauty had first taught her to be selfish and cruel, indifferent to the joys and sorrows of others, cold-hearted and capricious, greedy of admiration, exacting and tyrannical, with that petty woman's tyranny which is the worst of despotisms? Did she trace every sin of her life back to its true source? and did she discover that poisoned fountain in her own exaggerated estimate of the value of a pretty face? Surely, if her thoughts wandered so far along the backward current of her life, she must have repented in bitterness and despair of that first day in which the master-passions of her life had become her rulers, and the three demons of Vanity, Selfishness, and Ambition had joined hands and said, 'This woman is our slave; let us see what she will become under our guidance.'

How small these first youthful errors seemed as my lady looked back upon them in that long reverie by the lonely hearth! What small vanities, what petty cruelties! A triumph over a schoolfellow, a flirtation with the lover of a friend, an assertion of the right divine invested in blue eyes and shimmering golden-tinted hair. But how terribly that narrow pathway had widened out into the broad high-road of sin, and how swift the footsteps had become upon the now familiar way!

My lady twined her fingers in her loose amber curls, and made as if she would have torn them from her head. But even in that moment of mute despair the unyielding dominion of beauty asserted itself, and she released the poor tangled glitter of ringlets, leaving them to make a halo round her head in the dim firelight.

'I was not wicked when I was young,' she thought, as she stared gloomily at the fire, 'I was only thoughtless. I never did any harm – at least, never wilfully. Have I ever been really *wicked*, I wonder?' she mused. 'My worst wickednesses have been the result of wild impulses, and not of deeply laid plots. I am not like the women I have read of, who have lain night after night in the horrible dark and stillness, planning out treacherous deeds, and arranging every circumstance of an appointed crime. I wonder whether they suffered – those women – whether they ever suffered as—'

Her thoughts wandered away into a weary maze of confusion. Suddenly she drew herself up with a proud defiant gesture, and her eyes glittered with a light that was not entirely reflected from the fire.

'You are mad, Mr. Robert Audley,' she said, 'you are mad, and your fancies are a madman's fancies. I know what madness is. I know its signs and tokens, and I say that you are mad.'

She put her hand to her head, as if thinking of something which confused and bewildered her, and which she found it difficult to contemplate with calmness.

'Dare I defy him?' she muttered. 'Dare I? dare I? Will he stop now that he has once gone so far? Will he stop for fear of me? Will he stop for fear of me when the thought of what his uncle must suffer has not stopped him? Will anything stop him – but death?'

She pronounced the last two words in an awful whisper, and with her head bent forward, her eyes dilated, and her lips still parted as they had been parted in her utterance of that final word 'death,' she sat blankly staring at the fire.

'I can't plot horrible things,' she muttered presently; 'my brain isn't strong enough, or I'm not wicked enough, or brave enough. If I met Robert Audley in those lonely gardens, as I—'

The current of her thoughts was interrupted by a cautious knocking at her door. She rose suddenly, startled by any sound in the stillness of her room. She rose, and threw herself into a low chair near the fire. She flung her beautiful head back upon the soft cushions, and took a book from the table near her.

Insignificant as this action was it spoke very plainly. It spoke very plainly of ever-recurring fears – of fatal necessities for concealment – of a mind that in its silent agonies was ever alive to the importance of outward effect. It told more plainly than anything else could have told, how complete an actress my lady had been made by the awful necessity of her life.

The modest rap at the boudoir-door was repeated.

'Come in,' cried Lady Audley, in her liveliest tone.

The door was opened with that respectful noiselessness peculiar to a well-bred servant, and a young woman plainly dressed, and carrying some of the cold March winds in the folds of her garments, crossed the threshold of the apartment and lingered near the door, waiting permission to approach the inner regions of my lady's retreat.

It was Phœbe Marks, the pale-faced wife of the Mount Stanning innkeeper.

'I beg pardon, my lady, for intruding without leave,' she said; 'but I thought I might venture to come straight up without waiting for permission.'

'Yes, yes, Phœbe, to be sure. Take off your bonnet, you wretched cold-looking creature, and come and sit down here.'

Lady Audley pointed to the low ottoman upon which she had herself been seated a few minutes before. The lady's-maid had often sat upon it listening to her mistress's prattle in the old days, when she had been my lady's chief companion and *confidante*.

'Sit down here, Phœbe,' Lady Audley repeated; 'sit down here and talk to me. I'm very glad you came here to-night. I was horribly lonely in this dreary place.'

My lady shivered, and looked round the luxurious chamber very much as if the Sèvres and bronze, the buhl and ormolu, had been the mouldering adornments of some ruined castle. The dreary wretchedness of her thoughts had communicated itself to every object about her, and all outer things took their colour from that weary inner life which held its slow course of secret anguish in her breast. She had spoken the entire truth in saying that she was glad of her lady's-maid's visit. Her frivolous nature clung to this weak shelter in the hour of her fear and suffering. There were sympathies between her and this girl, who was like herself inwardly as well as outwardly – like herself, selfish, and cold, and cruel, eager for her own advancement, and greedy of opulence and elegance, angry with the lot that had been cast her, and weary of dull dependence. My lady hated Alicia for her frank, passionate, generous, daring nature; she hated her step-daughter, and clung to this pale-faced, pale-haired girl, whom she thought neither better nor worse than herself.

Phœbe Marks obeyed her late mistress's commands, and took off her bonnet before seating herself on the ottoman at Lady Audley's feet. Her smooth bands of light hair were unruffled by the March winds; her trimly-made drab dress and linen collar were as neatly arranged as they could have been had she only that moment completed her toilet.

'Sir Michael is better, I hope, my lady?' she said.

'Yes, Phœbe, much better. He is asleep. You may close that door,' added Lady Audley with a motion of her head towards the door of communication between the rooms, which had been left open.

Mrs. Marks obeyed submissively, and then returned to her seat.

'I am very, very unhappy, Phœbe,' my lady said, fretfully; 'wretchedly miserable.'

'About the secret?' asked Mrs. Marks, in a half-whisper.

My lady did not notice that question. She resumed in the same complaining tone. She was glad to be able to complain even to this lady's-maid. She had brooded over her fears, and had suffered so long in secret, that it was an inexpressible relief to her to bemoan her fate aloud.

'I am cruelly persecuted and harassed, Phœbe Marks,' she said. 'I am pursued and tormented by a man whom I never injured, whom I have never wished to injure. I am never suffered to rest by this relentless tormentor, and I—'

She paused, staring at the fire again, as she had done in her loneliness. Lost again in the dark intricacies of thoughts which wandered hither and thither in a dreadful chaos of terrified bewilderment, she could not come to any fixed conclusion.

Phœbe Marks watched my lady's face, looking upward at her late mistress with pale, anxious eyes, that only relaxed their watchfulness when Lady Audley's glance met that of her companion.

'I think I know whom you mean, my lady,' said the innkeeper's wife after a pause; 'I think I know who it is who is so cruel to you.'

'Oh, of course,' answered my lady, bitterly; 'my secrets are everybody's secrets. You know all about it, no doubt.'

'The person is a gentleman, is he not, my lady?'

'Yes.'

'A gentleman who came to the Castle Inn two months ago, when I warned you—'

'Yes, yes,' answered my lady impatiently.

'I thought so. The same gentleman is at our place to-night, my lady.'

Lady Audley started up from her chair – started up as if she would have done something desperate in her despairing fury; but she sank back again with a weary, querulous sigh. What warfare could such a feeble creature wage against her fate? What could she do but wind like a hunted hare till she found her way back to the starting-point of the cruel chase, to be there trampled down by her pursuers?

'At the Castle Inn?' she cried. 'I might have known as much. He has gone there to wring my secrets from your husband. Fool!' she exclaimed, suddenly turning upon Phœbe Marks in a transport of anger, 'do you want to destroy me that you have left those two men together?'

Mrs. Marks clasped her hands piteously.

'I didn't come away of my own free will, my lady,' she said; 'no one could have been more unwilling to leave the house than I was this night. I was sent here.'

'Who sent you here?'

'Luke, my lady. You can't tell how hard he can be upon me if I go against him.'

'Why did he send you?'

The innkeeper's wife dropped her eyelids under Lady Audley's angry glances, and hesitated confusedly before she answered this question.

'Indeed, my lady,' she stammered, 'I didn't want to come. I told Luke that it was too bad for us to worry you, first asking this favour, and then asking that, and never leaving you alone for a month together; but – but – he drove me down with his loud blustering talk, and he made me come.'

'Yes, yes,' cried Lady Audley, impatiently, 'I know that. I want to know why you have come.'

'Why, you know, my lady,' answered Phœbe, half reluctantly, 'Luke is very extravagant; and all I can say to him, I can't get him to be careful or steady. He's not sober; and when he's drinking with a lot of rough countrymen, and drinking, perhaps, even more than they do, it isn't likely that his head can be very clear for accounts. If it hadn't been for me we should have been ruined before this; and hard as I've tried, I haven't been able to keep the ruin off. You remember giving me the money for the brewer's bill, my lady.'

'Yes, I remember very well,' answered Lady Audley, with a bitter laugh, 'for I wanted that money to pay my own bills.'

'I know you did, my lady, and it was very, very hard for me to have to come and ask you for it, after all that we'd received from you before. But that isn't the worst; when Luke sent me down here to beg the favour of that help, he never told me that the Christmas rent was still owing; but it was, my lady, and it's owing now, and – and there's a bailiff in the house to-night, and we're to be sold up to-morrow unless—'

'Unless I pay your rent, I suppose,' cried Lady Audley. 'I might have guessed what was coming.'

'Indeed, indeed, my lady, I wouldn't have asked it,' sobbed Phœbe Marks, 'but he made me come.'

'Yes,' answered my lady bitterly, 'he made you come; and he will make you come whenever he pleases, and whenever he wants money for the gratification of his low vices; and you and he are my pensioners as long as I live, or as long as I have any money to give; for I suppose when my purse is empty and my credit ruined, you and your husband will turn upon me and sell me to the highest bidder. Do you know, Phœbe Marks, that my jewel-case has been half emptied to meet your claims? Do you know that my pin money, which I thought such a princely allowance when my marriage settlement was made, and when I was a poor governess at Mr. Dawson's – Heaven help me – my pin money has been overdrawn half a year to satisfy your demands? What can I do to appease you? Shall I sell my Marie Antoinette cabinet, or my Pompadour china, Leroy's and Benson's ormolu clocks, or my Gobelin tapestried chairs and ottomans? How shall I satisfy you next?'

'Oh, my lady, my lady,' cried Phœbe, piteously, 'don't be so cruel to me; you know, you know that it isn't I who want to impose upon you.'

'I know nothing,' exclaimed Lady Audley, 'except that I am the most miserable of women. Let me think,' she cried, silencing Phœbe's consolatory murmurs with an imperious gesture. 'Hold your tongue, girl, and let me think of this business, if I can.'

She put her hands to her forehead, clasping her slender fingers across her brow, as if she would have controlled the action of her brain by their convulsive pressure.

'Robert Audley is with your husband,' she said, slowly, speaking to herself rather than to her companion. 'Those two men are together, and there are bailiffs in the house, and your brutal husband is no doubt brutally drunk by this time, and brutally obstinate and ferocious in his drunkenness. If I refuse to pay this money his ferocity will be multiplied by a hundred-fold. There's little use in discussing that matter. The money must be paid.'

'But if you do pay it, my lady,' said Phœbe, very earnestly, 'I hope you will impress upon Luke that it is the last money you will ever give him while he stops in that house.'

'Why?' asked Lady Audley, letting her hands fall on her lap, and looking inquiringly at Mrs. Marks.

'Because I want Luke to leave the Castle.'

'But why do you want him to leave?'

'Oh, for ever so many reasons, my lady,' answered Phœbe. 'He's not fit to be the landlord of a public-house. I didn't know that when I married him, or I would have gone against the business, and tried to persuade him to take to the farming line. Not that I suppose he'd have given up his own fancy, though, either; for he's obstinate enough, as you know, my lady. He's not fit for his present business, though. He's scarcely ever sober after dark, and when he's drunk he gets almost wild, and doesn't seem to know what he does. We've had two or three narrow escapes with him already.'

'Narrow escapes!' repeated Lady Audley. 'What do you mean?'

'Why, we've run the risk of being burnt in our beds through his carelessness.'

'Burnt in your beds through his carelessness! Why, how was that?' asked my lady, rather listlessly. She was too selfish, and too deeply absorbed in her own troubles, to take much interest in any danger which had befallen her sometime lady's-maid.

'You know what a queer old place the Castle is, my lady; all tumble-down woodwork, and rotten rafters, and such like. The Chelmsford Insurance Company won't insure it, for they say if the place did happen to catch fire upon a windy night it would blaze away like so much tinder, and nothing in the world could save it. Well, Luke knows this, and the landlord has warned him of it times and often, for he lives close against us, and he keeps a pretty sharp eye upon all my husband's goings on, but when Luke's tipsy he doesn't know what he's about, and only a week ago he left a candle burning in one of the out-houses, and the flame caught one of the rafters of the sloping roof, and if it hadn't been for me finding it out when I went round the house the last thing, we should have all been burnt to death perhaps. And that's the third time the same kind of thing has happened in the six months we've had the place, and you can't wonder that I'm frightened; can you, my lady?'

My lady had not wondered, she had not thought about the business at all. She had scarcely listened to these common-place details; why should she care for this low-born waiting-woman's perils and troubles? Had she not her own terrors, her own soul-absorbing perplexities to usurp every thought of which her brain was capable?

She did not make any remark upon that which poor Phœbe had just told her; she scarcely comprehended what had been said, until some moments after the girl had finished speaking, when the words assumed their full meaning, as some words do two or three minutes after they have been heard without being heeded.

'Burnt in your beds,' said my lady, at last. 'It would have been a good thing for me if that precious creature, your husband, had been burnt in his bed before to-night.'

A vivid picture flashed upon her as she spoke. The picture of that frail wooden tenement, the Castle Inn, reduced to a roofless chaos of lath and plaster, vomiting flames from its black mouth and spitting sparks of fire upward towards the cold night sky.

She gave a weary sigh as she dismissed this image from her restless brain. She would be no better off even if this enemy should be for ever silenced. She had another and far more dangerous foe – a foe who was not to be bribed or bought off, though she had been as rich as an empress.

'I'll give you the money to send this bailiff away,' my lady said, after a pause. 'I must give you the last sovereign in my purse, but what of that? You know as well as I do that I dare not refuse you.'

Lady Audley rose and took the lighted lamp from her writing-table. 'The money is in my dressing-room,' she said; 'I will go and fetch it.'

'Oh, my lady,' exclaimed Phœbe, suddenly. 'I forget something; I was in such a way about this business that I quite forgot it.'

'Quite forgot what?'

'A letter that was given me to bring to you, my lady, just before I left home.'

'What letter?'

'A letter from Mr. Audley. He heard my husband mention that I was coming down here, and he asked me to carry this letter.'

Lady Audley set the lamp down upon the table nearest to her, and held out her hand to receive the letter. Phœbe Marks could scarcely fail to observe that the little jewelled hand shook like a leaf.

'Give it me – give it me,' cried my lady; 'let me see what more he has to say.'

She almost snatched the letter from Phœbe's hand in her wild impatience. She tore open the envelope and flung it from her; she could scarcely unfold the sheet of note-paper in her eager excitement.

The letter was very brief. It contained only these words:–

'Should Mrs. George Talboys really have survived the date of her supposed death, as recorded in the public prints, and upon the tomb-stone in Ventnor churchyard, and should she exist in the person of the lady suspected and accused by the writer of this, there can be no great difficulty in finding some one able and willing to identify her. Mrs. Barkamb, the owner of North Cottages, Wildernsea, would no doubt consent to throw some

*light upon this matter, either to dispel a delusion or to confirm
a suspicion.'*

'ROBERT AUDLEY.

'March 3rd, 1859.

'The Castle Inn, Mount Stanning.'

My lady crushed the letter fiercely in her hand, and flung it
from her into the flames.

'If he stood before me now, and I could kill him,' she
muttered in a strange inward whisper, 'I would do it – I would
do it!' She snatched up the lamp and rushed into the adjoining
room. She shut the door behind her. She could not endure
any witness of her horrible despair – she could endure nothing;
neither herself nor her surroundings.

END OF VOL. II.

VOLUME III

CHAPTER I
The red light in the sky

The door between my lady's dressing-room and the bed-chamber in which Sir Michael lay, had been left open. The baronet slept peacefully, his noble face plainly visible in the subdued lamplight. His breathing was low and regular, his lips curved in a half smile – a smile of tender happiness which he often wore when he looked at his beautiful wife, the smile of an all-indulgent father, who looked admiringly at his favourite child.

Some touch of womanly feeling, some sentiment of compassion softened Lady Audley's glance as it fell upon that noble reposing figure. For a moment the horrible egotism of her own misery yielded to her pitying tenderness for another. It was perhaps only a semi-selfish tenderness after all, in which pity for herself was as powerful as pity for her husband; but for once in a way, her thoughts ran out of the narrow groove of her own terrors and her own troubles to dwell with prophetic grief upon the coming sorrows of another.

'If they make him believe, how wretched he will be,' she thought.

But intermingled with that thought there was another – there was the thought of her lovely face, her bewitching manner, her arch smile, her low musical laugh, which was like a peal of silvery bells ringing across a broad expanse of flat pasture, and a rippling river in the misty summer evening. She thought of all these things with a transient thrill of triumph, which was stronger even than her terror.

If Sir Michael Audley lived to be a hundred years old, whatever he might learn to believe of her, however he might grow to despise her, would he ever be able to disassociate her from these attributes? No; a thousand times, no. To the last hour of his life his memory would present her to him invested with the loveliness that had first won his enthusiastic admiration, his devoted affection. Her worst enemies could not rob her of that fairy dower which had been so fatal in its influence upon her frivolous mind.

She paced up and down the dressing-room in the silvery lamplight, pondering upon the strange letter which she had received from Robert Audley. She walked backwards and forwards in that monotonous wandering for some time before she was able to steady her thoughts – before she was able to bring the scattered forces of her narrow intellect to bear upon the one all-important subject of the threat contained in the barrister's letter.

'He will do it,' she said, between her set teeth; 'he will do it, unless I get him into a lunatic asylum first; or unless—'

She did not finish the thought in words. She did not even think out the sentence; but some new and unnatural pulse in her heart seemed to beat out each separate syllable against her breast.

The thought was this: 'He will do it, unless some strange calamity befalls him and silences him for ever.' The red blood flashed up into my lady's face with as sudden and transient a blaze as the flickering flame of a fire, and died as suddenly away, leaving her more pale than winter snow. Her hands, which had before been locked convulsively together, fell apart and dropped heavily at her sides. She stopped in her rapid pacing to and fro – stopped as Lot's wife may have stopped, after that fatal backward glance at the perishing city, with every pulse slackening, with every drop of blood congealing in her veins, in the terrible process that was to transform her from a woman into a statue.

Lady Audley stood still for about five minutes in that strangely statuesque attitude, her head erect, her eyes staring straight before her – staring far beyond the narrow boundary of her chamber wall, into dark distances of peril and horror.

But, by-and-by, she started from that rigid attitude almost as abruptly as she had fallen into it. She roused herself from that semi-lethargy, and walked rapidly to her dressing-table, and seating herself before it, pushed away the litter of golden-stoppered bottles, and delicate china essence-boxes, and looked at her reflection in the large oval glass. She was very pale; but there was no other trace of agitation visible in her girlish face. The lines of her exquisitely-moulded lips were so beautiful, that it was only a very close observer who could have perceived a certain rigidity that was unusual to them. She saw this herself, and tried to smile away that statue-like immobility; but to-night the rosy lips refused to obey her: they were firmly locked, and were no longer the slaves of her will and pleasure. All the latent forces of her character concentrated themselves in this one feature. She might command her eyes; but she could not control the muscles of her mouth. She rose from before her dressing-table and took a dark velvet cloak and bonnet from the recesses of her wardrobe, and dressed herself for walking. The little ormolu clock on the chimney-piece struck the quarter after eleven while Lady Audley was employed in this manner; five minutes afterwards, she re-entered the room in which she had left Phœbe Marks.

The innkeeper's wife was sitting before the low hearth very much in the same attitude as that in which her late mistress had brooded over that lonely hearth earlier in the evening. Phœbe had replenished the fire, and had reassumed her bonnet and shawl. She was anxious to get home to that brutal husband, who was only too apt to fall into some mischief in her absence. She looked up as Lady Audley entered the room, and uttered an exclamation of surprise at seeing her mistress in a walking costume.

'My lady,' she cried, 'you are not going out to-night?'

'Yes, I am Phœbe,' Lady Audley answered, very quietly; 'I am going to Mount Stanning with you, to see this bailiff, and to pay and dismiss him myself.'

'But, my lady, you forget what the time is; you can't go out at such an hour.'

Lady Audley did not answer. She stood, with her fingers resting lightly upon the handle of the bell, meditating quietly.

'The stables are always locked, and the men in bed by ten o'clock,' she murmured, 'when we are at home. It will make a terrible hubbub to get a carriage ready; but yet I dare say one of the servants could manage the matter quietly for me.'

'But why should you go to-night, my lady?' cried Phœbe Marks. 'To-morrow will do quite as well. A week hence will do as well. Our landlord would take the man away if he had your promise to settle the debt.'

Lady Audley took no notice of this interruption. She went hastily into the dressing-room, and flung off her bonnet and cloak, and then returned to the boudoir, in her simple dinner costume, with her curls brushed carelessly away from her face. 'Now, Phœbe Marks, listen to me,' she said, grasping her *confidante*'s wrist, and speaking in a low, earnest voice, but with a certain imperious air that challenged contradiction, and commanded obedience.

'Listen to me, Phœbe,' she said, 'I am going to the Castle Inn, to-night; whether it is early or late is of very little consequence to me; I have set my mind upon going, and I shall go. You have asked me why, and I have told you. I am going in order that I may pay this debt myself, and that I may see for myself that the money I give is applied to the purpose for which I give it. There is nothing out of the common course of life in my doing this. I am going to do what other women in my position very often do. I am going to assist a favourite servant.'

'But it's getting on for twelve o'clock, my lady,' pleaded Phœbe.

Lady Audley frowned impatiently at this interruption.

'If my going to your house to pay this man should be known,' she continued, still retaining her hold of Phœbe's wrist, 'I am ready to answer for my conduct: but I would rather that the business would be kept quiet. I think that I can leave this house and return to it without being seen by any living creature, if you will do as I tell you.'

'I will do anything that you wish, my lady,' answered Phœbe, submissively.

'Then you will wish me good night presently, when my maid comes into the room, and you will suffer her to show you out of the house. You will cross the courtyard and wait for me in the avenue upon the other side of the archway. It may be half-an-hour before I am able to join you, for I must not leave my room till the servants have all gone to bed; but you may wait for me patiently, for come what may, I will join you.'

Lady Audley's face was no longer pale. An unnatural crimson spot burned in the centre of each rounded cheek, and an unnatural lustre gleamed in her great blue eyes. She spoke with an unnatural clearness, and an unnatural rapidity. She had altogether the appearance and manner of a person who has yielded to the dominant influence of some overpowering excitement. Phœbe Marks stared at her late mistress in mute bewilderment. She began to fear that my lady was going mad.

The bell which Lady Audley rang was answered by the smart lady's-maid, who wore rose-coloured ribbons and black silk gowns, and other adornments which were unknown to the humble people who sat below the salt in the good old days when servants wore linsey-woolsey.

'I did not know that it was so late, Martin,' said my lady, in that gentle tone which always won for her the willing service of her inferiors. 'I have been talking with Mrs. Marks, and have let the time slip by me. I shan't want anything to-night, so you may go to bed when you please.'

'Thank you, my lady,' answered the girl, who looked very sleepy, and had some difficulty in repressing a yawn even in her mistress's presence, for the Audley household usually kept very early hours. 'I'd better show Mrs. Marks out, my lady, hadn't I,' asked the maid, 'before I go to bed?'

'Oh, yes, to be sure, you can let Phœbe out. All the other servants have gone to bed, then, I suppose?'

'Yes, my lady.'

Lady Audley laughed as she glanced at the time-piece.

'We have been terribly dissipated up here, Phœbe,' she said. 'Good night. You may tell your husband that his rent shall be paid.'

'Thank you very much, my lady, and good night,' murmured Phœbe, as she backed out of the room followed by the lady's-maid.

Lady Audley listened at the door, waiting till the muffled sound of their footsteps died away in the octagon chamber, and on the carpeted staircase.

'Martin sleeps at the top of the house,' she said, 'ever so far away from this room. In ten minutes I may safely make my escape.'

She went back into her dressing-room, and put on her cloak and bonnet for the second time. The unnatural colour still burnt like a flame in her cheeks, the unnatural light still glittered in her eyes. The excitement which she was under held her in so strong a spell that neither her mind nor her body seemed to have any consciousness of fatigue. However verbose I may be in my description of her feelings, I can never describe a tithe of her thoughts or her sufferings. She suffered agonies that would fill closely printed volumes, bulky with a thousand pages, in that one horrible night. She underwent volumes of anguish, and doubt, and perplexity; sometimes repeating the same chapters of her torments over and over again; sometimes hurrying through a thousand pages of her misery without one pause, without one moment of breathing time. She stood by the low fender in her boudoir, watching the minute hand of the clock, and waiting till it should be time for her to leave the house in safety.

'I will wait ten minutes,' she said, 'not a moment beyond, before I enter upon my new peril.'

She listened to the wild roaring of the March wind, which seemed to have risen with the stillness and darkness of the night.

The hand slowly made its inevitable way to the figures which told that the ten minutes were past. It was exactly a quarter to twelve when my lady took her lamp in her hand, and stole softly from the room. Her footfall was as light as that of some graceful wild animal, and there was no fear of that airy step awakening any echo upon the carpeted stone corridors and staircase. She did not pause until she reached the vestibule upon the ground floor. Several doors opened out of this vestibule, which was an octagon, like my lady's ante-chamber. One of these doors led into the library, and it was this door which Lady Audley opened softly and cautiously.

To have attempted to leave the house secretly by any of the principal outlets would have been simple madness, for the housekeeper herself superintended the barricading of the great doors, back and front. The secrets of the bolts, and bars, and chains, and bells which secured these doors, and provided for the safety of Sir Michael Audley's plate-room, the door of which was lined with sheet-iron, were known only to the servants who had to deal with them. But although all these precautions were taken with the principal entrances to the citadel, a wooden shutter and a slender iron bar, light enough to be lifted by a child, were considered sufficient safeguard for the half-glass door which opened out of the breakfast-room into the gravelled pathway and smooth turf in the courtyard.

It was by this outlet that Lady Audley meant to make her escape. She could easily remove the bar and unfasten the shutter, and she might safely venture to leave the window ajar while she was absent. There was little fear of Sir Michael's awaking for some time, as he was a heavy sleeper in the earlier part of the night, and had slept more heavily than usual since his illness.

Lady Audley crossed the library, and opened the door of the breakfast-room which communicated with it. This latter apartment was one of the modern additions to the Court. It was a simple, cheerful chamber, with brightly-papered walls and pretty maple furniture, and was more occupied by Alicia than any one else. The paraphernalia of that young lady's favourite pursuits were scattered about the room – drawing materials, unfinished scraps of work, tangled skeins of silk, and all the other tokens of a careless damsel's presence; while Miss Audley's picture – a pretty crayon sketch of a rosy-faced hoyden in a riding-habit and hat – hung over the quaint Wedgwood ornaments on the chimney-piece. My lady looked upon these familiar objects with scornful hatred flaming in her blue eyes.

'How glad *she* will be if any disgrace befalls me!' she thought; 'how *she* will rejoice if I am driven out of this house!'

Lady Audley set the lamp upon a table near the fire-place, and went to the window. She removed the iron bar and the light wooden shutter, and then opened the glass door. The March night was black and moonless, and a gust of wind blew in upon her as she opened this door, and filled the room with its chilly breath, extinguishing the lamp upon the table.

'No matter,' my lady muttered, 'I could not have left it burning. I shall know how to find my way through the house when I come back. I have left all the doors ajar.'

She stepped quickly out upon the smooth gravel, and closed the glass door behind her. She was afraid lest that treacherous wind should blow-to the door opening into the library, and thus betray her.

She was in the quadrangle now, with that chill wind sweeping against her, and swirling her silken garments round her with a shrill rustling noise, like the whistling of a sharp breeze against the sails of a yacht. She crossed the quadrangle and looked back – looked back for a moment at the fire-light gleaming through the rosy-tinted curtains in her boudoir, and the dim gleam of the lamp behind the mullioned windows in the room where Sir Michael Audley lay asleep.

'I feel as if I was running away,' she thought. 'I feel as if I was running away secretly in the dead of the night, to lose myself and be forgotten. Perhaps it would be wiser in me to run away, to take this man's warning, and escape out of his power for ever. If I were to run away and disappear – as George Talboys disappeared. But where could I go? What would become of me? I have no money: my jewels are not worth a couple of hundred pounds, now that I have got rid of the best part of them. What could I do? I must go back to the old life, the old, hard, cruel, wretched life – the life of poverty, and humiliation, and vexation, and discontent. I should have to go back and wear myself out in that long struggle, and die – as my mother died, perhaps.'

My lady stood still for a moment on the smooth lawn between the quadrangle and the archway, with her head drooping upon her breast and her hands locked together, debating this question in the unnatural activity of her mind.

Her attitude reflected the state of that mind – it expressed irresolution and perplexity. But presently a sudden change came over her; she lifted her head – lifted it with an action of defiance and determination.

'No, Mr. Robert Audley,' she said aloud, in a low, clear voice; 'I will not go back – I will not go back. If the struggle between us is to be a duel to the death, you shall not find me drop my weapon.'

She walked with a firm and rapid step under the archway. As she passed under that massive arch, it seemed as if she disappeared into some black gulf that had waited open to receive her. The stupid clock struck twelve, and the solid masonry seemed to vibrate under its heavy strokes, as Lady Audley emerged upon the other side, and joined Phœbe Marks, who had waited for her late mistress very near the gateway of the Court.

'Now, Phœbe,' she said, 'it is three miles from here to Mount Stanning, isn't it?'

'Yes, my lady.'

'Then we can walk it in an hour.'

Lady Audley had not stopped to say this: she was walking quickly along the avenue with her humble companion by her side. Fragile and delicate as she was in appearance, she was a very good walker. She had been in the habit of taking long country rambles with Mr. Dawson's children in her old days of dependence, and she thought very little of a distance of three miles.

'Your beautiful husband will sit up for you, I suppose, Phœbe?' she said, as they struck across an open field that was used as a short cut from Audley Court to the high road.

'Oh, yes, my lady; he's sure to sit up. He'll be drinking with the man, I dare say.'

'The man! What man?'

'The man that's in possession, my lady.'

'Ah, to be sure,' said Lady Audley, indifferently.

It was strange that Phœbe's domestic troubles should seem so very far away from her thoughts at the time she was taking such an extraordinary step towards setting things right at the Castle Inn.

The two women crossed the field and turned into the high road. The way to Mount Stanning was very hilly, and the long road looked black and dreary in the dark night; but my lady walked on with a desperate courage, which was no common constituent in her selfish, sensuous nature; but a strange faculty born out of her great despair. She did not speak again to her companion until they were close upon the glimmering lights at the top of the hill, one of which village lights, gleaming redly through a crimson curtain, marked out the particular window behind which it was likely that Luke Marks sat nodding drowsily over his liquor, and waiting for the coming of his wife.

'He has not gone to bed, Phœbe,' said my lady, eagerly. 'But there is no other light burning at the inn. I suppose Mr. Audley is in bed and asleep.'

'Yes, my lady, I suppose so.'

'You are sure he was going to stay at the Castle to-night?'

'Oh, yes, my lady. I helped the girl to get his room ready before I came away.'

The wind, boisterous everywhere, was shriller and more pitiless in the neighbourhood of that bleak hill-top upon which the Castle Inn reared its rickety walls. The cruel blasts danced wildly round that frail erection. They disported themselves with the shattered pigeon-house, the broken weathercock, the loose tiles, and unshapely chimneys; they rattled at the window-panes, and whistled in the crevices; they mocked the feeble building from foundation to roof, and battered and banged and tormented it in their fierce gambols, until it trembled and rocked with the force of their rough play.

Mr. Luke Marks had not troubled himself to secure the door of his dwelling-house before sitting down to drink with the man who held provisional possession of his goods and chattels. The landlord of the Castle Inn was a lazy, sensual brute, who had no thought higher than a selfish concern for his own enjoyments, and a virulent hatred of anybody who stood in the way of his gratification.

Phœbe pushed open the door with her hand, and went into the house, followed by my lady. The gas was flaring in the bar, and smoking the low, plastered ceiling. The door of the bar-parlour was half open, and Lady Audley heard the brutal laughter of Mr. Marks as she crossed the threshold of the inn.

'I'll tell him you're here, my lady,' whispered Phœbe to her late mistress. 'I know he'll be tipsy. You – you won't be offended, my lady, if he should say anything rude. You know it wasn't my wish that you should come.'

'Yes, yes,' answered Lady Audley, impatiently, 'I know that. What should I care for his rudeness? Let him say what he likes.'

Phœbe Marks pushed open the parlour door, leaving my lady in the bar close behind her.

Luke sat with his clumsy legs stretched out upon the hearth; with a glass of gin-and-water in one hand and the poker in the other. He had just thrust the poker into a great heap of black coals, and was shattering them to make a blaze, when his wife appeared upon the threshold of the room.

He snatched the poker from between the bars, and made a half-drunken, half-threatening motion with it as he saw her.

'So you've condescended to come home at last, ma'am,' he said; 'I thought you was never coming no more.'

He spoke in a thick and drunken voice, and was by no means too intelligible. He was steeped to the very lips in alcohol. His eyes were dim and watery; his hands were unsteady; his voice was choked and muffled with drink. A brute, even when most sober; a brute, even when on his best behaviour; he was ten times more brutal in his drunkenness, when the few restraints which held his ignorant, every-day brutality in check were flung aside in the insolent recklessness of intoxication.

'I – I've been longer than I intended to be, Luke,' Phœbe answered, in her most conciliatory manner; 'but I've seen my lady, and she's been very kind, and – and she'll settle this business for us.'

'She's been very kind, has she?' muttered Mr. Marks, with a drunken laugh; 'thank her for nothing. I know the vally of her kindness. She'd be oncommon kind, I dessay, if she warn't obligated to be it.'

The man in possession, who had fallen into a maudlin and semi-unconscious state of intoxication upon about a third of the liquor that Mr. Marks had consumed, only stared in feeble wonderment at his host and hostess. He sat near the table. Indeed, he had hooked himself on to it with his elbows, as a safeguard against sliding under it, and he was making inane attempts to light his pipe at the flame of a guttering tallow candle near him.

'My lady has promised to settle the business for us,' Phœbe repeated, without noticing Luke's remarks; she knew her husband's dogged nature well enough by this time to know that it was worse than useless to try to stop him from doing or saying anything which his own stubborn will led him to do or say; 'and she's come down here to see about it to-night, Luke,' she added.

The poker dropped from the landlord's hand, and fell clattering amongst the cinders on the hearth.

'My Lady Audley come here to-night,' he said.

'Yes, Luke.'

My lady appeared upon the threshold of the door as Phœbe spoke.

'Yes, Luke Marks,' she said, 'I have come to pay this man, and to send him about his business.'

Lady Audley said these words in a strange semi-mechanical manner, very much as if she had learned the sentence by rote, and were repeating it without knowing what she said.

Mr. Marks gave a discontented growl, and set his empty glass down upon the table, with an impatient gesture.

'You might have given the money to Phœbe,' he said, 'as well as have brought it yourself. We don't want no fine ladies up here, pryin' and pokin' their precious noses into everythink.'

'Luke, Luke,' remonstrated Phœbe, 'when my lady has been so kind!'

'Oh, damn her kindness!' cried Mr. Marks; 'it ain't her kindness as we want, gal, it's her money. She won't get no snivellin' gratitood from me. Whatever she does for us she does because she is obliged, and if she warn't obliged she wouldn't do it—'

Heaven knows how much more Luke Marks might have said, had not my lady turned upon him suddenly, and awed him into silence by the unearthly glitter of her beauty. Her hair had been blown away from her face, and, being of a light, feathery quality, had spread itself into a tangled mass that surrounded her forehead like a yellow flame. There was another flame in her eyes – a greenish light, such as might flash from the changing hued orbs of an angry mermaid.

'Stop,' she cried. 'I didn't come up here in the dead of the night to listen to your insolence. How much is this debt?'

'Nine pound.'

Lady Audley produced her purse – a toy of ivory, silver, and turquoise – and took from it a bank-note and four sovereigns. She laid these upon the table.

'Let that man give me a receipt for the money,' she said, 'before I go.'

It was some time before the man could be roused into sufficient consciousness for the performance of this simple duty, and it was only by dipping a pen into the ink and pushing it between his clumsy fingers, that he was at last made to comprehend that his autograph was wanted at the bottom of the receipt which had been made out by Phœbe Marks. Lady Audley took the document as soon as the ink was dry, and turned to leave the parlour. Phœbe followed her.

'You musn't go home alone, my lady,' she said. 'You'll let me go with you?'

'Yes, yes, you shall go home with me.'

The two women were standing near the door of the inn as my lady said this. Phœbe stared wonderingly at her patroness. She had expected that Lady Audley would be in a hurry to return home after settling this business which she had capriciously taken upon herself; but it was not so; my lady stood leaning against the inn door and staring into vacancy, and again Mrs. Marks began to fear that trouble had driven her late mistress mad.

A little Dutch clock in the bar struck one while Lady Audley lingered in this irresolute, absent manner.

She started at the sound and began to tremble violently.

'I think I am going to faint, Phœbe,' she said; 'where can I get some cold water?'

'The pump is in the washhouse, my lady, I'll run and get you a glass of water.'

'No, no, no,' cried my lady, clutching Phœbe's arm as she was about to run away upon this errand, 'I'll get it myself. I must dip my head in a basin of water if I want to save myself from fainting. In which room does Mr. Audley sleep?'

There was something so irrelevant in this question that Phœbe Marks stared aghast at her mistress before she answered it.

'It was number three that I got ready, my lady – the front

room – the room next to ours,' she replied, after that pause of astonishment.

'Give me a candle,' said my lady; 'I'll go into your room, and get some water for my head. Stay where you are,' she added authoritatively, as Phœbe Marks was about to show the way – 'stay where you are, and see that that brute of a husband of yours doesn't follow me!'

She snatched the candle which Phœbe had lighted from the girl's hand; and ran up the rickety, winding staircase which led to the narrow corridor upon the upper floor. Five bed-rooms opened out of this low-ceilinged, close-smelling corridor: the numbers of these rooms were indicated by squat black figures painted upon the upper panels of the doors. Lady Audley had driven to Mount Stanning to inspect the house, when she had bought the business for her servant's bridegroom, and she knew her way about the dilapidated old place; she knew where to find Phœbe's bed-room; but she stopped before the door of that other chamber which had been prepared for Mr. Robert Audley.

She stopped and looked at the number on the door. The key was in the lock, and her hand dropped upon it as if unconsciously. Then she suddenly began to tremble again, as she had trembled a few minutes before at the striking of the clock. She stood for a few moments trembling thus, with her hand still upon the key; then a horrible expression came over her face, and she turned the key in the lock; she turned it twice, double locking the door.

There was no sound from within; the occupant of the chamber made no sign of having heard that ominous creaking of the rusty key in the rusty lock.

Lady Audley hurried into the next room. She set the candle on the dressing-table, flung off her bonnet and slung it loosely across her arm; she went to the wash-hand-stand and filled the basin with water. She plunged her golden hair into this

362

water, and then stood for a few moments in the centre of the room looking about her, with a white earnest face, and an eager gaze that seemed to take in every object in the poorly furnished chamber. Phœbe's bed-room was certainly very shabbily furnished; she had been compelled to select all the most decent things for those best bed-rooms which were set apart for any chance traveller who might stop for a night's lodging at the Castle Inn. But Mrs. Marks had done her best to atone for the lack of substantial furniture in her apartment by a superabundance of drapery. Crisp curtains of cheap chintz hung from the tent-bedstead; festooned draperies of the same material shrouded the narrow window, shutting out the light of day, and affording a pleasant harbour for tribes of flies and predatory bands of spiders. Even the looking-glass, a miserably cheap construction which distorted every face whose owner had the hardihood to look into it, stood upon a draperied altar of starched muslin and pink glazed calico, and was adorned with frills of lace and knitted work.

My lady smiled as she looked at the festoons and furbelows which met her eye upon every side. She had reason, perhaps, to smile, remembering the costly elegance of her own apartments; but there was something in that sardonic smile that seemed to have a deeper meaning than any natural contempt for Phœbe's poor attempts at decoration. She went to the dressing-table and smoothed her wet hair before the looking-glass, and then put on her bonnet. She was obliged to place the flaming tallow candle very close to the lace furbelows about the glass, so close that the starched muslin seemed to draw the flame towards it by some power of attraction in its fragile tissue.

Phœbe waited anxiously by the inn-door for my lady's coming. She watched the minute hand of the little Dutch clock, wondering at the slowness of its progress. It was only ten minutes past one when Lady Audley came down-stairs, with her bonnet on and her hair still wet, but without the candle.

Phœbe was immediately anxious about this missing candle.

'The light, my lady,' she said; 'you have left it up-stairs!'

'The wind blew it out as I was leaving your room,' Lady Audley answered, quietly. 'I left it there.'

'In my room, my lady?'

'Yes.'

'And it was quite out?'

'Yes, I tell you; why do you worry me about your candle? It is past one o'clock. Come.'

She took the girl's arm, and half-led, half-dragged her from the house. The convulsive pressure of her slight hand held her companion as firmly as an iron vice could have held her. The fierce March wind banged-to the door of the house, and left the two women standing outside it. The long black road lay bleak and desolate before them, dimly visible between the leafless hedges.

A walk of three miles' length upon a lonely country road, between the hours of one and two on a cold winter's morning, is scarcely a pleasant task for a delicate woman – a woman whose inclinations lean towards ease and luxury. But my lady hurried along the hard dry highway, dragging her companion with her as if she had been impelled by some horrible demoniac force which knew no abatement. With the black night above them – with the fierce wind howling round them, sweeping across a broad expanse of hidden country, blowing as if it had arisen simultaneously from every point of the compass, and making those wretched wanderers the focus of its ferocity – the two women walked through the darkness down the hill upon which Mount Stanning stood, along a mile and a half of flat road, and then up another hill, on the western side of which Audley Court lay in that sheltered valley, which seemed to shut in the old house from all the clamour and hubbub of the every-day world.

My lady stopped upon the summit of this hill to draw breath and to clasp her hands upon her heart, in the vain hope that she might still its cruel beating. They were now within three-quarters of a mile of the Court, and they had been walking for nearly an hour since they had left the Castle Inn.

Lady Audley stopped to rest with her face still turned towards the place of her destination. Phœbe Marks, stopping also, and very glad of a moment's pause in that hurried journey, looked back into the far darkness beneath which lay that dreary shelter which had given her so much uneasiness. As she did so, she uttered a shrill cry of horror, and clutched wildly at Lady Audley's cloak.

The night sky was no longer all dark. The thick blackness was broken by one patch of lurid light.

'My lady, my lady,' cried Phœbe, pointing to this lurid patch, 'do you see?'

'Yes, child, I see,' answered Lady Audley, trying to shake the clinging hands from her garments. 'What is the matter?'

'It is a fire! – a fire, my lady.'

'Yes, I'm afraid it is a fire. At Brentwood most likely. Let me go, Phœbe, it is nothing to us.'

'Yes, yes, my lady, it's nearer than Brentwood – much nearer; it's at Mount Stanning.'

Lady Audley did not answer. She was trembling again, with the cold, perhaps, for the wind had torn her heavy cloak away from her shoulders, and had left her slender figure exposed to the blast.

'It's at Mount Stanning, my lady,' cried Phœbe Marks. 'It's the Castle that's on fire – I know it is, I know it is. I thought of fire to-night, and I was fidgety and uneasy, for I knew this would happen some day. I wouldn't mind if it was only the wretched place, but there'll be life lost; there'll be life lost,' sobbed the girl, distractedly. 'There's Luke, too tipsy to help himself, unless others help him; there's Mr. Audley asleep—'

Phœbe Marks stopped suddenly at the mention of Robert's name, and fell upon her knees, clasping her uplifted hands, and appealing wildly to Lady Audley.

'Oh, my God!' she cried. 'Say it's not true, my lady; say it isn't true. It's too horrible, it's too horrible, it's too horrible!'

'What's too horrible?'

'The thought that's in my mind; the dreadful thought that's in my mind.'

'What do you mean, girl?' cried my lady, fiercely.

'Oh, God forgive me if I'm wrong!' the kneeling woman gasped, in detached sentences, 'and God grant I may be! Why did you go up to the Castle to-night, my lady? Why were you so set on going, against all I could say – you who are so bitter against Mr. Audley and against Luke, and who knew they were both under that roof ? Oh, tell me that I do you a cruel wrong, my lady; tell me so – tell me; for as there is a heaven above me, I think that you went to that place to-night on purpose to set fire to it. Tell me that I'm wrong, my lady; tell me that I'm doing you a wicked wrong.'

'I will tell you nothing except that you are a madwoman,' answered Lady Audley, in a cold, hard voice. 'Get up, fool, idiot, coward! Is your husband such a precious bargain that you should be grovelling there, lamenting and groaning for him? What is Robert Audley to you, that you behave like a maniac, because you think he is in danger? How do you know that the fire is at Mount Stanning? You see a red patch in the sky, and you cry out directly that your own paltry hovel is in flames; as if there were no place in the world that could burn except that. The fire may be at Brentwood, or further away – at Romford, or still further away; on the eastern side of London, perhaps. Get up, madwoman, and go back and look

366

after your goods and chattels, and your husband and your lodger. Get up and go; I don't want you.'

'Oh, my lady, my lady, forgive me,' sobbed Phœbe; 'there's nothing you can say to me that's hard enough for having done you such a wrong, even in my thoughts. I don't mind your cruel words – I don't mind anything if I'm wrong.'

'Go back and see for yourself,' answered Lady Audley, sternly. 'I tell you again I don't want you.'

She walked away in the darkness, leaving Phœbe Marks still kneeling upon the hard road, where she had cast herself in that agony of supplication. Sir Michael's wife walked towards the house in which her husband slept, with the red blaze lighting up the skies behind her, and with nothing but the blackness of the night before.

CHAPTER II

The bearer of the tidings

It was very late the next morning when Lady Audley emerged from her dressing-room, exquisitely dressed in a morning costume of delicate muslin, elaborate laces, and embroideries; but with a very pale face, and with half-circles of purple shadow under her eyes. She accounted for this pale face and these hollow eyes by declaring that she had sat up reading until a very late hour on the previous night.

Sir Michael and his young wife breakfasted in the library at a comfortable round table, wheeled close to the blazing fire; and Alicia was compelled to share this meal with her step-mother, however she might avoid that lady in the long interval between breakfast and dinner.

The March morning was bleak and dull, and a drizzling rain fell incessantly, obscuring the landscape, and blotting out the distance. There were very few letters by the morning's post; the daily newspapers did not arrive until noon; and such aids to conversation being missing, there was very little talk at the breakfast-table.

Alicia looked out at the drizzling rain drifting against the broad window-panes.

'No riding to-day,' she said; 'and no chance of any callers to enliven us; unless that ridiculous Bob comes crawling through the wet from Mount Stanning.'

Have you ever heard anybody, whom you knew to be dead, alluded to in a light, easy-going manner by another person who did not know of his death – alluded to as doing that or this – as performing some trivial every-day operation – when *you* know that he has vanished away from the face of this earth, and separated himself for ever from all living creatures and their common-place pursuits, in the awful solemnity of death? Such a chance allusion, insignificant though it may be, is apt to send a strange thrill of pain through the mind. The ignorant remark jars discordantly upon the hyper-sensitive brain; the King of Terrors is desecrated by that unwitting disrespect. Heaven knows what hidden reason my lady may have had for experiencing some such revulsion of feeling on the sudden mention of Mr. Audley's name; but her pale face blanched to a sickly white as Alicia Audley spoke of her cousin.

'Yes, he will come down here in the wet, perhaps,' the young lady continued, 'with his hat sleek and shining as if it had been brushed with a pat of fresh butter; and with white vapours steaming out of his clothes, and making him look like an awkward genie just let out of his bottle. He will come down here and print impressions of his muddy boots all over the carpet, and he'll sit on your Gobelin tapestry, my lady, in his wet overcoat; and he'll abuse you if you remonstrate, and will ask why people have chairs that are not to be sat upon, and why you don't live in Fig-tree Court, and—'

Sir Michael Audley watched his daughter with a thoughtful countenance as she talked of her cousin. She very often talked of him, ridiculing him and inveighing against him in no very measured terms. But, perhaps, the baronet thought of a certain Signora Beatrice who very cruelly entreated a gentleman called Benedick, but who was, it may be, heartily in love with him at the same time.

'What do you think Major Melville told me when he called here yesterday, Alicia?' Sir Michael asked, presently.

'I haven't the remotest idea,' replied Alicia, rather disdainfully. 'Perhaps he told you that we should have another war before long, by Ged, sir; or, perhaps, he told you that we should have a new ministry, by Ged, sir, for that those fellows are getting themselves into a mess, sir; or that those other fellows were reforming this, and cutting down that, and altering the other in the army, until, by Ged, sir, we shall have no army at all, by-and-by – nothing but a pack of boys, sir, crammed up to the eyes with a lot of senseless school-masters' rubbish, and dressed in shell-jackets and calico helmets. Yes, sir, they're fighting in Oudh in calico helmets at this very day, sir.'

'You're an impertinent minx, miss,' answered the baronet. 'Major Melville told me nothing of the kind; but he told me that a very devoted admirer of yours, a certain Sir Harry Towers, has forsaken his place in Hertfordshire, and his hunting stable, and has gone on the Continent for a twelvemonth's tour.'

Miss Audley flushed up suddenly at the mention of her old adorer, but recovered herself very quickly.

'He has gone on the Continent, has he?' she said, indifferently. 'He told me that he meant to do so – if – if he didn't have everything his own way. Poor fellow! he's a dear, good-hearted, stupid creature, and twenty times better than that peripatetic, patent refrigerator, Mr. Robert Audley.'

'I wish, Alicia, you were not so fond of ridiculing Bob,' Sir Michael said, gravely. 'Bob is a very good fellow, and I'm as fond of him as if he'd been my own son; and – and – I've been very uncomfortable about him lately. He has changed very much within the last few days, and he has taken all sorts of absurd ideas into his head, and my lady has alarmed me about him. She thinks—'

Lady Audley interrupted her husband with a grave shake of her head.

'It is better not to say too much about it yet awhile,' she said; 'Alicia knows what I think.'

'Yes,' rejoined Miss Audley, 'my lady thinks that Bob is

going mad; but I know better than that. He's not at all the sort of person to go mad. How should such a sluggish ditch-pond of an intellect as his ever work itself into a tempest? He may moon about for the rest of his life, perhaps, in a tranquil state of semi-idiotcy, imperfectly comprehending who he is, and where he's going, and what he's doing; but he'll never go mad.'

Sir Michael did not reply to this. He had been very much disturbed by his conversation with my lady on the previous evening, and had silently debated the painful question in his mind ever since.

His wife – the woman he best loved and most believed in – had told him with all appearance of regret and agitation, her conviction of his nephew's insanity. He tried in vain to arrive at the conclusion he wished most ardently to attain; he tried in vain to think that my lady was misled by her own fancies, and had no foundation for what she said. But then, again, it suddenly flashed upon him, to think this was to arrive at a worse conclusion; it was to transfer the horrible suspicion from his nephew to his wife. She appeared to be possessed with an actual conviction of Robert's insanity. To imagine her wrong was to imagine some weakness in her own mind. The longer he thought of the subject the more it harassed and perplexed him. It was most certain that the young man had always been eccentric. He was sensible, he was tolerably clever, he was honourable and gentlemanlike in feeling, though perhaps a little careless in the performance of certain minor social duties; but there were some slight differences, not easily to be defined, that separated him from other men of his age and position. Then, again, it was equally true that he had very much changed within the period that had succeeded the disappearance of George Talboys. He had grown moody and thoughtful, melancholy and absent-minded. He had held himself aloof from society; had sat for hours without speaking; had talked at other times by fits and starts; and had excited himself unusually in the discussion of subjects which apparently lay far out of the region of his own life and interests. Then there was even another point which seemed to strengthen my lady's case against this unhappy young man. He had been brought up in the frequent society of his cousin, Alicia – his pretty, genial cousin – to whom interest, and one would have thought affection, naturally pointed as his most fitting bride. More than this, the girl had shown him, in the innocent guilelessness of a transparent nature, that on her side at least, affection was not wanting; and yet, in spite of all this, he had held himself aloof, and had allowed other men to propose for her hand, and to be rejected by her, and had still made no sign.

Now love is so very subtle an essence, such an indefinable metaphysical marvel, that its due force, though very cruelly felt by the sufferer himself, is never clearly understood by those who look on at his torments and wonder why he takes the common fever so badly. Sir Michael argued that because Alicia was a pretty girl and an amiable girl it was therefore extraordinary and unnatural in Robert Audley not to have duly fallen in love with her. This baronet – who, close upon his sixtieth birthday, had for the first time encountered that one woman who out of all the women in the world had power to quicken the pulses of his heart – wondered why Robert failed to take the fever from the first breath of contagion that blew towards him. He forgot that there are men who go their ways unscathed amidst legions of lovely and generous women, to succumb at last before some harsh-featured virago, who knows the secret of that only philter which can intoxicate and bewitch him. He forgot that there are certain Jacks who go through life without meeting the Jill appointed for them by Nemesis, and die old bachelors perhaps, with poor Jill pining an old maid upon the other side of the party-wall. He forgot that love, which is a madness, and a scourge, and a fever, and a delusion, and a snare, is also a mystery, and very imperfectly understood by every one except the individual sufferer who writhes under its tortures. Jones, who is wildly enamoured of Miss Brown, and who lies awake at night until he loathes his comfortable pillow and tumbles his sheets into two twisted rags of linen in his agonies, as if he were a prisoner and wanted to wind them into impromptu ropes; this same Jones, who thinks Russell Square a magic place because his divinity inhabits it; who thinks the trees in that enclosure and the sky above it greener and bluer than any other trees or sky; and who feels a pang, yes, an actual pang, of mingled hope, and joy, and expectation, and terror when he emerges from Guilford Street, descending from the heights of Islington, into those sacred precincts; this very Jones is hard and callous towards the torments of Smith, who adores Miss Robinson, and cannot imagine what the infatuated fellow can see in the girl. So it was with Sir Michael Audley. He looked at his nephew as a sample of a very large class of young men, and his daughter as a sample of an equally extensive class of feminine goods; and could not see why the two samples should not make a very respectable match. He ignored all those infinitesimal differences in nature which make the wholesome food of one man the deadly poison of another. How difficult it is to believe sometimes that a man doesn't like such and such a favourite dish! If, at a dinner-party, a meek-looking guest refuses early salmon and cucumber, or green peas in February, we set him down as a poor relation whose instincts warn him off those expensive plates. If an alderman were to declare that he didn't like green fat, he would be looked upon as a social martyr, a Marcus Curtius of the dinner-table, who immolated himself for the benefit of his kind. His fellow aldermen would believe in anything rather than an heretical distaste for the city ambrosia of the soup tureen. But there are people who dislike salmon, and whitebait, and spring ducklings, and all manner of old-established delicacies, and there are other people who affect eccentric and despicable dishes generally stigmatised as nasty.

Alas, my pretty Alicia, your cousin did not love you! He admired your rosy English face, and had a tender affection for you which might perhaps have expanded by-and-by into something warm enough for matrimony; that every-day jog-trot species of union which demands no very passionate devotion; but for a sudden check which it had received in Dorsetshire. Yes, Robert Audley's growing affection for his cousin, a plant of very slow growth, I am fain to confess, had been suddenly dwarfed and stunted upon that bitter February day on which he had stood beneath the pine-trees talking to Clara Talboys. Since that day the young man had experienced an unpleasant sensation in thinking of poor Alicia. He looked at her as being in some vague manner an incumbrance upon the freedom of his thoughts; he had a haunting fear that he was in some tacit way pledged to her; that she had a species of claim upon him, which forbade to him the right of even thinking of another woman. I believe it was the image of Miss Audley presented to him in this light that goaded the young barrister into those outbursts of splenetic rage against the female sex which he was liable to at certain times. He was strictly honourable, so honourable that he would rather have immolated himself upon the altar of truth and Alicia than have done her the remotest wrong, though by so doing he might have secured his own happiness.

'If the poor little girl loves me,' he thought, 'and if she thinks that I love her, and has been led to think so by any word or act of mine, I am in duty bound to let her think so to the end of time, and to fulfil any tacit promise which I may have unconsciously made. I thought once – I meant once to – to make her an offer by-and-by, when this horrible mystery about George Talboys should have been cleared up and every-thing peacefully settled – but now—'

His thoughts would ordinarily wander away at this point of his reflections, carrying him where he never had intended to go; carrying him back under the pine-trees in Dorsetshire, and setting him once more face to face with the sister of his missing friend, and it was generally a very laborious journey by which he travelled back to the point from which he had strayed. It was so difficult for him to tear himself away from the stunted turf and the pine-trees.

'Poor little girl!' he would think on coming back to Alicia. 'How good it is of her to love me; and how grateful I ought to be for her tenderness. How many fellows would think such a generous, loving heart the highest boon that earth could give them. There's Sir Harry Towers stricken with despair at his rejection. He would give me half his estate, all his estate, twice his estate, if he had it, to be in the shoes which I am so anxious to shake off my ungrateful feet. Why don't I love her? Why is it that although I know her to be pretty, and pure, and good, and truthful, I don't love her? Her image never haunts me, except reproachfully. I never see her in my dreams. I never wake up suddenly in the dead of the night with her eyes shining upon me and her warm breath upon my cheek, or with the fingers of her soft hand clinging to mine. No, I'm not in love with her; I *can't* fall in love with her.'

He raged and rebelled against his ingratitude. He tried to argue himself into a passionate attachment for his cousin, but he failed ignominiously; and the more he tried to think of Alicia the more he thought of Clara Talboys. I am speaking now of his feelings in the period that elapsed between his return from Dorsetshire and his visit to Grange Heath.

Sir Michael sat by the library fire after breakfast upon this wretched rainy morning, writing letters and reading the newspapers. Alicia shut herself in her own apartment to read the third volume of a novel. Lady Audley locked the door of the octagon ante-chamber, and roamed up and down the suite of rooms from the bed-room to the boudoir all through that weary morning.

She had locked the door to guard against the chance of any one coming in suddenly and observing her before she was aware – before she had had sufficient warning to enable her to face their scrutiny. Her pale face seemed to grow paler as the morning advanced. A tiny medicine-chest was open upon the dressing-table, and little stoppered bottles of red lavender, sal volatile, chloroform, chlorodyne, and ether were scattered about. Once my lady paused before this medicine-chest, and took out the remaining bottles, half absently perhaps, until she came to one which was filled with a thick dark liquid, and labelled, 'Opium—Poison.'

She trifled a long time with this last bottle; holding it up to the light, and even removing the stopper and smelling the sickly liquid. But she put it from her suddenly with a shudder.

'If I could!' she muttered, 'if I could only do it! And yet why should I; *now*?'

She clenched her small hands as she uttered the last words, and walked to the window of the dressing-room, which looked straight towards that ivied archway under which any one must come who came from Mount Stanning to the Court.

There were smaller gates in the gardens which led into the meadows behind the Court; but there was no other way of coming from Mount Stanning or Brentwood than by the principal entrance.

The solitary hand of the clock over the archway was midway between one and two when my lady looked at it.

'How slow the time is,' she said, wearily; 'how slow, how slow! Shall I grow old like this, I wonder, with every minute of my life seeming like an hour?'

She stood for a few minutes watching the archway; but

no one passed under it while she looked; and she turned impatiently away from the window to resume her weary wandering about the rooms.

Whatever fire that had been, which had reflected itself vividly in the black sky, no tidings of it had as yet come to Audley Court. The day was miserably wet and windy; altogether the very last day upon which even the most confirmed idler and gossip would care to venture out. It was not a market-day, and there were therefore very few passengers upon the road between Brentwood and Chelmsford; so that as yet no news of the fire, which had occurred in the dead of the wintry night, had reached the village of Audley, or travelled from the village to the Court.

The girl with the rose-coloured ribbons came to the door of the ante-room to summon her mistress to luncheon; but Lady Audley only opened the door a little way, and intimated her intention of taking no luncheon.

'My head aches terribly, Martin,' she said; 'I shall go and lie down till dinner time. You may come at five to dress me.'

Lady Audley said this with the predetermination of dressing at four, and thus dispensing with the services of her attendant. Amongst all privileged spies, a lady's-maid has the highest privileges. It is she who bathes Lady Theresa's eyes with eau-de-cologne after her ladyship's quarrel with the colonel; it is she who administers sal volatile to Miss Fanny when Count Beaudesert, of the Blues, has jilted her. She has a hundred methods for the finding out of her mistress's secrets. She knows by the manner in which her victim jerks her head from under the hair-brush, or chafes at the gentlest administration of the comb, what hidden tortures are racking her breast – what secret perplexities are bewildering her brain. That well-bred attendant knows how to interpret the most obscure diagnoses of all mental diseases that can afflict her mistress; she knows when the ivory complexion is bought and paid for – when the pearly teeth are foreign substances fashioned by the dentist – when the glossy plaits are the relics of the dead, rather than the property of the living; and she knows other and more sacred secrets than these. She knows when the sweet smile is more false than Madame Levison's enamel, and far less enduring – when the words that issue from between gates of borrowed pearl are more disguised and painted than the lips which help to shape them. When the lovely fairy of the ball-room re-enters her dressing-room after the night's long revelry, and throws aside her voluminous Burnous and her faded bouquet, and drops her mask; and like another Cinderella loses the glass-slipper, by whose glitter she has been distinguished, and falls back into her rags and dirt; the lady's-maid is by to see the transformation. The valet who took wages from the prophet of Korazin, must have seen his master sometimes unveiled; and must have laughed in his sleeve at the folly of the monster's worshippers.

Lady Audley had made no *confidante* of her new maid, and on this day of all others she wished to be alone.

She did lie down, she cast herself wearily upon the luxurious sofa in the dressing-room, and buried her face in the down pillows and tried to sleep. Sleep! – she had almost forgotten what it was, that tender restorer of tired nature, it seemed so long now since she had slept. It was only about eight-and-forty hours, perhaps, but it appeared an intolerable time. Her fatigue of the night before, and her unnatural excitement, had worn her out at last. She did fall asleep; she fell into a heavy slumber that was almost like stupor. She had taken a few drops out of the opium bottle in a glass of water before lying down.

The clock over the mantel-piece chimed the quarter before four as she woke suddenly and started up, with the cold perspiration breaking out in icy drops upon her forehead. She had dreamt that every member of the household was clamouring at the door, eager to tell her of a dreadful fire that had happened in the night.

There was no sound but the flapping of the ivy leaves against the glass, the occasional falling of a cinder, and the steady ticking of the clock.

'Perhaps I shall be always dreaming these sort of dreams,' my lady thought, 'until the terror of them kills me!'

The rain had ceased, and the cold spring sunshine was glittering upon the windows. Lady Audley dressed herself rapidly but carefully. I do not say that even in her supremest hour of misery she still retained her pride in her beauty. It was not so; she looked upon that beauty as a weapon, and she felt that she had now double need to be well armed. She dressed herself in her most gorgeous silk; a voluminous robe of silvery, shimmering blue, that made her look as if she had been arrayed in moonbeams. She shook out her hair into feathery showers of glittering gold; and with a cloak of white cashmere about her shoulders, went down-stairs into the vestibule.

She opened the door of the library and looked in. Sir Michael Audley was asleep in his easy-chair. As my lady softly closed this door Alicia descended the stairs from her own room. The turret door was open, and the sun was shining upon the wet grass-plat in the quadrangle. The firm gravel-walks were already very nearly dry, for the rain had ceased for upwards of two hours.

'Will you take a walk with me in the quadrangle?' Lady Audley asked, as her step-daughter approached. The armed neutrality between the two women admitted of any chance civility such as this.

'Yes, if you please, my lady,' Alicia answered, rather list-lessly. 'I have been yawning over a stupid novel all the morning, and shall be very glad of a little fresh air.'

Heaven help the novelist whose fiction Miss Audley had been perusing, if he had no better critics than that young lady.

She had read page after page without knowing what she had been reading; and had flung aside the volumes half-a-dozen times to go to the window and watch for that visitor whom she had so confidently expected.

Lady Audley led the way through the low doorway and on to the smooth gravel drive, by which carriages approached the house. She was still very pale, but the brightness of her dress and of her feathery golden ringlets distracted an observer's eyes from her pallid face. All mental distress is, with some show of reason, associated in our minds with loose, disordered garments, and dishevelled hair, and an appearance in every way the reverse of my lady's. Why had she come out into the chill sunshine of the March afternoon to wander up and down that monotonous pathway with the step-daughter she hated? She came because she was under the dominion of a horrible restlessness, which would not suffer her to remain within the house waiting for certain tidings which she knew must too surely come. At first she had wished to ward them off – at first she had wished that strange convulsions of nature might arise to hinder their coming – that abnormal winter lightnings might wither and destroy the messenger who carried them – that the ground might tremble and yawn beneath his hastening feet, and that impassable gulfs might separate the spot from which the tidings were to come, and the place to which they were to be carried. She wished that the earth might stand still, and the paralysed elements cease from their natural functions; that the progress of time might stop; that the Day of Judgment might come, and that she might thus be brought before an unearthly tribunal, and so escape the intervening shame and misery of any earthly judgment. In the wild chaos of her brain, every one of these thoughts had held its place, and in her short slumber on the sofa in her dressing-room, she had dreamed all these things and a hundred other things, all bearing upon the same subject.

She had dreamed that a brook, a tiny streamlet when she first saw it, flowed across the road between Mount Stanning and Audley, and gradually swelled into a river, and from a river became an ocean, till the village on the hill receded far away out of sight and only a great waste of waters rolled where it once had been. She dreamt that she saw the messenger; now one person, now another, but never any probable person; hindered by a hundred hindrances; now startling and terrible; now ridiculous and trivial; but never either natural or probable; and going down into the quiet house with the memory of these dreams strong upon her, she had been bewildered by the stillness which had betokened that the tidings had not yet come.

And now her mind underwent a complete change. She no longer wished to delay that dreaded intelligence. She wished the agony, whatever it was to be, over and done with, the pain suffered, and the release attained. It seemed to her as if the intolerable day would never come to an end, as if her mad wishes had been granted, and the progress of time had actually stopped.

'What a long day it has been!' exclaimed Alicia, as if taking up the burden of my lady's thoughts; 'nothing but drizzle and mist and wind! And now that it's too late for anybody to go out, it must needs be fine,' the young lady added, with an evident sense of injury.

Lady Audley did not answer. She was looking at the stupid one-handed clock; and waiting for the news which must come sooner or later; which could not surely fail to come very speedily.

'They have been afraid to come and tell him,' she thought; 'they have been afraid to break the news to Sir Michael. Who will come to tell it, at last, I wonder? The rector of Mount Stanning, perhaps; or the doctor; some important person, at least.'

If she could have gone out into the leafless avenues, or on to the high road beyond them; if she could have gone so far as that hill upon which she had so lately parted with Phœbe, she would have gladly done so. She would rather have suffered anything than that slow suspense, that corroding anxiety, that metaphysical dry-rot in which heart and mind seemed to decay under an insufferable torture. She tried to talk; and by a painful effort contrived now and then to utter some common-place remark. Under any ordinary circumstances her companion would have noticed her embarrassment; but Miss Audley, happening to be very much absorbed by her own vexations, was quite as well inclined to be silent as my lady herself. The monotonous walk up and down the gravelled pathway suited Alicia's humour. I think that she even took a malicious pleasure in the idea that she was very likely catching cold; and that her cousin Robert was answerable for her danger. If she could have brought upon herself inflammation of the lungs, or ruptured blood-vessels, by that exposure to the chill March atmosphere, I think she would have felt a gloomy satisfaction in her sufferings.

'Perhaps Robert might care for me, if I had inflammation of the lungs,' she thought. 'He couldn't insult me by calling me a Bouncer then. Bouncers don't have inflammation of the lungs.'

I believe she drew a picture of herself in the last stage of consumption, propped up by pillows in a great easy-chair, looking out of a window in the afternoon sunshine, with medicine bottles, a bunch of grapes and a Bible upon a table by her side; and with Robert, all contrition and tenderness, summoned to receive her farewell blessing. She preached a whole chapter to him in that parting benediction, talking a great deal longer than was in keeping with her prostrate state, and very much enjoying her dismal castle in the air. Employed in this sentimental manner, Miss Audley took very little notice of her step-mother, and the one hand of the blundering clock had slipped to six by the time Robert had been blessed and dismissed.

'Good gracious me,' she cried, suddenly – 'six o'clock, and I'm not dressed.'

The half-hour bell rang in a cupola upon the roof while Alicia was speaking.

'I must go in, my lady,' she said. 'Won't you come?'

'Presently,' answered Lady Audley. 'I'm dressed, you see.'

Alicia ran off, but Sir Michael's wife still lingered in the quadrangle; still waited for those tidings which were so long coming.

It was nearly dark. The blue mists of evening had slowly risen from the ground. The flat meadows were filled with a grey vapour, and a stranger might have fancied Audley Court a castle on the margin of a sea. Under the archway the shadows of fast-coming night lurked darkly; like traitors waiting for an opportunity to glide stealthily into the quadrangle. Through the archway a patch of cold blue sky glimmered faintly, streaked by one line of lurid crimson, and lighted by the dim glitter of one wintry-looking star. Not a creature was stirring in the quadrangle but the restless woman, who paced up and down the straight pathways, listening for a footstep, whose coming was to strike terror to her soul. She heard it at last! – a footstep in the avenue upon the other side of the archway. But was it *the* footstep? Her sense of hearing, made unnaturally acute by excitement, told her that it was a man's footstep – told even more, that it was the tread of a gentleman; no slouching, lumbering pedestrian in hobnailed boots; but a gentleman who walked firmly and well.

Every sound fell like a lump of ice upon my lady's heart. She could not wait, she could not contain herself; she lost all self-control, all power of endurance, all capability of self-restraint; and she rushed towards the archway.

She paused beneath its shadow, for the stranger was close upon her. She saw him: O God! she saw him, in that dim evening light. Her brain reeled; her heart stopped beating. She uttered no cry of surprise, no exclamation of terror, but staggered backwards and clung for support to the ivied buttress of the archway. With her slender figure crouched into the angle formed by this buttress and the wall which it supported, she stood staring at the new-comer.

As he approached her more closely her knees sank under her, and she dropped to the ground; not fainting, or in any manner unconscious; but sinking into a crouching attitude, and still crushed into the angle of the wall; as if she would have made a tomb for herself in the shadow of that sheltering brickwork.

'My lady!'

The speaker was Robert Audley. He whose bed-room door she had double-locked seventeen hours before at the Castle Inn.

'What is the matter with you?' he said, in a strange, constrained manner. 'Get up, and let me take you in-doors.'

He assisted her to rise; and she obeyed him, very submissively. He took her arm in his strong hand and led her across the quadrangle and into the lamp-lit hall. She shivered more violently than he had ever seen any woman shiver before; but she made no attempt at resistance to his will.

CHAPTER III
My lady tells the truth

'Is there any room in which I can talk to you alone?' Robert
Audley asked, as he looked dubiously round the hall.

My lady only bowed her head in answer. She pushed open
the door of the library, which had been left ajar. Sir Michael
had gone to his dressing-room to prepare for dinner after a
day of lazy enjoyment; perfectly legitimate for an invalid. The
apartment was quite empty, and only lighted by the blaze of
the fire, as it had been upon the previous evening.

Lady Audley entered this room, followed by Robert, who
closed the door behind him. The wretched, shivering woman
went to the fire-place and knelt down before the blaze, as if
any natural warmth could have power to check that unnatural
chill. The young man followed her, and stood beside her upon
the hearth, with his arm resting upon the chimney-piece.

'Lady Audley,' he said, in a voice whose icy sternness held
out no hope of any tenderness or compassion, 'I spoke to you
last night very plainly; but you refused to listen to me. To-night
I must speak to you still more plainly; and you must no longer
refuse to listen to me.'

My lady, crouching before the fire with her face hidden in
her hands, uttered a low sobbing sound which was almost a
moan, but made no other answer.

'There was a fire last night at Mount Stanning, Lady Audley,'
the pitiless voice proceeded; 'the Castle Inn, the house in
which I slept, was burned to the ground. Do you know how
I escaped perishing in that destruction?'

'No.'

'I escaped by a most providential circumstance, which seems a very simple one. I did not sleep in the room which had been prepared for me. The place seemed wretchedly damp and chilly; the chimney smoked abominably when an attempt was made at lighting a fire; and I persuaded the servant to make me up a bed upon the sofa in the small ground-floor sitting-room which I had occupied during the evening.'

He paused for a moment, watching the crouching figure. The only change in my lady's attitude was that her head had fallen a little lower.

'Shall I tell you by whose agency the destruction of the Castle Inn was brought about, my lady?'

There was no answer.

'Shall I tell you?'

Still the same obstinate silence.

'My Lady Audley,' cried Robert, suddenly, '*you* were the incendiary. It was you whose murderous hand kindled those flames. It was you who thought by that thrice-horrible deed to rid yourself of me, your enemy and denouncer. What was it to you that other lives might be sacrificed? If by a second massacre of Saint Bartholomew you could have ridded yourself of *me*, you would have freely sacrificed an army of victims. The day is past for tenderness and mercy. For you I can no longer know pity or compunction. So far as by sparing your shame I can spare others who must suffer by your shame, I will be merciful; but no further. If there were any secret tribunal before which you might be made to answer for your crimes, I would have little scruple in being your accuser: but I would spare that generous and high-born gentleman upon whose noble name your infamy would be reflected.'

His voice softened as he made this allusion, and for a moment he broke down, but he recovered himself by an effort and continued –

'No life was lost in the fire of last night. I slept lightly, my lady, for my mind was troubled, as it has been for a long time, by the misery which I knew was lowering upon this house. It was I who discovered the breaking out of the fire in time to give the alarm and to save the servant girl and the poor drunken wretch, who was very much burnt in spite of my efforts, and who now lies in a precarious state at his mother's cottage. It was from him and from his wife that I learned who had visited the Castle Inn in the dead of the night. The woman was almost distracted when she saw me, and from her I discovered the particulars of last night. Heaven knows what other secrets of yours she may hold, my lady, or how easily they might be extorted from her if I wanted her aid, which I do not. My path lies very straight before me. I have sworn to bring the murderer of George Talboys to justice: and I will keep my oath. I say that it was by your agency my friend met with his death. If I have wondered sometimes, as it was only natural I should, whether I was not the victim of some horrible hallucination; whether such an alternative was not more probable than that a young and lovely woman should be capable of so foul and treacherous a murder, all wonder is past. After last night's deed of horror, there is no crime you could commit, however vast and unnatural, which could make me wonder. Henceforth you must seem to me no longer a woman; a guilty woman with a heart which in its worst wickedness has yet some latent power to suffer and feel; I look upon you henceforth as the demoniac incarnation of some evil principle. But you shall no longer pollute this place by your presence. Unless you will confess what you are, and who you are, in the presence of the man you have deceived so long; and accept from him and from me such mercy as we may be inclined to extend to you; I will gather together the witnesses who shall swear to your identity, and at peril of any shame to myself and those I love, I will bring upon you the punishment of your crime.'

The woman rose suddenly and stood before him erect and resolute; with her hair dashed away from her face and her eyes glittering.

'Bring Sir Michael!' she cried; 'bring him here, and I will confess anything – everything! What do I care? God knows I have struggled hard enough against you, and fought the battle patiently enough; but you have conquered, Mr. Robert Audley. It is a great triumph, is it not? a wonderful victory! You have used your cool, calculating, frigid, luminous intellect to a noble purpose. You have conquered – a MADWOMAN!'

'A madwoman!' cried Mr. Audley.

'Yes, a madwoman. When you say that I killed George Talboys, you say the truth. When you say that I murdered him treacherously and foully, you lie. I killed him because I AM MAD! because my intellect is a little way upon the wrong side of that narrow boundary-line between sanity and insanity; because when George Talboys goaded me, as you have goaded me; and reproached me, and threatened me; my mind, never properly balanced, utterly lost its balance; and *I was mad!* Bring Sir Michael; and bring him quickly. If he is to be told one thing, let him be told everything; let him hear the secret of my life!'

Robert Audley left the room to look for his uncle. He went in search of that honoured kinsman with God knows how heavy a weight of anguish at his heart, for he knew he was about to shatter the day-dream of his uncle's life; and he knew that our dreams are none the less terrible to lose, because they have never been the realities for which we have mistaken them. But even in the midst of his sorrow for Sir Michael, he could not help wondering at my lady's last words – 'the secret of my life.' He remembered those lines in the letter written by Helen Talboys upon the eve of her flight from Wildernsea, which had so puzzled him. He remembered those appealing sentences – 'You should forgive me, for you know *why* I have been so. You know the *secret* of my life.'

He met Sir Michael in the hall. He made no attempt to prepare the way for the terrible revelation which the baronet was to hear. He only drew him into the fire-lit library, and there for the first time addressed him quietly thus:–

'Lady Audley has a confession to make to you, sir – a confession which I know will be a most cruel surprise, a most bitter grief. But it is necessary for your present honour, and for your future peace, that you should hear it. She has deceived you, I regret to say, most basely; but it is only right you should hear from her own lips any excuses which she may have to offer for her wickedness. May God soften this blow for you,' sobbed the young man, suddenly breaking down; 'I cannot!'

Sir Michael lifted his hand as if he would have commanded his nephew to be silent; but that imperious hand dropped feeble and impotent at his side. He stood in the centre of the fire-lit room, rigid and immovable.

'Lucy!' he cried, in a voice whose anguish struck like a blow upon the jarred nerves of those who heard it, as the cry of a wounded animal pains the listener – 'Lucy! tell me that this man is a madman! tell me so, my love, or I shall kill him!'

There was a sudden fury in his voice as he turned upon Robert, as if he could indeed have felled his wife's accuser to the earth with the strength of his uplifted arm.

But my lady fell upon her knees at his feet; interposing herself between the baronet and his nephew, who stood leaning upon the back of an easy-chair, with his face hidden by his hand.

'He has told you the truth,' said my lady, 'and he is not mad! I have sent for you that I may confess everything to you. I should be sorry for you if I could; for you have been very, very good to me; much better to me than I ever deserved; but I can't, I can't – I can feel nothing but my own misery. I told you long ago that I was selfish; I am selfish still – more selfish than ever in my misery. Happy, prosperous people may feel for others. I laugh at other people's sufferings; they seem so small compared to my own.'

When first my lady had fallen on her knees, Sir Michael had attempted to raise her, and had remonstrated with her; but as she spoke he dropped into a chair close to the spot upon which she knelt, and with his hands clasped together, and with his head bent to catch every syllable of those horrible words, he listened as if his whole being had been resolved into that one sense of hearing.

'I must tell you the story of my life; in order to tell you why I have become the miserable wretch who has no better hope than to be allowed to run away and hide in some desolate corner of the earth. I must tell you the story of my life,' repeated my lady, 'but you need not fear that I shall dwell long upon it. It has not been so pleasant to me that I should wish to remember it. When I was a very little child I remember asking a question which it was natural enough that I should ask, God help me! I asked where my mother was. I had a faint remembrance of a face, like what my own is now, looking at me when I was very little better than a baby; but I had missed the face suddenly, and had never seen it since. They told me that my mother was away. I was not happy, for the woman who had charge of me was a disagreeable woman, and the place in which we lived was a lonely place, a village upon the Hampshire coast, about seven miles from Portsmouth. My father, who was in the navy, only came now and then to see me; and I was left almost entirely to the charge of this woman, who was irregularly paid; and who vented her rage upon me when my father was behind-hand in remitting her money. So you see that at a very early age I found out what it was to be poor.

'Perhaps it was more from being discontented with my dreary life than from any wonderful impulse of affection, that I asked very often the same question about my mother. I always received the same answer – she was away. When I asked where, I was told that that was a secret. When I grew old enough to understand the meaning of the word death, I asked if my mother was dead, and I was told – "No, she was not dead; she was ill, and she was away." I asked how long she had been ill, and I was told that she had been so some years; ever since I was a baby.

'At last the secret came out. I worried my foster-mother with the old question one day when the remittances had fallen very much in arrear, and her temper had been unusually tried. She flew into a passion; and told me that my mother was a madwoman; and that she was in a mad-house forty miles away. She had scarcely said this when she repented, and told me that it was not the truth, and that I was not to believe it, or to say that she had told me such a thing. I discovered afterwards that my father had made her promise most solemnly never to tell me the secret of my mother's fate.

'I brooded horribly upon the thought of my mother's madness. It haunted me by day and night. I was always picturing to myself this madwoman pacing up and down some prison cell, in a hideous garment that bound her tortured limbs. I had exaggerated ideas of the horror of her situation. I had no knowledge of the different degrees of madness; and the image that haunted me was that of a distraught and violent creature, who would fall upon me and kill me if I came within her reach. This idea grew upon me until I used to awake in the dead of the night, screaming aloud in an agony of terror, from a dream in which I had felt my mother's icy grasp upon my throat, and heard her ravings in my ear.

'When I was ten years old my father came to pay up the arrears due to my protectress, and to take me to school. He had left me in Hampshire longer than he had intended, from his inability to pay this money. So there again I felt the bitterness of poverty, and ran the risk of growing up an ignorant creature amongst coarse rustic children, because my father was poor.'

My lady paused for a moment, but only to take breath, for she had spoken rapidly, as if eager to tell this hated story, and to have done with it. She was still on her knees, but Sir Michael made no effort to raise her.

He sat silent and immovable. What was this story that he was listening to? Whose was it, and to what was it to lead? It could not be his wife's; he had heard her simple account of her youth, and had believed it as he had believed in the Gospel. She had told him a very brief story of an early orphanage, and a long quiet, colourless youth spent in the conventual seclusion of an English boarding-school.

'My father came at last, and I told him what I had discovered. He was very much affected when I spoke of my mother. He was not what the world generally calls a good man, but I learned afterwards that he had loved his wife very dearly; and that he would have willingly sacrificed his life to her, and constituted himself her guardian, had he not been compelled to earn the daily bread of the madwoman and her child by the exercise of his profession. So here again I beheld what a bitter thing it is to be poor. My mother, who might have been tended by a devoted husband, was given over to the care of hired nurses.

'Before my father sent me to school at Torquay, he took me to see my mother. This visit served at least to dispel the idea which had so often terrified me. I saw no raving, strait-waistcoated maniac, guarded by zealous gaolers; but a golden-haired, blue-eyed, girlish creature, who seemed as frivolous as a butterfly, and who skipped towards us with her yellow curls decorated with natural flowers, and saluted us with radiant smiles, and gay, ceaseless chatter.

'But she didn't know us. She would have spoken in the same manner to any stranger who had entered the gates of the garden about her prison-house. Her madness was an hereditary disease transmitted to her from her mother, who had died mad. She, my mother, had been, or had appeared, sane up to the hour of my birth; but from that hour her intellect had decayed, until she had become what I saw her.

'I went away with the knowledge of this, and with the knowledge that the only inheritance I had to expect from my mother was – insanity!

'I went away with this knowledge in my mind, and with something more – a secret to keep. I was only a child of ten years old; but I felt all the weight of that burden. I was to keep the secret of my mother's madness; for it was a secret that might affect me injuriously in after-life. I was to remember this.

'I did remember this; and it was, perhaps, this that made me selfish and heartless; for I suppose I am heartless. As I grew older I was told that I was pretty – beautiful – lovely – bewitching. I heard all these things at first indifferently; but by-and-by I listened to them greedily, and began to think that in spite of the secret of my life I might be more successful in the world's great lottery than my companions. I had learnt that which in some indefinite manner or other every schoolgirl learns sooner or later – I learned that my ultimate fate in life depended upon my marriage, and I concluded that if I was indeed prettier than my schoolfellows, I ought to marry better than any of them.

'I left school before I was seventeen years of age with this thought in my mind; and I went to live at the other extremity of England with my father, who had retired upon his half-pay, and had established himself at Wildernsea, with the idea that the place was cheap and select.

'The place was indeed select. I had not been there a month before I discovered that even the prettiest girl might wait a long time for a rich husband. I wish to hurry over this part of my life: I dare say I was very despicable. You and your nephew, Sir Michael, have been rich all your lives, and can very well afford to despise me; but I knew how far poverty can affect a life, and I looked forward with a sick terror to a life so affected. At last the rich suitor – the wandering prince – came.'

She paused for a moment, and shuddered convulsively. It was impossible to see any of the changes of her countenance, for her face was obstinately bent towards the floor. Through-out her long confession she never lifted it; throughout her long confession her voice was never broken by a tear. What she had to tell she told in a cold, hard tone; very much the tone in which some criminal, dogged and sullen to the last, might have confessed to a gaol chaplain.

'The wandering prince came,' she repeated; 'he was called George Talboys.'

For the first time since his wife's confession had begun, Sir Michael Audley started. He began to understand it all now. A crowd of unheeded words and forgotten circumstances that had seemed too insignificant for remark or recollection, flashed back upon him as vividly as if they had been the leading incidents of his past life.

'Mr. George Talboys was a cornet in a dragoon regiment. He was the only son of a rich country gentleman. He fell in love with me, and married me three months after my seventeenth birthday. I think I loved him as much as it was in my power to love anybody; not more than I have loved you, Sir Michael; not so much; for when you married me you elevated me to a position that he could never have given me.'

The dream was broken. Sir Michael Audley remembered that summer's evening, nearly two years ago, when he had first declared his love for Mr. Dawson's governess; he remembered the sick, half-shuddering sensation of regret and disappoint-ment that had come over him then; and he felt as if it had in some manner dimly foreshadowed the agony of to-night.

But I do not believe that even in his misery he felt that entire and unmitigated surprise, that utter revulsion of feeling that is felt when a good woman wanders away from herself, and becomes the lost creature whom her husband is bound in honour to abjure. I do not believe that Sir Michael Audley had ever *really* believed in his wife. He had loved her and admired her; he had been bewitched by her beauty and bewildered by her charms; but that sense of something wanting, that vague feeling of loss and disappointment which had come upon him on the summer's night of his betrothal, had been with him more or less distinctly ever since. I cannot believe that an honest man, however pure and single may be his mind, however simply trustful his nature, is ever really deceived by falsehood. There is beneath the voluntary confidence an involuntary distrust; not to be conquered by any effort of the will.

'We were married,' my lady continued, 'and I loved him very well, quite well enough to be happy with him as long as his money lasted, and while we were on the Continent, travelling in the best style and always staying at the best hotels. But when we came back to Wildernsea and lived with papa, and all the money was gone, and George grew gloomy and wretched, and was always thinking of his troubles, and appeared to neglect me, I was very unhappy; and it seemed as if this fine marriage had only given me a twelvemonth's gaiety and extravagance after all. I begged George to appeal to his father; but he refused. I persuaded him to try and get employment; and he failed. My baby was born, and the crisis which had been fatal to my mother arose for me. I escaped; but I was more irritable perhaps after my recovery; less inclined to fight the hard battle of the world; more disposed to complain of poverty and neglect. I did complain one day, loudly and bitterly. I upbraided George Talboys for his cruelty in having allied a helpless girl to poverty and misery; and he flew into a passion with me and ran out of the house. When I awoke the next morning I found a letter lying on the table by my bed, telling me that he was going to the Antipodes to seek his fortune, and that he would never see me again until he was a rich man.

'I looked upon this as a desertion, and I resented it bitterly – I resented it by hating the man who had left me with no protector but a weak, tipsy father, and with a child to support. I had to work hard for my living, and in every hour of labour – and what labour is more wearisome than the dull slavery of a governess? – I recognised a separate wrong done me by George Talboys. His father was rich; his sister was living in luxury and respectability; and I, his wife, and the mother of his son, was a slave allied for ever to beggary and obscurity. People pitied me; and I hated them for their pity. I did not love the child; for he had been left a burden upon my hands. The hereditary taint that was in my blood had never until this time showed itself by any one sign or token; but at this time I became subject to fits of violence and despair. At this time I think my mind first lost its balance, and for the first time I crossed that invisible line which separates reason from madness. I have seen my father's eyes fixed upon me in horror and alarm. I have known him soothe me as only mad people and children are soothed, and I have chafed against his petty devices, I have resented even his indulgence.

'At last these fits of desperation resolved themselves into a desperate purpose. I determined to run away from this wretched home which my slavery supported. I determined to desert this father who had more fear of me than love for me. I determined to go to London, and lose myself in that great chaos of humanity.

'I had seen an advertisement in the *Times* while I was at Wildernsea, and I presented myself to Mrs. Vincent, the advertiser, under a feigned name. She accepted me, waiving all question as to my antecedents. You know the rest. I came here, and you made me an offer, the acceptance of which would lift me at once into the sphere to which my ambition had pointed ever since I was a schoolgirl, and heard for the first time that I was pretty.

'Three years had passed, and I had received no token of my husband's existence; for I argued that if he had returned to England, he would have succeeded in finding me under any name and in any place. I knew the energy of his character well enough to know this.

'I said, "I have a right to think that he is dead, or that he wishes me to believe him dead, and his shadow shall not stand between me and prosperity." I said this, and I became your wife, Sir Michael, with every resolution to be as good a wife as it was in my nature to be. The common temptations that assail and shipwreck some women had no terror for me. I would have been your true and pure wife to the end of time, though I had been surrounded by a legion of tempters. The mad folly that the world calls love had never had any part in my madness; and here at least extremes met, and the vice of heartlessness became the virtue of constancy.

'I was very happy in the first triumph and grandeur of my new position, very grateful to the hand that had lifted me to it. In the sunshine of my own happiness I felt, for the first time in my life, for the miseries of others. I had been poor myself, and I was now rich, and could afford to pity and relieve the poverty of my neighbours. I took pleasure in acts of kindness and benevolence. I found out my father's address and sent him large sums of money, anonymously, for I did not wish him to discover what had become of me. I availed myself to the full of the privilege your generosity afforded me. I dispensed happiness on every side. I saw myself loved as well as admired; and I think I might have been a good woman for the rest of my life, if fate would have allowed me to be so.

'I believe that at this time my mind regained its just balance. I had watched myself very closely since leaving Wildernsea; I had held a check upon myself. I had often wondered, while sitting in the surgeon's quiet family circle, whether any suspicion of that invisible hereditary taint had ever occurred to Mr. Dawson.

'Fate would not suffer me to be good. My destiny compelled me to be a wretch. Within a month of my marriage, I read in one of the Essex papers of the return of a certain Mr. Talboys, a fortunate gold-seeker, from Australia. The ship had sailed at the time I read the paragraph. What was to be done?

'I said just now that I knew the energy of George's character. I knew that the man who had gone to the Antipodes, and won a fortune for his wife, would leave no stone unturned in his efforts to find her. It was hopeless to think of hiding myself from him.

'Unless he could be induced to believe that I was dead, he would never cease in his search for me.

'My brain was dazed as I thought of my peril. Again the balance trembled; again the invisible boundary was passed; again I was mad.

'I went down to Southampton and found my father, who was living there with my child. You remember how Mrs. Vincent's name was used as an excuse for this hurried journey, and how it was contrived that I should go with no other escort than Phœbe Marks, whom I left at the hotel while I went to my father's house.

'I confided to my father the whole secret of my peril. He was not very much shocked at what I had done, for poverty had perhaps blunted his sense of honour and principle. He was not very much shocked; but he was frightened; and he promised to do all in his power to assist me in my horrible emergency.

'He had received a letter addressed to me at Wildernsea,

by George, and forwarded from there to my father. This letter had been written within a few days of the sailing of the *Argus*, and it announced the probable date of the ship's arrival at Liverpool. This letter gave us, therefore, data upon which to act.

'We decided at once upon the first step. This was that on the date of the probable arrival of the *Argus*, or a few days later, an advertisement of my death should be inserted in the *Times*.

'But almost immediately after deciding upon this, we saw that there were fearful difficulties in the carrying out of such a simple plan. The date of the death, and the place in which I died, must be announced, as well as the death itself. George would immediately hurry to that place, however distant it might be, however comparatively inaccessible, and the shallow falsehood would be discovered.

'I knew enough of his sanguine temperament, his courage and determination, his readiness to hope against hope, to know that unless he saw the grave in which I was buried, and the register of my death, he would never believe that I was lost to him.

'My father was utterly dumbfounded and helpless. He could only shed childish tears of despair and terror. He was of no use to me in this crisis.

'I was hopeless of any issue out of my difficulty. I began to think that I must trust to the chapter of accidents; and hope that amongst other obscure corners of the earth, Audley Court might remain undreamt-of by my husband.

'I sat with my father, drinking tea with him in his miserable hovel, and playing with the child, who was pleased with my dress and jewels, but quite unconscious that I was anything but a stranger to him. I had the boy in my arms, when a woman who attended him came to fetch him that she might make him more fit to be seen by the lady, as she said.

'I was anxious to know how the boy was treated, and I detained this woman in conversation with me, while my father dozed over the tea-table.

'She was a pale-faced, sandy-haired woman, of about five-and-forty; and she seemed very glad to get the chance of talking to me as long as I pleased to allow her. She soon left off talking of the boy, however, to tell me her own troubles. She was in very great trouble, she told me. Her eldest daughter had been obliged to leave her situation from ill-health; in fact, the doctor said the girl was in a decline; and it was a hard thing for a poor widow who had seen better days to have a sick daughter to support, as well as a family of young children.

'I let the woman run on for a long time in this manner, telling me the girl's ailments, and the girl's age, and the girl's doctor's stuff, and piety, and sufferings, and a great deal more. But I neither listened to her nor heeded her. I heard her, but only in a far-away manner, as I heard the traffic in the street, or the ripple of the stream at the bottom of it. What were this woman's troubles to me? I had miseries of my own; and worse miseries than *her* coarse nature could ever have to endure. These sort of people always had sick husbands or sick children, and expected to be helped in their illnesses by the rich. It was nothing out of the common. I was thinking this; and I was just going to dismiss the woman with a sovereign for her sick daughter; when an idea flashed upon me with such painful suddenness that it sent the blood surging up to my brain, and set my heart beating, as it only beats when I am mad.

'I asked the woman her name. She was a Mrs. Plowson, and she kept a small general shop, she said, and only ran in now and then to look after Georgey, and to see that the little maid-of-all-work took care of him. Her daughter's name was Matilda. I asked her several questions about this girl Matilda, and I ascertained that she was four-and-twenty, that she had always been consumptive, and that she was now, as the doctor said, going off in a rapid decline. He had declared that she could not last much more than a fortnight.

'It was in three weeks that the ship that carried George Talboys was expected to anchor in the Mersey.

'I need not dwell much upon this business. I visited the sick girl. She was fair and slender. Her description, carelessly given, might tally nearly enough with my own; though she bore no shadow of resemblance to me, except in these two particulars. I was received by the girl as a rich lady who wished to do her service. I bought the mother, who was poor and greedy, and who for a gift of money, more money than she had ever before received, consented to submit to anything I wished. Upon the second day after my introduction to this Mrs. Plowson, my father went over to Ventnor, and hired lodgings for his invalid daughter and her little boy. Early the next morning he carried over the dying girl and Georgey, who had been bribed to call her "mamma." She entered the house as Mrs. Talboys; she was attended by a Ventnor medical man as Mrs. Talboys; she died, and her death and burial were registered in that name. The advertisement was inserted in the *Times*, and upon the second day after its insertion George Talboys visited Ventnor, and ordered the tombstone which at this hour records the death of his wife, Helen Talboys.'

Sir Michael Audley rose slowly, and with a stiff, constrained action, as if every physical sense had been benumbed by that one sense of misery.

'I cannot hear any more,' he said, in a hoarse whisper; 'if there is anything more to be told, I cannot hear it. Robert, it is you who have brought about this discovery, as I understand. I want to know nothing more. Will you take upon yourself the duty of providing for the safety and comfort of this lady, whom I have thought my wife? I need not ask you to remember in all you do, that I have loved her very dearly and truly. I cannot say farewell to her. I will not say it until I can think of her without bitterness – until I can pity her; as I now pray that God may pity her this night.'

Sir Michael walked slowly from the room. He did not trust himself to look at that crouching figure. He did not wish to see the creature whom he had cherished. He went straight to his dressing-room, rang for his valet, and ordered him to pack a portmanteau, and make all necessary arrangements for accompanying his master by the last up-train.

CHAPTER IV

The hush that succeeds the tempest

Robert Audley followed his uncle into the vestibule after Sir
Michael had spoken those few quiet words which sounded the
death-knell of his hope and love. Heaven knows how much
the young man had feared the coming of this day. It had come;
and though there had been no great outburst of despair, no
whirlwind of stormy grief, no loud tempest of anguish and
tears, Robert took no comforting thought from the unnatural
stillness. He knew enough to know that Sir Michael Audley
went away with the barbed arrow, which his nephew's hand
had sent home to its aim, rankling in his tortured heart; he
knew that this strange and icy calm was the first numbness of
a heart stricken by a grief so unexpected as for a time to
be rendered almost incomprehensible by a blank stupor of
astonishment. He knew that when this dull quiet had passed
away, when little by little, and one by one, each horrible
feature of the sufferer's sorrow became first dimly apparent
and then terribly familiar to him, the storm would burst in
fatal fury, and tempests of tears and cruel thunder-claps of
agony would rend that generous heart.

Robert had heard of cases in which men of his uncle's age
had borne some great grief, as Sir Michael had borne this, with
a strange quiet; and had gone away from those who would
have comforted them, and whose anxieties have been relieved
by this patient stillness, to fall down upon the ground and die
under the blow which at first had only stunned them. He
remembered cases in which paralysis and apoplexy had

stricken men as strong as his uncle in the first hour of the horrible affliction; and he lingered in the lamp-lit vestibule, wondering whether it was not his duty to be with Sir Michael – to be near him, in case of any emergency, and to accompany him wherever he went.

Yet, would it be wise to force himself upon that grey-headed sufferer in this cruel hour, in which he had been awakened from the one delusion of a blameless life to discover that he had been the dupe of a false face, and the fool of a nature which was too coldly mercenary, too cruelly heartless, to be sensible of its own infamy?

'No,' thought Robert Audley, 'I will not intrude upon the anguish of this wounded heart. There is humiliation mingled with this bitter grief. It is better he should fight the battle alone. I have done what I believe to have been my solemn duty, yet I should scarcely wonder if I had rendered myself for ever hateful to him. It is better he should fight the battle alone. I can do nothing to make the strife less terrible. Better that it should be fought alone.'

While the young man stood with his hand upon the library door, still half doubtful whether he should follow his uncle or re-enter the room in which he had left that more wretched creature, whom it had been his business to unmask, Alicia Audley opened the dining-room door, and revealed to him the old-fashioned oak-panelled apartment, the long table covered with snowy damask, and bright with a cheerful glitter of glass and silver.

'*Is* papa coming to dinner?' asked Miss Audley. 'I'm *so* hungry; and poor Tomlins has sent up three times to say the fish will be spoiled. It must be reduced to a species of isinglass soup by this time, I should think,' added the young lady, as she came out into the vestibule with the *Times* newspaper in her hand.

She had been sitting by the fire reading the paper, and waiting for her seniors to join her at the dinner-table.

'Oh, it's you, Mr. Robert Audley,' she remarked, indifferently. 'You dine with us, of course. Pray go and find papa. It must be nearly eight o'clock, and we are supposed to dine at six.'

Mr. Audley answered his cousin rather sternly. Her frivolous manner jarred upon him, and he forgot in his irrational displeasure that Miss Audley had known nothing of the terrible drama which had been so long enacting under her very nose.

'Your papa has just endured a very great grief, Alicia,' the young man said, gravely.

The girl's arch, laughing face changed in a moment to a tenderly earnest look of sorrow and anxiety. Alicia Audley loved her father very dearly.

'A grief!' she exclaimed; 'papa grieved? Oh! Robert, what has happened?'

'I can tell you nothing yet, Alicia,' Robert answered, in a low voice.

He took his cousin by the wrist, and drew her into the dining-room as he spoke. He closed the door carefully behind him before he continued:–

'Alicia, can I trust you?' he asked, earnestly.

'Trust me to do what?'

'To be a comfort and a friend to your poor father under a very heavy affliction.'

'YES!' cried Alicia, passionately. 'How can you ask me such a question? Do you think there is anything I would not do to lighten any sorrow of my father's? Do you think there is anything I would not suffer if my suffering could lighten his?'

The rushing tears rose to Miss Audley's bright grey eyes as she spoke.

'Oh, Robert! Robert! could you think so badly of me as to think that I would not try to be a comfort to my father in his grief ?' she said, reproachfully.

'No, no, my dear,' answered the young man, quietly; 'I never doubted your affection, I only doubted your discretion. May I rely upon that?'

'You may, Robert,' said Alicia, resolutely.

'Very well, then, my dear girl, I will trust you. Your father is going to leave the Court, for a time at least. The grief which he has just endured – a sudden and an unlooked-for sorrow, remember – has no doubt made this place hateful to him. He is going away; but he must not go alone, must he, Alicia?'

'Alone? No! No! But I suppose my lady—'

'Lady Audley will not go with him,' said Robert, gravely; 'he is about to separate himself from her.'

'For a time?'

'No; for ever.'

'Separate himself from her for ever!' exclaimed Alicia. 'Then this grief—'

'Is connected with Lady Audley. Lady Audley is the cause of your father's sorrow.'

Alicia's face, which had been pale before, flushed crimson. Sorrow, of which my lady was the cause – a sorrow which was to separate Sir Michael for ever from his young wife! There had been no quarrel between them – there had never been anything but harmony and sunshine between Lucy Audley and her generous husband. This sorrow must surely then have arisen from some sudden discovery; it was, no doubt, a sorrow associated with disgrace. Robert Audley understood the meaning of that vivid blush.

'You will offer to accompany your father wherever he may choose to go, Alicia,' he said. 'You are his natural comforter at such a time as this, but you will best befriend him in this hour of trial by avoiding all intrusion upon his grief. Your very ignorance of the particulars of that grief will be a security for your discretion. Say nothing to your father that you might not have said to him two years ago, before he married a second wife. Try and be to him what you were before the woman in yonder room came between you and your father's love.'

'I will,' murmured Alicia, 'I will.'

'You will naturally avoid all mention of Lady Audley's name. If your father is often silent, be patient; if it sometimes seems to you that the shadow of this great sorrow will never pass away from his life, be patient still; and remember that there can be no better hope of a cure for his grief than the hope that his daughter's devotion may lead him to remember there is one woman upon this earth who will love him truly and purely until the last.'

'Yes, yes, Robert, dear cousin, I will remember.'

Mr. Audley, for the first time since he had been a schoolboy, took his cousin in his arms and kissed her broad forehead.

'My dear Alicia,' he said, 'do this, and you will make me happy. I have been in some measure the means of bringing this sorrow upon your father. Let me hope that it is not an enduring one. Try and restore my uncle to happiness, Alicia, and I will love you more dearly than brother ever loved a noble-hearted sister; and a brotherly affection may be worth having, perhaps, after all, my dear, though it is very different to poor Sir Harry's enthusiastic worship.'

Alicia's head was bent and her face hidden from her cousin while he spoke; but she lifted her head when he had finished, and looked him full in the face with a smile that was only the brighter for her eyes being filled with tears.

'You are a good fellow, Bob,' she said: 'and I've been very foolish and wicked to feel angry with you, because—'

The young lady stopped suddenly.

'Because what, my dear?' asked Mr. Audley.

'Because I'm silly, cousin Robert,' Alicia said quickly; 'never mind that, Bob; I'll do all you wish, and it shall not be my fault if my dearest father doesn't forget his troubles before long. I'd go to the end of the world with him, poor darling, if I thought there was any comfort to be found for him in the journey. I'll go and get ready directly. Do you think papa will go to-night?'

'Yes, my dear; I don't think Sir Michael will rest another night under this roof, yet awhile.'

'The mail goes at twenty minutes past nine,' said Alicia; 'we must leave the house in an hour if we are to travel by it. I shall see you again before we go, Robert.'

'Yes, dear.'

Miss Audley ran off to her room to summon her maid, and make all necessary preparations for the sudden journey, of whose ultimate destination she was as yet quite ignorant.

She went heart and soul into the carrying out of the duty which Robert had dictated to her. She assisted in the packing of her portmanteaus, and hopelessly bewildered her maid by stuffing silk dresses into her bonnet boxes, and satin shoes into her dressing-case. She roamed about her rooms gathering together drawing materials, music-books, needlework, hair-brushes, jewellery, and perfume-bottles, very much as she might have done had she been about to sail for some savage country devoid of all civilised resources. She was thinking all the time of her father's unknown grief; and perhaps a little of the serious face and earnest voice which had that night revealed her cousin Robert to her in a new character.

Mr. Audley went up-stairs after his cousin, and found his way to Sir Michael's dressing-room. He knocked at the door and listened, heaven knows how anxiously, for the expected answer. There was a moment's pause, during which the young man's heart beat loud and fast, and then the door was opened by the baronet himself. Robert saw that his uncle's valet was already hard at work preparing for his master's hurried journey.

Sir Michael came out into the corridor.

'Have you anything more to say to me, Robert?' he asked, quietly.

'I only came to ascertain if I could assist in any of your arrangements. You go to London by the mail?'

'Yes.'

'Have you any idea of where you will stay?'

'Yes, I shall stop at the Clarendon; I am known there. Is that all you have to say?'

'Yes; except that Alicia will accompany you.'

'Alicia!'

'She could not very well stay here, you know, just now. It would be best for her to leave the Court until—'

'Yes, yes, I understand,' interrupted the baronet; 'but is there nowhere else that she could go – must she be with me?'

'She could go nowhere else so immediately; and she would not be happy anywhere else.'

'Let her come, then,' said Sir Michael, 'let her come.'

He spoke in a strange subdued voice, and with an apparent effort; as if it were painful to him to have to speak at all. As if all this ordinary business of life were a cruel torture to him; and jarred so much upon his grief as to be almost worse to bear than that grief itself.

'Very well, my dear uncle, then all is arranged; Alicia will be ready to start at nine o'clock.'

'Very good, very good,' muttered the baronet; 'let her come if she pleases; poor child, let her come.'

He sighed heavily as he spoke in that half-pitying tone of his daughter. He was thinking how comparatively indifferent he had been towards that only child for the sake of the woman now shut in the fire-lit room below.

'I shall see you again before you go, sir,' said Robert; 'I will leave you till then.'

'Stay!' said Sir Michael, suddenly; 'have you told Alicia?'

'I have told her nothing; except that you are about to leave the Court for some time.'

'You are very good, my boy, you are very good,' the baronet murmured in a broken voice.

He stretched out his hand. His nephew took it in both his own, and pressed it to his lips.

'Oh, sir! how can I ever forgive myself ?' he said; 'how can I ever cease to hate myself for having brought this grief upon you?'

'No, no, Robert, you did right – you did right; I wish that God had been so merciful to me as to take my miserable life before this night; but you did right.'

Sir Michael re-entered his dressing-room, and Robert slowly returned to the vestibule. He paused upon the threshold of that chamber in which he had left Lucy, Lady Audley; otherwise Helen Talboys, the wife of his lost friend.

She was lying upon the floor; upon the very spot on which she had crouched at her husband's feet telling her guilty story. Whether she was in a swoon; or whether she lay there in the utter helplessness of her misery; Robert scarcely cared to know. He went out into the vestibule, and sent one of the servants to look for her maid, the smart be-ribboned damsel, who was loud in wonder and consternation at the sight of her mistress.

'Lady Audley is very ill,' he said; 'take her to her room and see that she does not leave it to-night. You will be good enough to remain near her; but do not either talk to her, or suffer her to excite herself by talking.'

My lady had not fainted; she allowed the girl to assist her, and rose from the ground upon which she had grovelled. Her golden hair fell in loose, dishevelled masses about her ivory throat and shoulders; her face and lips were colourless; her eyes terrible in their unnatural light.

'Take me away,' she said, 'and let me sleep! Let me sleep, for my brain is on fire!'

As she was leaving the room with her maid, she turned and looked at Robert. 'Is Sir Michael gone?' she asked.

'He will leave in half-an-hour.'

'There were no lives lost in the fire at Mount Stanning?'

'None.'

'I am glad of that.'

'The landlord of the house, Marks, was very terribly burned, and lies in a precarious state at his mother's cottage; but he may recover.'

'I am glad of that – I am glad no life was lost. Good night, Mr. Audley.'

'I shall ask to see you for half-an-hour's conversation in the course of to-morrow, my lady?'

'Whenever you please. Good night.'

'Good night.'

She went away, quietly leaning upon her maid's shoulder, and leaving Robert with a sense of strange bewilderment that was very painful to him.

He sat down by the broad hearth upon which the red embers were fading, and wondered at the change in that old house which, until the day of his friend's disappearance, had been so pleasant a home for all who sheltered beneath its hospitable roof. He sat brooding over that desolate hearth, and trying to decide upon what must be done in this sudden crisis. He sat, helpless and powerless to determine upon any course of action, lost in a dull reverie, from which he was aroused by the sound of carriage wheels driving up to the little turret entrance.

The clock in the vestibule struck nine as Robert opened the library-door. Alicia had just descended the stairs with her maid, a rosy-faced country girl.

'Good-by, Robert,' said Miss Audley, holding out her hand to her cousin; 'good-by, and God bless you! You may trust me to take care of papa.'

'I am sure I may. God bless you, my dear.'

For the second time that night Robert Audley pressed his lips to his cousin's candid forehead; and for the second time the embrace was of a brotherly or paternal character; rather than the rapturous proceeding which it would have been had Sir Harry Towers been the privileged performer.

It was five minutes past nine when Sir Michael came downstairs, followed by his valet, grave and grey-haired like himself. The baronet was pale, but calm and self-possessed. The hand which he gave to his nephew was as cold as ice; but it was with a steady voice that he bade the young man good-by.

'I leave all in your hands, Robert,' he said, as he turned to leave the house in which he had lived so long. 'I may not have heard the end; but I have heard enough. Heaven knows I have no need to hear more. I leave all to you, but you will not be cruel – you will remember how much I loved—'

His voice broke huskily before he could finish the sentence.

'I will remember you in everything, sir,' the young man answered. 'I will do everything for the best.'

A treacherous mist of tears blinded him and shut out his uncle's face, and in another minute the carriage had driven away, and Robert Audley sat alone in the dark library, where only one red spark glowed amongst the pale-grey ashes. He sat alone, trying to think what he ought to do, and with the awful responsibility of a wicked woman's fate upon his shoulders.

'Good heavens,' he thought; 'surely this must be God's judgment upon the purposeless, vacillating life I led up to the seventh day of last September. Surely this awful responsibility has been forced upon me in order that I may humble myself to an offended Providence, and confess that a man cannot choose his own life. He cannot say, "I will take existence lightly, and keep out of the way of the wretched, mistaken, energetic creatures, who fight so heartily in the great battle."

He cannot say, "I will stop in the tents while the strife is fought, and laugh at the fools who are trampled down in the useless struggle." He cannot do this. He can only do, humbly and fearfully, that which the Maker who created him has appointed for him to do. If he has a battle to fight, let him fight it faithfully; but woe betide him if he skulks when his name is called in the mighty muster-roll; woe betide him if he hides in the tents when the tocsin summons him to the scene of war!'

One of the servants brought candles into the library, and relighted the fire; but Robert Audley did not stir from his seat by the hearth. He sat as he had often sat in his chambers in Fig-tree Court, with his elbows resting upon the arms of his chair, and his chin upon his hand.

But he lifted his head as the servant was about to leave the room.

'Can I send a telegram from here to London?' he asked.

'It can be sent from Brentwood, sir – not from here.'

Mr. Audley looked at his watch, thoughtfully.

'One of the men can ride over to Brentwood, sir, if you wish any message to be sent.'

'I do wish to send a message; will you manage it for me, Richards?'

'Certainly, sir.'

'You can wait, then, while I write the message?'

'Yes, sir.'

The man brought writing materials from one of the side-tables, and placed them before Mr. Audley.

Robert dipped a pen in the ink, and stared thoughtfully at one of the candles for a few moments before he began to write.

The message ran thus:–

'From Robert Audley, of Audley Court, Essex, to Francis
Wilmington, of Paper Buildings, Temple.

'Dear Wilmington, if you know any physician, experienced in cases of mania, and to be trusted with a secret, be so good as to send me his address by telegraph.'

Mr. Audley sealed this document in a stout envelope, and handed it to the man, with a sovereign.

'You will see that this is given to a trustworthy person, Richards,' he said, 'and let the man wait at the station for the return message. He ought to get it in an hour and a half.'

Mr. Richards, who had known Robert Audley in jackets and turn-down collars, departed to execute his commission. Heaven forbid that we should follow him into the comfortable servants' hall at the Court, where the household sat round the blazing fire, discussing in utter bewilderment the events of the day.

Nothing could be wider from the truth than the speculations of these worthy people. What clue had they to the mystery of that fire-lit room in which a guilty woman had knelt at their master's feet to tell the story of her sinful life? They only knew that which Sir Michael's valet had told them of his sudden journey. How his master was as pale as a sheet, and spoke in a strange voice that didn't sound like his own, somehow, and how you might have knocked him – Mr. Parsons, the valet – down with a feather, if you had been minded to prostrate him by the aid of so feeble a weapon.

The wiseheads of the servants' hall decided that Sir Michael had received sudden intelligence through Mr. Robert – they were wise enough to connect the young man with the catastrophe – either of the death of some near and dear relation – the elder servants decimated the Audley family in their endeavours to find a likely relation – or of some alarming fall in the funds; or of the failure of some speculation or bank in which the greater part of the baronet's money was invested. The general leaning was towards the failure of a bank; and every member of the assembly seemed to take a dismal and raven-like delight in the fancy; though such a supposition involved their own ruin in the general destruction of that liberal household.

Robert sat by the dreary hearth, which seemed dreary even now when the blaze of a great wood-fire roared in the wide chimney, and listened to the low wail of the March wind, moaning round the house and lifting the shivering ivy from the walls it sheltered. He was tired and worn out, for remember that he had been awakened from his sleep at two o'clock that morning by the hot breath of blazing timber and the sharp crackling of burning woodwork. But for his presence of mind and cool decision, Mr. Luke Marks would have died a dreadful death. He still bore the traces of the night's peril, for the dark hair had been singed upon one side of his forehead, and his left hand was red and inflamed from the effect of the scorching atmosphere, out of which he had dragged the landlord of the Castle Inn. He was thoroughly exhausted with fatigue and excitement, and he fell into a heavy sleep in his easy-chair before the bright fire, from which he was only awakened by the entrance of Mr. Richards with the return message.

This return message was very brief.

'Dear Audley, always glad to oblige. Alwyn Mosgrave, M.D., 12, Savile Row. Safe.'

This, with names and addresses, was all that it contained.

'I shall want another message taken to Brentwood to-morrow morning, Richards,' said Mr. Audley, as he folded the telegram. 'I should be glad if the man would ride over with it before breakfast. He shall have half-a-sovereign for his trouble.'

Mr. Richards bowed.

'Thank you, sir – not necessary, sir; but as you please, of course, sir,' he murmured. 'At what hour might you wish the man to go?'

Mr. Audley might wish the man to go as early as he could; so it was decided that he should go at six.

'My room is ready I suppose, Richards?' said Robert.

'Yes, sir – your old room.'

'Very good. I shall go to bed at once. Bring me a glass of brandy-and-water as hot as you can make it, and wait for the telegram.'

The second message was only a very earnest request to Doctor Mosgrave to pay an immediate visit to Audley Court on a matter of serious moment.

Having written this message, Mr. Audley felt that he had done all that he could do. He drank his brandy-and-water. He had actual need of the diluted alcohol, for he had been chilled to the bone by his adventures during the fire. He slowly sipped the pale golden liquid and thought of Clara Talboys, of that earnest girl whose brother's memory was now avenged, whose brother's destroyer was humiliated in the dust. Had she heard of the fire at the Castle Inn? How could she have done otherwise than hear of it in such a place as Mount Stanning? But had she heard that *he* had been in danger, and that he had distinguished himself by the rescue of a drunken boor? I fear that, even sitting by that desolate hearth, and beneath the roof whose noble owner was an exile from his own house, Robert Audley was weak enough to think of these things – weak enough to let his fancy wander away to the dismal fir-trees under the cold February sky, and the dark-brown eyes that were so like the eyes of his lost friend.

CHAPTER V

Dr. Mosgrave's advice

My lady slept. Through that long winter night she slept
soundly. Criminals have often so slept their last sleep upon
earth; and have been found in the grey morning slumbering
peacefully by the gaoler who came to wake them.

The game had been played and lost. I do not think that
my lady had thrown away a card, or missed the making of a
trick which she might by any possibility have made: but
her opponent's hand had been too powerful for her, and he
had won.

She was more at peace now than she had ever been since
that day – so soon after her second marriage – on which she
had seen the announcement of the return of George Talboys
from the gold-fields of Australia. She might rest now, for they
now knew the worst of her. There were no new discoveries
to be made. She had flung the horrible burden of an almost
unendurable secret off her shoulders, and her selfish sensuous
nature resumed its mastery of her. She slept, peacefully nestled
in her downy bed, under the soft mountain of silken coverlet,
and in the sombre shade of the green velvet curtains. She had
ordered her maid to sleep on a low couch in the same room,
and she had also ordered that a lamp should be kept burning
all night.

Not that I think she had any fear of shadowy visitations in
the still hours of the night. She was too thoroughly selfish to
care very much for anything that could not hurt her; and she
had never heard of a ghost doing any actual and palpable

harm. She had feared Robert Audley, but she feared him no longer. He had done his worst; she knew that he could do no more without bringing everlasting disgrace upon the name he venerated.

'They'll put me away somewhere, I suppose,' my lady thought, 'that is the worst they can do for me.'

She looked upon herself as a species of state prisoner, who would have to be taken good care of. A second Iron Mask who must be provided for in some comfortable place of confinement. She abandoned herself to a dull indifference. She had lived a hundred lives within the space of the last few days of her existence, and she had worn out her capacity for suffering; for a time at least.

She took a cup of strong green tea and a few delicate fragments of toast the next morning with the same air of quiet relish common to condemned creatures who eat their last meal, while the gaolers look on to see that they do not bite fragments off the crockery, or swallow the tea-spoon, or do any other violent act tending to the evasion of Mr. Jack Ketch. She ate her breakfast, and took her morning bath, and emerged, with perfumed hair, and in the most exquisitely careless of morning toilets, from her luxurious dressing-room. She looked round at all the costly appointments of the room with a yearning lingering gaze before she turned to leave it; but there was not one tender recollection in her mind of the man who had caused the furnishing of the chamber, and who in every precious toy that was scattered about in the reckless profusion of magnificence, had laid before her a mute evidence of his love. My lady was thinking how much the things had cost, and how painfully probable it was that the luxurious apartment would soon pass out of her possession.

She looked at herself in the cheval-glass before she left the room. A long night's rest had brought back the delicate rose-tints of her complexion, and the natural lustre of her blue eyes. That unnatural light which had burned so fearfully the day before had gone, and my lady smiled triumphantly as she contemplated the reflection of her beauty. The days were gone in which her enemies could have branded her with white-hot irons, and burned away the loveliness which had done such mischief. Whatever they did to her, they must leave her her beauty, she thought. At the worst they were powerless to rob her of that.

The March day was bright and sunny, with a cheerless sunshine certainly. My lady wrapped herself in an Indian shawl; a shawl that had cost Sir Michael a hundred guineas. I think she had an idea that it would be well to wear this costly garment; so that if hustled suddenly away, she might carry at least one of her possessions with her. Remember how much she had perilled for a fine house and gorgeous furniture, for carriages and horses, jewels and laces; and do not wonder if she clung with a desperate tenacity to gauds and gew-gaws in the hour of her despair. If she had been Judas she would have held to her thirty pieces of silver to the last moment of her shameful life.

Mr. Robert Audley breakfasted in the library. He sat long over his solitary cup of tea, smoking his meerschaum pipe, and meditating darkly upon the task that lay before him.

'I will appeal to the experience of this Dr. Mosgrave,' he thought; 'physicians and lawyers are the confessors of this prosaic nineteenth century. Surely he will be able to help me.'

The first fast train from London arrived at Audley at half-past ten o'clock, and at five minutes before eleven, Richards, the grave servant, announced Dr. Alwyn Mosgrave.

The physician from Savile Row was a tall man, of about fifty years of age. He was thin and sallow, with lantern jaws, and eyes of a pale feeble grey, that seemed as if they had once been blue, and had faded by the progress of time to their present neutral shade. However powerful the science of medicine as wielded by Dr. Alwyn Mosgrave, it had not been strong enough to put flesh upon his bones, or brightness into his face. He had a strangely expressionless, and yet strangely attentive, countenance. He had the face of a man who had spent the greater part of his life in listening to other people, and who had parted with his own individuality and his own passions at the very outset of his career.

He bowed to Robert Audley, took the opposite seat indicated by him, and addressed his attentive face to the young barrister. Robert saw that the physician's glance for a moment lost its quiet look of attention, and became earnest and searching.

'He is wondering whether I am the patient,' thought Mr. Audley, 'and is looking for the diagnoses of madness in my face.'

Dr. Mosgrave spoke as if in answer to this thought.

'It is not about your own – health – that you wish to consult me?' he said interrogatively.

'Oh, no!'

Dr. Mosgrave looked at his watch, a fifty guinea Benson-made chronometer, which he carried loose in his waistcoat pocket as carelessly as if it had been a potato.

'I need not remind you that my time is precious,' he said; 'your telegram informed me that my services were required in a case of – danger – as I apprehend, or I should not be here this morning.'

Robert Audley had sat looking gloomily at the fire, wondering how he should begin the conversation, and had needed this reminder of the physician's presence.

'You are very good, Dr. Mosgrave,' he said, rousing himself by an effort, 'and I thank you very much for having responded to my summons. I am about to appeal to you upon a subject which is more painful to me than words can describe. I am about to implore your advice in a most difficult case, and I trust, almost blindly, to your experience to rescue me, and others who are very dear to me, from a cruel and complicated position.'

The business-like attention in Dr. Mosgrave's face grew into a look of interest as he listened to Robert Audley.

'The revelation made by the patient to the physician is I believe as sacred as the confession of a penitent to his priest?' Robert asked gravely.

'Quite as sacred.'

'A solemn confidence, to be violated under no circumstances?'

'Most certainly.'

Robert Audley looked at the fire again. How much should he tell, or how little, of the dark history of his uncle's second wife.

'I have been given to understand, Dr. Mosgrave, that you have devoted much of your attention to the treatment of insanity.'

'Yes, my practice is almost confined to the treatment of mental diseases.'

'Such being the case, I think I may venture to conclude that you sometimes receive strange, and even terrible revelations.'

Dr. Mosgrave bowed.

He looked like a man who could have carried, safely locked in his passionless breast, the secrets of a nation, and who would have suffered no inconvenience from the weight of such a burden.

'The story which I am about to tell you is not my own story,' said Robert, after a pause; 'you will forgive me therefore if I once more remind you that I can only reveal it upon the understanding that under no circumstances, or upon no apparent justification, is that confidence to be betrayed.'

Dr. Mosgrave bowed again. A little sternly perhaps this time.

'I am all attention, Mr. Audley,' he said, coldly.

Robert Audley drew his chair nearer to that of the physician, and in a low voice began the story which my lady had told upon her knees in the same chamber upon the previous night. Dr. Mosgrave's listening face, turned always towards the speaker, betrayed no surprise at that strange revelation. He smiled once, a grave quiet smile, when Mr. Audley came to that part of the story which told of the conspiracy at Ventnor, but he was not surprised. Robert Audley ended his story at the point at which Sir Michael Audley had interrupted my lady's confession. He told nothing of the disappearance of George Talboys, nor of the horrible suspicions that had grown out of that disappearance. He told nothing of the fire at the Castle Inn.

Dr. Mosgrave shook his head gravely when Mr. Audley came to the end of his story.

'You have nothing further to tell me?' he said.

'No. I do not think there is anything more that need be told,' Robert answered, rather evasively.

'You would wish to prove that this lady is mad, and therefore irresponsible for her actions, Mr. Audley?' said the physician.

Robert Audley stared wondering at the mad doctor. By what process had he so rapidly arrived at the young man's secret desire?"

'Yes, I would rather, if possible, think her mad. I should be glad to find that excuse for her.'

'And to save the *esclandre* of a Chancery suit, I suppose, Mr. Audley,' said Dr. Mosgrave.

Robert shuddered, as he bowed an assent to this remark. It was something worse than a Chancery suit that he dreaded, with a horrible fear. It was a trial for murder that so long had haunted his dreams. How often he had awoken in an agony of shame from a vision of a crowded court-house, and his uncle's wife, in a criminal dock, hemmed in on every side by a sea of eager faces.

'I fear that I shall not be of any use to you,' the physician said quietly. 'I will see the lady if you please, but I do not believe that she is mad.'

'Why not?'

'Because there is no evidence of madness in anything that she has done. She ran away from her home, because her home was not a pleasant one, and she left it in the hope of finding a better. There is no madness in that. She committed the crime of bigamy, because by that crime she obtained fortune and position. There is no madness there. When she found herself in a desperate position, she did not grow desperate. She employed intelligent means, and she carried out a conspiracy which required coolness and deliberation in its execution. There is no madness in that.'

'But the taints of hereditary insanity—'

'May descend to the third generation and appear in the lady's children, if she have any. Madness is not necessarily transmitted from mother to daughter. I should be glad to help you, if I could, Mr. Audley, but I do not think there is any proof of insanity in the story you have told me. I do not think any jury in England would accept the plea of insanity in such a case as this. The best thing that you can do with this lady is to send her back to her first husband; if he will have her.'

Robert started at this sudden mention of his friend. 'Her first husband is dead –' he answered, 'at least he has been missing for some time – and I have reason to believe that he is dead.'

Dr. Mosgrave saw the startled movement, and heard the embarrassment in Robert Audley's voice as he spoke of George Talboys.

'The lady's first husband is missing,' he said, with a strange emphasis on the word – 'you think that he is dead.'

He paused for a few moments and looked at the fire, as Robert had looked before.

'Mr. Audley,' he said presently, 'there must be no half-confidences between us. You have not told me all.'

Robert, looking up suddenly, plainly expressed in his face the surprise he felt at these words.

'I should be very poorly able to meet the contingencies of my professional experience,' said Dr. Mosgrave, 'if I could not perceive where confidence ends and reservation begins. You have only told me half this lady's story, Mr. Audley. You must tell me more before I can offer you any advice. What has become of the first husband?'

He asked this question in a decisive tone. As if he knew it to be the key-stone of an arch.

'I have already told you, Dr. Mosgrave, that I do not know.'

'Yes,' answered the physician, 'but your face has told me what you would have withheld from me; it has told me that you *suspect!*'

Robert Audley was silent.

'If I am to be of use to you, you must trust me, Mr. Audley,' said the physician. 'The first husband disappeared – how and when? I want to know the history of his disappearance.'

Robert paused for some time before he replied to this speech; but by-and-by, he lifted his head, which had been bent in an attitude of earnest thought, and addressed the physician.

'I will trust you, Dr. Mosgrave,' he said, 'I will confide entirely in your honour and goodness. I do not ask you to do any wrong to society; but I ask you to save our stainless name from degradation and shame, if you can do so conscientiously.'

He told the story of George's disappearance, and of his own doubts and fears, heaven knows how reluctantly.

Dr. Mosgrave listened as quietly as he had listened before. Robert concluded with an earnest appeal to the physician's best feelings. He implored him to spare the generous old man, whose fatal confidence in a wicked woman had brought such misery upon his declining years.

It was impossible to draw any conclusion either favourable or otherwise from Dr. Mosgrave's attentive face. He rose when Robert had finished speaking, and looked at his watch once more.

'I can only spare you twenty minutes,' he said. 'I will see the lady if you please. You say her mother died in a mad-house?'

'She did. Will you see Lady Audley alone?'

'Yes, alone if you please.'

Robert rang for my lady's maid, and under convoy of that smart young damsel the physician found his way to the octagon ante-chamber, and the fairy boudoir with which it communicated.

Ten minutes afterwards he returned to the library in which Robert sat waiting for him.

'I have talked to the lady,' he said quietly, 'and we understand each other very well. There is latent insanity! Insanity which might never appear; or which might appear only once or twice in a life-time. It would be *dementia* in its worst phase perhaps: acute mania; but its duration would be very brief, and it would only arise under extreme mental pressure. The lady is not mad; but she has the hereditary taint in her blood. She has the cunning of madness, with the prudence of intelligence. I will tell you what she is, Mr. Audley. She is dangerous!'

Dr. Mosgrave walked up and down the room once or twice before he spoke again.

'I will not discuss the probabilities of the suspicion that distresses you, Mr. Audley,' he said presently, 'but I will tell you this much. I do not advise any *esclandre*. This Mr. George Talboys has disappeared, but you have no evidence of his death. If you could produce evidence of his death, you could produce no evidence against this lady, beyond the one fact that she had a powerful motive for getting rid of him. No jury in the United Kingdom would condemn her upon such evidence as that.'

Robert Audley interrupted Doctor Mosgrave hastily.

'I assure you, my dear Sir,' he said, 'that my greatest fear is the necessity of any exposure – any disgrace.'

'Certainly, Mr. Audley,' answered the physician coolly, 'but you cannot expect me to assist you to condone one of the worst offences against society. If I saw adequate reason for believing that a murder had been committed by this woman, I should refuse to assist you in smuggling her away out of the reach of justice, although the honour of a hundred noble families might be saved by my doing so. But I do not see adequate reason for your suspicions; and I will do my best to help you.'

Robert Audley grasped the physician's hands in both his own.

'I will thank you when I am better able to do so,' he said, with emotion. 'I will thank you in my uncle's name as well as in my own.'

'I have only five minutes more, and I have a letter to write,' said Dr. Mosgrave, smiling at the young man's energy.

He seated himself at a writing-table in the window, dipped his pen in the ink and wrote rapidly for about seven minutes. He had filled three sides of a sheet of note-paper when he threw down his pen and folded his letter.

He put this letter into an envelope and delivered it, unsealed, to Robert Audley.

The address which it bore was –

> Monsieur Val,
> Villebrumeuse,
> Belgium.

Mr. Audley looked rather doubtfully from this address to the doctor, who was putting on his gloves as deliberately as if his life had never known a more solemn purpose than the proper adjustment of them.

'That letter,' he said, in answer to Robert Audley's inquiring look, 'is written to my friend Monsieur Val, the proprietor and medical superintendent of a very excellent *maison de santé* in the town of Villebrumeuse. We have known each other for many years, and he will no doubt willingly receive Lady Audley into his establishment, and charge himself with the full responsibility of her future life; it will not be a very eventful one!'

Robert Audley would have spoken, he would have once more expressed his gratitude for the help which had been given to him, but Dr. Mosgrave checked him with an authoritative gesture.

'From the moment in which Lady Audley enters that house,' he said, 'her life, so far as life is made up of action and variety, will be finished. Whatever secrets she may have will be secrets for ever! Whatever crimes she may have committed she will be able to commit no more. If you were to dig a grave for her in the nearest churchyard and bury her alive in it, you could not more safely shut her from the world and all worldly associations. But as a physiologist and as an honest man I believe you could do no better service to society than by doing this; for physiology is a lie if the woman I saw ten minutes ago is a woman to be trusted at large. If she could have sprung at my throat and strangled me with her little hands, as I sat talking to her just now, she would have done it.'

'She suspected your purpose, then!'

'She knew it. "You think I am mad like my mother, and you have come to question me," she said. "You are watching for some sign of the dreadful taint in my blood." Good day to you, Mr. Audley,' the physician added hurriedly; 'my time was up ten minutes ago, it is as much as I shall do to catch the train.'

CHAPTER VI
Buried alive

Robert Audley sat alone in the library with the physician's letter upon the table before him, thinking of the work which was still to be done.

The young barrister had constituted himself the denouncer of this wretched woman. He had been her judge; and he was now her gaoler. Not until he had delivered the letter which lay before him to its proper address, not until he had given up his charge into the safe keeping of the foreign mad-house doctor, not until then would the dreadful burden be removed from him and his duty done.

He wrote a few lines to my lady, telling her that he was going to carry her away from Audley Court to a place from which she was not likely to return, and requesting her to lose no time in preparing for the journey. He wished to start that evening, if possible, he told her.

Miss Susan Martin, the lady's-maid, thought it a very hard thing to have to pack her mistress's trunks in such a hurry, but my lady assisted in the task. It seemed a pleasant excitement to her, this folding and refolding of silks and velvets, this gathering together of jewels and millinery. They were not going to rob her of her possessions, she thought. They were going to send her away to some place of exile; but even exile was not hopeless, for there was scarcely any spot upon this wide earth in which her beauty would not constitute a little royalty, and win her liege knights and willing subjects. She toiled resolutely in directing and assisting her servant, who scented bankruptcy and ruin in all this packing up and hurrying away, and was therefore rather languid and indifferent in the discharge of her duties; and at six o'clock in the evening she sent her attendant to tell Mr. Audley that she was ready to depart as soon as he pleased.

Robert had consulted a volume of *Bradshaw*, and had discovered that Villebrumeuse lay out of the track of all railway traffic, and was only approachable by diligence from Brussels. The mail for Dover left London Bridge at nine o'clock, and could be easily caught by Robert and his charge, as the seven o'clock up-train from Audley reached Shoreditch at a quarter past eight. Travelling by the Dover and Calais route, they would reach Villebrumeuse by the following afternoon or evening.

What need have we to follow them upon that dismal night journey? My lady lay on one of the narrow cabin couches, comfortably wrapped in her furs; she had not forgotten her favourite Russian sables even in this last hour of shame and misery. Her mercenary soul hankered greedily after the costly and beautiful things of which she had been mistress. She had hidden away fragile teacups and covered vases of Sèvres and Dresden among the folds of her silken dinner dresses. She had secreted jewelled and golden drinking-cups amongst her delicate linen. She would have taken the pictures from the walls, and the Gobelin tapestry from the chairs, had it been possible for her to do so. She had taken all she could, and she accompanied Mr. Audley with a sulky submission, that was the despondent obedience of despair.

Robert Audley paced the deck of the steamer as the Dover clocks were striking twelve, and the town glimmered like a luminous crescent across the widening darkness of the sea. The vessel flew swiftly through the rolling waters towards the friendly Gallic shore, and Mr. Audley sighed a long sigh of relief as he remembered how soon his work would be done. He thought of the wretched creature lying forlorn and friendless in the cabin below. But when he pitied her most, and he could not but sometimes pity her for her womanhood and her helplessness, his friend's face came back upon him, bright and hopeful as he had seen it only on that first day of George's return from the Antipodes, and with that memory there returned his horror of the shameful lie that had broken the husband's heart.

'Can I ever forget it?' he thought; 'can I ever forget his blank white face as he sat opposite to me at the coffee-house, with the *Times* newspaper in his hand? There are some crimes that can never be atoned for, and this is one of them. If I could bring George Talboys to life to-morrow, I could never heal that horrible heart-wound; I could never make him the man he was before he read that printed lie.'

It was late in the afternoon of the next day when the diligence bumped and rattled over the uneven paving of the principal street in Villebrumeuse. The old ecclesiastical town, always dull and dreary, seemed more than ordinarily dreary under the grey evening sky. The twinkling lamps, lighted early, and glimmering feebly, long distances apart, made the place seem darker rather than lighter, as glow-worms intensify the blackness of a hedge by their shining presence. The remote Belgian city was a forgotten, old world place, and bore the dreary evidence of decay upon every façade in the narrow streets, on every dilapidated roof, and feeble pile of chimneys. It was difficult to imagine for what reason the opposite rows of houses had been built so close together as to cause the lumbering diligence to brush the foot passengers off the wretched *trottoir*, unless they took good care to scrape the shop windows with their garments, for there was building room enough and to spare upon the broad expanse of flat country that lay behind the old city. Hyper-critical travellers might have wondered why the narrowest and most uncomfortable streets were the busiest and most prosperous, while the nobler and broader thoroughfares were empty and deserted. But Robert Audley thought of none of these things. He sat in a corner of the mouldy carriage, watching my lady in the opposite corner, and wondering what the face was like that was so carefully hidden beneath her veil.

They had had the *coupé* of the diligence to themselves for the whole of the journey, for there were not many travellers between Brussels and Villebrumeuse, and the public conveyance was supported by the force of tradition rather than by any great profit attaching to it as a speculation.

My lady had not spoken during the journey, except to decline some refreshments which Robert had offered her at a halting-place upon the road. Her heart sank when they left Brussels behind, for she had hoped that city might have been the end of her journey, and she had turned with a feeling of sickness and despair from the dull Belgian landscape.

She looked up at last as the vehicle jolted into a great stony quadrangle, which had been the approach to a monastery once, but which was now the courtyard of a dismal hotel, in whose cellars legions of rats skirmished and squeaked even while the broad sunshine was bright in the chambers above.

Lady Audley shuddered as she alighted from the diligence, and found herself in that dreary courtyard. Robert was surrounded by chattering porters, who clamoured for his 'baggages,' and disputed amongst themselves as to the hotel at which he was to rest. One of these men ran away to fetch a hackney-coach at Mr. Audley's behest, and reappeared presently, urging on a pair of horses – which were so small as to suggest the idea that they had been made out of one ordinary-sized animal – with wild shrieks and whoops that had a demoniac sound in the darkness.

Mr. Audley left my lady in a dreary coffee-room in the care

of a drowsy attendant while he drove away to some distant part of the quiet city. There was official business to be gone through before Sir Michael's wife could be quietly put away in the place suggested by Dr. Mosgrave. Robert had to see all manner of important personages; and to take numerous oaths; and to exhibit the English physician's letter; and to go through much ceremony of signing and countersigning, before he could take his lost friend's cruel wife to the home which was to be her last upon earth. Upwards of two hours elapsed before all this was arranged and the young man was free to return to the hotel, where he found his charge staring absently at a pair of wax candles, with a cup of untasted coffee standing cold and stagnant before her.

Robert handed my lady into the hired vehicle, and took his seat opposite to her once more.

'Where are you going to take me?' she asked, at last. 'I am tired of being treated like some naughty child, who is put into a dark cellar as a punishment for its offences. Where are you taking me?'

'To a place in which you will have ample leisure to repent the past, Mrs. Talboys,' Robert answered, gravely.

They had left the paved streets behind them, and had emerged out of a great gaunt square, in which there appeared to be about half-a-dozen cathedrals, into a smooth boulevard, a broad lamp-lit road, on which the shadows of the leafless branches went and came tremblingly, like the shadows of paralytic skeletons. There were houses here and there upon this boulevard; stately houses, *entre cour et jardin*, and with plaster vases of geraniums on the stone pillars of the ponderous gateways. The rumbling hackney-carriage drove upwards of three-quarters of a mile along this smooth roadway before it drew up against a gateway, older and more ponderous than any of those they had passed.

My lady gave a little scream as she looked out of the coach

window. The gaunt gateway was lighted by an enormous lamp; a great structure of iron and glass, in which one poor little shivering flame struggled with the March wind.

The coachman rang the bell, and a little wooden door at the side of the gate was opened by a grey-haired man, who looked out at the carriage, and then retired. He reappeared three minutes afterwards behind the folding iron gates which he unlocked and threw back to their full extent, revealing a dreary desert of stone-paved courtyard.

The coachman led his wretched horses into this courtyard, and piloted the vehicle to the principal doorway of the house, a great mansion of grey stone, with several long ranges of windows, many of which were dimly lighted, and looked out like the pale eyes of weary watchers upon the darkness of the night.

My lady, watchful and quiet as the cold stars in the wintry sky, looked up at these casements with an earnest and scrutinising gaze. One of the windows was shrouded by a scanty curtain of faded red; and upon this curtain there went and came a dark shadow, the shadow of a woman with a fantastic head-dress, the shadow of a restless creature, who paced perpetually backwards and forwards before the window.

Sir Michael Audley's wicked wife laid her hand suddenly upon Robert's arm, and pointed with the other hand to this curtained window.

'I know where you have brought me,' she said. 'This is a MAD-HOUSE.'

Mr. Audley did not answer her. He had been standing at the door of the coach when she addressed him, and he quietly assisted her to alight, and led her up a couple of shallow stone-steps, and into the entrance-hall of the mansion. He handed Doctor Mosgrave's letter to a neatly-dressed, cheerful-looking, middle-aged woman, who came tripping out of a little chamber which opened out of the hall, and was very much like the bureau of an hotel. This person smilingly welcomed Robert and his charge; and after despatching a servant with the letter, invited them into her pleasant little apartment, which was gaily furnished with bright amber curtains and heated by a tiny stove.

'Madame finds herself very much fatigued?' the Frenchwoman said, interrogatively, with a look of intense sympathy, as she placed an arm-chair for my lady.

'Madame' shrugged her shoulders wearily, and looked round the little chamber with a sharp glance of scrutiny that betokened no very great favour.

'WHAT is this place, Robert Audley?' she cried fiercely. 'Do you think I am a baby, that you may juggle with and deceive me – what is it? It is what I said just now, is it not?'

'It is a *maison de santé*, my lady,' the young man answered gravely. 'I have no wish to juggle with or to deceive you.'

My lady paused for a few moments, looking reflectively at Robert.

'A *maison de santé*,' she repeated. 'Yes, they manage these things better in France. In England we should call it a madhouse. This is a house for mad people, this, is it not, Madame?' she said, in French, turning upon the woman, and tapping the polished floor with her foot.

'Ah, but no, Madame,' the woman answered, with a shrill scream of protest. 'It is an establishment of the most agreeable, where one amuses oneself—'

She was interrupted by the entrance of the principal of this agreeable establishment, who came beaming into the room with a radiant smile illuminating his countenance, and with Dr. Mosgrave's letter open in his hand.

It was impossible for him to say *how* enchanted he was to make the acquaintance of M'sieu. There was nothing upon earth which he was not ready to do for M'sieu in his own person, and nothing under heaven which he would not strive

434

to accomplish for him, as the friend of his acquaintance, so very much distinguished, the English doctor. Dr. Mosgrave's letter had given him a brief synopsis of the case, he informed Robert, in an undertone, and he was quite prepared to undertake the care of the charming and very interesting Madame – Madame—

He rubbed his hands politely, and looked at Robert. Mr. Audley remembered, for the first time, that he had been recommended to introduce his wretched charge under a feigned name.

He affected not to hear the proprietor's question. It might seem a very easy matter to have hit upon a heap of names, any one of which would have answered his purpose; but Mr. Audley appeared suddenly to have forgotten that he had ever heard any mortal appellation except that of himself and his lost friend.

Perhaps the proprietor perceived and understood his embarrassment. He at any rate relieved it by turning to the woman who had received them, and muttering something about No. 14, Bis. The woman took a key from a long range of others that hung over the mantel-piece, and a wax candle from a bracket in a corner of the room, and having lighted the candle, led the way across the stone-paved hall, and up a broad slippery staircase of polished wood.

The English physician had informed his Belgian colleague that money would be of minor consequence in any arrangements made for the comfort of the English lady who was to be committed to his care. Acting upon this hint, Monsieur Val opened the outer door of a stately suite of apartments, which included a lobby, paved with alternate diamonds of black and white marble, but of a dismal and cellarlike darkness; a saloon furnished with gloomy velvet draperies, and with a certain funereal splendour which is not peculiarly conducive to the elevation of the spirits; and a bed-chamber, containing a bed

435

so wondrously made, as to appear to have no opening whatever in its coverings, unless the counterpane had been split asunder with a penknife.

My lady stared dismally round at the range of rooms, which looked dreary enough in the wan light of a single wax candle. This solitary flame, pale and ghostlike in itself, was multiplied by paler phantoms of its ghostliness, which glimmered everywhere about the rooms; in the shadowy depths of the polished floors and wainscot, or the window-panes, in the looking-glasses, or in those great expanses of glimmering something which adorned the rooms, and which my lady mistook for costly mirrors, but which were in reality wretched mockeries of burnished tin.

Amid all the faded splendour of shabby velvet, and tarnished gilding, and polished wood, the woman dropped into an arm-chair, and covered her face with her hands. The whiteness of them, and the starry light of diamonds trembling about them, glittered in the dimly-lighted chamber. She sat silent, motionless, despairing, sullen, and angry, while Robert and the French doctor retired into an outer chamber, and talked together in undertones. Mr. Audley had very little to say that had not been already said for him, with a far better grace than he himself could have expressed it, by the English physician. He had, after great trouble of mind, hit upon the name of Taylor, as a safe and simple substitute for that other name to which alone my lady had a right. He told the Frenchman that this Mrs. Taylor was distantly related to him – that she had inherited the seeds of madness from her mother, as indeed Dr. Mosgrave had informed Monsieur Val, and that she had shown some fearful tokens of the lurking taint that was latent in her mind; but that she was not to be called 'mad.' He begged that she might be treated with all tenderness and compassion; that she might receive all reasonable indulgences; but he impressed upon Monsieur Val, that under no circumstances was she to be permitted to leave the house and grounds without the protection of some reliable person, who should be answerable for her safe keeping. He had only one other point to urge, and that was that Monsieur Val, who, as he had understood, was himself a Protestant – the doctor bowed – would make arrangements with some kind and benevolent Protestant clergyman, through whom spiritual advice and consolation might be secured for the invalid lady; who had especial need, Robert added, gravely, of such advantages.

This – with all necessary arrangements as to pecuniary matters, which were to be settled from time to time between Mr. Audley and the doctor, unassisted by any agents whatever – was the extent of the conversation between the two men, and occupied about a quarter of an hour. My lady sat in the same attitude when they re-entered the bed-chamber in which they had left her, with her ringed hands still clasped over her face.

Robert bent over her to whisper in her ear.

'Your name is Madame Taylor here,' he said. 'I do not think you would wish to be known by your real name.'

She only shook her head in answer to him, and did not even remove her hands from over her face.

'Madame will have an attendant entirely devoted to her service,' said Monsieur Val. 'Madame will have all her wishes obeyed; her *reasonable* wishes, but that goes without saying,' Monsieur adds, with a quaint shrug. 'Every effort will be made to render Madame's sojourn at Villebrumeuse agreeable, and as much profitable as agreeable. The inmates dine together when it is wished. I dine with the inmates, sometimes; my subordinate, a clever and a worthy man, always. I reside with my wife and children in a little pavilion in the grounds; my subordinate resides in the establishment. Madame may rely upon our utmost efforts being exerted to ensure her comfort.'

Monsieur is saying a great deal more to the same effect,

rubbing his hands and beaming radiantly upon Robert and his charge, when Madame rises suddenly, erect and furious, and dropping her jewelled fingers from before her face, tells him to hold his tongue.

'Leave me alone with the man who has brought me here,' she cried between her set teeth. 'Leave me!'

She points to the door with a sharp imperious gesture; so rapid that the silken drapery about her arm makes a swooping sound as she lifts her hand. The sibilant French syllables hiss through her teeth as she utters them, and seem better fitted to her mood and to herself than the familiar English she has spoken hitherto.

The French doctor shrugs his shoulders as he goes out into the dark lobby, and mutters something about a 'beautiful devil,' and a gesture worthy of 'the Mars.' My lady walked with a rapid footstep to the door between the bed-chamber and the saloon; closed it, and with the handle of the door still in her hand, turned and looked at Robert Audley.

'You have brought me to my grave, Mr. Audley,' she cried; 'you have used your power basely and cruelly, and have brought me to a living grave.'

'I have done that which I thought just to others and merciful to you,' Robert answered, quietly; 'I should have been a traitor to society had I suffered you to remain at liberty after – after the disappearance of George Talboys and the fire at the Castle Inn. I have brought you to a place in which you will be kindly treated by people who have no knowledge of your story – no power to taunt or to reproach you. You will lead a quiet and peaceful life, my lady, such a life as many a good and holy woman in this Catholic country freely takes upon herself, and happily endures unto the end. The solitude of your existence in this place will be no greater than that of a king's daughter, who, flying from the evil of the time, was glad to take shelter in a house as tranquil as this. Surely it is a small atonement which I ask you to render for your sins, a light penance which I call upon you to perform. Live here and repent; nobody will assail you, nobody will torment you. I only say to you, repent!'

'I *cannot*!' cried my lady, pushing her hair fiercely from her white forehead, and fixing her dilated eyes upon Robert Audley, 'I *cannot*! Has my beauty brought me to *this*? Have I plotted and schemed to shield myself, and laid awake in the long deadly nights trembling to think of my dangers, for *this*? I had better have given up at once, since *this* was to be the end. I had better have yielded to the curse that was upon me, and given up when George Talboys first came back to England.'

She plucked at the feathery golden curls as if she would have torn them from her head. It had served her so little after all, that gloriously glittering hair; that beautiful nimbus of yellow light that had contrasted so exquisitely with the melting azure of her eyes. She hated herself and her beauty.

'I would laugh at you and defy you if I dared,' she cried; 'I would kill myself and defy you if I dared. But I am a poor, pitiful coward, and have been so from the first. Afraid of my mother's horrible inheritance; afraid of poverty; afraid of George Talboys; afraid of *you*.'

She was silent for a little while, but she still held her place by the door, as if determined to detain Robert as long as it was her pleasure to do so.

'Do you know what I am thinking of?' she said presently. 'Do you know what I am thinking of, as I look at you in the dim light of this room? I am thinking of the day upon which George Talboys – disappeared.'

Robert started as she mentioned the name of his lost friend; his face turned pale in the dusky light, and his breathing grew quicker and louder.

'He was standing opposite me as you are standing now,' continued my lady. 'You said that you would raze the old

439

house to the ground; that you would root up every tree in the gardens to find your dead friend. You would have had no need to do so much; the body of George Talboys lies at the bottom of the old well, in the shrubbery beyond the lime-walk.'

Robert Audley flung up his hands and clasped them above his head, with one loud cry of horror.

'Oh, my God!' he said, after a dreadful pause, 'have all the ghastly things that I have thought prepared me so little for the ghastly truth, that it should come upon me like this at last?'

'He came to me in the lime-walk,' resumed my lady, in the same hard, dogged tone as that in which she had confessed the wicked story of her life. 'I knew that he would come, and I had prepared myself, as well as I could, to meet him. I was determined to bribe him, to cajole him, to defy him; to do anything sooner than abandon the wealth and the position I had won, and go back to my old life. He came, and he reproached me for the conspiracy at Ventnor. He declared that so long as he lived he would never forgive me for the lie that had broken his heart. He told me that I had plucked his heart out of his breast and trampled upon it; and that he had now no heart in which to feel one sentiment of mercy for me. That he would have forgiven me any wrong upon earth, but that one deliberate and passionless wrong that I had done him. He said this and a great deal more, and he told me that no power on earth should turn him from his purpose, which was to take me to the man I had deceived, and make me tell my wicked story. He did not know the hidden taint that I had sucked in with my mother's milk. He did not know that it was possible to drive me mad. He goaded me as you have goaded me; he was as merciless as you have been merciless. We were in the shrubbery at the end of the lime-walk. I was seated upon the broken masonry at the mouth of the well. George Talboys was leaning upon the disused windlass, in which the rusty iron spindle rattled loosely whenever he shifted his position. I rose at last, and turned upon him to defy him, as I had determined to defy him at the worst. I told him that if he denounced me to Sir Michael, I would declare him to be a madman or a liar, and I defied him to convince the man who loved me – blindly, as I told him – that he had any claim to me. I was going to leave him after having told him this, when he caught me by the wrist and detained me by force. You saw the bruises that his fingers made upon my wrist and noticed them, and did not believe the account I gave of them. I could see that, Mr. Robert Audley, and I saw that you were a person I should have to fear.'

She paused, as if she had expected Robert to speak; but he stood silent and motionless waiting for the end.

'George Talboys treated me as you treated me,' she said presently. 'He swore that if there was but one witness of my identity, and that witness was removed from Audley Court by the width of the whole earth, he would bring him there to swear to my identity, and to denounce me. It was then that I was mad. It was then that I drew the loose iron spindle from the shrunken wood, and saw my first husband sink with one horrible cry into the black mouth of the well. There is a legend of its enormous depth. I do not know how deep it is. It is dry, I suppose; for I heard no splash; only a dull thud. I looked down and I saw nothing but black emptiness. I knelt down and listened, but the cry was not repeated, though I waited for nearly a quarter of an hour – God knows how long it seemed to me – by the mouth of the well.'

Robert Audley uttered no word of horror when the story was finished. He moved a little nearer towards the door against which Helen Talboys stood. Had there been any other means of exit from the room, he would gladly have availed himself of it. He shrank from even a momentary contact with this creature.

'Let me pass you, if you please,' he said, in an icy voice.

'You see I do not fear to make my confession to you,' said Helen Talboys, 'for two reasons. The first is that you dare not use it against me, because you know it would kill your uncle to see me in a criminal dock; the second is, that the law could pronounce no worse sentence than this, a life-long imprisonment in a mad-house. You see I do not thank you for your mercy, Mr. Robert Audley, for I know exactly what it is worth.'

She moved away from the door, and Robert passed her, without a word, without a look.

Half-an-hour afterwards he was in one of the principal hotels at Villebrumeuse, sitting at a neatly-ordered supper-table, with no power to eat; with no power to distract his mind, even for a moment, from the image of that lost friend who had been treacherously murdered in the thicket at Audley Court.

CHAPTER VII
Ghost-haunted

No feverish sleeper travelling in a strange dream ever looked out more wonderingly upon a world that seemed unreal than Robert Audley, as he stared absently at the flat swamps and dismal poplars between Villebrumeuse and Brussels. Could it be that he was returning to his uncle's house without the woman who had reigned in it for nearly two years as queen and mistress? He felt as if he had carried off my lady, and had made away with her secretly and darkly, and must now render up an account to Sir Michael of the fate of that woman, whom the baronet had so dearly loved.

'What shall I tell him?' he thought; 'shall I tell the truth – the horrible ghastly truth? No; that would be too cruel. His generous spirit would sink under the hideous revelation. Yet, in his ignorance of the extent of this wretched woman's wickedness, he may think perhaps that I have been hard with her.'

Brooding thus, Mr. Robert Audley absently watched the cheerless landscape from his seat in the shabby *coupé* of the diligence, and thought how great a leaf had been torn out of his life, now that the dark story of George Talboys was finished.

What had he to do next? A crowd of horrible thoughts rushed into his mind as he remembered the story that he had heard from the white lips of Helen Talboys. His friend – his murdered friend – lay hidden amongst the mouldering ruins of the old well at Audley Court. He had lain there for six long months, unburied, unknown; hidden in the darkness of the old convent well. What was to be done?

To institute a search for the remains of the murdered man was to inevitably bring about a coroner's inquest. Should such an inquest be held, it was next to impossible that the history of my lady's crime could fail to be brought to light. To prove that George Talboys met with his death at Audley Court was to prove almost as surely that my lady had been the instrument of that mysterious death; for the young man had been known to follow her into the lime-walk upon the day of his disappearance.

'My God!' Robert exclaimed, as the full horror of this position became evident to him, 'is my friend to rest in his unhallowed burial-place because I have condoned the offences of the woman who murdered him?'

He felt that there was no way out of this difficulty. Sometimes he thought that it little mattered to his dead friend whether he lay entombed beneath a marble monument, whose workmanship should be the wonder of the universe, or in that obscure hiding-place in the thicket at Audley Court. At another time he would be seized with a sudden horror at the wrong that had been done to the murdered man, and would fain have travelled even more rapidly than the express between Brussels and Paris could carry him, in his eagerness to reach the end of his journey, that he might set right this cruel wrong.

He was in London at dusk on the second day after that on which he had left Audley Court, and he drove straight to the Clarendon, to inquire after his uncle. He had no intention of seeing Sir Michael, as he had not yet determined how much or how little he should tell him, but he was very anxious to ascertain how the old man had sustained the cruel shock he had so lately endured.

'I will see Alicia,' he thought; 'she will tell me all about her father. It is only two days since he left Audley. I can scarcely expect to hear of any favourable change.'

But Mr. Audley was not destined to see his cousin that evening, for the servants at the Clarendon told him that Sir Michael and his daughter had left by the morning mail for Paris, on their way to Vienna.

Robert was very well pleased to receive this intelligence; it afforded him a welcome respite, for it would be decidedly better to tell the baronet nothing of his guilty wife until he returned to England, with his health unimpaired, and his spirits re-established, it was to be hoped.

Mr. Audley drove to the Temple. The chambers which had seemed dreary to him ever since the disappearance of George Talboys were doubly so to-night. For that which had been only a dark suspicion had now become a horrible certainty. There was no longer room for the palest ray, the most transitory glimmer of hope. His worst terrors had been too well founded.

George Talboys had been cruelly and treacherously murdered by the wife he had loved and mourned.

There were three letters waiting for Mr. Audley at his chambers. One was from Sir Michael, and another from Alicia. The third was addressed in a hand the young barrister knew only too well, though he had seen it but once before. His face flushed redly at the sight of the superscription, and he took the letter in his hand, carefully and tenderly, as if it had been a living thing, and sentient to his touch. He turned it over and over in his hands, looking at the crest upon the envelope, at the post-mark, at the colour of the paper, and then put it into the bosom of his waistcoat with a strange smile upon his face.

'What a wretched and unconscionable fool I am,' he thought. 'Have I laughed at the follies of weak men all my life, and am I to be more foolish than the weakest of them at last? The beautiful brown-eyed creature! Why did I ever see her? Why did my relentless Nemesis ever point the way to that dreary house in Dorsetshire?'

He opened the two first letters. He was foolish enough to keep the last for a delicious morsel – a fairy-like dessert after the common-place substantialities of a dinner.

Alicia's letter told him that Sir Michael had borne his agony with such a persevering tranquillity that she had become at last far more alarmed by his patient calmness than by any stormy manifestation of despair. In this difficulty she had secretly called upon the physician who attended the Audley household in any cases of serious illness, and had requested this gentleman to pay Sir Michael an apparently accidental visit. He had done so, and after stopping half-an-hour with the baronet, had told Alicia that there was no present danger of any serious consequence from this quiet grief, but that it was necessary that every effort should be made to arouse Sir Michael, and to force him, however unwillingly, into action.

Alicia had immediately acted upon this advice, had resumed her old empire as a spoiled child, and reminded her father of a promise he had made of taking her through Germany. With considerable difficulty she had induced him to consent to fulfilling this old promise, and having once gained her point, she had contrived that they should leave England as soon as it was possible to do so, and she told Robert, in conclusion, that she would not bring her father back to his old house until she had taught him to forget the sorrows associated with it.

The Baronet's letter was very brief. It contained half-a-dozen blank cheques on Sir Michael Audley's London bankers.

'You will require money, my dear Robert,' he wrote,

'for such arrangements as you may think fit to make for the future comfort of the person I committed to your care. I need scarcely tell you that those arrangements cannot be too liberal. But perhaps it is as well that I should tell you now, for the first and only time,

that it is my earnest wish never again to hear that person's name.
I have no wish to be told the nature of the arrangements you may
make for her. I am sure that you will act conscientiously and
mercifully. I seek to know no more. Whenever you want money,
you will draw upon me for any sums that you may require; but you
will have no occasion to tell me for whose use you want that money.'

Robert Audley breathed a long sigh of relief as he folded
this letter. It released him from a duty which it would have
been most painful for him to perform, and it for ever decided
his course of action with regard to the murdered man.

George Talboys must lie at peace in his unknown grave,
and Sir Michael Audley must never learn that the woman he
had loved bore the red brand of murder on her soul.

Robert had only the third letter to open – the letter which
he had placed in his bosom while he read the others; he tore
open the envelope, handling it carefully and tenderly as he
had done before.

The letter was as brief as Sir Michael's. It contained only
these few lines:–

'Dear Mr. Audley, –
  'The rector of this place has been twice to see Marks, the man
you saved in the fire at the Castle Inn. He lies in a very precarious
state at his mother's cottage, near Audley Court, and is not
expected to live many days. His wife is attending him, and both he
and she have expressed a most earnest desire that you should see
him before he dies. Pray come without delay.
                      'Yours very sincerely,
                         'CLARA TALBOYS.'
'Mount Stanning Rectory, March 6.'

Robert Audley folded this letter very reverently, and
replaced it underneath that part of his waistcoat which might

447

be supposed to cover the region of his heart. Having done this, he seated himself in his favourite arm-chair, filled and lighted a pipe, and smoked it out, staring reflectively at the fire as long as his tobacco lasted. The lazy light that glimmered in his handsome grey eyes told of a dreamy reverie that could have scarcely been either gloomy or unpleasant. His thoughts wandered away upon the blue clouds of hazy tobacco smoke, and carried him into a bright region of unrealities, in which there was neither death nor trouble, grief nor shame; only himself and Clara Talboys in a world that was made all their own by the great omnipotence of their loves.

It was not till the last shred of pale Turkish tobacco had been consumed, and the grey ashes knocked out upon the topmost bar of the grate, that this pleasant dream floated off into the great storehouse in which the visions of things that never have been and never are to be, are kept locked and guarded by some stern enchanter, who only turns the keys now and then and opens the door of his treasure-house a little way for the brief delight of mankind. But the dream fled, and the heavy burden of dismal realities fell again upon Robert's shoulders, more tenacious than any old man of the sea. 'What can that man Marks want with me?' thought the barrister. 'He is afraid to die until he has made a confession, perhaps. He wishes to tell me that which I know already – the story of my lady's crime. I knew that he was in the secret. I was sure of it even upon the night on which I first saw him. He knew the secret, and he traded on it.'

Robert Audley shrank strangely from returning to Essex. How should he meet Clara Talboys now that he knew the secret of her brother's fate? How many lies he should have to tell, or how much equivocation he must use in order to keep the truth from her? Yet would there be any mercy in telling her that horrible story, the knowledge of which must cast a blight upon her youth, and blot out every hope she had ever secretly cherished? He knew by his own experience how possible it was to hope against hope, and to hope unconsciously; and he could not bear that her heart should be crushed as his had been by the knowledge of the truth. 'Better that she should hope vainly to the last,' he thought; 'better that she should go through life seeking the clue to her lost brother's fate, than that I should give that clue into her hands and say, "Our worst fears are realised. The brother you loved has been foully murdered in the early promise of his youth."'

But Clara Talboys had written to him imploring him to return to Essex without delay. Could he refuse to do her bidding, however painful its accomplishment might be? And again, the man was dying, perhaps, and had implored to see him. Would it not be cruel to refuse to go, to delay an hour unnecessarily? He looked at his watch. It wanted only five minutes to nine. There was no train to Audley after the Ipswich mail, which left London at half-past eight; but there was a train that left Shoreditch at eleven, and stopped at Brentwood between twelve and one. Robert decided upon going by this train, and walking the distance between Brentwood and Audley, which was upwards of six miles.

He had a long time to wait before it would be necessary to leave the Temple on his way to Shoreditch, and he sat brooding darkly over the fire and wondering at the strange events which had filled his life within the last year and a half, coming like angry shadows between his lazy inclinations and himself, and investing him with purposes that were not his own.

'Good heavens!' he thought, as he smoked his second pipe, 'how can I believe that it was I who used to lounge all day in this easy-chair reading Paul de Kock, and smoking mild Turkish, who used to drop in at half-price to stand amongst the press men at the back of the boxes, and see a new burlesque, and finish the evening with the "Chough and Crow," and chops and pale ale at Evans's? Was it I to whom life was such an easy merry-go-round? Was it I who was one of the boys who sit at ease upon the wooden horses, while other boys run barefoot in the mud, and work their hardest in the hope of a ride when their work is done? Heaven knows I have learnt the business of life since then; and now I must needs fall in love and swell the tragic chorus which is always being sung by the poor addition of my pitiful sighs and groans. Clara Talboys! Clara Talboys! Is there any merciful smile latent beneath the earnest light of your brown eyes? What would you say to me if I told you that I love you as earnestly and truly as I have mourned for your brother's fate – that the new strength and purpose of my life which has grown out of my friendship for the murdered man grows even stronger as it turns to you, and changes me until I wonder at myself? What would she say to me? Ah! Heaven knows. If she happened to like the colour of my hair, or the tone of my voice, she might listen to me, perhaps. But would she hear me any more because I love her truly and purely; because I would be constant, and honest, and faithful to her? Not she! These things might move her, perhaps, to be a little pitiful to me; but they would move her no more! If a girl with freckles and white eyelashes adored me, I should only think her a nuisance; but if Clara Talboys had a fancy to trample upon my uncouth person I should think she did me a favour. I hope poor little Alicia may pick up with some fair-haired Saxon in the course of her travels. I hope—' His thoughts wandered away wearily, and lost themselves. How could he hope for anything, or think of anything, while the memory of his dead friend's unburied body haunted him like a horrible spectre? He remembered a story – a morbid, hideous, yet delicious story, which had once pleasantly congealed his blood on a social winter's evening – the story of a man, a monomaniac, perhaps, who had been haunted at every turn by the image of an unburied kinsman who *could* not rest in his unhallowed hiding-place. What if that dreadful story had its double in reality? What if he were henceforth to be haunted by the phantom of murdered George Talboys?

He pushed his hair away from his face with both his hands, and looked rather nervously around the snug little apartment. There were lurking shadows in the corners of the room that he scarcely liked. The door opening into his little dressing-room was ajar; he got up to shut it, and turned the key in the lock with a sharp click.

'I haven't read Alexandre Dumas and Wilkie Collins for nothing,' he muttered. 'I'm up to their tricks, sneaking in at doors behind a fellow's back, and flattening their white faces against window-panes, and making themselves all eyes in the twilight. It's a strange thing that your generous-hearted fellow, who never did a shabby thing in his life, is capable of any meanness the moment he becomes a ghost. I'll have the gas laid on to-morrow, and engage Mrs. Maloney's eldest son to sleep under the letter-box in the lobby. The youth plays popular melodies upon a piece of tissue paper and a small-tooth comb, and will be quite pleasant company.'

Mr. Audley walked wearily up and down the room, trying to get rid of the time. It was no use leaving the Temple until ten o'clock, and even then he would be sure to reach the station half-an-hour too early. He was tired of smoking. The soothing narcotic influence might be pleasant enough in itself, but the man must be of a singularly unsocial disposition who does not, after half-a-dozen lonely pipes, feel the need of some friendly companion, at whom he can stare dreamily athwart the pale grey mists, and who will stare kindly back at him in return. Do not think that Robert Audley was without friends, because he so often found himself alone in his quiet chambers. The solemn purpose which had taken so powerful a hold upon his careless life had separated him from old associations, and it was for this reason that he was alone. He had dropped away from his old friends. How could he sit amongst them, at social wine parties, perhaps, or at pleasant little dinners, that were washed down with Nonpareil and Chambertin, Pomard and Champagne? How could he sit amongst them, listening to their careless talk of politics and opera, literature and racing, theatres and science, scandal, and theology, and yet carry in his mind the horrible burden of those dark terrors and suspicions that were with him by day and night? He could not do it! He had shrunk from these men as if he had, indeed, been a detective police officer, stained with vile associations, and unfit company for honest gentlemen. He had drawn himself away from all familiar haunts, and had shut himself in his lonely rooms with the perpetual trouble of his mind for his sole companion, until he had grown as nervous as habitual solitude will eventually make the strongest and the wisest man, however he may vaunt himself of his strength and wisdom.

The clock of the Temple Church and the clocks of St. Dunstan's, St. Clement Danes, and a crowd of other churches, whose steeples uprear themselves above the house-tops by the river, struck ten at last, and Mr. Audley, who had put on his hat and overcoat nearly half-an-hour before, let himself out of the little lobby, and locked his door behind him. He mentally reiterated his determination to engage 'Parthrick,' as Mrs. Maloney's eldest son was called by his devoted mother. The youth should enter upon his functions the very next night after, and if the ghost of hapless George Talboys should invade these gloomy apartments, the phantom must make its way across Patrick's body before it could reach the inner chamber in which the proprietor of the premises slept.

Do not laugh at poor Robert because he grew hypochondriacal, after hearing the horrible story of his friend's death. There is nothing so delicate, so fragile, as that invisible balance upon which the mind is always trembling. Mad to-day and sane to-morrow.

Who can forget that almost terrible picture of Dr. Samuel Johnson? The awful disputant of the club-room, solemn, ponderous, severe, and merciless, the admiration and the terror of humble Bozzy, the stern monitor of gentle Oliver, the friend of Garrick and Reynolds to-night: and before sunset to-morrow a weak miserable old man, discovered by good Mr. and Mrs. Thrale, kneeling upon the floor of his lonely chamber, in an agony of childish terror and confusion, and praying to a merciful God for the preservation of his wits. I think the memory of that dreadful afternoon, and of the tender care he then received, should have taught the doctor to keep his hand steady at Streatham, when he took his bed-room candlestick, from which it was his habit to shower rivulets of molten wax upon the costly carpet of his beautiful protectress; and might have even had a more enduring effect, and taught him to be merciful, when the brewer's widow went mad in her turn, and married that dreadful creature, the Italian singer. Who has not been, or is not to be, mad in some lonely hour of life? Who is quite safe from the trembling of the balance?

Fleet Street was quiet and lonely at this late hour, and Robert Audley being in a ghost-seeing mood would have been scarcely astonished had he seen Johnson's set come roystering westward in the lamplight, or blind John Milton groping his way down the steps before Saint Bride's church.

Mr. Audley hailed a Hansom at the corner of Farringdon Street, and was rattled rapidly away across tenantless Smithfield market, and into a labyrinth of dingy streets that brought him out upon the broad grandeur of Finsbury Pavement.

'Nobody ever saw a ghost in a Hansom cab,' Robert thought, 'and even Dumas hasn't done *that* as yet. Not but that he's capable of doing it if the idea occurred to him. *Un revenant en fiacre*. Upon my word, the title doesn't sound bad. The story would be something about a dismal gentleman, in black, who took the vehicle by the hour, and was contumacious upon the subject of fares, and beguiled the driver into lonely neighbourhoods, beyond the barriers, and made himself otherwise unpleasant.'

The Hansom rattled up the steep and stony approach to the Shoreditch station, and deposited Robert at the doors of that unlovely temple. There were very few people going to travel by this midnight train, and Robert walked up and down the long wooden platform, reading the huge advertisements whose gaunt lettering looked wan and ghastly in the dim lamplight.

He had the carriage in which he sat all to himself. All to himself, did I say? Had he not lately summoned to his side that ghostly company which of all companionship is the most tenacious? The shadow of George Talboys pursued him, even in the comfortable first-class carriage, and was behind him when he looked out of the window, and was yet far away ahead of him and the rushing engine, in that thicket towards which the train was speeding, by the side of the unhallowed hiding-place in which the mortal remains of the dead man lay, neglected and uncared for.

'I must give my lost friend decent burial,' Robert thought, as a chill wind swept across the flat landscape, and struck him with such frozen breath as might have emanated from the lips of the dead. 'I must do it; or I shall die of some panic like this which has seized upon me to-night. I must do it; at any peril; at any cost. Even at the price of that revelation which will bring the madwoman back from her safe hiding-place, and place her in a criminal dock.' He was glad when the train stopped at Brentwood at a few minutes after twelve. Only one other person got out at the little station – a burly grazier, who had been to one of the theatres to see a tragedy. Country people always go to see tragedies. None of your flimsy vaude-villes for them! None of your pretty drawing-room, moderator lamp and French window pieces, with a confiding husband, a frivolous wife, and a smart lady's-maid, who is always accommodating enough to dust the furniture and announce visitors; no such gauzy productions; but a good monumental five-act tragedy, in which their ancestors have seen Garrick and Mrs. Abington, and in which they themselves can remember the O'Neil, the beautiful creature whose lovely neck and shoulders became suffused with a crimson glow of shame and indignation, when the actress was Mrs. Beverley, and insulted by Stukeley in her poverty and sorrow. I think our modern O'Neils scarcely feel their stage wrongs so keenly; or, perhaps, those brightly indignant blushes of to-day struggle ineffectually against the new art of Madame Rachel, and are lost to the public beneath the lily purity of priceless enamel.

Robert Audley looked hopelessly about him as he left the pleasant town of Brentwood, and descended the lonely hill into the valley which lay between the town he had left behind him and that other hill, upon which that frail and dismal tenement – the Castle Inn – had so long struggled with its enemy, the wind, only to succumb at last, and to be shrivelled and consumed away like a withered leaf, by the alliance of that old adversary with a newer and a fiercer foe.

'It's a dreary walk,' Mr. Audley said, as he looked along the smooth high road that lay before him, lonely as the track across a desert. 'It's a dreary walk for a dismal wretch to take between twelve and one, upon a cheerless March night, with not so much moonlight in all the black sky as might serve to convince one of the existence of such a luminary. But I'm very glad I came,' thought the barrister, 'if this poor creature is dying, and really wishes to see me. I should have been a wretch had I held back. Besides, *she* wishes it; she wishes it; and what can I do but obey her, Heaven help me!'

He stopped by the wooden fence which surrounded the gardens of Mount Stanning rectory, and looked across a laurel hedge towards the lattice windows of that simple habitation.

There was no glimmer of light in any one of these windows, and Mr. Audley was fain to go away, after having had no better satisfaction than such cold comfort as was to be obtained from a long lingering contemplation of the house that sheltered the one woman before whose invincible power the impregnable fortress of his heart had surrendered. Only a heap of blackened ruins stood upon the spot on which the Castle Inn had once done battle with the winds of Heaven. The cold night breezes had their way with the few fragments that the fire had left, and whirled them hither and thither as they would, scattering a shower of dust and cinders and crumbling morsels of charred wood upon Robert Audley as he passed.

It was half-past one o'clock when the night wanderer entered the village of Audley, and it was only there that he remembered that Clara Talboys had omitted to give him any direction by which he might find the cottage in which Luke Marks lay.

'It was Dawson who recommended that the poor creature should be taken to his mother's cottage,' Robert thought, by-and-by, 'and I dare say Dawson has attended him ever since the fire. He'll be able to tell me the way to the cottage.'

Acting upon this idea, Mr. Audley stopped at the house in which Helen Talboys had lived before her second marriage. The door of the little surgery was ajar, and there was a light burning within. Robert pushed the door open and peeped in. The surgeon was standing at the mahogany counter, mixing a draught in a glass measure, with his hat close beside him. Late as it was, he had evidently only just come in. The harmonious snoring of his assistant sounded from a little room within the surgery.

'I am sorry to disturb you, Mr. Dawson,' Robert said, apologetically, as the surgeon looked up and recognised him, 'but I have come down to see Marks, who, I hear, is in a very bad way, and I want you to tell me the way to his mother's cottage.'

'I'll show you the way, Mr. Audley,' answered the surgeon, 'I am going there this minute.'

'The man is very bad then?'

'So bad that he can be no worse. The only change that can happen is that change which will take him beyond the reach of any earthly suffering.'

'Strange!' exclaimed Robert. 'He did not appear to be much burnt.'

'He was not much burnt. Had he been, I should never have recommended his being removed from Mount Stanning. It is the shock that has done the business. His health had been long undermined by habits of intoxication, and has completely given way under the sudden terror of that night. He has been in a raging fever for the last two days; but to-night he is much calmer, and I'm afraid, before to-morrow night, we shall have seen the last of him.'

'He has asked to see me, I am told,' said Mr. Audley.

'Yes,' answered the surgeon, carelessly. 'A sick man's fancy, no doubt. You dragged him out of the house, and did your best to save his life. I dare say, rough and boorish as the poor fellow is, he thinks a good deal of that.'

They had left the surgery, the door of which Mr. Dawson had locked behind him. There was money in the till, perhaps, for surely the village apothecary could not have feared that the most daring housebreaker would imperil his liberty in the pursuit of blue pill and colocynth, or salts and senna.

The surgeon led the way along the silent street, and presently turned into a lane at the end of which Robert Audley saw the wan glimmer of a light. A light which told of the watch that is kept by the sick and dying; a pale, melancholy light, which always has a dismal aspect when looked upon in this silent hour betwixt night and morning. It shone from the window of the cottage in which Luke Marks lay, watched by his wife and mother.

Mr. Dawson lifted the latch, and walked into the common room of the little tenement, followed by Robert Audley. It was empty, but a feeble tallow candle, with a broken back and a long, cauliflower-headed wick sputtered upon the table. The sick man lay in the room above.

'Shall I tell him you are here?' asked Mr. Dawson.

'Yes, yes, if you please. But be cautious how you tell him, if you think the news likely to agitate him. I am in no hurry. I can wait. You can call me when you think I can safely come up-stairs.'

The surgeon nodded, and softly ascended the narrow wooden stairs leading to the upper chamber. Mr. Dawson was a good man, and indeed a parish surgeon has need to be good, and tender, and kindly, and gentle, or the wretched patients who have no neatly folded fees or gold and silver to offer, may suffer petty slights and insignificant cruelties, not easily to be proved before a board of well-to-do poor-law guardians, but not the less bitter to bear in the fretful and feverish hours of sickness and pain.

Robert Audley seated himself in a Windsor chair, by the cold hearth-stone, and stared disconsolately about him. Small as the room was, the corners were dusky and shadowy in the dim light of the cauliflower-headed candle. The faded face of an eight-day clock, which stood opposite Robert Audley, seemed to stare him out of countenance. The awful sounds which can emanate from eight-day clocks after midnight are too generally known to need description. The young man listened in awe-stricken silence to the heavy, monotonous ticking, which sounded as if the clock had been counting out the seconds which yet remained for the dying man, and checking them off with gloomy satisfaction. 'Another minute gone! another minute gone! another minute gone!' the clock seemed to say, until Mr. Audley felt inclined to throw his hat at it, in the wild hope of stopping that melancholy and monotonous noise.

But he was relieved at last by the low voice of the surgeon, who looked down from the top of the little staircase to tell him that Luke Marks was awake and would be glad to see him.

Robert immediately obeyed this summons. He crept softly up the stairs and took off his hat before he bent his head to enter at the low doorway of the humble rustic chamber. He took off his hat in the presence of this common peasant-man because he knew that there was another and a more awful presence hovering about the room, and eager to be admitted.

Phœbe Marks was sitting at the foot of the bed, with her eyes fixed upon her husband's face. Not with any very tender expression in their pale light, but with a sharp, terrified anxiety, which showed that it was the coming of death itself that she dreaded, rather than the loss of her husband. The old woman was busy at the fire-place, airing linen, and preparing some mess of broth which it was not likely the patient would ever eat. The sick man lay with his head propped up by pillows, his coarse face deadly pale, and his great hands wandering uneasily about the coverlet. Phœbe had been reading to him, for an open Testament lay amongst the medicine and lotion bottles upon the table near the bed. Every object in the room was neat and orderly, and bore witness of that delicate precision which had always been a distinguishing characteristic of Phœbe.

The young woman rose as Robert Audley crossed the threshold, and hurried towards him.

'Let me speak to you for a moment, sir, before you talk to Luke,' she said, in an eager whisper. 'Pray let me speak to you first.'

'What's the gal a sayin', there?' asked the invalid in a subdued roar, which died away hoarsely on his lips. He was feebly savage, even in his weakness. The dull glaze of death was gathering over his eyes, but they still watched Phœbe with a sharp glance of dissatisfaction. 'What's she up to there?'

he said. 'I won't have no plottin' and no hatchin' agen me. I want to speak to Mr. Audley my own self; and whatever I done I'm a goin' to answer for. If I done any mischief, I'm a goin' to try and undo it. What's she a sayin'?'

'She ain't a sayin' nothin', lovey,' answered the old woman, going to the bedside of her son, who, even when made more interesting than usual by illness, did not seem a very fit subject for this tender appellation.

'She's only a tellin' the gentleman how bad you've been, my pretty.'

'What I'm a goin' to tell I'm only a goin' to tell to him, remember,' growled Mr. Marks; 'and ketch me a tellin' of it to him if it warn't for what he done for me the other night.'

'To be sure not, lovey,' answered the old woman, soothingly.

Her intellect was rather limited in its scope, and she attached no more importance to her son's eager words now, than she had attached to the wild ravings of delirium. That horrible delirium in which Luke had described himself as being dragged through miles of blazing brick and mortar; and flung down wells; and dragged out of deep pits by the hair of the head; and suspended in the air by giant hands that came out of the clouds to pluck him from off the solid earth and hurl him into chaos; with many other wild terrors and delusions which ran riot in his distempered brain.

Phœbe Marks had drawn Mr. Audley out of the room and on to the narrow landing at the top of the little staircase. This landing was a platform of about three feet square, and it was as much as the two could manage to stand upon it without pushing each other against the white-washed wall, or backwards down the stairs.

'Oh, sir, I wanted to speak to you so badly,' Phœbe whispered eagerly; 'you know what I told you when I found you safe and well upon the night of the fire?'

'Yes, yes.'

'I told you what I suspected; what I think still.'

'Yes, I remember.'

'But I never breathed a word of it to anybody but you, sir; and I think that Luke has forgotten all about that night; I think that what went before the fire has gone clean out of his head altogether. He was tipsy you know when my la– when she came to the Castle; and I think he was so dazed and scared like by the fire that it all went out of his memory. He doesn't suspect what I suspect at any rate, or he'd have spoken of it to anybody and everybody; but he's dreadful spiteful against my lady, for he says if she'd have let him have a place at Brentwood or Chelmsford, this wouldn't have happened. So what I wanted to beg of you, sir, is not to let a word drop before Luke.'

'Yes, yes, I understand; I will be careful.'

'My lady has left the Court, I hear, sir?'

'Yes.'

'Never to come back, sir?'

'Never to come back.'

'But she has not gone where she'll be cruelly treated; where she'll be ill-used?'

'No, she will be very kindly treated.'

'I'm glad of that, sir; I beg your pardon for troubling you with the question, sir, but my lady was a kind mistress to me.'

Luke's voice, husky and feeble, was heard within the little chamber at this period of the conversation, demanding angrily when 'that gal would have done jawing,' upon which Phœbe put her finger to her lips, and led Mr. Audley back into the sick room.

'I don't want *you*,' said Mr. Marks, decisively, as his wife re-entered the chamber, 'I don't want *you*, you've no call to hear what I've got to say; I only want Mr. Audley, and I wants to speak to him all alone, with none o' your sneakin' listenin' at doors, d'ye hear, so you may go down-stairs and keep there till you're wanted; and you may take mother – no, mother may stay, I shall want her presently.'

The sick man's feeble hand pointed to the door, through which his wife departed very submissively.

'I've no wish to hear anything, Luke,' she said, 'but I hope you won't say anything against those that have been good and generous to you.'

'I shall say what I like,' answered Mr. Marks, fiercely, 'and I'm not agoin' to be ordered by you. You ain't the parson, as I've ever heerd of; nor the lawyer neither.'

The landlord of the Castle Inn had undergone no moral transformation by his death-bed sufferings, fierce and rapid as they had been. Perhaps some faint glimmer of a light that had been far off from his life, now struggled feebly through the black obscurities of ignorance that darkened his soul. Perhaps a half angry, half sullen penitence urged him to make some rugged effort to atone for a life that had been selfish and drunken and wicked. Be it how it might, he wiped his white lips, and turning his haggard eyes earnestly upon Robert Audley, pointed to a chair by the bedside.

'You've made game of me in a general way, Mr. Audley,' he said, presently, 'and you've drawed me out, and you've tumbled and tossed me about like in a gentlemanly way, till I was nothink or anythink in your hands; and you've looked me through and through, and turned me inside out till you thought you knowed as much as I knowed. I'd no particular call to be grateful to you, not before the fire at the Castle t'other night. But I am grateful to you for that. I'm not grateful to folks in a general way, p'raps, because the things as gentlefolks have give me have a'most allus been the very things I didn't want. They've give me soup, and tracks, and flannel, and coals; but, Lord, they've made such a precious noise about it that I'd have been glad to send 'em all back to

462

'em. But when a gentleman goes and puts his own life in danger to save a drunken brute like me, the drunkenest brute as ever was feels grateful like to that gentleman, and wishes to say before he dies – which he sees in the doctor's face as he ain't got long to live – "Thank ye, Sir, I'm obliged to you." '

Luke Marks stretched out his left hand – the right had been injured by the fire, and was wrapped in linen – and groped feebly for that of Mr. Robert Audley.

The young man took the coarse but shrunken hand in both his own, and pressed it cordially.

'I need no thanks, Luke Marks,' he said, 'I was very glad to be of service to you.'

Mr. Marks did not speak immediately. He was lying quietly upon his side, staring reflectingly at Robert Audley.

'You was oncommon fond of that gent as disappeared at the Court, warn't you, Sir?' he said at last.

Robert started at the mention of his dead friend.

'You was oncommon fond of this Mr. Talboys, I've heerd say, Sir,' repeated Luke.

'Yes, yes,' answered Robert, rather impatiently, 'he was my very dear friend.'

'I've heerd the servants at the Court say how you took on when you couldn't find him. I've heerd the landlord of the Sun Inn say how cut up you was when you first missed him. "If the two gents had been brothers," the landlord said, "our gent," meanin' you, Sir, "couldn't have been more cut up when he missed the other." '

'Yes, yes, I know, I know,' said Robert; 'pray do not speak any more of this subject; I cannot tell you how much it distresses me.'

Was he to be haunted for ever by the ghost of his unburied friend? He came here to comfort this sick man, and even here he was pursued by that relentless shadow; even here he was reminded of the secret crime which had darkened his life.

'Listen to me, Marks,' he said, earnestly; 'believe me, that I appreciate your grateful words, and that I am very glad to have been of service to you. But before you say anything more, let me make one most solemn request. If you have sent for me that you may tell me anything of the fate of my lost friend, I entreat you to spare yourself and to spare me that horrible story. You can tell me nothing which I do not already know. The worst you can tell me of the woman who was once in your power, has already been revealed to me by her own lips. Pray then be silent upon this subject; I say again, you can tell me nothing which I do not know.'

Luke Marks looked musingly at the earnest face of his visitor, and some shadowy expression which was almost like a smile flitted feebly across the sick man's haggard features.

'I can't tell you nothin' you don't know?' he asked.

'Nothing.'

'Then it ain't no good for me to try,' said the invalid, thoughtfully. 'Did *she* tell you?' he asked after a pause.

'I must beg, Marks, that you will drop the subject,' Robert answered, almost sternly; 'I have already told you that I do not wish to hear it spoken of. Whatever discoveries you made, you made your market out of them. Whatever guilty secrets you got possession of, you were paid for keeping silence. You had better keep silence to the end.'

'Had I?' cried Luke Marks in an eager whisper. 'Had I really now better hold my tongue to the last?'

'I think so, most decidedly. You traded on your secret, and you were paid to keep it. It would be more honest to hold to your bargain, and keep it still.'

'Would it now?' said Mr. Marks with a ghastly grin; 'but suppose my lady had one secret and I another. How then?'

'What do you mean?'

'Suppose I could have told something all along; and would have told it, perhaps, if I'd been a little better treated; if what

464

was give to me had been give a little more liberal like, and not flung at me as if I was a dog, and was only give it to be kep' from bitin'. Suppose I could have told somethin', and would have told it but for that? How then?'

It is impossible to describe the ghastliness of the triumphant grin that lighted up the sick man's haggard face.

'His mind is wandering,' Robert thought; 'I had need be patient with him, poor fellow. It would be strange if I could not be patient with a dying man.'

Luke Marks lay staring at Mr. Audley for some moments with that triumphant grin upon his face. The old woman, wearied out with watching her dying son, had dropped into a doze, and sat nodding her sharp chin over the handful of fire, upon which the broth that was never to be eaten, still bubbled and simmered.

Mr. Audley waited very patiently until it should be the sick man's pleasure to speak. Every sound was painfully distinct in that dead hour of the night. The dropping of the ashes on the hearth, the ominous crackling of the burning coals, the slow and ponderous ticking of the sulky clock in the room below, the low moaning of the March wind (which might have been the voice of an English Banshee, screaming her dismal warning to the watchers of the dying), the hoarse breathing of the sick man – every sound held itself apart from all other sounds, and made itself into a separate voice, loud with a gloomy portent in the solemn stillness of the house.

Robert sat with his face shaded by his hands, thinking what was to become of him now that the secret of his friend's fate had been told, and the dark story of George Talboys and his wicked wife had been finished in the Belgian mad-house. What was to become of him?

He had no claim upon Clara Talboys; for he had resolved to keep the horrible secret that had been told to him. How then could he dare to meet her with that secret held back from her? How could he ever look into her earnest eyes, and yet withhold the truth? He felt that all power of reservation would fail before the searching glance of those calm brown eyes. If he was indeed to keep this secret he must never see her again. To reveal it would be to embitter her life. Could he, for any selfish motive of his own, tell her this terrible story? – or could he think that if he told her she would suffer her murdered brother to lie unavenged and forgotten in his unhallowed grave?

Hemmed in on every side by difficulties which seemed utterly insurmountable; with the easy temperament which was natural to him embittered by the gloomy burden he had borne so long, Robert Audley looked hopelessly forward to the life which lay before him, and thought that it would have been better for him had he perished among the burning ruins of the Castle Inn.

'Who would have been sorry for me? No one but my poor little Alicia,' he thought, 'and hers would have only been an April sorrow. Would Clara Talboys have been sorry? No! She would have only regretted me as a lost link in the mystery of her brother's death. She would only—'

CHAPTER VIII

That which the dying man had to tell

Heaven knows whither Mr. Audley's thoughts might have wandered had he not been startled by a sudden movement of the sick man, who raised himself up in his bed, and called to his mother.

The old woman woke up with a jerk, and turned sleepily enough to look at her son.

'What is it, Luke, deary?' she asked soothingly. 'It ain't time for the doctor's stuff yet. Mr. Dawson said as you weren't to have it till two hours after he went away, and he ain't been gone an hour yet.'

'Who said it was the doctor's stuff I wanted?' cried Mr. Marks, impatiently. 'I want to ask you something, mother. Do you remember the seventh of last September?'

Robert started, and looked eagerly at the sick man. Why did he harp upon this forbidden subject? Why did he insist upon recalling the date of George's murder? The old woman shook her head in feeble confusion of mind.

'Lord, Luke,' she said, 'how can'ee ask me such questions? My memory's been a failin' me this eight or nine year; and I never was one to remember the days of the month, or aught o' that sort. How should a poor workin' woman remember such things?'

Luke Marks shrugged his shoulders impatiently.

'You're a good un to do what's asked you, mother,' he said, peevishly. 'Didn't I tell you to remember that day? Didn't I tell you as the time might come when you'd be called upon to bear witness about it, and put upon your Bible oath about it? Didn't I tell you that, mother?'

The old woman shook her head hopelessly.

'If you say so, I make no doubt you did, Luke,' she said, with a conciliatory smile; 'but I can't call it to mind, lovey. My memory's been failin' me this nine year, sir,' she added, turning to Robert Audley, 'and I'm but a poor crittur.'

Mr. Audley laid his hand upon the sick man's arm.

'Marks,' he said, 'I tell you again, you have no cause to worry yourself about this matter. I ask you no questions; I have no wish to hear anything.'

'But suppose I want to tell somethin',' cried Luke, with feverish energy, 'suppose I feel that I can't die with a secret on my mind, and have asked to see you on purpose that I might tell you. Suppose that, and you'll suppose nothing but the truth. I'd have been burnt alive before I'd have told *her*.' He spoke these words between his set teeth, and scowled savagely as he uttered them. 'I'd have been burnt alive first. I made her pay for her pretty insolent ways; I made her pay for her airs and graces; I'd never have told her – never, never! I had my power over her, and I kept it; I had my secret, and I was paid for it; and there wasn't a petty slight as she ever put upon me or mine that I didn't pay her out for twenty times over!'

'Marks, Marks, for heaven's sake be calm,' said Robert, earnestly; 'what are you talking of ? What is it that you could have told?'

'I'm agoin' to tell you,' answered Luke, wiping his dry lips. 'Give us a drink, mother.'

The old woman poured out some cooling drink into a mug, and carried it to her son.

He drank it in an eager hurry, as if he felt that the brief remainder of his life must be a race with the pitiless pedestrian, Time.

'Stop where you are,' he said to his mother, pointing to a chair at the foot of the bed.

The old woman obeyed, and seated herself meekly opposite to Mr. Audley. She took out her spectacle case, polished her spectacles, put them on and beamed placidly upon her son, as if she cherished some faint hope that her memory might be assisted by this process.

'I'll ask you another question, mother,' said Luke, 'and I think it'll be strange if you can't answer it. Do you remember when I was at work upon Atkinson's farm; before I was married, you know, and when I was livin' down here along of you?'

'Yes, yes,' Mrs. Marks answered, nodding triumphantly, 'I remember that, my dear. It were last fall, just about as the apples was bein' gathered in the orchard across our lane, and about the time as you had your new sprigged wesket. I remember, Luke, I remember.'

Mr. Audley wondered where all this was to lead to, and how long he would have to sit by the sick man's bed hearing a conversation that had no meaning to him.

'If you remember that much, maybe you'll remember more, mother,' said Luke. 'Can you call to mind my bringing some one home here one night, while Atkinsons was stackin' the last o' their corn?'

Once more Mr. Audley started violently, and this time he looked up earnestly at the face of the speaker, and listened, with a strange, breathless interest, that he scarcely understood himself, to what Luke Marks was saying.

'I rek'lect your bringin' home Phœbe,' the old woman answered with great animation; 'I rek'lect your bringin' Phœbe home to take a cup o' tea, or a little snack o' supper, a mort o' times.'

'Bother Phœbe,' cried Mr. Marks, 'whose a talkin' of Phœbe? What's Phœbe that anybody should go to put theirselves out

469

about her? Do you remember my bringin' home a gentleman arter ten o'clock one September night; a gentleman as was wet through to the skin, and was covered with mud and slush, and green slime and black muck, from the crown of his head to the sole of his foot, and had his arm broke, and his shoulder swelled up awful; and was such a objeck that nobody would ha' knowed him? A gentleman as had to have his clothes cut off him in some places, and as sat by the kitchen fire, starin' at the coals as if he'd gone mad or stupid-like, and didn't know where he was, or who he was: and as had to be cared for like a baby, and dressed and dried, and washed, and fed with spoonfuls of brandy that had to be forced between his locked teeth, before any life could be got into him. Do you remember that, mother?'

The old woman nodded, and muttered something, to the effect that she remembered all these circumstances most vividly, now that Luke happened to mention them.

Robert Audley uttered a wild cry, and fell down upon his knees by the side of the sick man's bed.

'My God!' he ejaculated, 'I thank Thee for Thy wondrous mercies. George Talboys is alive!'

'Wait a bit,' said Mr. Marks, 'don't you be too fast. Mother, give us down that tin-box on the shelf over against the chest of drawers, will you?'

The old woman obeyed, and after fumbling amongst broken tea-cups and milk-jugs, lidless wooden cotton-boxes, and a miscellaneous litter of rags and crockery, produced a tin snuff-box with a sliding lid; a shabby, dirty-looking box enough.

Robert Audley still knelt by the bedside with his face hidden by his clasped hands. Luke Marks opened the tin box.

'There ain't no money in it, more's the pity,' he said, 'or if there had been it wouldn't have been let stop very long. But there's summat in it that perhaps you'll think quite as vallible as money, and that's what I'm goin' to give you as a proof that a drunken brute can feel thankful to them as is kind to him.'

He took out two folded papers, which he gave into Robert Audley's hands.

They were two leaves torn out of a pocket-book, and they were written upon in pencil, and in a handwriting that was quite strange to Mr. Audley. A cramped, stiff and yet scrawling hand, such as some ploughman might have written.

'I don't know this writing,' Robert said, as he eagerly unfolded the first of the two papers. 'What has this to do with my friend? Why do you show me these?'

'Suppose you read 'em first,' said Mr. Marks, 'and ask me questions about 'em afterwards.'

The first paper which Robert Audley had unfolded contained the following lines, written in that cramped, yet scrawling hand which was so strange to him.

'My dear friend, – I write to you in such utter confusion of mind as perhaps no man ever before suffered. I cannot tell you what has happened to me, I can only tell you that something has happened which will drive me from England, a broken-hearted man, to seek some corner of the earth in which I may live and die unknown and forgotten. I can only ask you to forget me. If your friendship could have done me any good, I would have appealed to it. If your counsel could have been of any help to me, I would have confided in you. But neither friendship nor counsel can help me; and all I can say to you is this, God bless you for the past, and teach you to forget me in the future.   G. T.'

The second paper was addressed to another person, and its contents were briefer than those of the first.

'Helen, – May God pity and forgive you for that which you have done to-day, as truly as I do. Rest in peace. You shall never

471

hear of me again; to you and to the world, I shall henceforth be
that which you wished me to be to-day. You need fear no
molestation from me. I leave England, never to return.   G.T.'

Robert Audley sat staring at these lines in hopeless bewilderment. They were not in his friend's familiar hand; and yet they purported to be written by him, and were signed with his initials.

He looked scrutinisingly at the face of Luke Marks, thinking that perhaps some trick was being played upon him.

'This was not written by George Talboys,' he said.

'It was,' answered Luke Marks, 'it was written by Mr. Talboys, every line of it; he wrote it with his own hand; but it was his left hand, for he couldn't use his right because of his broken arm.'

Robert Audley looked up suddenly, and the shadow of suspicion passed away from his face.

'I understand,' he said, 'I understand. Tell me all; tell me how it was that my poor friend was saved.'

He could scarcely realise to himself yet that what he had heard could be true. He could scarcely believe that this friend whom he had so bitterly regretted might still clasp him by the hand in a happy future, when the darkness of the past should have cleared away. He was dazed and bewildered at first, and not able to understand this new hope which had dawned so suddenly upon him.

'Tell me all,' he cried, 'for mercy's sake tell me everything, and let me try to understand it if I can.'

'I was at work up at Atkinson's farm last September,' said Luke Marks, 'helpin' to stack the last o' the corn, and as the nighest way from the farm to mother's cottage was through the meadows at the back o' the Court, I used to come that way; and Phœbe used to stand at the gate in the garden wall beyond the lime-walk, sometimes, to have a chat with me,

472

knowin' my time o' comin' home. Sometimes she wouldn't be there, and sometimes I've leapt the dry moat as parts the kitchen gardens from the meadows alongside of 'em, and have dropped in at the servants' hall to have a glass of ale or a bit o' supper, as it might be.

'I don't know what Phœbe was a doin' upon the evenin' of the seventh o' September – I rek'lect the date because Farmer Atkinson paid me my wages all of a lump on that day, and I'd had to sign a bit of a receipt for the money he give me – I don't know what she was a doin', but she warn't at the gate agen the lime-walk, so I went round to the other side o' the gardens and jumped across the dry ditch; for I wanted partic'ler to see her that night, as I was goin' away to work upon a farm beyond Chelmsford the next day. Audley church clock struck nine as I was crossin' the meadows between Atkinson's and the Court, and it must have been about a quarter past nine when I got into the kitchen garden.

'I crossed the garden, and went into the lime-walk; the nighest way to the servants' hall took me through the shrubbery and past the dry well. It was a dark night, but I knew my way well enough about the old place, and the light in the window of the servants' hall looked red and comfortable through the darkness. I was close against the mouth of the dry well when I heard a sound that made my blood creep. It was a groan; a groan of a man in pain, as was lyin' somewhere hid among the bushes. I warn't afraid of ghosts, and I warn't afraid of anythink in a general way, but there was somethin' in hearin' this groan as chilled me to the very heart, and for a minute I was struck all of a heap and didn't know what to do. But I heard the groan again, and then I began to search amongst the bushes. I found a man lyin' hidden under a lot o' laurels, and I thought at first he was up to no good, and I was a goin' to collar him and take him to the house, when he caught me by the wrist without gettin' up from the ground, but lookin' at me very earnest, as I could see by the way his face was turned towards me in the darkness, and asked me who I was, and what I was, and what I had to do with the folks at the Court.

'There was somethin' in the way he spoke that told me he was a gentleman, though I didn't know him from Adam, and couldn't see his face; and I answered his questions civil.

' "I want to get away from this place," he said, "without bein' seen by any livin' creetur, remember that. I've been lyin' here ever since four o'clock to-day, and I'm half dead, but I want to get away without bein' seen, mind that."

'I told him that was easy enough, but I began to think my first thoughts of him might have been right enough after all, and that he couldn't have been up to no good to want to sneak away so precious quiet.

' "Can you take me to any place where I can get a change of dry clothes," he says, "without half-a-dozen people knowin' it?"

'He'd got up into a sittin' attitude by this time, and I could see that his right arm hung loose by his side, and that he was in pain.

'I pointed to his arm, and asked him what was the matter with it; but he only answered very quiet like, "Broken, my lad, broken. Not that that's much," he says in another tone, speaking to himself like, more than to me. "There's broken hearts as well as broken limbs, and they're not so easy mended."

'I told him I could take him to mother's cottage, and that he could dry his clothes there and welcome.

' "Can your mother keep a secret?" he asked.

' "Well she could keep one well enough, if she could remember it," I told him; "but you might tell her the secrets of all the Freemasons, and Foresters, and Buffalers, and Oddfellers as ever was, to-night; and she'd have forgotten all about 'em to-morrow mornin'."

474

'He seemed satisfied with this, and he got himself up by holdin' on to me, for it seemed as if his limbs was so cramped, the use of 'em was almost gone. I felt as he came agen me, that his clothes were wet and mucky.

' "You haven't been and fell into the fish-pond, have you, Sir?" I asked.

'He made no answer to my question; he didn't seem even to have heard it. I could see now he was standin' upon his feet that he was a tall, fine-made man, a head and shoulders higher than me.

' "Take me to your mother's cottage," he said, "and get me some dry clothes if you can; I'll pay you well for your trouble."

'I knew that the key was mostly left in the wooden gate in the garden wall, so I led him that way. He could scarcely walk at first, and it was only by leanin' heavily upon my shoulder that he managed to get along. I got him through the gate, leavin' it unlocked behind me, and trustin' to the chance of that not bein' noticed by the under-gardener, who had the care of the key, and was a careless chap enough. I took him across the meadows, and brought him up here, still keepin' away from the village, and in the fields, where there wasn't a creature to see us at that time o' night; and so I got him into the room down-stairs, where mother was a sittin' over the fire gettin' my bit o' supper ready for me.

'I put the strange chap in a chair agen the fire, and then for the first time I had a good look at him. I never see anybody in such a state before. He was all over green damp and muck, and his hands was scratched and cut to pieces. I got his clothes off him how I could, for he was like a child in my hands, and sat starin' at the fire as helpless as any baby; only givin' a long heavy sigh now and then, as if his heart was a goin' to bust. He didn't seem to know where he was; he didn't seem to hear us nor to see us; he only sat starin' straight before him, with his poor broken arm hanging loose by his side.

'Thinkin' he was in a very bad way, I wanted to go and fetch Mr. Dawson to him, and I said somethin' about it to mother. But queer as he seemed in his mind, he looked up quickly, as sharp as possible, and said No, No; nobody was to know of his bein' there except us two.

'I asked if I should run and fetch a drop of brandy; and he said, yes, I might do that. It was close upon eleven o'clock when I went into the public-house, and it was strikin' eleven as I got back home.

'It was a good thing I'd fetched the brandy, for he was shiverin' awful, and the edge of the mug rattled against his teeth. I had to force the spirit between 'em, they were so tight locked, before he could drink it. At last he dropped into a kind of a doze, a stupid sort of sleep, and began to nod over the fire, so I ran and got a blanket and wrapped him in it, and got him to lie down upon the press bedstead in the room under this. I sent mother to bed, and I sat by the fire and watched him, and kep' the fire up till it was just upon daybreak, when he 'woke up all of a sudden with a start, and said he must go, directly that minute.

'I begged him not to think of such a thing, and told him he warn't fit to move for ever so long; but he said he must go, and he got up, and though he staggered like, and at first could hardly stand steady two minutes together, he wouldn't be beat, and he got me to dress him in his clothes as I'd dried and cleaned as well as I could while he laid asleep. I did manage it at last, but the clothes was awful spoiled, and he looked a dreadful objeck, with his pale face and a great cut on his forehead that I'd washed and tied up with a handkercher. He could only get his coat on by buttoning it on round his neck, for he couldn't put a sleeve upon his broken arm. But he held out agen everything, though he groaned every now and then; and what with the scratches and bruises on his hands, and the cut upon his forehead and his stiff limbs and his broken arm

476

he'd plenty of call to groan; and by the time it was broad daylight he was dressed and ready to go.

'"What's the nearest town to this upon the London road?" he asked me.

'I told him as the nighest town was Brentwood.

'"Very well then," he says, "if you'll go with me to Brentwood, and take me to some surgeon as'll set my arm, I'll give you a five-pound note for that and all your other trouble."

'I told him that I was ready and willin' to do anything as he wanted done; and asked him if I shouldn't go and see if I could borrow a cart from some of the neighbours to drive him over in, for I told him it was a good six miles' walk.

'He shook his head, No, no, no, he said, he didn't want anybody to know anything about him; he'd rather walk it.

'He did walk it; and he walked it like a good un too; though I know as every step he took o' them six mile he took in pain; but he held out as he'd held out before; I never see such a chap to hold out in all my blessed life. He had to stop sometimes and lean agen a gateway to get his breath; but he held out still, till at last we got into Brentwood, and then he says "Take me to the nighest surgeon's," and I took him, and I waited while he had his arm set in splints, which took a precious long time. The surgeon wanted him to stay in Brentwood till he was better, but he said it warn't to be heard on, he must get up to London without a minute's loss of time; so the surgeon made him as comfortable as he could, considerin', and tied up his arm in a sling.'

Robert Audley started. A circumstance connected with his visit to Liverpool flashed suddenly back upon his memory. He remembered the clerk who had called him back to say that there was a passenger who took his berth on board the *Victoria Regia* within an hour or so of the vessel's sailing; a young man with his arm in a sling, who had called himself by some common name, which Robert had forgotten.

'When his arm was dressed,' continued Luke, 'he says to the surgeon, can you give me a pencil to write something before I go away. The surgeon smiles and shakes his head. "You'll never be able to write with that there hand to-day," he says, pointin' to the arm as had just been dressed. "P'raps not," the young chap answers quiet enough, "but I can write with the other." "Can't I write it for you?" says the surgeon. "No thank you," answers the other, "what I've got to write is private. If you can give me a couple of envelopes I'll be obliged to you."

'With that the surgeon goes to fetch the envelopes, and the young chap takes a pocket-book out of his coat pocket with his left hand; the cover was wet and dirty, but the inside was clean enough, and he tears out a couple of leaves and begins to write upon 'em as you see; and he writes dreadful awk'ard with his left hand, and he writes slow, but he contrives to finish what you see, and then he puts the two bits o' writin' into the envelopes as the surgeon brings him, and he seals 'em up, and he puts a pencil cross upon one of 'em, and nothin' on the other; and then he pays the surgeon for his trouble; and the surgeon says, ain't there nothin' more he can do for him, and can't he persuade him to stay in Brentwood till his arm's better; but he says no, no, it ain't possible; and then he says to me, "Come along o' me to the railway-station and I'll give you what I've promised."

'So I went to the station with him. We was in time to catch the train as stops at Brentwood at half-after eight, and we had five minutes to spare. So he takes me into a corner of the platform, and he says: "I wants you to deliver these here letters for me," which I told him I was willin'. "Very well, then," he says, "look here, you know Audley Court?" "Yes," I says, "I ought to, for my sweetheart lives lady's-maid there." "Whose lady's-maid?" he says. So I tells him "My lady's, the new lady what was governess at Mr. Dawson's." "Very well, then," he says, "this here letter with the cross upon the envelope is for Lady Audley, but you're to be sure to give it into her own hands; and remember to take care as nobody sees you give it." I promises to do this, and he hands me the first letter. And then he says, "Do you know Mr. Audley, as is nevy to Sir Michael?" and I said, "Yes, I've heerd tell on him, and I'd heerd as he was a reg'lar swell, but affable and free spoken" (for I had heerd tell on you, you know),' Luke added parenthetically. '"Now look here," the young chap says, "you're to give this other letter to Mr. Robert Audley, whose a stayin' at the Sun Inn, in the village;" and I tells him it's all right, as I've know'd the Sun ever since I was a baby. So then he gives me the second letter, what's got nothink wrote upon the envelope, and he gives me a five-pound note, accordin' to promise; and then he says "Good day, and thank you for all your trouble," and he gets into a second-class carriage, and the last I sees of him is a face as white as a sheet of writin' paper, and a great patch of stickin' plaster criss-crossed upon his forehead.'

'Poor George! poor George!'

'I went back to Audley, and I went straight to the Sun Inn, and asked for you, meanin' to deliver both letters faithful, so help me God, then; but the landlord told me as you'd started off that mornin' for London, and he didn't know when you'd come back, and he didn't know the name o' the place where you lived in London, though he said he thought it was in one o' them Law Courts, such as Westminster Hall or Doctors' Commons, or somethin' like that. So what was I to do? I couldn't send the letter by post, not knowin' where to direct to, and I couldn't give it into your own hands, and I'd been told partikler not to let anybody else know of it; so I'd nothin' to do but to wait and see if you come back, and bide my time for givin' of it to you.

'I thought I'd go over to the Court in the evenin' and see Phœbe, and find out from her when there'd be a chance of my seein' her lady, for I know'd she could manage it if she liked. So I didn't go to work that day, though I ought to ha' done, and I lounged and idled about until it was nigh upon dusk, and then I goes down to the meadows behind the Court, and there I finds Phœbe sure enough waitin' agen the wooden door in the wall, on the look-out for me.

'Well I went into the shrubbery with her, and I was a turnin' towards the old well, for we'd been in the habit of sittin' upon the brickwork about it often of a summer's evening, but Phœbe comes over as pale as a ghost all of a sudden, and says, "Not there! not there!" So I asks, "Why not there?" and she answers as she don't know, but she feels nervous like this evenin', and she's heerd as the well's haunted. I tells her as that's all a pack o'gammon, but she says, whether it is, or whether it isn't, she won't go agen the well. So we goes back to the gate, and she leans upon it talkin' to me.

'I hadn't been talkin' to her long before I see there was somethink wrong with her, and I told her as much.

'"Well," she says, "I ain't quite myself this evenin', for I had a upset, yesterday, and I ain't got over it yet."

'"A upset," I says. "You had a quarrel with your missus, I suppose."

'She didn't answer me directly, but she smiled the queerest smile as ever I see, and presently she says,

'"No, Luke, it weren't nothin' o' that kind; and what's more, nobody could be friendlier towards me than my lady; I think she'd do anythink for me a'most, and I think whether it was a bit o' farming stock and furniture or such like, or whether it was the goodwill of a public-house, she wouldn't refuse me anythink as I asked her."

'I couldn't make out this, for it was only a few days before, as she'd told me her missus was selfish and extravagant, and we might wait a long time before we could get what we wanted from her.

'So I says to her, "Why, this is rather sudden like, Phœbe," and she says, "Yes, it is sudden;" and she smiles again, just the same sort of smile as before. Upon that I turns round upon her sharp, and says, "I'll tell you what it is, my gal, you're a keepin' somethink from me; somethink you've been told, or somethink you've found out; and if you think you're a goin' to try that game on with me, you'll find you're very much mistaken; and so I give you warnin'."

'But she laughed it off like, and says, "Lor, Luke, what could have put such fancies into your head?"

'I says, "If I've got fancies in my head it's you that have put 'em there; and I tell you once more I won't stand no nonsense, and if you want to keep secrets from the man as you're a goin' to marry, you'd better marry somebody else and keep secrets from him, for you won't do it from me, and so I tell you."

'Upon which she begins to whimper a bit, but I takes no notice o' that, but begins to question her about my lady. I had the letter marked with the pencil cross in my pocket, and I wanted to find out how I was to deliver it.

'"Perhaps other people can keep secrets as well as you," I said, "and perhaps other people can make friends as well as you. There were a gentleman came here to see your missus yesterday, warn't there; a tall young gentleman with a brown beard?"

'Instead of answering of me like a Christian, my cousin Phœbe bursts out a cryin', and wrings her hands, and goes on awful, until I'm dashed if I can make out what she's up to.

'But little by little I got it out of her, for I wouldn't stand no nonsense; and she told me how she'd been sittin' at work at the window of her little room, which was at the top of the house, right up in one of the gables, and overlooked the lime-walk and the shrubbery and the well, when she see my lady walkin' with a strange gentleman, and they walked together for a long time, until by-and-by they—'

481

'Stop,' cried Robert Audley, 'I know the rest.'

'Well Phœbe told me all about what she see, and she told me as she'd met her lady almost directly afterwards, and somethin' had passed between 'em, not much, but enough to let her missus know that the servant what she looked down upon had found out that as would put her in that servant's power to the last day of her life.

'"And she is in my power, Luke," says Phœbe, "and she'll do anythin' in the world for us if we keep her secret."

'So you see both my Lady Audley and her maid thought as the gentleman as I'd seen safe off by the London train was lyin' dead at the bottom of the well. If I was to give the letter they'd find out the contrairy of this, and if I was to give the letter, Phœbe and me would lose the chance of gettin' started in life by her missus.

'So I kep' the letter and kep' my secret, and my lady kep' hern. But I thought if she acted liberal by me, and gave me the money I wanted, free like, I'd tell her everythink and make her mind easy.

'But she didn't. Whatever she give me she throwed me as if I'd been a dog. Whenever she spoke to me, she spoke as she might have spoken to a dog; and a dog she couldn't abide the sight on. There was no word in her mouth that was too bad for me. There was no toss as she could give her head that was too proud and scornful for me; and my blood biled agen her, and I kep' my secret, and let her keep hern. I opened the two letters and I read 'em, but I couldn't make much sense out of 'em, and I hid 'em away; and not a creature but me has see 'em until this night.'

Luke Marks had finished his story, and lay quietly enough, exhausted by having talked so long. He watched Robert Audley's face, fully expecting some reproof, some grave lecture; for he had a vague consciousness that he had done wrong.

But Robert did not lecture him; he had no fancy for an office which he did not think himself fitted to perform.

'The clergyman will talk to him and comfort him when he comes to-morrow morning,' Mr. Audley thought; 'and if the poor creature needs a sermon it will come better from his lips than from mine. What should I say to him? His sin has recoiled upon his own head; for had my lady's mind been set at ease, the Castle Inn would not have been burned down. Who shall dare to try and order his own life after this? who can fail to recognise God's hand in this strange story?'

He thought very humbly of the deductions he had made and acted upon. He remembered how implicitly he had trusted in the pitiful light of his own reason; but he was comforted by remembering also that he had tried simply and honestly to do his duty; faithfully alike to the dead and to the living.

Robert Audley sat until long after daybreak with the sick man, who fell into a heavy slumber a short time after he had finished his story. The old woman had dozed comfortably throughout her son's confession. Phœbe was asleep upon the press bedstead in the room below; so the young barrister was the only watcher.

He could not sleep; he could only think of the story he had heard. He could only thank God for his friend's preservation, and pray that he might be able to go to Clara Talboys, and say, 'Your brother still lives, and has been found.'

Phœbe came up-stairs at eight o'clock, ready to take her place at the sick bed, and Robert Audley went away to get a bed at the Sun Inn. He had had no more comfortable rest than such odd snatches of sleep as are to be got in railway carriages and on board steamers, during the last three nights, and he was completely worn out. It was nearly dusk when he awoke out of a long dreamless slumber, and dressed himself before dining in the little sitting-room, in which he and George had sat together a few months before.

The landlord waited upon him at dinner, and told him that Luke Marks had died at five o'clock that afternoon. 'He went off rather sudden like,' the man said, 'but very quiet.'

Robert Audley wrote a long letter that evening, addressed to Madame Taylor, care of Monsieur Val, Villebrumeuse; a long letter in which he told the wretched woman who had borne so many names and was to bear a false one for the rest of her life, the story that the dying man had told him.

'It may be some comfort to her to hear that her husband did not perish in his youth by her wicked hand,' he thought, 'if her selfish soul can hold any sentiment of pity or sorrow for others.'

CHAPTER IX
Restored

Clara Talboys returned to Dorsetshire to tell her father that his only son had sailed for Australia upon the 9th of September, and that it was most probable he yet lived, and would return to claim the forgiveness of the father he had never very particularly injured; except in the matter of having made that terrible matrimonial mistake which had exercised so fatal an influence upon his youth.

Mr. Harcourt Talboys was fairly nonplussed. Junius Brutus had never been placed in such a position as this, and seeing no way of getting out of this dilemma by acting after his favourite model, Mr. Talboys was fain to be natural for once in his life, and to confess that he had suffered much uneasiness and pain of mind about his only son, since his conversation with Robert Audley; and that he would be heartily glad to take his poor boy to his arms, whenever he should return to England. But when was he likely to return? and how was he to be communicated with? That was the question. Robert Audley remembered the advertisement which he had caused to be inserted in the Melbourne and Sydney papers. If George had re-entered either city alive, how was it that no notice had ever been taken of that advertisement? Was it likely his friend would be indifferent to his uneasiness? But, then again, it was just possible that George Talboys had not happened to see this advertisement; and, as he had travelled under a feigned name, neither his fellow-passengers nor the captain of the vessel would have been able to identify him with the person advertised for. What was to be done? Must they wait patiently till George grew weary of his exile, and returned to the friends who loved him; or were there any means to be taken by which his return might be hastened? Robert Audley was at fault! Perhaps, in the unspeakable relief of mind which he had experienced upon the discovery of his friend's escape, he was unable to look beyond the one fact of that providential preservation.

In this state of mind he went down to Dorsetshire to pay a visit to Mr. Talboys, who had given way to a perfect torrent of generous impulses, and had gone so far as to invite his son's friend to share the prim hospitality of the square, red-brick mansion.

Mr. Talboys had only two sentiments upon the subject of George's story; one was a natural relief and happiness in the thought that his son had been saved; the other was an earnest wish that my lady had been *his* wife, and that he might thus have had the pleasure of making a signal example of her.

'It is not for me to blame you, Mr. Audley,' he said, 'for having smuggled this guilty woman out of the reach of justice, and thus, as I may say, paltered with the laws of your country. I can only remark that, had the lady fallen into *my* hands, she would have been very differently treated.'

It was in the middle of April when Robert Audley found himself once more under those black fir-trees beneath which his wandering thoughts had so often strayed since his first meeting with Clara Talboys. There were primroses and early violets in the hedges now, and the streams which, upon his first visit, had been hard and frost-bound as the heart of Harcourt Talboys had thawed, like that gentleman, and ran merrily under the black-thorn bushes in the capricious April sunshine.

Robert had a prim bed-room, and an uncompromising dressing-room allotted to him in the square house, and he woke every morning upon a metallic spring-mattress which always gave him the idea of sleeping upon some musical instrument, to see the sun glaring in upon him through the square white blinds, and lighting up the two lacquered urns which adorned the foot of his blue iron bedstead, until they blazed like two tiny brazen lamps of the Roman period.

A visit to Mr. Harcourt Talboys was perhaps rather more like a return to boyhood and boarding-school than is quite consonant with the Sybarite view of human enjoyment. There were the same curtainless windows, and narrow strips of bedside carpet; the same clanging bell in the early morning; the same uncompromising servants filing into a long dining-room to assist at perhaps the same prayers; and there was altogether rather too much of the 'private academy for the sons of gentlemen preparing for the church and the army' in the Talboys establishment.

But if the square-built, red-brick mansion had been the palace of Armida, and the prim, linen-jacketed man represented by a legion of houris, Robert Audley could have scarcely seemed better satisfied with his entertainment.

He awoke to the sound of the clanging bell, and made his toilet in the cruel early morning sunshine, which is bright without being cheerful, and makes you wink without making you warm. He emulated Mr. Harcourt Talboys in the matter of shower-baths and cold water, and emerged prim and blue as that gentleman himself, as the clock in the hall struck seven, to join the master of the house in his ante-breakfast constitutional under the fir-trees in the stiff plantation.

But there was generally a third person who assisted in these constitutional promenades, and that third person was Clara Talboys, who used to walk by her father's side, more beautiful than the morning – for that was sometimes dull and cloudy, while she was always fresh and bright – in a broad-leaved straw hat and flapping blue ribbons, one quarter of an inch of which Mr. Audley would have esteemed a prouder decoration than ever adorned a favoured creature's button-hole.

Absent George was often talked of in these morning walks, and Robert Audley seldom took his place at the long breakfast-table without remembering the morning upon which he had first sat in that room, telling his friend's story, and hating Clara Talboys for her cold self-possession. He knew her better now, and knew that she was one of the most noble and beautiful of women. But had she yet discovered how dear she was to her brother's friend? Robert used to wonder sometimes if it were possible that he had not yet betrayed himself; if it could be possible that the love which made her very presence a magical influence to him, had failed to make itself known by some inadvertent glance, by some unconscious tremble in the voice, that seemed to take another tone when he addressed her.

The dull life in the square-built house was only relieved now and then by a stiff dinner party, at which a few country people assembled to bore each other by mutual consent; and by occasional inroads of morning callers, who took the drawing-room by storm, and held it for about an hour, to the utter discomfiture of Mr. Audley. That gentleman nourished sentiments of peculiar malevolence upon the subject of the fresh-coloured young country squires, who generally appeared with their mammas and sisters upon these occasions.

It was impossible, of course, that these young men could come within the radius of Clara's brown eyes without falling wildly in love with her; and it was impossible, therefore, that Robert Audley could do otherwise than furiously hate them as impertinent rivals and interlopers. He was jealous of any-body and everybody who came into the region inhabited by those calm brown eyes; jealous of a fat widower of eight-and-forty; of an elderly baronet with purple whiskers; of the old women about the neighbourhood whom Clara Talboys visited and ministered to; of the flowers in the conservatory, which occupied so much of her time and distracted her attention from him.

At first they were very ceremonious towards each other, and were only familiar and friendly upon the one subject of George's adventures; but, little by little, a pleasant intimacy arose between them, and before the first three weeks of Robert's visit had elapsed, Miss Talboys made him happy, by taking him seriously in hand and lecturing him on the purposeless life he had led so long, and the little use he had made of the talents and opportunities that had been given to him.

How pleasant it was to be lectured by the woman he loved! How pleasant it was to humiliate himself and depreciate himself before her! How delightful it was to get such splendid opportunities of hinting that if his life had been sanctified by an object, he might indeed have striven to be something better than an idle *flâneur* upon the smooth pathways that have no particular goal; that, blessed by the ties which would have given a solemn purpose to every hour of his existence, he might indeed have fought the battle earnestly and unflinchingly. He generally wound up with a gloomy insinuation to the effect that it was only likely he would drop quietly over the edge of the Temple Gardens some afternoon, when the river was bright and placid in the low sunlight, and the little children had gone home to their tea.

'Do you think I can read French novels and smoke mild Turkish until I am three-score-and-ten, Miss Talboys?' he asked. 'Do you think that there will not come a day in which my meerschaums will be foul, and the French novels more than usually stupid, and life altogether such a dismal monotony that I shall want to get rid of it somehow or other?'

I am sorry to say that while this hypocritical young barrister was holding forth in this despondent way, he had mentally sold up his bachelor possessions, including all Michel Lévy's

489

publications and half-a-dozen solid silver-mounted meer-schaums, pensioned off Mrs. Maloney, and laid out two or three thousand pounds in the purchase of a few acres of verdant shrubbery and sloping lawn, embosomed amid which there should be a fairy cottage *ornée*, whose rustic casements should glimmer out of bowers of myrtle and clematis to see themselves reflected in the purple bosom of a lake.

Of course Clara Talboys was far from discovering the drift of these melancholy lamentations. She recommended Mr. Audley to read hard and think seriously of his profession, and begin life in real earnest. It was a hard, dry sort of existence perhaps which she recommended; a life of serious work and application, in which he should strive to be useful to his fellow-creatures, and win a reputation for himself. Mr. Audley almost made a wry face at the thought of such a barren prospect.

'I'd do all that,' he thought, 'and do it earnestly, if I could be sure of a reward for my labour. If she would accept my reputation when it was won, and support me in the struggle by her beloved companionship. But what if she sends me away to fight the battle, and marries some hulking country squire while my back is turned?'

Being naturally of a vacillating and dilatory disposition, there is no saying how long Mr. Audley might have kept his secret, fearful to speak and break the charm of that uncertainty which, though not always hopeful, was very seldom quite despairing, had not he been hurried by the impulse of an unguarded moment into a full confession of the truth.

He had stayed five weeks at Grange Heath, and felt that he could not, in common decency, stay any longer; so he had packed his portmanteau one pleasant May morning, and had announced his departure.

Mr. Talboys was not the sort of man to utter any passionate lamentations at the prospect of losing his guest, but he expressed himself with a cool cordiality which served with him as the strongest demonstration of friendship.

'We have got on very well together, Mr. Audley,' he said, 'and you have been pleased to appear sufficiently happy in the quiet routine of our orderly household; nay, more, you have conformed to our little domestic regulations in a manner which I cannot refrain from saying I take as an especial compliment to myself.'

Robert bowed. How thankful he was to the good fortune which had never suffered him to oversleep the signal of the clanging bell, or led him away beyond the ken of clocks at Mr. Talboys' luncheon hour.

'I trust as we have got on so remarkably well together,' Mr. Talboys resumed, 'you will do me the honour of repeating your visit to Dorsetshire whenever you feel inclined. You will find plenty of sport amongst my farms, and you will meet with every politeness and attention from my tenants, if you like to bring your gun with you.'

Robert responded most heartily to these friendly overtures. He declared that there was no earthly occupation that was more agreeable to him than partridge shooting, and that he should be only too delighted to avail himself of the privilege so kindly offered to him. He could not help glancing towards Clara as he said this. The perfect lids drooped a little over the brown eyes, and the faintest shadow of a blush illuminated the beautiful face.

But this was the young barrister's last day in Elysium, and there must be a dreary interval of days and nights and weeks and months before the first of September would give him an excuse for returning to Dorsetshire. A dreary interval which fresh-coloured young squires, or fat widowers of eight-and-forty might use to his disadvantage. It was no wonder, therefore, that he contemplated this dismal prospect with moody despair, and was bad company for Miss Talboys that morning.

But in the evening after dinner, when the sun was low in the west, and Harcourt Talboys closeted in his library upon some judicial business with his lawyer and a tenant farmer, Mr. Audley grew a little more agreeable. He stood by Clara's side in one of the long windows of the drawing-room watching the shadows deepening in the sky and the rosy light growing every moment rosier as the day died out. He could not help enjoying that quiet *tête-à-tête*, though the shadow of the next morning's express which was to carry him away to London loomed darkly across the pathway of his joy. He could not help being happy in her presence; forgetful of the past, reckless of the future.

They talked of the one subject which was always a bond of union between them. They talked of her lost brother George. She spoke of him in a very melancholy tone this evening. How could she be otherwise than sad, remembering that if he lived – and she was not even sure of that – he was a lonely wanderer far away from all who loved him, and carrying the memory of a blighted life wherever he went? In the sombre twilight stillness she spoke of him thus, with her hands clasped and the tears trembling in her eyes.

'I cannot think how papa can be so resigned to my poor brother's absence,' she said, 'for he does love him, Mr. Audley; even you must have seen lately that he does love him. But I cannot think how he can so quietly submit to his absence. If I were a man, I would go to Australia, and find him, and bring him back; if he was still to be found among the living,' she added in a lower voice.

She turned her face away from Robert, and looked out at the darkening sky. He laid his hand upon her arm. It trembled in spite of him, and his voice trembled, too, as he spoke to her.

'Shall *I* go to look for your brother?' he said.

'*You!*' She turned her head, and looked at him earnestly

through her tears. 'You, Mr. Audley! Do you think that I could ask you to make such a sacrifice for me, or for those I love?'

'And do you think, Clara, that I should think any sacrifice too great an one if it were made for you? Do you think there is any voyage I would refuse to take, if I knew that you would welcome me when I came home, and thank me for having served you faithfully? I will go from one end of the continent of Australia to the other to look for your brother, if you please, Clara; and will never return alive unless I bring him with me, and will take my chance of what reward you shall give me for my labour.'

Her head was bent, and it was some moments before she answered him.

'You are very good and generous, Mr. Audley,' she said, at last, 'and I feel this offer too much to be able to thank you for it. But – what you speak of could never be. By what right could I accept such a sacrifice?'

'By the right which makes me your bounden slave for ever and ever, whether you will or no. By the right of the love I bear you, Clara,' cried Mr. Audley, dropping on his knees – rather awkwardly, it must be confessed – and covering a soft little hand, that he had found half-hidden among the folds of a silken dress, with passionate kisses.

'I love you, Clara,' he said, 'I love you. You may call for your father, and have me turned out of the house this moment, if you like; but I shall go on loving you all the same; and I shall love you for ever and ever, whether you will or no.'

The little hand was drawn away from his, but not with a sudden or angry gesture, and it rested for one moment lightly and tremulously upon his dark hair.

'Clara, Clara!' he murmured, in a low pleading voice, 'shall I go to Australia to look for your brother?'

There was no answer. I don't know how it is, but there is scarcely anything more delicious than silence in such cases.

Every moment of hesitation is a tacit avowal; every pause is a tender confession.

'Shall we both go, dearest? Shall we go as man and wife? Shall we go together, my dear love, and bring our brother back between us?'

Mr. Harcourt Talboys, coming into the lamp-lit room a quarter of an hour afterwards, found Robert Audley alone, and had to listen to a revelation which very much surprised him. Like all self-sufficient people, he was tolerably blind to everything that happened under his nose, and he had fully believed that his own society, and the Spartan regularity of his household, had been the attractions which had made Dorsetshire delightful to his guest.

He was rather disappointed, therefore; but he bore his disappointment pretty well, and expressed a placid and rather stoical satisfaction at the turn which affairs had taken.

'I have only one more point upon which I wish to obtain your consent, my dear sir,' Robert said, when almost everything had been pleasantly settled. 'Our honeymoon trip, with your permission, will be to Australia.'

Mr. Talboys was taken aback by this. He brushed something like a tearful mist away from his hard grey eyes as he offered Robert his hand.

'You are going to look for my son,' he said. 'Bring me back my boy, and I will freely forgive you for having robbed me of my daughter.'

So Robert Audley went back to London, to surrender his chambers in Fig-tree Court, and to make all due inquiries about such ships as sailed from Liverpool for Sydney in the month of June.

He went back a new man, with new hopes, new cares, new prospects, new purposes; with a life that was so entirely changed that he looked out upon a world in which everything wore a radiant and rosy aspect, and wondered how it could ever have seemed such a dull, neutral-tinted universe.

He had lingered until after luncheon at Grange Heath, and it was in the dusky twilight that he entered the shady Temple courts and found his way to his chambers. He found Mrs. Maloney scrubbing the stairs, as was her wont upon a Saturday evening, and he had to make his way upward amidst an atmosphere of soapy steam, that made the bannisters greasy under his touch.

'There's lots of letthers, yer honour,' the laundress said, as she rose from her knees and flattened herself against the wall to enable Robert to pass her, 'and there's some parrcels, and there's a gentleman which has called ever so many times, and is waitin' to-night, for I towld him you'd written to me to say your rooms were to be airred.'

'Very good, Mrs. M.; you may get me some dinner and a pint of sherry as soon as you like, and see that my luggage is all right if you please.'

He walked quietly up to his room to see who his visitor was. He was not likely to be anybody of consequence. A dun, perhaps; for he had left his affairs in the wildest confusion when he ran off in answer to Mr. Talboys' invitation, and had been much too high up in the sublime Heaven of love, to remember any such sublunary matters as unsettled tailors' bills.

He opened the door of his sitting-room, and walked in. The canaries were singing their farewell to the setting sun, and the faint, yellow light was flickering upon the geranium leaves. The visitor, whoever he was, sat with his back to the window and his head bent upon his breast. But he started up as Robert Audley entered the room, and the young man uttered a great cry of delight and surprise, and opened his arms to his lost friend, George Talboys.

Mrs. Maloney had to fetch more wine and more dinner from the tavern which she honoured with her patronage, and the two young men sat deep into the night by the hearth which had so long been lonely.

We know how much Robert had to tell. He touched lightly and tenderly upon that subject which he knew was cruelly painful to his friend; he said very little of the wretched woman who was wearing out the remnant of her wicked life in the quiet suburb of the forgotten Belgian city.

George Talboys spoke very briefly of that sunny seventh of September, upon which he had left his friend sleeping by the trout stream while he went to accuse his false wife of that conspiracy which had well nigh broken his heart.

'God knows that from the moment in which I sank into the black pit, knowing the treacherous hand that had sent me to what might have been my death, my chief thought was of the safety of the woman who had betrayed me. I fell upon my feet upon a mass of slush and mire, but my shoulder was bruised, and my arm broken against the side of the well. I was stunned and dazed for a few minutes, but I roused myself by an effort, for I felt that the atmosphere I breathed was deadly. I had my Australian experiences to help me in my peril, and I could climb like a cat. The stones of which the well was built were rugged and irregular, and I was able to work my way upwards by planting my feet in the interstices of the stones, and resting my back at times against the opposite side of the well, helping myself as well as I could with my hands, though one arm was crippled. It was hard work, Bob, and it seems strange enough that a man who had long professed himself weary of his life should take so much trouble to preserve it. I think I must have been working upwards of half-an-hour before I got to the top; I know the time seemed an eternity of pain and peril. It was impossible for me to leave the place until after dark without being observed, so I hid myself behind a clump of laurel bushes and laid down on the grass faint and exhausted to wait for nightfall. The man who found me there told you the rest, Robert.'

'Yes, my poor old friend – yes, he told me all.'

George had never returned to Australia after all. He had gone on board the *Victoria Regia*, but had afterwards exchanged his berth for one in another vessel belonging to the same owners, and had gone to New York, where he had stayed as long as he could support the weariness of his exile; as long as he could endure the loneliness of an existence which separated him from every friend he had ever known.

'Jonathan was very kind to me, Bob,' he said; 'I had enough money to enable me to get on pretty well in my own quiet way, and I meant to have started on the Californian gold-fields to get more when that was gone. I might have made plenty of friends had I pleased, but I carried the old bullet in my breast; and what sympathy could I have with men who knew nothing of my grief? I yearned for the strong grasp of your hand, Bob; the friendly touch of the hand which had guided me through the darkest passage of my life.'

CHAPTER X

At peace

Two years have passed since the May twilight in which Robert found his old friend; and Mr. Audley's dream of a fairy cottage has been realised between Teddington Lock and Hampton Bridge, where, amid a little forest of foliage, there is a fantastical dwelling-place of rustic woodwork, whose latticed windows look out upon the river. Here amongst the lilies and the rushes on the sloping bank, a brave boy of eight years old plays with a toddling baby who peeps wonderingly from its nurse's arms at that other baby in the purple depth of the quiet water.

Mr. Audley is a rising man upon the home circuit by this time, and has distinguished himself in the great breach of promise case of Hobbs *v.* Nobbs, and has convulsed the Court by his deliciously comic rendering of the faithless Nobbs's amatory correspondence. The handsome dark-eyed boy is Master George Talboys, who declines *musa* at Eton, and fishes for tadpoles in the clear water under the spreading umbrage beyond the ivied walls of his academy. But he comes very often to the fairy cottage to see his father, who lives there with his sister and his sister's husband; and he is very happy with his uncle Robert, his aunt Clara, and the pretty baby who has just begun to toddle on the smooth lawn that slopes down to the water's brink, upon which there is a little Swiss boat-house and landing stage where Robert and George moor their slender wherries.

Other people come to the cottage near Teddington. A

bright, merry-hearted girl, and a grey-bearded gentleman, who has survived the trouble of his life, and battled with it as a Christian should.

It is more than a year since a black-edged letter, written upon foreign paper, came to Robert Audley, to announce the death of a certain Madame Taylor, who had expired peacefully at Villebrumeuse, dying after a long illness, which Monsieur Val described as a *maladie de langueur*.

Another visitor comes to the cottage in this bright summer of 1861 – a frank, generous-hearted young man, who tosses the baby, and plays with Georgey, and is especially great in the management of the boats, which are never idle when Sir Harry Towers is at Teddington.

There is a pretty rustic smoking-room over the Swiss boat-house, in which the gentlemen sit and smoke in the summer evenings, and whence they are summoned by Clara and Alicia to drink tea, and eat strawberries and cream upon the lawn.

Audley Court is shut up, and a grim old housekeeper reigns paramount in the mansion which my lady's ringing laughter once made musical. A curtain hangs before the pre-Raphaelite portrait; and the blue mould which artists dread gathers upon the Wouvermans and Poussins, the Cuyps and Tintorettos. The house is often shown to inquisitive visitors, though the baronet is not informed of that fact, and people admire my lady's rooms, and ask many questions about the pretty, fair-haired woman, who died abroad.

Sir Michael has no fancy to return to the familiar dwelling-place in which he once dreamed a brief dream of impossible happiness. He remains in London until Alicia shall be Lady Towers, when he is to remove to a house he has lately bought in Hertfordshire, on the borders of his son-in-law's estate. George Talboys is very happy with his sister and his old friend. He is a young man yet, remember, and it is not quite impossible that he may by-and-by find some one who will be able to console him for the past. That dark story of the past fades little by little every day, and there may come a time in which the shadow my lady's wickedness has cast upon the young man's life, will utterly vanish away.

The meerschaums and the French novels have been presented to a young Templar, with whom Robert Audley had been friendly in his bachelor days, and Mrs. Maloney has a little pension paid her quarterly for her care of the canaries and geraniums.

I hope no one will take objection to my story because the end of it leaves the good people all happy and at peace. If my experience of life has not been very long, it has at least been manifold; and I can safely subscribe to that which a mighty king and a great philosopher declared, when he said that neither the experience of his youth nor of his age had ever shown him 'the righteous forsaken, nor his seed begging their bread.'

FINIS

PENGUIN CLASSICS

THE CASTLE OF OTRANTO
HORACE WALPOLE

A haunted castle and a ruined bloodline …

Manfred, wicked lord of Otranto Castle, is horrified when his son is crushed to death on his wedding day. But rather than witness the end of his line, as foretold in a curse, he resolves to send his own wife to a convent and marry the intended bride himself.

However, Manfred's lustful greed will be disturbed by the terrifying omens that now haunt his castle: bleeding statues, skeletal ghouls and a giant sword – as well as the arrival of the rightful prince of Otranto.

www.penguinclassics.com

PENGUIN CLASSICS

A SICILIAN ROMANCE
ANN RADCLIFFE

A desolate castle hides a family's shameful secrets …

On the rocky northern shores of Sicily stands a lonely castle, the
home of the aristocratic Mazzini family. The Marquis of Mazzini has
remarried and gone away to live with his new wife, abandoning his
two daughters – sweet-natured Emilia and lively, imaginative Julia – to
wander the labyrinthine corridors alone. His only involvement with
their lives is to arrange a marriage between Julia and the cruel Duke de
Luovo, even though she loves another.

But that is not the end of Julia's troubles. Strange lights and unearthly
groaning noises are coming from parts of the castle that have been
locked up for years. Is it occupied by some terrible supernatural power?
Or do even darker secrets lie within its depths?

www.penguinclassics.com

He just wanted a decent book to read ...

Not too much to ask, is it? It was in 1935 when Allen Lane, Managing Director of Bodley Head Publishers, stood on a platform at Exeter railway station looking for something good to read on his journey back to London. His choice was limited to popular magazines and poor-quality paperbacks – the same choice faced every day by the vast majority of readers, few of whom could afford hardbacks. Lane's disappointment and subsequent anger at the range of books generally available led him to found a company – and change the world.

'We believed in the existence in this country of a vast reading public for intelligent books at a low price, and staked everything on it'
Sir Allen Lane, 1902–1970, founder of Penguin Books

The quality paperback had arrived – and not just in bookshops. Lane was adamant that his Penguins should appear in chain stores and tobacconists, and should cost no more than a packet of cigarettes.

Reading habits (and cigarette prices) have changed since 1935, but Penguin still believes in publishing the best books for everybody to enjoy. We still believe that good design costs no more than bad design, and we still believe that quality books published passionately and responsibly make the world a better place.

So wherever you see the little bird – whether it's on a piece of prize-winning literary fiction or a celebrity autobiography, political tour de force or historical masterpiece, a serial-killer thriller, reference book, world classic or a piece of pure escapism – you can bet that it represents the very best that the genre has to offer.

Whatever you like to read – trust Penguin.